The ART of LOVING YOU

The ART of LOVING YOU

NATASHA BISHOP

SLOWBURN
A zando IMPRINT
NEW YORK

The characters and events in this book are fictitious.
Any similarity to real persons, living or dead, is coincidental
and not intended by the author.

Slowburn is an imprint of Zando.
zandoprojects.com

First Edition: April 2026

Text design by Neuwirth & Associates, Inc.
Cover illustration by Michael Machira Mwagi
Photos via Depositphotos.com: (New York) UTBP; (Colorado) snehitdesign; (Chicago) dibrova; (South Carolina) alexlmx; (Baltimore) sepavone; (California) focqus; (Virginia) fireandstone

Library of Congress Control Number: 2025948079

978-1-63893-274-1 (Paperback)
978-1-63893-275-8 (ebook)

1 3 5 7 9 10 8 6 4 2
Manufactured in the United States of America
LKS

For all the Black girls with jagged edges,
I hope you find your sandpaper to come along
and tell you how beautiful they are.

Author's Note

I wrote this book to show a story of two people learning how to love themselves through their grief and finding solace in each other. I think Dani and Micah's journey is beautiful and hard-earned, but it's also a heavy one. If these triggers are too much for you, please take care of yourself and maybe catch me in the next book.

Love you all!

Trigger warnings: grief/loss, death of loved ones, mentions of gun violence, mentions of fatal car accidents, mentions of stillbirth/miscarriage, mentions of suicide

Playlist

1. Beyoncé – "Heaven"
2. Beyoncé, Tanner Adell, Brittney Spencer, Reyna Roberts, Tiera Kennedy – "BLACKBIIRD"
3. Ed Sheeran – "Dive"
4. JP Saxe – "Blurry"
5. Brandy – "Almost Doesn't Count"
6. PARTYOF2, Jadagrace, SWIM, TJOnline – "smiles :)"
7. Teyana Taylor, Erykah Badu – "Lowkey"
8. SiR – "Satisfaction"
9. ESTA, Leon Thomas III – "dangerous game"
10. Justin Nozuka – "Insecure"
11. Isaiah Falls, Sasha Keable – "NIGHT OFF"
12. H.E.R., Bryson Tiller – "Could've Been"
13. Omar Apollo – "Dispose of Me"
14. GIVĒON – "Make You Mine"
15. Babyface, Coco Jones – "Simple"
16. Hozier – "Movement"
17. Justin Bieber, Kehlani – "Get Me"
18. Jessie Reyez – "HITTIN"
19. JoJo – "Comeback"

20. Lucky Daye, Masego, Alex Isley, Jack Dine – Good & Plenty—Remix"
21. Tyla – "ART"

Scan the QR Code for Apple and Spotify Links

Apple

Spotify

The ART of LOVING YOU

Prologue

Dani

WHY DO PEOPLE FALL IN LOVE?

What do they get out of handing their heart to another human being?

Is companionship really worth the pain of exposure—exposure of your deepest vulnerabilities?

Who decided that was a good idea?

I look around the resort suite I've called home for the last two weeks. You would think after attending a wedding as gorgeous as this, I'd see the appeal of all this shit. I don't.

All I see is a beautiful backdrop marred by the ugliness of the bride's insecurities and the groom's cowardice. Is this what love has to offer? Transforming into the worst version of yourself in its name?

No thank you.

I spent most of this trip trying to keep the bride from flying off the handle about the dumbest shit while she treated us like errand girls and ruined her relationship with her sister. I am beyond ready to get out of Tulum, having resolved to never attend another wedding ever again. My suitcase doesn't seem to be getting that message, though. I've been sitting here trying to zip it shut for the past five minutes, but it keeps getting stuck.

Another attempt snags my nail, damn near ripping it off.

Stupid piece of . . .

A knock on my door stops my thought in its tracks.

"You good? It's time to get the fuck out of here," Evie says as I open the door to her and Janelle, both smiling yet looking exhausted.

It's been a trying two weeks for all of us.

When we were younger, I used to compare us to the element benders in *Avatar: The Last Airbender*.

Evie was a firebender. Her features make her look like a Southern belle, but she is all bite and no bark. Her spirit is forged in flames.

Nelle was an earthbender, unwavering in her resilience and loyalty. It also helped that her bohemian style on her curvy body always made her look like an earthly goddess too.

Amerie was an airbender, cunning in her movements and free-spirited in her thinking.

I was a waterbender. My peacekeeping ways kept the flow of the group steady.

It's been a long time since I referred to us that way, but seeing them standing here—Evie wearing a red sleeveless jumpsuit and her twists pulled into a high ponytail, and Nelle with her face-framing boho braids and waist beads below a sage-colored crop top—I have to laugh at the imagery.

"Almost. My suitcase won't close."

Nelle laughs. "What'd you buy?"

"Nothing!" I defend. I travel way too often to get sucked into souvenir hell. I didn't overpack and I only bought eight small souvenirs—two for my mom, two for my dad, two for my assistant, Nisha, and two for my mentor, Tanya.

No, I'm not the problem here. The problem is I need a new suitcase because this one up and quit on the job.

Nelle turns up her nose at me only to immediately give up the act and let out a soft chuckle that lets me know she didn't mean it.

"Okay, let's see if we can get it," she says.

"I can help her."

A rich baritone voice drifts around the corner, and I unfortunately know who I'm going to see before he shows his face.

Micah Wright.

The man who took my world by storm eleven years ago.

The man who set the bar for all the rest.

A man I just can't seem to escape.

The universe doesn't seem to know what to do with us—constantly bringing us together, only to rip us apart in ways that change me every time.

I don't want to change anymore.

I'm content with this version of myself. I like being the decider of my fate and answering to no one but myself.

Micah knew the model: the girl who commanded runways and graced magazine covers but never felt in charge of her own life. But he doesn't know the content creator: the woman who posts only what she wants when she wants. And he doesn't know the business owner who commands boardrooms as well as she did runways—maybe even better.

And that's why Micah can never be anything more than another secret in my vault, another thread of my past.

Rome, the best man, walks around the corner to join Micah, his hand landing on Nelle's hip.

That's one good thing to come out of Amerie and Arnold's nuptials. I haven't seen my girl this happy in a long time, and no one deserves that more. She's always sacrificing her happiness for the good of others, and no one has benefitted from that more than Ri. I mean, I can't think of anyone else who would agree to be her sister's maid-of-honor when the groom is her ex-boyfriend. I can't think of anyone else who—after all that—would put up with her sister's nasty attitude toward her.

I love these girls. I've been friends with Ri, Nelle, and Evie since high school, but I've always felt that the blood in their veins runs in mine. Watching this wedding unfold has shown me, however, that I've allowed that connection to blind me to the harsh reality of what was happening within Ri and Nelle's relationship. I was too focused on keeping my family together, failing to see that Janelle was suffering under the weight of that tether.

Rome pulled her from under that rock and for that, I'll always be grateful to him.

"Just the man we needed," Evie chuckles, slapping Micah's shoulder. "You're in good hands, boo."

She ushers Rome and Nelle away before I have a chance to object.

"Umm, yeah, thanks." I step aside, giving Micah a wide berth into my room.

His tall frame feels so imposing in my space. Everything about him is so familiar yet so foreign to me. His locs look the same as they have for years, but I don't remember what they feel like between my fingers. He still smells of lavender and musk, but it's been far too long since I've been alone with him, engulfed in the scent from this close.

It's been that way by design and I need to remember that.

"You ready to go home?" he asks while hunched over my suitcase, his brow furrowed in concentration.

Oh, we're doing small talk.

I hate small talk.

"Yep," I offer.

His eyes float over to me, unamused.

Sighing, I step into my armor. "Are you?"

His fingers tug at the zipper of my bag with all the gentleness you'd expect from an artist. Every ounce of patience I don't have exists within Micah. I probably would've given up and asked our concierge, Javier, for help getting a new suitcase at this point, but Micah doesn't even flinch.

He takes his sweet time slowly coaxing the zipper to bend to his will. And it does. Because most things do.

He pats the top of the suitcase before setting it upright. "Absolutely. I don't know how it's possible, but I'm more tired after spending two weeks on the beach than I am after getting a commission done."

I force out a polite laugh when all I want to do is grab my bag and put some space between us. I'll be damned if I let him know that any part of his presence unsettles me.

"Right. I'm tired too," I say, dryly.

He makes another attempt at conversation, which I only half listen to in favor of checking the text that just came through on my phone.

Tanya: Love you, Dani Girl

Random declarations of love aren't usually Tanya's style of drama, but given that we haven't spoken on the phone since I've been in Tulum and haven't seen each other in a while due to her own traveling adventures, I guess she's feeling sentimental.

I run my hands over the necklace she passed down to me from her mom—one form of Tanya's sentimentality. Out of all the things she's ever given me, this is by far my favorite; I haven't taken it off since the day she gave it to me three years ago.

Me: Love you, too. Maybe when I get back you'll sit still long enough for me to visit? With gifts, of course

I pocket my phone before she can start hounding me about what I got her. Micah closes the gap between us, but when I expect him to put the handle of my bag in my hands, he walks past me with it still in his grasp.

"Oh. Thanks for getting the zipper for me, Micah. I can take it from here."

"Let's go, Dani."

My back goes ramrod straight at the force in his tone.

His eyes drift down my frame. Not in a sexual way—I've been the subject of that stare from him before. This is different. Like he doesn't know what to make of me.

Good.

I've spent the years since we were together honing this armor, perfecting it until it was ironclad. I've overcome the heartache he left me with and I'm better on my own. I don't need him to perceive me, and I damn sure don't need his comfort or his love.

There is nothing for him to know.

Chapter One

Micah

"DID I EVER TELL YOU YOU'RE MY HERO?" MY SISTER, Bailey, asks half sarcastically as I hand her a cup of ginger hibiscus tea.

"Conveniently, the only time you do is when I bring your ass tea," I joke.

"Mmm, well, what can ya do?" She smacks her lips with a cheeky smile. I watch as she lowers her standing desk to its lowest setting before sitting down and sipping her tea. She hums contentedly and then sets her mug on the heated coaster beside her. She looks back at her computer and leans her arms against the forearm support pads connected to her desk before typing a long email. While she's focused, I take a look around her space to see what upgrades can be made. I've wanted to get her a new chair with better adjustments, since she's had this one for a couple of years. The ergonomic chair helps her muscles not be so tight after a long day of being sedentary. When I get back to my office, I'll search for some options to show her.

I've always been protective of Bailey—that's just the nature of being a decade older than your sibling. Since her multiple sclerosis diagnosis four years ago, I've done my best to consider ways to help her feel comfortable.

To be honest, I never knew what MS was before Bailey's diagnosis. I had heard of it, but I knew nothing of its causes, symptoms, or—most important—treatments. When I researched it and learned it's a disease where the immune system attacks the protective covering of nerves, and that there's no cure, I was devastated for her.

Bailey hits send on her email and turns her focus back to me. "So, guess what?"

"Do I wanna know?"

She rolls her eyes. "Why can't you ever just say 'what'?"

"Because you want me to." I shrug, moving out of the way before the back of her hand can connect with my ribs.

"Anyway, Roc just booked an interview with *Essence*. I just found out from Zariah."

A sense of pride washes over me at Roc's accomplishment. He's a newer artist who specializes in contemporary art. He often uses photographs or everyday objects in his paintings. We met three years ago when neither of us were in a good place. I had just opened my gallery, Spring House, and what should have been a moment of pure joy and bliss felt hollow. I was surrounded by so much love, but the one person I wanted by my side as I realized my dreams wanted nothing to do with me, and that cast a cloud of anguish over the space.

Roc's best friend had just been killed, and he needed somewhere to channel that pain. I offered him my studio to work in and a spot in the gallery to show his finished paintings, and the rest was history. I'm immensely happy to see him thriving now.

"That's what's up. I'ma go call him when we're done."

"Tell him I said hey and congratulations," she says, her voice subdued.

I squint at her. "You know he'd rather hear that from you directly."

She squirms in her seat, which makes me chuckle. Everyone knows Roc has a thing for my sister. He's a good guy, so I don't have any issues with it, but Bailey refuses to talk to me about it.

"Goodbye, Chopper." She spits my nickname at me.

I hold my hand up in surrender. "Ay, I was just saying, Franky. It's cool, I'm done." I laugh, softening my tone with her nickname. "What you got for me?"

She looks me over as if she's contemplating whether or not she wants to continue the silent treatment. The sound of her sucking her teeth lets me know she decided against it. "You have a new commission request." As she turns her computer screen to show the request, my phone pings with a new email. I grab it to turn the volume down, but the lock screen preview makes me automatically unlock the phone to read the entire message. This has to be a joke.

Please be a joke.

From: vtownsend@harkerlegalgroup.com
To: micahwright@springhouse.com
Subject: ATTENTION REQUIRED - Tanya Holden Estate

Hello Mr. Wright,
I hope this message finds you well.
My name is Victor Townsend. I am Tanya Holden's lawyer, and I am contacting you with unfortunate news.
Tanya passed away this past Tuesday after a long battle with colon cancer. Per Tanya's last wishes, I would like to request your presence at her funeral and reading of the will.
Please see the details attached and let me know if you have any questions.
I look forward to meeting with you.
Sincerely,
Victor Townsend, Esq.

It's not a joke. I click on the attachment, and smiling back at me is the woman I consider a second mother. Underneath her name is her birthdate, but the sight of her death date right next to it is jarring.

How could Tanya not be here anymore? Death comes for everyone. I've understood that from a very young age, but Tanya is . . . Tanya was larger than life. Like an asshole, I assumed she'd have more time.

The lawyer mentions in his message that she had colon cancer. We hadn't talked in the last two weeks while I was away for Arnold and Amerie's wedding. I had wanted to visit in the weeks before leaving, but she said she was out of town and would let me know when she got back.

She never followed up, and I let life get in the way of reaching back out to her.

Fuck. She was one of the most important people in the world to me, and I didn't even know she had cancer. The gravity of that sends me crashing face-first into the pool of regrets never far from my mind.

My hands feel impossibly heavy, so I let them drop, forgetting I was holding my phone. The sound of the screen hitting the floor is so dull it barely registers. I can hear the worry in Bailey's voice calling out, but I don't have it in me to answer. Something pulls at the sleeve of my shirt, and it isn't until I catch sight of Bailey's shoes that I realize she's dragged me to sit in her chair.

She bends down so we're at eye level. "Micah, you're scaring me. What's going on?"

I look back at her and force words from my mouth that I'm in no way prepared to process. "It's Tanya. She's dead."

I hate the sound of disingenuous tears.

About fifty people are standing inside Huber Memorial Church, each one a worse actor than the last. The woman who worked beside Tanya at the Baltimore Museum of Art and undermined her at every turn stands by her casket, wailing into a handkerchief. I recognize the woman consoling her as the one who cursed Tanya out in the parking lot after she fired her from the museum.

The man sneaking sips of what smells like whiskey between his sniffles, meant to look like he's choked up, is the man who used to run the rec center. Tanya always said she hated the man because he had a rotten soul.

None of these people cared about Tanya, and she didn't care about them. There were so many people who loved Tanya, so many whose lives she changed.

Why aren't they here?

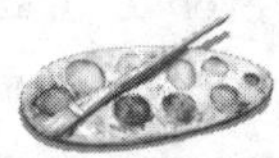

My hands curl into fists when I hear someone ask why bad things always happen to good people, so I move to find a seat in the back of the church, hidden away from prying eyes. The sooner I can get out of here, the better.

As soon as I find a seat, the wailing woman moves away from Tanya's casket, and there *she* is. The shining beacon who makes swimming in this sea of inauthenticity worth it.

From the moment I first saw Dani Jenkins, I knew I had been bested. I knew nothing I could create with my own hands would ever come close to her beauty. Looking at her now, standing by Tanya's casket in silence, sunglasses covering her eyes, I still believe that wholeheartedly. I've never met anyone quite as radiant as her.

A part of me knows I should go on as if I don't see her. Considering the way she avoided me in Tulum in the face of joy, approaching her in the face of grief is bound to send her running. But a bigger part of me needs to talk to her. Tanya was a considerable part of both of our lives, and her loss is devastating. I can't leave here without knowing how Dani is coping.

My feet feel heavier with every step toward the front of the church. Every cough, sniffle, and whisper I hear as I walk up the aisle grates on every nerve I have left. It doesn't feel natural to see Tanya so still. The woman was in constant motion, always searching for her next great adventure. I don't know who decided to dress her in the hot pink dress draped over her body. Knowing her, she probably arranged it herself; whether to unsettle attendees or not is anyone's guess. But, without her boisterous energy as the final accessory, the outfit loses its charm, instead serving as the cruel reminder that she's really gone.

Needing to ground myself, I turn to Dani. Not an inch of skin is showing on her body, yet when my palm touches the small of her back, a wave of heat hits my spine. "Dani," I whisper. Her body remains perfectly still, and with her shades on, I can't even tell if she heard me.

I start to say her name one more time when words finally fall from her lips. "I was at brunch." Her voice is hoarse, as if she hasn't spoken in days, so I lean closer to ensure I heard her right.

"What?"

Finally, she turns her body toward me. "That's where I was when I got the email," she says, lowering her sunglasses just enough for me to see her bloodshot eyes. The pain etched across her features makes me want to pull her into me, but I drop my hands to my sides instead. "I was at brunch with the girls."

She must have gotten the same email from Mr. Townsend that I did. "I was at the gallery laughing with Bailey," I offer, hoping the answer can somehow assuage any guilt she might be feeling.

She tilts her head as if really seeing me for the first time. "I didn't even know she was sick. Did you know?"

There's a plea in her voice. An anguished prayer that she's not alone, that she wasn't the only one robbed of her chance to say goodbye.

"I didn't know. I would've told you." Whether she wanted to pretend the connection between us was invisible or not, I would've never hid this from her.

Her chin drops to her chest, the tension slowly leaving her shoulders. The pastor makes his way to the podium, signaling that the service is about to begin.

Despite the attendees, the service is pleasant. Dani and I shared a moment of levity when the slideshow of Tanya heavily featured the two of us but not a single other person here today. Only Tanya would manage one final *fuck you* from beyond the grave.

Tanya is being cremated, so there's no procession to any burial site, and to my knowledge, no one is hosting a repast, so it's just . . . over.

I step outside and put my hand up to block the sun's unforgiving rays. Everyone files out of the church, seemingly content with going back to their lives. I have no desire to do that.

Without a word, Dani and I migrate so that we're standing side by side, facing the street. I don't think Dani sought me out consciously. Like me, she's seeking stillness among the chaos. Trying to find a path back to normalcy, whatever that looks like now.

Whenever I experienced a loss this great, it was Tanya who saved me from my own recklessness. Loss has driven me to act so far out of my character I didn't recognize myself. I treated the world like it didn't matter.

Who is going to save me now that she's the one who's lost? Do I even want to be saved?

We stand there until there's virtually no one left in the parking lot. The threads of grief binding us unravel with every car that pulls off. Dani hides it well, but I can feel her calm demeanor shifting to a base instinct to flee.

She turns to do just that, but her path is blocked by an older Black man of average height in a black suit. His hair is mostly white, while his beard and mustache are salt-and-pepper. His hooded eyes don't look unkind, just serious. Before he can speak to her, I position myself in front of Dani.

He looks back and forth between us, his mouth muscles twitching but never quite reaching a smile.

Clearing his throat, he focuses his attention on me. "Mr. Wright"—then on Dani—"Ms. Jenkins. My name is Victor Townsend. I emailed the two of you."

Recognition hits both of us, and we each shake his hand.

"Thank you for coming," he says.

"Of course," I respond.

"Yes, well, I'm just glad we were informed about it before it was too late," Dani adds.

I turn to look at her, finding her brows knitted together and her gaze set on Mr. Townsend. Her anger is misplaced, but damn if I'll tell her that. I turn back to Mr. Townsend, folding my arms against my chest.

"Right. Here's my card. It has my office address on it." He reaches into his pocket, pulls out two business cards, and extends them to us. "Would you both be able to head there now for the reading of the will?"

"Right now?" I ask.

"Correct."

There's nothing in Tanya's will I want. What I want is something I can never have again. I can never call her for advice, open my email to find artists and events she recommends, or get my ass whooped in chess on random visits. Her will won't bring her back, so it's pointless to me, but clearly there's something she wants me to have, so I agree to come.

Mr. Townsend looks to Dani for confirmation, and based on the resolve that takes over his features, he must get it. He gives us both a stern nod and heads off to his car.

He's a very frigid man. I imagine Tanya probably gave him hell regularly. I chuckle at the thought, then look over to Dani, who stares unblinkingly at the card.

I rest my hand on top of her wrist. The effect is almost instantaneous; her fingers twitch beneath my hold, and her eyes flutter, slowly at first and then rapidly until they're focused on mine. It's been a long time since I've seen her eyes this close. They're still red-rimmed, but they're no less breathtaking. Pitch-black and iridescent. They're bewitching in a terrifying way because one look from her could bring you to your knees or have you following her off the ship to your cold, watery death. Even knowing this, I'd still stare into her eyes every time.

"Do you want to ride with me over there?"

The question seems to remind her who she's talking to and where we are because her neck snaps in both directions frantically. The tug of her wrist against my hand isn't forceful. It's almost gentle but enough to make me immediately relent.

"No, thank you," she says, shaking her head vehemently. And with that, she walks away from me . . . again.

Chapter Two

Dani

HOW COULD I HAVE MISSED IT?

How could I not know she was sick?

The last time we talked on the phone, she didn't sound good. Her breathing was labored and she kept coughing, but she assured me she was fine, that travel fatigue had caught up to her and she was recovering from an upper respiratory infection.

She lied.

Why wouldn't she have told me what was going on? I could've been there. I could've helped in some way. Taken her to treatments. Something. Anything.

I could've said goodbye.

The last text I sent her haunts my dreams. I should've driven straight from the airport to her house so I could put eyes on her. Instead, I waited for her to initiate the conversation about her schedule.

I went on with life as if we had all the time in the world. What a sick joke.

A loud horn rips me from my thoughts just in time to swerve out of the way of an oncoming truck. The steering wheel fights against my overcorrection as I make a sharp right over a curb in front of a gas station off the Alameda.

Ignoring the stares from people at the pumps, I throw my car in park and rest my head against the top of the steering wheel.

You're okay. You're fine. Everything's fine.

A cruel laugh falls from my lips. That mantra usually drags me back from the edge of ruin, but now it's dangling me off the side of the cliff with every intention of letting me fall.

Everything's not fucking fine.

There's a rap against my window and I prepare myself to put on a show for whatever stranger is inserting themselves in my business.

I would've taken a nosy stranger over seeing Micah standing outside. I wonder how much of that he saw.

Let's get this over with.

I roll my window down at his silent instruction and wait.

"Move over."

"Excuse me?" I ask.

"Move over. I'm driving."

I let out a deep breath that does absolutely nothing to calm my nerves and let my head fall against the headrest. "I don't need you to drive. Were you following me?"

"We're going to the same place. Was I supposed to find an alternate route because you don't wanna be in the same vicinity as me for some reason?"

For some reason. Ha. He makes it seem like I have some petty grudge against him. I don't have a grudge at all; I'm just the only one of us with any sense. It's pointless for us to build any sort of connection when history has shown what happens every time we go down that road.

I'm not in the habit of wasting my time.

"I don't have a problem with you, Micah."

"Right. Move over."

"Micah. No."

"Danielle. Yes."

Oh, we're pulling out the government now, I see.

"You almost crashed thirty seconds ago. Let's be forreal."

I wave him off. "I was distracted for a second, damn. I'm fine." I know I'm not fine. I don't know how long it will take for anything to be fine again, but I know it will be. I don't have any other choice. Tanya was the main person in my life who made me feel okay in my skin. Without her to push me out of my failure mindset, I would've given up on my modeling dreams before they had a chance to take off. For all the bad and ugly that world brought me, it also gave me too much good to discard. As encouraging as she was, she could also play hardball and she would have my ass if she thought I let her death make me give up on my own life.

Micah opens my door and stoops until he's at my eye level. "I hate to break it to you, but this is gonna end with me getting my way this time. We don't have to talk on the ride over, but please don't make me stand around helpless to help someone else."

The severity of his words and his pained expression take the wind out of my sails. On one knee in front of me, fists balled like he's barely holding on, ready to beg me for salvation that I can't give, he leaves me no choice but to unbuckle my seat belt and climb over the middle console.

After climbing in, he adjusts my seat and mirrors.

"What about your car?" I ask, looking back at his impeccably clean white Audi SQ8 parked right behind me, waiting for someone to come along and fuck with it.

"Not worried about it." He locks eyes with me, tossing any follow-up question I might've had to the back of my mind, and pulls off.

Mr. Townsend's office is as boring as I expect it to be. The walls are plain, his various degrees serving as the only decorations. His oak desk is traditional, neatly organized, and lacking anything worth taking a second look at.

As a matter of fact, the only note of color in this entire office is a pink rose preserved in a glass-covered vase sitting on the bookshelf behind him.

That had to be from Tanya. I highly doubt she'd work with this man without trying to add at least a little color to his space.

"How did she do it?" I ask, forsaking all pleasantries.

I feel Micah's eyes on me, but I don't look his way. My attention stays on Mr. Townsend, watching his every move for any signs of deception.

"How did she do what?"

I pull out my phone and open my texts with Tanya. I navigate to our photos as quickly as possible to avoid rereading that final exchange once again. Stretching my arm across his desk, I swipe through the numerous pictures Tanya sent me while supposedly on her travels. There are pictures of her on the beaches of Italy, at Madame Tussauds in New York, at the Musée d'Orsay in Paris, and so on.

"She told me she was traveling. She sent me all these pictures. Clearly that wasn't true, so how did she do it?"

He stops watching my slideshow and adjusts his suit jacket. "She did do some traveling when she was first diagnosed. But she also arranged a photoshoot to make it look like she was in all these places when her condition progressed. They were all places she'd been to before, so she'd be able to answer any questions you might ask."

He says it matter-of-factly, oblivious to how it flays me wide open that someone I treasured went to such lengths to hide her health from me.

Maybe he's not oblivious. Maybe he just doesn't care. I'm well aware that this man doesn't deserve my judgment or my ire. He is only doing his job, after all, but someone has to hold this rage in my chest and it can't be me.

"Why would she do that?"

"She didn't want either of you to know about her diagnosis. She said it was important that you go on living your lives without seeing her like that."

"Like a human?" I ask. No matter how hard I try, I can't wrap my head around the fact that she would leave us without saying goodbye. Yes, she was the textbook definition of fabulous, so I'm sure seeing her sick would've been a shock, but I would take that shock a million times just to give her one last hug.

Fuck. These beige ass walls are not going to see my tears.

"I suppose so," Mr. Townsend says. His nonchalant tone makes my blood boil.

"Right. And you're a lawyer, so of course you don't mind perpetuating lies."

He leans his weight against his desk, his gaze seething.

I match his energy and lean in as well. I feel the weight of Micah at my back, silently conveying to both Mr. Townsend and me that he's on my side. I probably don't deserve that from him, but I'll take it.

"Let me be clear," Mr. Townsend starts. "My priority was and still is Tanya. It was my duty to carry out her last wishes however she saw fit. You may not like it—and believe me, I understand why you wouldn't—but that's not my problem."

We stare at each other until he looks away to grab a file off his desk. That should feel like a win, but instead it feels like he couldn't be bothered to engage in my childish games.

"Let's get started," Mr. Townsend announces.

"Wait a minute," I interrupt.

He pulls his eyes away from the file, seemingly ready for another insult to be hurled his way.

"Shouldn't we wait for whoever else is coming?" I motion around Micah and myself to the otherwise empty office.

"No one else is coming, Ms. Jenkins." He waits for me to take a seat before continuing. "Mrs. Holden left everything to the two of you."

Micah and I share a look of disbelief. Tanya had other family and friends, causes that meant a lot to her. Why would she leave everything to us?

"That can't be right," Micah interjects.

"I wrote the will up for her, Mr. Wright. I assure you, it's correct. There are some caveats, though."

He hands over a letter that we grab in unison.

Dear Dani and Micah,

If you're reading this, I'm dead.

I would apologize for the dramatics, but really, what were you expecting?

Now, I know the two of you well enough to know you're beating yourselves up for being unaware of my illness. To that I say, get over yourselves. How could you know something I purposefully didn't tell you?

I'm sorry for keeping it from you. Micah, you're probably sitting there internalizing everything, wondering how you could've saved me. Dani, you're probably burning with anger and taking it out on poor Victor. Stop that.

Trust me when I say, I did what I thought was best. Watching the life slowly fade from my eyes is a fate I could never put on you. I did it with my mother and some days I remember those final moments more than I remember her life. I don't want that for you.

Truthfully, I wasn't expecting the two of you. You stormed into my life and completely decimated my carefully laid plans to be the aloof bombshell that everyone wanted to be around yet no one really knew. I swear George sent you. The bastard had the audacity to make me a widow at the age of thirty-six, and over two decades later—instead of sending me a new man to occupy my golden years—he sent me two ambitious kids with tender hearts that sucked me in.

Dani, you showed up at the rec center with so much bravado. Anyone who even thought of stepping on your dreams of becoming a model felt your wrath. You had a laser focus that demanded attention and I couldn't help but to give it to you.

Micah, we may have met under unusual circumstances, but at a young age you had this quiet confidence about you. I've come across many arrogant artists in my day, and when you walked into my class, your smirk made me think you'd be no different. I've never been more happy to be wrong. You kept to yourself, but you were always watching, observing. You always knew exactly what you wanted to do with your work, but you were also always the first to help someone when they didn't.

Life has thrown you both curveball after curveball, and it's molded you in different ways. Dani, you've become scared of letting yourself have anything good, for fear of losing it. You deserve all the good things. Grab them and hold on tight. Micah, you've become convinced that you don't deserve the good things that have come to you. I'm sure I'm not the first person to tell you this, but let me reiterate the point: you have earned every bit of your success. Do not let anyone, including yourself, steal your joy.

I have watched you both grow from young hopefuls with dreams and ambitions to still young but older hopefuls who have actually seen their dreams realized. Some of those dreams haven't been what you thought and some have been more than you imagined, but you've accomplished them all the same. If I could give you any advice? It would be to never stop dreaming. If you stop, what reason is there to wake up?

Okay . . .

Well, now that I've buttered you up, I figured it's time to make my final requests.

Here's the first:

I instructed Victor to give you this letter after the funeral so that this would make more sense. I'm sure you noticed that my funeral was far from anything I would've ever associated my name with, full of phony try-hards I absolutely despised in life.

That's because the funeral was for appearances only. People love to act like they give a damn about you once you're gone when they wouldn't piss on you if you were on fire when you were alive. That's fine, let the frauds shed their crocodile tears. I don't want them anywhere near my real homegoing.

That's where you come in. There isn't anyone else I'd want to plan my homegoing than you two, so should you choose to accept, I leave this and the task of cleaning out my house in your hands. I want you to hold a gala in my name and auction off my things for charity. I've been fortunate enough to accumulate quite a few gems over my lifetime, and it would mean the world to me for them to find new homes that will cherish them as I did.

Whatever you do, do it up big. When you think you've gone overboard, do a little more.

I only have two rules:

1. *Do it together. It's important to me that you're together on this every step of the way. No dividing and conquering, no passing the planning off to a professional. The*

two of you are capable of creating magic together, and that's exactly how I want to go out.

2. *Make magic. I want you to auction off something together. I don't care what it is as long as you do it as a unit.*

Easy enough? Here's the catch:

There's some things I need you to do for me. Some places you'll need to go, people you'll need to meet, and things you'll need to get.

If you're going to throw a gala in my honor, you'll need a more complete picture of me. You're probably thinking what else could I have possibly hidden from you. I lived quite a life, and there are parts of my story you don't know. I want to share them with you now.

Victor will have the details of your first task, but it'll be up to you to find the rest along the way. I trust you'll rise to the challenge.

Anyhoo, I guess I'm done rambling on now. This is a lot to take in, I'm sure, and I'm sorry for that. I know that I've had more time to process the end of my life than you have, but please don't be sad for me. I'm ready to be with George and my family again. I've lived a full life with no regrets.

How many people get to say that?

Thank you for honoring an old woman with the gift of family.

Love you deeply,
Tanya

A scavenger hunt. She's sending us on a damn scavenger hunt. That woman really left us a multitude of assignments like a professor going on sabbatical. I'm half expecting Mr. Townsend to pop up with a Blackboard login page next. It wouldn't surprise me if Tanya told him to grade our performances when this is over.

Micah laughs. It starts off like a slow rumble, gradually becoming a full guffaw. "I was worried that she might've lost her light at the end, but this is so fucking Tanya. I'm glad."

I take him in before turning to see Mr. Townsend with a restrained smile on his face.

He's right. This illness stole everything from her, but she held on to her fire until the very end.

I cling to that shred of relief with everything in me.

Micah and Mr. Townsend talk more about formalities, but I have nothing left to contribute. I reread the letter three more times before we finally bring this meeting to an end.

I practically run out of the office before I remember I have to wait for Micah or else be the biggest bitch for leaving him stranded.

He strolls out of the office, hands in his pockets, and stands by my side. "She clocked you," he says.

"What?"

"She said you were probably taking your anger out on the lawyer. She was right."

"And she said you were probably trying to create a time machine to go back and save her. So what?"

He sucks his teeth. "She ain't say nothing about no time machine."

"Might as well. Look, I don't know about you, but I need a minute to process this, so are you ready to go?"

He hangs his head. "You okay to drive?"

"I'm fine." As always.

"Then I don't need a ride." He holds my keys out for me to take.

I balk in his direction. "What about your car?"

He points toward the back of the parking lot where Rome waits in Micah's car. He must've texted him to bring it here.

"I figured you'd want to go our separate ways after this."

He thought right.

"Thank you." I pause. "And thank you for getting me here."

"You're welcome, Dani." He pats me on my shoulder and steps away from me.

I don't know what makes me do it, but I grab his wrist. "That's it? You've been fighting to be in my space all day." Not that I want him to. Of course I don't. It's just odd.

He smirks. "Didn't you read the letter? We're about to be seeing a lot of each other."

His words ring in my ears long after he pulls out of the parking lot.

Chapter Three

Micah

FOR AS LONG AS I CAN REMEMBER, LITTLE SUNSHINE'S Daycare has been as much a fixture in our family as any person. I went there. Bailey went there. My mom worked there for a long time, and then I bought it for her, so now she owns it.

I've watched this place transform and adapt over the years. It's grown with the times and with the leadership, but one thing that's always been the same is the dedication to the kids there. My mom has boxes and boxes of every piece of artwork ever given to her.

Right now, I'm helping her gather a few of those boxes to take home from the closet in her office. A couple of the kids are aging out of the center, as it serves children only up to ten years old, so my mom wants to make them something using their own art.

She tried to convince me not to come, but being around family is what I need right now.

"How was the service, Mi?" she asks once we're settled in the car.

"It was . . . a lot." I sigh. My head is still spinning from Tanya's letter and everything thrown at Dani and me. "Can I ask you a question about Chi Chi?"

Chi Chi was my aunt Monica. I have no idea where I got that name from. I started calling her that when I was little and it just stuck. Mom was distraught when she lost her only sister. We all were, but the mere mention of her name visibly pierced a hole in my mom's heart for a long time after. I was a teenage ball of rage when she died, but my mom was a mass of pure despair. Now, she says it brings her peace to talk about Chi Chi, but I like to test the waters first.

The orbs of her eyes well with tears. "Of course you can."

I've been thinking about her a lot more since Tanya's passing. Tanya and Chi Chi would've liked each other; they were cut from the same cloth. I have no doubt that they've become the best of friends in the afterlife.

"Was there anything you learned about her after she died that surprised you?"

"Hmm, I learned she had terrible taste in dresses."

"Dresses?" I need to make sure I heard her right, because I think I saw Chi Chi in a dress only once in my life.

"Yep. When I finally found the will to clean out her house, she had a stash of dresses in the back of her closet. I don't know what she had them for, but every single one of them was hideous. One of them was literally the color of vomit. Do you remember when we had pot roast for Easter one year and you threw it up? You were so disgusted that you could see pieces of beef and carrots in the toilet that you refused to eat anything beef-related for months? It looked like that."

"That's . . . descriptive." I shiver as she snickers. "And she had never mentioned them to you before?"

"Nope. Why do you ask?"

I tell her about Tanya's will and the scavenger hunt Dani and I will need to embark on.

"Are you worried about what you're gonna find out about her?"

"No. Well, yes." Having to plan the gala and auction is daunting, but I'm confident we can put something together that will make Tanya proud. Her letter made it sound like what we would learn on this scavenger hunt would tear our worlds apart, and that has me a bit on edge. Finding out about her cancer when it was already too late was shocking enough.

"Well, let me ask you this. Is there anything you could learn about Tanya that would make you love her less?"

"No." That's never been a question.

"Then, you just have to take each discovery as it comes. Most people take their secrets with them to the grave. She's trusting you to care for them the way you cared for her. Take solace in that."

I nod along with her. I pull into my parents' driveway, throwing the car in park before turning to face her. "Thanks, Mom."

She pats my cheek. "Anytime, Mi. And for the record, when I die I want a parade."

A shocked laugh escapes me. "Are we talking Macy's level or the fairgrounds?"

She purses her lips and tilts her head. "Macy's, of course." Without another word, she slips out of the car and up to the front door.

Shaking my head, I grab the boxes from the back before heading inside, where I follow the sound of raised voices down the hallway and stumble upon one hell of a scene.

My cousins, Paris and Penelope, are in the living room. Penelope has Paris pinned to the ground with her leg in the air, while Bailey slams her palm on the ground.

Right before her palm hits the carpet a third time, Paris kicks her leg up and swings her body to the side.

"Bullshit!" Penelope screams out.

My dad's eyes go wide as he looks on from the couch.

Paris sticks her tongue out and her middle finger up. "Told you you couldn't pin me, bitch."

"I did pin you, dumb hoe. You just got away," Penelope chastises.

The shouts from all three ladies increase until Mom shows them she can shout the loudest. "Why are y'all always tearing my house up?!" she demands. "Old as you are," she mumbles under her breath.

Paris moves to stand, but Penelope swipes Paris's legs from under her and pushes her shoulder before jumping up.

Dad snorts as he gets up from the couch and wraps me up in a hug and then kisses Mom.

"Gigi, you know I can't let her show me up," Penelope says, donning an innocent voice.

They're only a year apart, and while they're the very best of friends, they always find something to compete over. Chi Chi always said they got that from their dad, because it definitely didn't come from her.

Mom turns her nose up and smacks both Penelope and Paris on the butts as she walks past them. Bailey slips her hand in Mom's and trails behind her to the kitchen.

"What up, Mikey?" Paris greets me.

"Hey, Pee Pee Girls."

Paris's nostrils flare and Penelope's lips turn to a sneer at the childhood nickname they've always hated. It's not my fault their mother gave them both *P* names. It was too easy.

"And to think, we came over to check on your ass," Penelope jeers.

I pull her into a bear hug, smacking a kiss on her forehead that she wipes off. "Oh, I thought you came over to fight for your championship."

She presses her index and middle fingers against my forehead. "My championship ain't ever been in danger."

Paris snaps her neck in Penelope's direction, lips primed to fire back an insult, but the scent of Mom's leftover homemade cinnamon rolls fill the air. Her nose practically lifts her off the ground.

She rushes over for a quick hug before turning to the kitchen. "Gigi, my neck hurts from that beating I took, I think some dessert would help heal me," she calls out as she goes.

"This bitch," Penelope mutters to herself.

"You know she don't care about shit once she smells my mom's cooking."

"True. How are you holding up?" she asks, looping her arm around my waist.

"Uh, you know, I've been better, but I'll be okay." Tanya said not to feel sad for her, because she was ready to go. But she didn't say not to be sad for myself, so I'm going to sit in this feeling for a little while longer.

"I know you will."

We walk into the kitchen to find Paris dancing around in circles with a cinnamon roll in her hands while Bailey records her and Mom does her best to ignore them both.

As Penelope runs into the fold, I feel confident that family is exactly what I needed today.

My thoughts keep drifting to Dani, wondering how she's holding up. Is she letting anyone be there for her?

I pull out my phone and send her a text. The only reason I have her new number is because Amerie insisted her wedding party have each other's contact information.

Before her number changed, the proof of our connection was easy to find. It shone through every text, voice note, and emoji. Now, as I start a brand-new text chain with her, the empty screen serves as a stark reminder of how far we've fallen.

> Me: Hey I know yesterday was a lot. I'm sure I'm not high on your list of confidants but I'm here if you need to talk

The "Delivered" status beneath my text is the only acknowledgment I receive.

Hours later, I'm in the kitchen making popcorn for everyone while Mom and Bailey make an executive decision on what movie we'll be watching.

The Pee Pee Girls stroll into the kitchen, arm in arm, only separating to stand on either side of me. Paris locks her arms with me while Penelope rests her head on my chest. The way they move through the world is not like Bailey and me. They function on a different wavelength, more like twins than anything. In the thirty years they've been in this world together, they've never even lived apart, so they are very much an extension of each other.

"What do you two want?" I ask, eyeing them both.

They look between themselves, telepathically communicating who's going to start. Paris wins. Or loses, depending on how you look at it.

"Well, we were just talking to Bails about OP's Family Day at the gallery this weekend."

"Okay?" I ask, uncertain. Spring Hill has hosted the kids of Our Place many times before. They don't usually have to butter me up for something beforehand.

"And it got us wondering," Penelope takes over. "If you had reconsidered our offer?"

I remove myself from the cocoon they tried to build around me. "I already gave you my answer." Reconsideration was never on the table.

About a year ago, they asked me to come on as a sort-of partner at Our Place. My parents are on the board, but they wanted me to have a bigger role. I flat-out refused.

Chi Chi was my best friend and Our Place meant the world to her, but I don't deserve to have a hand in that. I haven't earned my place in her legacy.

I thought I had shut this conversation down the first time they broached it. I didn't think I'd have to endure the look in their eyes when I shattered their perception of me again.

"We know, we just thought—"

I cut Paris off, not wanting to hear it. "No. The answer is still no." I hold my fist up to my chest, rubbing small circles there until the ache starts to subside.

"Could you tell us why?" Penelope asks.

The ping of the microwave saves me from having to answer them or myself. I grab the popcorn and pour it into the waiting bowl. "That's something I'll have to deal with one day." Probably the day I meet Chi Chi again. "But you don't. Leave it alone, okay?"

Unwilling to watch the disappointment flood their faces, I turn my back on them.

Later, when I've made it home and fallen into my bed, a text chimes on my phone.

Without even looking, I can feel that it's her.

Chapter Four

Dani

SPONSORED POST FOR A BLACK WOMAN–OWNED SHOE brand? Check.

Follow up with the distribution company for Promesa? Check.

Edit my upcoming YouTube video? Check.

After the funeral yesterday, work is the only thing that makes sense. If I stop working for a moment, the exhaustion will set in. The bomb Tanya set off on Micah and me will consume my thoughts.

Ugh, Micah.

What the hell was Tanya thinking?

Actually, I don't think I want to know.

Up until now, I was doing a wonderful job of barely acknowledging Micah's existence. Him being in my inner circle had no bearing on my life whatsoever, but now I have no choice but to acknowledge him. Tanya's death should've broken the invisible connection between us, but instead it's dug up the shallow grave I buried us in. Now, I have to figure out how to present the same indifference toward him while spending an absurd amount of time together.

My phone rings, and an involuntary sigh runs through my body when my mom's contact photo appears.

Answering her call is the last thing I need right now. Michelle Jenkins is a lot of things: a badass scientist, a musical connoisseur, a history nerd. We haven't always seen eye to eye, but I know what a capable woman she is. One thing she's not capable of? Letting me deflect.

She thinks the only way of coping is dealing with things head-on, so she'll push and push until your dam breaks. This dam of mine has been carefully constructed. Years of layering each concrete block of secrets and shame have ensured my survival. I'm not ready to give her a peek at the other side.

The phone rings for what feels like an eternity until her photo finally disappears, letting me catch my breath.

While I'm navigating back to the to-do list Nisha left in my email, another notification pops up on my phone. A text from Micah.

Micah: Hey I know yesterday was a lot. I'm sure I'm not high on your list of confidants but I'm here if you need to talk

Ha! That's probably my first genuine laugh of the day. Not high on my list of confidants. That list is incredibly short to begin with; losing Tanya has made it so I can count the names on one hand. Micah lost his place on that list six years ago, and if I have my way, he'll never find his way back on it.

Leaving him on delivered, I reopen my to-do list.

I still have to decide whether I want to partner with this new makeup company. All their products are vegan and their packaging looks like different desserts. Their blush sticks are shaped like chocolate truffles, their eyeshadow palettes like ice cream cones, with shades named for different ice cream flavors. The tagline is *Indulge in yourself.*

They want me to be a sponsored partner, but I never agree to partnerships without trying the products first and researching the company. I'll be damned if I attach my name to a brand with shitty products and even shittier leaders.

I keep all my PR packages that I haven't opened yet in my spare bedroom, so I head there to find the one from Indulgence Cosmetics. Their unique packaging had already sold me and the company seems to be on the up-and-up based on everything Nisha and I found. The last thing to do is figure out if their stuff is any good.

Pulling out the eyeshadow palettes, blush, and bronzer they sent along with my tried-and-true makeup products from other brands, I set up my vanity to record a video.

One hour later, I have a face beat to the gods and I know for a fact that I want to partner with this brand, but I also know I'm going to have to rerecord the entire thing.

I hated every second of recording that. I don't even have to watch it back to know how horrible it turned out and that no amount of editing is going to fix it.

I blow out a harsh breath. If there's one word I could use to describe my content lately, what would it be?

Stale.

It's just . . . stale. It feels like I'm ripping myself off over and over again, and though I know that's somewhat the point—as influencers we're not reinventing the wheel here—it shouldn't be this dry.

When I first decided to take a step back from runway and editorial modeling and focus more on working for myself, it was exhilarating. I could make the content I wanted how I wanted to without having to run it by a million other people first. I could be my own person.

Now, it's exhausting.

I want to still love it. I do still love it, but sometimes when I look at myself at thirty-one years old next to all the twentysomethings who are shaking shit up on a daily basis, I don't feel like I compare.

Damn, so much for work being the only thing that makes sense.

I switch focus to anything on my list involving my tequila brand, Promesa. That's much more manageable right now.

My fingers flinch at the sound of my phone ringing yet again. The face on the screen settles my nerves a bit though.

Omari Hughes is a friend of mine. A friend I see naked whenever the mood strikes, but a friend nonetheless.

"Well, well, well, I was just thinking about you." I wasn't. But a little goes a long way with this man.

"Oh, yeah? Guess I have perfect timing then, huh?"

"That depends."

"On?" he asks with raised brows.

"On if you plan on coming to see me tonight."

The white of his teeth cast a glow over the FaceTime call.

I met Omari last year while on a cruise. He's absolutely gorgeous. He's tall with golden-brown skin, hazel eyes, a wide-set nose, and lush lips that I know for a fact make great pillows to sit on. He's successful, making a name for himself in the finance industry, and he's a genuinely nice guy. He can be a yapper, so I tend to zone out, but I like that about him. It's a great distraction when I don't want to be alone and don't want to talk about myself—like tonight.

Staring at him on my screen now, though, I'm starting to notice certain things that don't appeal to me as much as they used to.

His box fade looks great on him, but my fingers long to grab hold of a head full of locs. I don't find myself getting lost in the flecks of gold in his eyes anymore nor do I admire the crisp suits he wears every single time I see him.

I have to get a fucking grip.

A night to turn off my heart and my brain and listen only to my pussy seems like the perfect remedy for this shitty week.

"Absolutely. You hungry?"

"I can be," I offer.

"I'm leaving the office now, but let me go home to shower and all that and then I can come pick you up?"

"Or"—I lean closer to the phone, lowering my voice to a breathy whisper—"we could order in." I'm not hungry for food anyway.

His responding smirk is downright devilish. "Even better."

Knowing what's coming gives me the motivation to push through the rest of my to-do list.

I'm twenty minutes into editing the video I made showcasing my favorite dupe perfumes when I hear the distinct click of my door unlocking. The girls are the only people who have a key to my place who use it without calling first, so I'm not surprised when I see Nelle and Evie walk into my bedroom.

"Well, hello, my babies. What are y'all up to?"

"I told you she was gonna act like everything was okay," Evie says offhandedly to Janelle.

"You did say that," Janelle cosigns.

"Do y'all wanna fill me in or talk around me?"

Janelle, clearly fresh off work in her pleated-waist dress, turns to me with a determined glint in her eyes. "Why didn't you tell us that Tanya passed away?"

My heart sinks.

I knew this was coming. I've been reacting to messages in the group chat and sending the occasional gifs, trying to appear normal. I was hoping I'd be able to fly under the radar for a few more days before I had to talk about this with them.

"Oh. How'd you find out?"

Evie's eyes lower to slits, investigating my every movement. "I ran into your mom at the store and she told me. What's going on, Dani?"

I sigh. I should've known my mom would find a way to get me to face my shit. "I guess I just wanted to be in denial for a while longer. Telling you guys makes it real." Irritation sets in as the burn of tears bubbles up. I press my nails into the palm of my hand to try to shift the pain somewhere else.

Anything to avoid crying.

Evie's eyes soften as she scoots closer to me. "Aww, I'm so sorry. I know she meant a lot to you."

"How can we help?" Janelle asks. "We don't have to talk about it if you don't want. We can just . . . sit. Exist. Whatever you need."

This is why a large piece of my heart has their names carved in it. They understand who I am and they accept me for it.

I wrap my arms around both their shoulders to pull them in for a group hug, and for one brief moment, I let my grief take over. The dam is still intact, but it doesn't feel like it's at capacity anymore.

Once we separate part and I'm satisfied I can speak without breaking, I tell them about Tanya's last wishes and confess Micah's part in it.

"Wait, wait. How is this the first time we're hearing that Micah knew Tanya too?" Evie questions.

"Right. So, y'all have known each other for a long time and just didn't say shit?"

I don't want to lie to my girls—any more than I already have, that is. But I also don't want to share that piece of my life with them. My history with Micah is just that: history. It should stay in the past where it belongs.

"We didn't know each other. Not really. We just both knew Tanya." I know from the look on their faces that they don't believe me. They shouldn't. But I'm able to distract them with another subject. "But anyway, enough about that headache. How are you doing, Nelle? Have you talked to Ri at all since she's been on her honeymoon?"

To say that I was appalled by Ri's behavior during her wedding would be an understatement. Going into the two-week affair, I was expecting the normal drama that comes with a wedding, especially a destination wedding. What I wasn't expecting was for Ri to spend the entire time being a bitch to everyone around her, Nelle most of all. If I were in Ri's shoes, I would probably kiss the ground she walked on instead of making her miserable. Maybe that's just me, but I highly doubt I'm alone.

Ri isn't always the easiest person to get along with, which is why I find myself being the peacemaker more often than not, but that trip stretched my abilities beyond their limits.

"Nope. And I have no desire to. When she gets back, we can figure out where we go from here, but until then I'm enjoying my peace away from her."

"That's fair. I'm really sorry if it felt like I was taking her side."

"Dani," Janelle says. "I'm gonna stop you right there. None of that shit is on you. This had been building for a while, so I'm glad everything finally came to a head."

I nod my understanding before she continues.

"And I hope y'all don't feel like you have to choose between us. I love y'all and I'm never coming up off you. So, even if me and her never figure our shit out, we'll"—she motions her index finger between the three of us—"always be good."

Evie raises her hand like she's in a classroom.

"Yes, Evie?" I ask with a snicker.

She lowers her hand and clears her throat. "That was so nice. Love you too, all that good shit, but um, I'm good on Amerie."

I can't say I'm surprised by her statement. Evie's always been less tolerant of Ri's antics than anyone else, but her tone of voice when she says it makes me laugh all the same.

Janelle joins in the laughter. "You're just done with her?"

"Been done, actually. We're just too old for the shit she pulls, and I'm over it. Apparently, we're gonna be tangled up with these men for a long time since you wanna slob down Rome, and you"—she points to me—"got whatever you got going on with Micah."

"Nothing's going on with me and Micah."

"Oh, so we're just not talking about you spending time with Jalen *and* his son?" Janelle adds.

"Your boyfriend tricked me into that!" Evie retorts.

"'Boyfriend' is crazy, first of all. Second of all, all he did was ask and you said yes."

My brows peak as I try to hide my amusement. Our last brunch was eventful to say the least. I received devastating news, and our chauffeur, Rome, asked Evie to help his nephew with some kind of video game competition. She agreed, but I think in her mimosa-filled haze she forgot that doing so would put her in Jalen's orbit. They were very flirty at the wedding. I'm curious to see if she'll do what she always does and push it away or fall into it.

"Not you defending a man. That's what's crazy. Your *boyfriend*"—she emphasizes the word—"took advantage of my drunken kindness and I won't forget it."

Janelle rolls her eyes. We know Evie's not actually mad, because if she was, everyone and their mama would know.

"Whatever, Evie," Janelle says.

"Whatever my ass. What was I saying before you two started ganging up on me?"

"Some nonsense," I tease.

She flips me off and the action seems to switch the light bulb on in her head. "Oh! Back to your raggedy sister. Since *y'all* got us tangled up with her conniving husband's friends for life, I'm not gonna stop coming around or not go somewhere just because she's there. But, she better not even think about hitting me up one-on-one. I don't wanna talk to her, see her, kick it with her, skate with her. Nothing." She folds her arms across her chest and turns up her nose.

"You get on my nerves." Janelle laughs.

We joke more about the entire situation and move on to grilling Janelle about how things are going with Rome, but in the back of my mind I keep thinking about how my relationship with Amerie will be going forward.

Evie may be ready to give up on her, but I can't do that. We've been friends for seventeen years. She's seen me at my worst and never gave up on me. I have to believe that person is still there.

Thinking about it is giving me a headache, so I tune back in to Janelle and Evie, sighing with relief when Janelle runs off to use my shower and Evie orders snacks and drinks for everyone.

I text Omari for a rain check on my dick appointment. Dicks come and go, but your girls are forever.

Hours after the girls and I have downed multiple bottles of wine, gorged ourselves on junk food, watched our favorite episodes of *Grey's Anatomy*, and raided my perfume collection to "help" me with my video edits, they're fast asleep in my bed.

Evie's soft snores match the pace of my heartbeat, and I count each one while staring at my ceiling. Sleep won't come for me, not when the words of Micah's text flash across my eyelids every time I close them.

I do have to face him eventually. Not for him, and definitely not for me. For Tanya.

Sighing, I roll over and grab my phone from the nightstand, shooting off a response before I change my mind.

Me: I'm okay, thanks. We should probably get started on Tanya's neverending list

Chapter Five

Micah

Tanya's street is disturbingly quiet when I pull onto it. I used to say that Tanya picked her house because the neighborhood was as loud as she was. Now, there's nothing. Not a single neighbor outside mowing their lawn or smoking. No kids riding their bikes up and down the hill. No music drifting out of various windows. It's like she took all the energy of this place with her.

I pull into her driveway, leaving enough space for Dani to park beside me when she gets here. After she finally texted me back the other day, we made a plan to start cleaning out Tanya's house.

She claims she doesn't have a problem with me, but we both know that's a lie. When we're in group settings, she can pretend with the best of them, most of the time opting to pretend I'm not there at all. It's the rare moment we're alone that she can't get away from me fast enough.

Moments later, her sleek black car pulls up.

When she steps out of the car, her greeting is short—not rude per se, but clipped. She rubs her palms against her jeans three times in quick succession and her bottom lip holds a permanent position between her teeth. Facing this house and its memories isn't going to be easy for either of us.

We both stop in our tracks the moment we step inside. Tanya never let anything be out of place when she was alive, so it's not like I was expecting the place to be in ruins, but this is like stepping into a time capsule.

Absolutely nothing has changed since the last time I was here. Her keys are still hanging on the rack by the door. The Moroccan rug she had in the entryway is still rolled up and sitting in the corner because after insisting on having it, she decided she didn't like how it looked on her floor.

I feel like I'm trespassing. Like I've disturbed the peace of a sacred shrine. My feet itch to run out of here. The sensation rises up my leg, making it impossible to stand still.

The door to the den is open and I can make out the corner of one of her many paintings. A sad smile creeps across my face, as I know I'll find all of her favorite artwork in there, but that she won't be there to talk about them with me for the hundredth time.

A loud gasp from Dani shakes my thought away. She's staring at the den as well.

Is it because she knows the piece that started us on this path is in there?

Does she think about that day as much as I do?

"Are you okay?" I ask. I shouldn't have asked. I can see the moment her walls go up, locking me on the other side.

"I'm fine," she mutters as she heads upstairs.

"Whoever's up there, please give me strength," I whisper as she disappears from my line of sight.

The portrait I made for Tanya follows me around the den as I go through boxes and make note of things I think she would want auctioned off, donated, or thrown out.

I've come a long way since I did this painting. I've come into my own as an artist and as a man, but looking at this portrait reminds me of all the mistakes I've made getting here.

As I make my way upstairs, I catch a glimpse of Dani sitting on the floor in one of the bedrooms. She's looking through a thick book and rubbing her finger back and forth across her brow.

If you look at Dani on social media, you'd think she's incredibly put-together and that she eats, sleeps, and breathes her brand. You'd think that nothing and no one affects her, that she's a one-woman army who doesn't need or want anyone to stand behind her. Maybe those things are true now, but I remember a different version of her.

I remember the Dani who felt deeply. The one who was unapologetic about who and what she loved. The one who appreciated adventure.

When I see her with her girls, I know that version still exists, I'm just not privy to it.

It shouldn't eat me up inside. I've been outside her circle of trust for far longer than I was ever inside it. It shouldn't bother me, but it does.

It bothers me that we never had a real chance.

Tanya's letter said that I don't feel I deserve good things. It's hard to feel deserving of good things when the people ten times better than you get cut down. My aunt had her life snatched away by a reckless driver. One of my best friends' life was cut short by a stray bullet. An autoimmune disease forced my sister to reimagine her dance dreams. And then there's me. I fucked up when I was younger, and Tanya handed me a second chance. I took the risky route in school and pursued my art dreams instead of the guaranteed future, yet I still ended up being successful enough to ensure my family's comfort for life. It doesn't seem right. Why me? Why not them?

If there's any real justification for how fortunate I've been, I'd say it has to be because life is making up for playing the cruelest trick it could: putting Dani in mine before either of us was ready.

Watching her now, uninhibited with her emotions, feels like a rare gift.

You didn't earn this.

That realization hits me like a ton of bricks. This peek behind Dani's curtain wasn't given, it was stolen. Shame washes over me as I purposefully slam my hand against the railing, wordlessly announcing my presence.

Dani snaps up from her bent-forward position. I catch the look of indecision on her face. She can't hide what she was looking at and wipe away her tears at the same time. She has to choose one: hide her memories or hide her emotions.

Her decision is made when I enter the room, her hand already lowering from her face back to her side, the book still in her lap.

"What'd you find?" I ask.

"It's, um"—she pauses to clear any sign of emotion out of her voice—"it's a photobook. I found it on her desk."

"Oh, that's cool. Can I look at it with you?"

She rushes to stand and practically slams the book against my chest. "Yeah, here you go. I'm gonna look at the other rooms."

She brushes past me, and I sigh in frustration. "Dani. Stop."

Surprisingly, she does, but she doesn't turn to face me.

"We don't have time for this. Tanya meant too much to both of us for us to fuck this up over our shit."

"Our shit? We don't have any shit."

"So you keep telling me," I counter.

She spins around, meeting my vexed expression with her own indignation. "What is it you want from me?"

She's definitely not ready for that conversation.

"I know we don't have the best track record, but I've never had animosity toward you. If I've done something to you, can you please put me out of my misery and tell me? Give me a chance to make it right."

She doesn't slap me or turn and run away, so I take a small step forward, and then another. It's a desperate move but that's exactly what I am—a desperate man wanting to understand how we got here. I'm not without fault for our missed opportunities, but she was the one who reduced us to strangers three years ago.

Why am I being punished for her decision?

Her eyes soften, but I don't dare make a move. She put us here, so she needs to be the one to set us right.

"I'm sorry," she says, her voice softer than a whisper.

"That I feel that way?" I question.

She lets out a soft chuckle. "No. I'm just sorry. It's not you."

I take another step closer and another until our breaths mingle as one. "You wanna tell me what it is, then?"

"Nothing I can't handle. And being here without Tanya didn't help, but I shouldn't have taken it out on you."

I nod slowly, taking in her words. Curiosity eats away at me as I wonder what it is that she's handling on her own and why she feels she has to do that. "It's all good. We all got our ways of dealing with shit. But let's make a deal?"

"What kind of deal?"

I hold out my hand to her. "Let's be partners in this."

She takes my hand in hers. Her posture is always perfect, but she somehow manages to stand even straighter. "For Tanya?"

"For Tanya." For now.

She lets our hands linger for a moment longer before she breaks our connection and steals the photobook still clutched in my other hand. "You should see this."

She flips past pages of Tanya in different stages of childhood. One particular photo catches my eye. It's a black-and-white one of her, looking no older than six, sitting on the hood of a Chevy convertible while fist-bumping an older man. I assume from the similarity in their noses that the man was her dad. It's good to know that she's always been the star of the show.

Dani keeps flipping through Tanya's memories until she gets to the one she wanted to show me. Tanya stands with Barack and Michelle Obama. While amazing, it's not surprising. Tanya lived an adventurous life, and those adventures got her in the room with a plethora of big names. What *is* surprising is that if you look closely at the photo, you can see that in Tanya's hands she's holding pictures of Dani and me. Dani's picture looks to be one of her magazine covers while mine is a snapshot in front of Spring Hill.

"Please tell me she didn't meet the Obamas and pull pictures of us out of her wallet." It's not a real question. We know that's exactly what she did.

"It's the printed photos for me, though. Like, Tanya, I know you had your phone on you," Dani adds.

We laugh and it feels good to laugh like this with her again. Another moment Tanya gives to us.

"She would've had them there for hours if she had pulled up pictures on her phone," I say through my laughter.

"Oooh, you're right. She would've hated being called any kind of grandma, but that's such a grandma thing to do. Carry pictures of your kids in your wallet."

Dani's chortle grows louder as she lets her chin fall to her chest, but when the rhythm of the sound changes and her shoulders start to shake, I know her laugh has morphed into tears.

The first choke of air from her prompts me to wrap my arms around her without question. If she doesn't want me touching her, she can push me away and I'll go, but I need the anchor as much as she does.

"It should've been us," she cries.

"What should've been us?"

"We should've been the ones taking care of her in the end." She looks up at me, the tears bubbling up but refusing to fall. "Who was there for her? Who cleaned up for her? You know she was big on cleaning. Who cooked her meals?"

"Well, not her, but it never was," I interject, wanting to take some of the weight off her shoulders. It works, if only for a moment, but I'll take it.

"Who held her hand when she took her last breath?"

These same questions have tormented me since learning of Tanya's death. Did she suffer for long? Did she get treatment, or was it too late? Was she alone when she died? So many questions that we may never get the answers to, unless Mr. Townsend can provide them. And even if he can, will it make us feel better to know or will it just add more fuel to the flames of our pain?

"I think that it would've hurt her more to see us see her that way than for us to not be there at all." It's the only solace I can offer.

"It's not fair."

Cancer never is.

"It's not."

She looks up at me, finding the same hurt in my eyes that lives in hers, and falls into me. Her body is overcome with sobs, my body the only thing keeping her off the ground.

Chapter Six

Dani

I CANNOT BELIEVE I CRIED ON THIS MAN'S SHOULDERS.

Fury courses through my veins as I lift my head, finding a small patch of my foundation on his shirt. Not only did I lose control with someone who's at the very top of the list of people I don't want to share feelings with, but the evidence of that loss of control is now staring me in the face—on display for everyone he encounters the rest of the day.

All this because the past doesn't know how to stay in the fucking past. Why couldn't it be my old life wiped from existence?

When I started my career, I was overly sensitive. Every rejection and criticism I received felt like a personal attack on my soul. I would spend hours reading every nasty comment made on posts and videos of me to the point where I could recite them verbatim.

My self-worth was in the gutter. I looked in the mirror and all I could see was everything people didn't like about me. I said yes to things I had no interest in doing that didn't serve me at all just because I was afraid I wouldn't get another opportunity.

When I left New York, I left that old version of myself behind. I toughened my skin until it was impenetrable.

I became known as the woman who oozed confidence out of her every pore and who didn't hesitate to eviscerate naysayers with her words. People stopped trying me because they knew it was a lost cause. I became the one in control.

People like Nigel Pierce are the reason I had to transform myself. He was—and unfortunately still is—a huge name in the modeling industry. He was responsible for making and breaking far too many of my peers, and I was one of the models he made—and almost broke—too.

He preyed on my insecurities and made me feel like I needed him, like I would fade into obscurity if he stopped seeing the value in me. After all, if he hadn't discovered me and booked my first show, I might still be in my shitty apartment with more roommates than bedrooms begging brands to notice me.

I haven't seen or spoken to him in years, but last night he commented on my latest post. He didn't even say anything worth getting upset about, just a simple "Dani Jenkins. It's been too long, beautiful," yet it sent me into a tailspin, sending my mood to the pits of hell.

The audacity to think he can just pop up out of nowhere and talk to me. And the one person I could talk to about it isn't here anymore.

Tanya was the one person who knew the details of my past with Nigel. I knew telling her would make her murderous, but I also knew I could trust her to keep it to herself if I asked. If she were here, I would've come over last night so we could open a bottle—or three—of wine and plot his downfall.

Instead, I'm here to do away with her.

Being in this house is fucking with me. Everything in here is a landmine, waiting to trigger an onslaught of emotions.

I can't do this.

I don't want to do this.

I don't want to be the person to go through all her things and determine their worth. All her things are priceless to me.

She was priceless to me.

And she hid everything from me.

She always did what she thought was best for me, so I'm trying my best not to be angry with her, but I'm so fucking angry with her.

Sucking in a deep breath, I try to ignore the increasing tightness in my chest and the fog spreading over all my thoughts.

Micah brushes his hands against my shoulders. I know he wants to see my eyes, but I can't let him. I can't let him see any more than he already has.

The sound of the doorbell is a welcome reprieve.

Micah lets out a small sigh, his breath ghosting across the shell of my ear, adding butterflies to my already rumbling stomach.

"That's, uh, Bailey. She said she'd meet us here to help go through stuff."

I wonder if he asked her to be here because he needed a buffer or because he thought I'd want one. Either way, her presence is a gift horse I won't look in the mouth.

"You should go let her in. I'll be down in a minute," I muster despite my dry tongue.

Micah tries observing me again, but I keep my eyes focused on that fucking spot of makeup.

"Dani," he starts.

"Micah," I cut him off, exasperated and barely holding on to what little control I have left.

The frustrated grunt from his lips lingers in the air around us, seeking validation and falling short of any acceptance. "You're fine. I know," he says as he ever so slowly releases his grip on me, unknowingly plummeting me into the darkness.

He darts downstairs as I stumble into the bathroom, shutting myself in.

The cold, smooth surface of the sink provides minimal relief against the clamminess of my skin, but I grip it for dear life to try to stave off the vomit clawing its way up my throat.

You're okay. You're fine. Everything's fine.

I recite the mantra to myself repeatedly until the soft tan of the walls stops spinning and the feeling returns to my lower limbs.

After another few minutes of self-assurances, I feel mostly back to normal aside from the tension headache that always follows moments like this.

The first time I lost control of my body, it was terrifying. I was running through the halls of a hotel, unsure if he was chasing me or if it was just the pounding of my heart against my chest I was hearing.

Had Nigel not gotten a random phone call, what would've happened in that room? Would I have given him the things he demanded from me? Would he have taken them by force?

Somehow my legs carried me to an empty stairway before they crumbled beneath me. I felt as if I were floating outside of my body, watching everything unfold. I was screaming at myself to get up, but my legs were frozen to the ground. My body was so unbearably hot, I thought I might melt from the inside out. I kept telling myself to breathe, but it felt as if rocks were sitting on my chest, making the task impossible.

I laid in that stairway powerless to move until my body decided it was safe to work again. The headache that followed was severe enough to leave me bedridden for a full twenty-four hours after. Eventually, losing control became part of my norm. The aftershock headaches became slightly less debilitating.

I didn't figure out a way to bring myself out of the haze sooner until my last confrontation with Nigel.

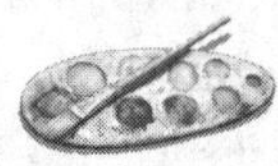

I hate being home.

I spent the last six months in London for work, and I had hoped that would've been long enough to ease the pain I felt at home, but being back in New York doesn't feel good.

Everywhere I look something reminds me of him.

Right as I'm about to unzip my suitcase, Leslie calls me.

There's a voice I haven't missed at all. While I was in London, Leslie left me alone for the most part. Most of my time was spent working on the shoe collaboration with occasional shows and photoshoots, so there was no need for her to be on my line every five minutes.

That might be what I'll miss the most about London.

"Leslie. Long time no talk. What a pleasure." Sarcasm drips from every word like venom. We're well past the point of pretending we're anything more than agent and client. We're a means to an end for each other, not friends.

"Are you at home?" She never bothers to say hello. It's always straight to the point.

"Yes."

"Good. There's a launch party for Dolce's newest fragrance tonight. I'm sending a glam squad your way."

I sigh. I definitely haven't missed this shit. "Leslie. I'm tired. I just got home and I'm jet-lagged. I don't want to go to a party tonight." The only plans I have are with my bed and my TV.

Leslie grunts her frustration. "You've been missing from the New York scene for six months. You need to make a reappearance, and it needs to be good."

"I've been working."

"No one gives a fuck what you're doing if they can't see you doing it."

We go back and forth until the conversation ends with me doing what I always do—giving in.

"Welcome home," I whisper to myself.

At the party, I order another glass of wine from the bar. If I could drown in this glass, I would.

This party is everything Leslie wanted it to be. It's loud and crowded. People have been bombarding me with welcome-back love from the moment I walked in while I've been trying my best to keep my eyes open. The mini knit Balmain dress I'm wearing is doing the heavy lifting for me tonight because I don't have the energy to give.

My model friend Anya and her husband, Pedro, are here, and though I usually always have fun when they're around, tonight is not that night. I should've put my foot down with Leslie because I can feel the exhaustion in my bones. My legs are about to give out and I can hear my words slowing down.

I excuse myself to the restroom, hoping a moment of quiet and a splash of cold water can bring me back, but the body I just bumped into is the coldest splash of water I could ask for.

"Dani Jenkins. You look fantastic." Nigel Pierce leans in to kiss me on the cheek.

I step out of his grasp just in time. "Nigel. What are you doing here?" Leslie is under strict instructions not to send me alone anywhere where Nigel is expected to be, so if he's here, I shouldn't be.

His hand lingers by my hip. My feet itch to run as far away as I can, so I dig my nails into my palm, reminding myself that we're in a room full of people, not a hotel room with no one to save me but myself.

He chuckles, clearly offended by my lack of enthusiasm. "I was invited, same as you. You really do look good, Dani." He makes no attempt to hide his sleazy gaze sliding down my frame. I feel like not even a scorching-hot shower could erase this feeling from my skin.

"Thank you. If you'll excuse me, I was headed to the restroom."

He grabs my wrist before I can step away, his grip forceful and demanding. "Hold on a minute. Let's catch up. We might be working together soon, so it'd be good for us to get reacquainted."

My lip curls against my will. "Excuse me? Working together on what?"

He lets me go, brushing his hands down his sides to regain his composure. "Haven't you talked to Leslie? She pitched you for my upcoming campaign. I told her I was still considering other models, but I've always felt strongly about your talent. Maybe we can get together to talk it over?"

All the blood drains from my body. The room starts to spin and I'm barely able to keep myself upright.

No. No. No. Not now. Not in front of him.

"I-I-I have to go." I push past him, sprinting to the bathroom and shutting myself inside the farthest stall.

I put my head between my legs to try to keep the vomit down. It's hard to breathe. It's hard to move. It's impossible to speak.

This is the one that gets me. I'm going to die here.

I squeeze my eyes shut and try to force air from my lungs. It takes only moments for everything to go black.

At some point, a quiet tap on the stall snaps my eyes open.

"Dani, it's me. Let me in," Ri whispers.

"Ri? What are you doing here?" I look down at my palms, red and angry with impressions of my nails.

"You texted me an SOS and then didn't say anything else, so I tracked your phone. Talked my way past security."

I don't remember pulling out my phone. I don't even know how long I've been in this bathroom. Has my absence been noticed?

I crack open the stall and pull Ri inside.

She holds up a small purse. "I have my travel sewing kit with me. I assumed this was some kind of wardrobe malfunction. What's going on?"

Tears well in my eyes as I release a shaky breath.

"Dani, hey. What's wrong? Talk to me." She grips my shoulders, concern marring her features.

The skin on my wrist feels hot, right where Nigel grabbed me. I claw at my skin, trying to scrape his touch away.

Ri puts her hand on top of mine. "Stop. Stop. You're gonna hurt yourself."

"Good," I cry. "He touched me."

"Who touched you?"

I ignore her, training my gaze on the tarnished spot of skin.

"Dani." She stops me once again. "Who touched you?"

I shake my head vehemently. I can't. I can't.

She takes my hands in hers, forcing me to meet her eyes as she initiates a deep breath, encouraging me to follow her. "You're okay," she coos. "You're okay." She shushes me like a baby on her shoulder when a sob breaks free. "You're okay, I'm here. You're fine. Everything's fine. Say it with me, Dani. Okay? Say you're okay."

"I'm okay," I say shakily.

"You're fine," she says.

"I'm fine," I spit out.

"Everything's fine," she says, rubbing circles on the inside of my palms.

"Everything's fine," I say, taking a steady breath.

She makes me stand in that stall repeating those words and deepening my breaths until it feels less like labor.

"I'm sorry," I croak.

She shakes her head. "No need to be sorry. Let's get you out of here, okay?"

"I can't go back out there."

"Well, if you don't, you'll have to move in here, and that's no good. I'll go out first. You take a minute and then follow me. Okay?"

When I zone out on the bathroom floor again, she grabs my chin and turns my face to hers. "Okay?"

"Okay."

She nods her approval. "One minute, Dani. Don't make me come back to get you."

I say okay again and count down to myself.

Ri leads me out of the party, and I abandon my coat in favor of a quick exit. She gets me home and tucked into my bed before joining me.

"How are you feeling?" she asks.

"Better. But my head is killing me," I say, rubbing my temples.

She goes to my bathroom and comes back with two pills and a glass of water, which I down without question.

"Thank you, Ri. For everything."

She waves me off. "You'd do it for me. What should we do now? Watch some reality TV?"

The words *you're okay, you're fine, everything's fine* became my haven. They saved me more times than I can count.

Micah and Bailey's voices drift upstairs, reminding me that I can't hide out here forever.

I hate being reintroduced to the woman staring back at me in the mirror. The sweat droplets lining my edges, the hard-set line of my mouth that refuses to tip in either direction, the glassy eyes. My least favorite version of myself. I had hoped to never see her again, but here she is reminding me that she's always there no matter who I mold myself into.

Looking around the bathroom, I spot my purse hanging on the doorknob. I must've grabbed it on autopilot when I ran out of the bedroom. I sift through its contents until I find my blotting papers, eye drops, and concealer. Never leave home without them.

Walking down the steps, Micah and Bailey's voices drift from the den. When I reach them, Micah is carefully taking Tanya's paintings off the wall while Bailey is wrapping them in bubble wrap.

She spots me first, throwing her hand up in a wave. "Hi, I'm Bailey."

I've never met Bailey in person—I've seen only pictures back when Micah and I knew each other—but she's grown into a beautiful woman. She and Micah could be twins even down to the smile. I wonder if they get it from their mom or dad.

"Dani, my sister, Bailey. Bailey, this is Dani. My . . . friend," Micah says, not moving from his spot. He doesn't look up, but he pauses, waiting for me to reject the concept of us being friends. I want to object, because we're not friends. We don't know how to be friends without blurring the lines, which always leads to our downfall. Something in me won't let me do it, though, so instead I turn my focus back to Bailey.

"Nice to meet you," I say.

"How are you holding up?"

"I'm okay, thanks for asking. And thanks for helping with all this."

She walks me through what they've done since she got there, and I realize I was locked in the bathroom for longer than I thought.

Our polite conversation keeps my emotions in check, despite my eyes flying to Tanya's paintings with Micah's every move.

Needing to do something to keep myself busy, I grab a box from the hall closet and start loading the paintings inside once Bailey finishes wrapping them.

"Have you guys started thinking about the gala? Themes and stuff?" she asks, eyes darting between us.

For the first time since I've walked downstairs, Micah looks at me.

We haven't discussed the gala or the scavenger hunt Tanya is sending us on. Cleaning out her house seemed like the safest place to start.

"Is drama a theme? That's what Tanya would want," Micah says.

Bailey rolls her eyes. "Well, no. Not exactly. What about a color scheme? What was Tanya's favorite color?"

"Teal and gold," we answer in unison.

That color combination is the definition of opulence, she used to say.

"Easy enough. Then we'll go with that." Bailey makes a note in her phone. I can see the wheels in her head turning, the gala perfectly falling into place.

"Franky, don't start," Micah warns.

She cuts her eyes over to him in a way only little sisters do. "Don't start what?"

"You don't have to do everything. Dani and I can do it."

"And you will. But I can help, so stop trying to bench me," she demands.

"I didn't say you couldn't. I'm just saying. You get all hype and you wanna take everything on by yourself."

I make no moves to hide my eyes ping-ponging back and forth between them, but they don't even seem to remember I'm here.

"I'm aware of my limitations. You don't have to keep reminding me," she snaps.

"Franky, I . . ."

"Umm, sorry," I interrupt. "What am I missing?" I regret the question as soon as Bailey looks at me in stunned silence.

She takes a minute to gather her thoughts. "I have MS and that means Micah sometimes forgets I'm still a capable adult."

The look on Micah's face is a stab to the gut. My heart goes out to both of them. I know Micah means well, that he adores his sister, but he clearly crosses the line to smothering.

"Maybe I should get Micah and my mom together while you and I plan this extravagant party." I don't know anything about multiple sclerosis and now isn't the appropriate time to ask my questions, but I can relate to the problem of overprotective family members. My mom and I fought constantly about her need to keep me safe when I didn't think I needed it. I didn't truly understand her struggle as a concerned mom until my late twenties. Right now, Bailey doesn't see Micah's overbearingness as care—she sees it as him underestimating her. That, I can help with.

She smirks. "That sounds perfect. Micah's a terrible party planner, anyway."

Micah looks like he wants to say something, but I catch his attention with a subtle shake of my head. His words won't help right now.

The tension between the siblings dissipates long enough for us to get back to work, until Micah picks up the painting. The painting he finished for Tanya on the day she introduced us. The day that changed our lives forever.

"Ooh, she's wearing teal and gold. We should hang that at the entrance," Bailey offers, not realizing what memories she just stumbled into.

Chapter Seven

Dani

Spending the morning at the farmer's market with my mom used to be one of my favorite weekend activities as a kid, so when she asked me to go with her today, I didn't hesitate to say yes.

After setting Micah's portrait of Tanya to the side yesterday, I was able to steer the conversation away from the realm of anything personal and focus on throwing out other ideas for the gala. I've officially tagged Nisha in to help as well because she insisted she had capacity for it on top of everything else she does for me, so the four of us are meeting again at Tanya's to get organized. Micah has things to do today concerning the Baltimore Collective, the foundation he runs with Rome, Christian, and Arnold, so that meeting isn't happening until tomorrow.

Today, I'm allowing myself a day of joy and no complications.

Mom shakes the cup of iced coffee she just got from our favorite local vendor before stopping to grab some apples. "Don't let me forget your father asked me to get him some hot sauce from Corey's stall," she says as she puts another apple in her roller bag.

That man needs a hot sauce intervention. I have no doubt he has about five bottles of the stuff sitting in their pantry right now, but of course, he wants more. We'll make sure he gets it, though, because it's all he ever asks for.

"I got you. How's he doing? I meant to return his call yesterday but I was so tired."

"Mhm, he told me not to buy you any truffle oil today since you didn't call him back." She shrugs as if either one of them would actually stand by that. Every time we come to a farmer's market, Mom insists on buying everything. I'm not mad at it. You never get too old or too successful to let your parents treat you.

"That don't sound like my daddy. He's not that petty."

She sucks her teeth. "That man is King Petty." She points to herself. "And I'm Queen Petty."

I point to myself. "But I'm the princess and that treatment is reserved for peasants."

She shoves my arm. "Be quiet, girl."

We move to the vendor who sells a few different types of truffle oils, and like I suspected, she puts a few bottles in her roller bag for me.

"Not a word to your daddy," she threatens.

I chuckle into my hand, silently agreeing. "Anyway, I'm thinking about getting Evie's car detailed for her birthday, so how many bottles of hot sauce you think I gotta get your husband for him to fit me in the schedule?" Dad's car detailing business is always booked.

Mom takes the last sip of her iced coffee and throws it in the nearby trash can. "Now, you tell me how it's supposed to be a gift from you when you're using your dad's services?"

"Because *I'm* the one bringing the car to him."

She rolls her eyes with a laugh.

I stop to look at some waist beads I think Nelle would like while Mom grabs us a couple of donuts from a pastry stall.

"Do you want to come over tomorrow night to make some recipes I found on Pinterest?" she asks.

"I can't. I gotta go to Tanya's for a planning meeting."

"How's that going?"

I can tell from her tone that this conversation could take a turn quickly. Would it be too much to ask for my truffle oils so I can go?

"It's fine," I say.

She waits until I have a mouth full of a cinnamon sugar donut to tell me what's on her mind. "I'm worried about you."

I cough around my bite, a cloud of cinnamon escaping my lips. Here we go. "Why are you worried?"

She bites into her jelly donut, using the time it takes her to chew to consider her next words. "We haven't talked about Tanya since she passed. I know you're planning her homegoing, but you haven't told me much about that. You haven't said much of anything. You haven't even cried—not that I'm saying you have to—I just wanna make sure you're coping with her death."

Why are tears the metric for sadness? I've cried plenty of times over Tanya, but because I don't bottle my tears in a jar and splash them in everyone's faces, I'm not grieving properly.

I know my mom means well. I know I probably shouldn't get so defensive with her, but it took us a long time to get our communication style figured out, and it can be easy to regress.

"I promise you, I'm facing Tanya's death head-on," I say, shoving another bite of donut in my mouth.

You could be doing better.

I slam my eyes shut against that thought. I'm doing the best I'm willing to do right now. Tanya made sure I couldn't sweep her death or my feelings about it under the rug, and part of me wants to thank her for that. The other part of me wants to bring her back to life just so I can strangle her.

"Okay, good. That's really good to hear. I'm here for you, Yelli. That's all I wanna say."

I bend down and wrap my arms around her middle and squeeze, careful not to get donut dust on her jacket. "I love you, Mom."

I hear her sniffle against my shoulder. "I love you too, baby."

When we separate, I lock my hand with hers and we walk to the hot sauce stall.

"I think three bottles would get you on the schedule in time for Evie's birthday," she offers with a wide smile.

"Just three? Say less."

After spending entirely too much time and money at the farmer's market, Mom and I drive back to my place.

While we unload my goods, I FaceTime Dad and he gives me shit for taking so long to reach out. When Mom starts ganging up on me, I throw her ass right under the bus and show Dad all the stuff she bought me.

Mom doesn't get a chance to rip into me once Dad hangs up because Nisha FaceTimes me.

I mouth a sarcastic "so sorry" before gleefully answering. "Oh heyyy, Nisha!"

Her face fills my screen. She takes me in, her dark eyes glowing with suspicion. "What's wrong? Usually you answer with 'ughhh, I don't wanna do work!'"

Her mocking tone draws out a giggle from my mom. "She's just happy you saved her from me tearing her ass up," she calls out.

Nisha's eyes light up. "Is that Mama Jenkins? Hey, girl!"

Mom snatches the phone from me so they can bond like always.

When I met Nisha, I hadn't been back in Baltimore long. I had decided to stay in a hotel until I found a place so I wouldn't impose on my parents or the girls. Nisha worked at the front desk. At the time, I was rumored to be dating a singer all because I had starred in his music video and someone decided to harass me about it in the lobby. She stepped in and told the guy off. From then on, she became somebody I could rely on.

It went beyond job responsibilities into friendship, and what's more, I felt safe with her. That was something I had been craving in my professional life, so I offered to double her salary if she came to work with me, and the rest is history.

My mom took to Nisha immediately. Mom said she could instantly tell Nisha had my best interests at heart—something she'd never said about anyone I'd surrounded myself with in New York.

Six years later, that still proves true.

"Um, hello?" I interrupt my mom midsentence.

She looks up at me with her mouth agape.

"She called my phone."

I hold my hand out, but she turns her back to me. "I swear I didn't raise her this way."

Nisha's laugh echoes off my walls. "You did the best you could, Mama. I was just watching my little Sim waiting for her location to say home, but if I knew she was out with you, I would've just hit you up."

"I know it," Mom responds.

Unbelievable, these two.

They continue to ignore me for another couple of minutes until Mom takes pity and announces her departure. She hands back the phone and kisses my forehead as she leaves.

"I swear the two of you together makes my ass itch," I say around a fake shudder.

She shoos her hand at the camera. "Oh stop, you love us."

"Separately," I say deadpan.

"That's just a lie," she counters.

"Right. So, anyway, why were you stalking my location? Because I really don't wanna work."

"You told me to track you down and make you review the Wallflower samples today."

Damn, I'd completely forgotten about my collaboration with the sunglasses brand, which had sent me prototypes of my designs for approval.

"Nishaaaaa. Don't make me," I say through a pained groan.

"I know, pookie," she says patronizingly. "Who's a pretty girl?"

I hold my hands over my head with a sigh. "Let me go grab the damn box."

"Those are cute!" Nisha says about the pair with rose-gold lenses I'm wearing.

So far, we've gone through eight of the twelve pairs they sent me, and I've been unhappy with only one of them.

This pair has a gold nose pad and gold arms to accent the lenses and a three-barrel hinge to keep the design sleek.

"This might be my favorite pair."

"What did you call that one again?" Nisha asks.

"Honeybee."

"Buzz buzz, bitch. Those are perfect," Nisha exclaims.

We fall into a fit of laughter over her corniness.

After I try on the final four pairs, I give Nisha a list of notes to send to Wallflower and ask her to schedule a follow-up meeting with them.

We go over a few other items before getting to the one I'm least looking forward to.

"Is there anything I need to know to be prepared for the meeting at Tanya's tomorrow?"

That Tanya is an asshole for making me do this . . . with him.

"Mmm, nope. Nothing I can think of."

"Okay, and it's just me, you, Micah, and Bailey, right?"

I nod my confirmation.

"And, so, who is Micah to you? Like how well do you know him?"

What a loaded question.

I've kept my history with Micah a secret from everybody. I never even told Tanya because I didn't want her rubbing it in our faces that she introduced us, and by the time I wanted to tell her, we were back to being strangers.

"We kind of dated," I mumble. I don't know what makes me do it, but I tell her damn near everything. I tell her how Tanya introduced us eleven years ago and we spent the most magical day together that led to a kiss in the rain. How I snuck out of his apartment that night for a job opportunity in New York and didn't see him again for five years. How attached at the hip we were when we found each other again until he went home to Baltimore and distanced himself from me. I even tell her how I felt seeing him at his gallery opening three years ago when I walked away from the possibility of us for the last time.

Nisha's eyes go wide with every confession until I'm finished. "I can't believe you asked him to go to London with you and he said no."

"Me either," I say. It's all I can offer. I don't know why things fell apart with us, and I don't care to find out.

She grumbles. "But then when you saw him years later, you didn't wanna hear him out?"

"He had a girlfriend, Nish."

She blows out a raspberry. "I can bet that girlfriend didn't have shit on fate!"

Fate? Oh brother, maybe I made a mistake telling her everything.

"Alright, well, that's enough of that."

"I mean, come on. What are the chances that your friend would marry the friend of the guy you had a passionate tryst with years ago? If that's not fate, I don't know what is."

I sigh. "And now that you're using words like *tryst*, I have got to end this conversation." She raises her finger in the air, but I interrupt before she can speak. "And it's not fate. It's Baltimore being too damn small."

She scowls at me and then shakes her head until her face morphs into a sly grin. "You're in denial, it's okay. Imagine knowing who your soulmate is for eleven years and nothing happening. This is like a movie."

I groan. "Imagine getting hung up on because you say silly things."

She huffs out a laugh. "You're lucky I have to go pick up Deux from the groomers. Can't wait to see you and *Micah* tomorrow." She says Micah's name like it's made of rainbows and unicorns.

"Goodbye, Nisha. Send me puppy pics when you pick up Deux."

She waves as she ends the call.

I need a drink after that.

A bottle of Promesa stares at me from the bar cart in my living room, daring me to indulge. Some people might think it's self-absorbed to have a bottle of my own tequila in my house. Those people are idiots. If I didn't think Promesa was the best tequila on the market, I wouldn't make it. I wouldn't have poured my energy into finding the right partner to make the highest-quality tequila possible. I wouldn't have poured my soul into making sure the product Promesa puts out not only tastes amazing, but evokes feelings. It's not just a tequila. It's passion. It's euphoria. It's power.

I don't drink this shit because I helped make it. I drink it because it's good.

The sweet aroma of the golden liquid permeates the air when I open the bottle. Holding it to my lips, I close my eyes and allow the bittersweet memories clouding my mind to guide the liquid down my throat to the pit of my stomach.

After two more shots, my apartment starts to feel hollow. Every sound—from the AC flowing through my vents to the icemaker in my fridge—seems filtered through a speaker.

I pick up my phone and text Omari. There's no reason I should enjoy these drinks alone.

Within moments, he agrees to come over, and thirty minutes later he's there knocking.

Omari stands at my door with hungry eyes. His standard formal attire is replaced with black sweatpants, a T-shirt, and a flannel. There's no pretense about what he's here for.

When I step aside to let him in, he grabs me by the waist and pushes me against the entrance to take my lips in a fiery kiss. He smells like cigars, sin, and warmth.

"Hi," he murmurs with a heady voice. "You've been busy."

I haven't really. Not too busy to answer his texts at least; I just haven't been answering them.

"I'm here now," I whisper back, pulling him inside and slamming the door shut. I don't want words. I don't want to talk about our days or hear about a single fucking investment. I want to be ravished and disrespected.

We fumble our way through the living room and into the kitchen where he pops me onto the counter the way he's done a million times before. My eyes roll to the back of my head when he starts that delectable exploration of my neck with his tongue that I love so much.

The pads of his hands are so soft as he runs them up my stomach to cup my breasts. I try to ignore the feeling that they're too soft, not marked by a single callus or blister. The feeling finally gets pushed to the back of my mind when he lifts my shirt over my head and tweaks my right nipple, swirling his tongue down to my chest to find its way to the left one. I moan when he bites down ever so gently.

This is good.

This is what I needed.

"You always feel so good," he says, his lips dancing across my skin.

"Mmm," I moan. I open my eyes to tell him to make me feel good, but it's not Omari's face I see. It's a pair of obsidian almond-shaped eyes against midnight skin, locs dangling over my breasts. I squeeze my eyes shut. "Fuck," I spit.

I can feel his hand hovering over my rib cage. "You okay?" he asks, concern hanging off his words.

I lean my head back against my cabinet and slowly let my eyes flutter open, relieved to see just Omari again. "Yep. Just a head rush. Take me to the bedroom."

"You sure? Do you need anything?"

I look at the forgotten bottle of Promesa sitting on the counter. I don't know if it's helping or hurting my hallucinations, but I take a swig. Grabbing Omari's chin between my fingers, I slide his lips apart to pour a shot down his throat. He lets me, licking his lips when he's done.

I lean over and kiss him deeply. "I just need you."

Satisfied with my response, he picks me up and carries me to my room, kicking the door closed behind him.

Once we're both kneeling on the bed, I rip his shirt over his head, trailing my fingers over his chest and enjoying how his skin ripples under my touch.

He grabs me by the throat and pulls me into him, kissing me behind the ear. "Don't get cocky, Dani. We're just getting started." The bite in his voice pulls a moan out of me.

Thank the lord we're back on track.

I push on his stomach until he releases his grip and then I lie down and pull my bottoms off, leaving me completely naked and splayed open for him. His eyes darken as he takes me in, leaning over to grip my thighs.

"You look so perfect for me," he says, his voice gruff.

Damnit. There he goes transforming before my eyes again.

Fuck this. I give him what I hope is a look of seduction and flip over to my stomach, hiking my ass in the air.

I don't need to see him for him to make me feel good.

"Fuck, Dani," he groans.

"How's this for perfect?"

When his tongue breaches my center, my body finally lets go and lets me get lost in the moment.

The blackout curtains in my room block out any trace of the sun's rays, but I know they're there because I've been staring at my clock for over an hour.

Sleep never fully came for me anyway. The wheels in my mind moved too fast for it to hold on to me.

Sometimes, I have these periods where I can't keep up with my thoughts, and everything around me becomes foggy.

If I stay in this bed any longer, I'll suffocate under the weight of the fog. Fighting the temptation to let it take me, I throw my feet off the side of the bed and stretch my arms up to the ceiling. I check to see if Omari's awake. He quietly smacks his lips and turns over to face away from me. Perfect.

I sneak off to the bathroom and prepare to start my day. The tightness in my chest settles with every step of my routine.

"Good morning," Omari greets me when I step out of the bathroom, making me jump out of my skin.

"Shit, good morning."

He chuckles. "Sorry. Didn't mean to scare you."

"You were just snoring so peacefully not that long ago. I wasn't expecting you to be up," I tease.

"Oh, wow. You lying on me now? I don't snore."

"You definitely snore. But it's a cute snore. Not a 'tap you on the shoulder and tell you to get the fuck out' kind of snore."

"Well, that's a relief, then," he jokes.

He gets out of the bed and excuses himself to the bathroom. I appreciate the gentle stroke of my arm he gives me as he passes by because he knows I don't accept morning-breath kisses.

When he comes out of the bathroom, I've just finished getting dressed.

"I was just going to make our coffees," I say. Normally, after Omari spends the night, I make us both coffee in the morning and we drink them on my balcony before he heads out for work or whatever it is he does in his free time.

He grabs my waist and pushes me against my dresser, taking my lips in a fiery kiss. "Have breakfast with me."

The words almost don't compute in my mind.

We do dinners. We know what comes after dinner.

We don't do breakfasts out in public. It's too . . . intimate. There's an implication that comes with it, that you're more than what you are.

Hell, even a trip would be better than breakfast. The same rules don't apply when you're on vacation, and Omari and I have taken plenty of sexcations together.

We've enjoyed sex on a cruise ship over Caribbean waters, under the stars in Paris, and on the beaches of Saint Lucia. We've let our bodies do the talking after wine tours in California and after nights of dancing in Nashville.

But breakfast? In our backyard?

"Oh. I don't know."

"I promise." He sticks three fingers up in a Scout's honor. "This is not me trying to break out of the friends-with-benefits zone. I'm just hungry and don't wanna eat breakfast alone."

Breakfast isn't a meal I typically eat unless my dad's making it or it's brunch and there are mimosas involved, so I can't even offer to make him something here.

It's just breakfast. Nothing more, nothing less. I don't have my planning meeting until later, so there's no real reason for me not to go.

"Fine. Wherever we go better have good coffee."

"Nothing beats yours, but I think I can come close. Let's go." He steps back and offers me his arm, so I take it.

We end up at a place called Days of the Week Café. It's a charming spot with picnic-style decor. The menu tells the story of how the owner chose the name because she has seven children, each one named after a day of the week.

We order coffee and he also orders a Bloody Mary as we sit and talk. My eyes start to glaze over when he starts talking about investments, but I manage to dial back in when he brings the conversation around to his elderly Labrador retriever, Barkley. I hate to admit it, but my favorite thing about Omari might be his dog. He's the sweetest, most gentle creature I've ever met. Anytime I've stayed over at Omari's place, I've almost been tempted to stay when Barkley hobbles over to me and lays his head in my lap.

"And how is the old man?" I ask.

"Old. He's starting to have trouble jumping on the couch."

My hand flies up to my mouth. "Oh no!"

"Yeah. It's okay, though. He's hangin' in there. I'm taking him to physical therapy."

"Aww, good. Only the best for Sir Barkley."

"You know, he told me to tell you he misses you."

I look into Omari's kind eyes. "Is that so? I didn't realize Barkley could talk."

He wipes the corner of his mouth with a napkin. "Oh yeah, he's real chatty. But only with me."

Yapper recognizes yapper, I guess. "Interesting. Well, tell Barkley I miss him too."

Something akin to hope overwhelms his features, sparking dread in my heart. My wish is for everything to stay the same between us and I have to believe he feels that way too.

As we're walking out of the restaurant, a familiar face comes into view. Three years of living in the same city again and I've never once run into Micah on the street. Why is this happening now? My desire for him to pretend he doesn't see me is crushed when a sly smirk flashes across his face as he gets closer.

"If I didn't know any better, I'd say you were stalking me, Dani," he says once we're finally within earshot.

"Good thing you do know better, Micah."

"Good thing. Just a fair warning, I know Bailey has a lot of ideas in mind, so be prepared for her to talk a mile a minute today."

"That's fine," I say curtly. Omari doesn't know Tanya passed away or what I've been tasked to do, and I want to keep it that way for no other reason than it's none of his business. So, whatever Micah has to say about today can wait until we're supposed to be together.

He seems to catch on to my brush-off, eyeing me up and down before turning to Omari. "My bad, bruh. I'm Micah. I'm Dani's—"

"He's my friend's husband's friend," I cut him off. Why is he trying to get this man all in my business? I should stomp on his big toe right now. From the corner of my eye, I can see Micah cast a side glance in my direction, and I can't lie, that makes me smile a bit. "And Micah, this is my . . . Omari."

Why did I stumble over the word *friend*? What the fuck was I about to say? Was I about to shove Omari into a box he doesn't belong in just to have something to say?

It's time for Micah to go.

"Nice to meet you, Myomari." Micah holds his hand out for Omari to dap him up.

Smartass.

Omari steps closer to Micah. "Omari," he corrects. "Yeah, you too, man."

The two of them chop it up for longer than necessary, leaving me standing there wondering what I did to deserve this dumb shit.

Enough is enough. "Omari, do you mind dropping me at home? I got some stuff to do before some meetings later."

Unfazed, Omari turns to me. "Yeah, that's no problem."

He says his goodbyes to Micah before ushering me to his car. When I look back in Micah's direction, his eyes are firmly planted on me.

Chapter Eight

Micah

THE DARK AND LIGHT SQUARES START BLENDING INTO each other on the board.

My hand hovers over the beautifully crafted wood pieces, trying to figure out what feels right.

"You always did take forever to make your first move." The slight rasp in her voice settles my spirit.

When I look up from the chessboard, she looks exactly as I remember her, down to the mole under her left eye. Her hairline is mostly white, while the rest of her tight curls are a blend of black and gray.

She's smiling at me with a glint of mischief twinkling in her gaze.

"Coming to me in my dreams now, Tanya?" I say, allowing myself to take one more look at my pieces before focusing on her.

She hums. *"Seemed like you needed me."*

That's more than a little true. Ever since Paris and Penelope brought up their proposal again, I've been warring with myself.

When they first asked me, I shut it down and never thought about it again. Now, it's all I can think about.

Why are they so insistent on just handing me things when I haven't earned them?

What have I done for them or for Our Place that would warrant such a gift?

I make my first move, looking to Tanya for any reaction. As usual, she doesn't have one. She simply surveys the board and quickly decides on her return.

"You know what your problem is, Micah?"

I chuckle. *"No, but I'm sure you're gonna tell me."*

She waits until after I've moved my pawn to respond. *"You're hard-headed. Did you even read my letter?"* she asks as she moves one of her bishops.

"Oh, I read it." Multiple times. I've pored over the words in my head repeatedly, and I know what she's about to say, but she can't undo my perception with the flick of her pen.

"Yet you're still denying yourself things that could bring you joy. Hence, you're hardheaded."

"Ah, well, I never denied that," I confess.

She stares me down, silently capturing one of my rooks. *"What would make you worthy in your eyes? What would you have to do?"*

I rub my hand over my beard, unsure of what to say. *"I honestly don't know."*

"Well, maybe you should figure that out instead of just accepting that you'll never reach this imaginary mountaintop."

She knows I don't have a rebuttal for that, so she continues with the game as if she didn't say a word. *"Check,"* she calls, making me retreat with my king.

"Why did you have to keep it a secret from us?"

She twists her lips to the side, her eyes looking down at the board. *"I don't think I should answer that."*

"Why not?"

She looks up to lock eyes with me. *"It won't give you any peace. You'll just be wondering if that's my real answer or just what you wanted me to say because you're dreaming."*

At least I know myself well enough to know that. *"Fair."* I pause, taking a moment to absorb having her in my presence. There are so many things I want to say to her, and yet there's only one question that seems worth asking. *"Are you happy now?"*

An aura of serenity glows around her as she puts her hand on top of mine. *"I'm very happy."* She reaches over to dab my eye, her fingers now damp with tears I didn't even realize had welled up.

"Good," I say.

We keep talking, laughing over me trying to get afterlife secrets out of her, until it's clear I stand no chance of winning. I try one last-ditch effort to keep myself in the game and keep this dream from ending, but she looks at me with resolve in her eyes.

"Micah-Angelo"—she pulls out the cheesy nickname she gave me after we met—*"I think our time is up."*

"Will I see you again?"

She shrugs her shoulders and winks. *"It's your mind. You tell me."* She makes her winning move. *"Checkmate."*

Slowly, I pull my eyelids apart and greet the darkness of my room. I can't believe I can't even beat Tanya in chess in my dreams.

I touch my face to make sure I'm really awake. Sitting up, I rub my arm across my bare chest. All I can hear are Tanya's words over and over again. *What would make you worthy in your eyes?* I wish I had an answer for that. I've done my best to not repeat the mistakes of my past, but that doesn't mean they don't still haunt my future.

All I can do is strive to be a better man now. As if knowing I needed a reminder of my progress, my phone starts ringing with a call from Tavion's school.

"Hello?"

A demure voice responds. "Hi, Mr. Wright. We've had an incident here at the school and need Tavion to be picked up, but we're unable to reach his mom."

I'm the second emergency contact for my godson when his mom, Samantha, is busy.

"I'm on my way," I rush to say before hanging up.

Sammy was the girlfriend of my childhood best friend, Taron, and the mother of his child. We were only eighteen and Tavion was just a newborn when Taron was gunned down during a drive-by. They were aiming for a guy we used to hoop with who lived nearby. They got him, and if it hadn't been for Taron, they might've gotten me too.

Taron clocked the shooters seconds before everything happened and he knocked me to the ground.

I didn't even see him get hit. All I know is that when it was over, I got up and Taron didn't. I tried to stop the bleeding, but there was so much of it, coming from too many different places. By the time the ambulance got to us, I knew he was gone. And while I have a good relationship with Sammy and Tavion now, those first four years of his life were rough.

I was supposed to be his godfather, but I couldn't look at Tavion's face knowing I was part of the reason he'd never know his dad. So, I ran. I went to school an hour away at Bowie State University, which is far when you have to rely on public transportation, and I used any excuse in the book to stay away.

When I think about those four years I let Sammy struggle alone, I'm disgusted with myself. She had plenty of help with Tavion. Her mom and grandmom supported her; my parents and her other friends looked after her too. They gave her all the support she needed to be a good mother, but she had no one to help her exist without Taron. Everyone knew him, but we were the only surviving family he had, so we were the only ones who truly understood how grim a world without him in it was. She thought we'd navigate that emptiness together, but I let her down.

I'm just grateful she let me back into their lives when I got my head out of my ass.

When I walk into Tavion's high school, he's sitting in the front office with his arms laid across the backs of the chairs next to him, not a care or ounce of remorse on his face.

His face morphs into that of innocence when he spots me. "Oh, hey, Micah. I told them not to bug Mom because she don't have her phone on her at work."

She works long hours as a nurse while going to school to be a neuropsychologist, so she can't always drop everything to get to his school.

"Don't worry, I'll make sure she knows everything they had to say."

His eyes stay glued to the floor after that. His principal calls me back to her office to explain that Tavion's been suspended due to fighting. Again. I'm not surprised—Tavion is no stranger to fights and most of them are in defense of someone else. He's always going out of his way to help the people around him. He's like his dad in that way.

Once I'm done talking to the principal and usher Tavion out to my car, he rushes to his own defense. "Hear me out. I had to do it. These kids were messing with this guy in our class. He's got a stutter and they thought it was funny to surround him and cut him off every time he stuttered."

"So you fought 'em all?"

"Nah, two of 'em ran away, but the last one, yeah, I did."

I can't be mad about that. I would've done the same thing. "Look, I get it. I really do. But how are you supposed to finish school when you spend half the time being suspended for being a vigilante?"

He stares out of the window, the weight of the world pressing down on his shoulders. "Some things are more important."

"You sound just like your dad." If Taron were here, he'd be celebrating. He'd probably take Tee to all of our spots around the city bragging to everyone how his son is basically *The Equalizer.*

Tee's jaw clenches, a storm brewing behind his eyes. "I wouldn't know."

A red light gives me a chance to really look at him. I recognize that pain on his face, that feeling of being adrift and not knowing who can throw you a lifeboat. Of being angry and not knowing where to aim it or even what's the point.

"Light's green," Tee says when I don't move.

I let the silence linger, the sound of my engine and the world outside these windows serving as a placeholder until I can figure out the right thing to say. "We don't talk about him much, huh?"

"At all," he huffs. "You don't talk about him at all. Every time I ask Mom a question about him, she shuts me down. When I go to the barbershop, the old heads always point out how much I look like him but never want to talk about him. Do you know what it's like to walk around and have everyone know more about where you come from than you do?"

Most of the people in the neighborhood who knew Taron don't speak about him. His death rocked a lot of people, but none more than Sammy. She thought the two of them would build a life together. She pictured them growing old side by side while raising Tee and probably giving him a sibling or two. When that dream was snatched away, she couldn't bring herself to talk about him or even think about him. She would lash out at anyone who tried to go down memory lane, until eventually everyone followed her lead and stopped talking about him altogether. Locking him away in a box was the only way she could stay strong enough to keep going for Tee. We all understood that.

Unbeknownst to us, all we've managed to do is put a Band-Aid over a wound that's still festering. We thought time alone would heal it, but it's only added to the infection.

The thing about death is that it's never final. The end of someone's life is merely the start of a quiet suffering that spans generations.

I can't bring Taron back to Tavion any more than I can bring Chi Chi back to my mom or Tanya back to Dani and myself. I can't bring them back and I can't make it right, but the cycle of staying silent about those we've lost in the hopes of easing our heartache has to end.

"What do you wanna know?" I ask.

His head snaps in my direction. "Really?"

"Ask away."

As I turn down another street, I watch as every question he's ever had about his dad floats to the front of his mind. He scratches his head with indecision as if my offer will turn back into a pumpkin at any moment and he'll lose his opportunity.

"Take your time," I add. "I'll answer any question you have."

His shoulders relax a bit. He's grown into a formidable young man, molded in his father's image, but when he looks at me like this, all I see is the little boy he used to be. The five-year-old who forced me to walk around with him wrapped around my leg. The seven-year-old who was overjoyed to be cast as a tree in his school play. The ten-year-old who learned the hard way that he was deathly afraid of roller coasters.

"What was he like?"

"Hmm," I ponder as I reverse into a parking spot at a diner close to Tee's house. "He was unintentionally funny. Like he wasn't the type to crack jokes, but he would just say the most off-the-wall stuff in earnest, and it would crack everybody up. He also loved anything to do with ghosts." I switch the car off. "Wanna hear how he forced me to help set a trap for a ghost he swore was living in his grandparents' house?"

His eyes widen as his grin stretches from ear to ear. "Absolutely."

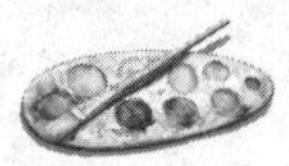

After our impromptu breakfast where Tee unleashed all the questions he's been holding in his whole life, I take him home and wait for Sammy to get there. It felt good to talk about Taron, to remember him. For so long, whenever I thought about him, the only thing I could picture was his lifeless eyes and the blood covering my hands.

Thinking about him has me thinking about Our Place. Taron, Sammy, and I spent so much time there growing up. It's where Sammy and Taron first met. Our best memories spawned there. He would hate the fact that Tee has never stepped foot inside that building.

I look to the ceiling with my hands in my lap. Maybe this is the reason Tanya is sending us on this excursion. So she doesn't become the next Pandora's box buried in the back of our closet.

Sammy comes through the door in light blue scrubs. Her eyes are puffy and her blowout looks worse for wear. "Where is he?" she asks.

"Upstairs playing *2K*. I stopped and got you this," I say, pulling an energy drink from behind my back.

Her eyes twinkle with joy. "You beautiful man."

She goes to take it, but I pull back at the last second, my eyebrows pinching. "But you're gonna save it for later because you'll be going to sleep soon, right?"

She shakes her head and pretends she's about to step on my toe before grabbing the can out of my hand. "Sleep. Ha. What is sleep? I gotta get some studying in before class later. And I have to discipline your godson."

"Well, before we get into that. How are classes going?"

"Good, good. I'm just tryna figure out how this is the same twenty-four hours we've always had in a day."

"Can't be, right?"

"Can't be. They're putting crack in these hours or somethin' now, because I can't keep the fuck up."

"How can I help?"

She casts a sidelong glance at me.

"What?"

"You know what. You're helping plenty."

In my eyes, paying for Sammy's tuition will never be enough. That's the very least I could do. "I beg to differ."

She huffs, grabbing a coconut water from the fridge for me. "I'm not gonna argue with your fat-headed self."

"That's good to hear, because you might not like what I have to say next."

I tell her about my conversation with Tee concerning his dad, some of the questions he asked me, and what I shared with him. The color drains from her face the longer I talk.

She buries her head in her hands, lifting it when she feels my hand against her shoulder. "I'm failing him."

"Sammy. No, you're not."

"Yes, I am. My baby was hurting and I couldn't see past my own pain."

"You're grieving."

She rolls her eyes and taps her foot impatiently. "For sixteen years?"

"There isn't a timeline for grief. Matter fact, I don't think grief ever stops. The ones left behind carry the loss around until it's their turn to leave this Earth. It never gets easier, you just get used to the ache. You learn to rebuild yourself around it because it's impossible to be the same person you were before."

"I was never supposed to do this alone." Her eyes shoot over to me. "No offense. I just mean parent-wise."

I take her hands in mine. "Don't apologize to me. You're right, you weren't supposed to be alone, but you've done an incredible job." Sammy is a damn good mom. There's never been a time when Tee hasn't been her number one priority. She learned how to be a mom while learning how to be an adult and her own person. "You raised a good kid. He's insanely smart with a good head on his shoulders and a heart of gold. I know we see a lot of Taron in him, but he is who he is because of you. Taron was the soil but you are the water that feeds him so he can grow."

Tears stream down her face. "Thank you. And thank you for looking out for him."

"It's my honor."

"So, what do I do? Every time I try to talk about him, it's like my heart is cracking all over again."

I'm not an authority on how to handle this. Penelope and Paris can attest to that. I have nothing to offer except my truth. "Maybe you don't have to hide that from him anymore. If he's telling you he can handle it, believe him."

She promises to consider my words, and I promise to support whatever plan she comes up with before leaving.

"Dani, long time no see," I greet her with a smile. When I ran into her earlier while she was with that Disney villain–looking motherfucker, it was bittersweet. I hated seeing her arm wrapped around his, but I liked the surprise of running into her. Sometimes, I think about the night she walked into my gallery. Of all the women in the world Arnold could've dated, he picked one that brought Dani waltzing back into my life. I spent the next three years praying for serendipity to intervene again, for a coincidental run-in away from the prying eyes and ears of our friends, because I knew she'd never meet up with me if I simply asked. I didn't even know what I would do or what I would say if I saw her. Maybe we could've restarted our friendship or maybe I would've gotten on my knees and begged her to give us another chance. I didn't know, but I didn't care either. I just wanted the possibility. Today was the first day my wish was granted.

Her lip curls. "Shut up, Micah."

I smile as Bailey's roaring laugh sounds from the kitchen. Moments later, she walks into Tanya's living room with her notebook and tablet. "Damn, what'd you do, Chopper?"

I shrug. "I have no idea why I'm being greeted with such hostility."

Dani side-eyes me.

Bailey looks back and forth between us. She turns to Dani. "I will turn a blind eye if you choose to hit him."

Before I can needle her anymore, the doorbell rings and Dani rushes off to answer it. She comes back with a tall woman who has a cheery smile and looks like she might be Indian. "Micah, Bailey, this is my assistant, Nisha. Nisha, this is my cohost, Micah, and his sister, Bailey."

Nisha greets me warmly, but there's a shift when she connects with Bailey. The moment their hands touch, their eyes snap up to each other's and hold. It goes on for so long I feel like I'm interrupting. I've known Bailey for her entire life, and I've never seen this look on her.

"Uh, sorry," Nisha says as she slowly extricates her hands from Bailey's. Her focus switches back to Dani and me, though her body language still appears off. "Let's talk gala, shall we? For catering, how about the service you used for the Promesa launch?"

Dani's eyes light up. "That food was amazing. That's perfect. Can you set up a meeting for us so we can check their availability and go over menu options? We would want something completely different than what we had for Promesa, so I wanna make sure they can accommodate."

"Yep, I'm typing up an email now."

"And for music, are we thinking live entertainment? I might know some people," Bailey adds.

"Who you got?" Dani asks.

"Depends on the vibe. Since we decided to host at Spring Hill, maybe something soft like Janessa Howard?"

"Ooh she's fire," Nisha applauds. Janessa Howard is a classic violinist who's also known on TikTok for her violin covers of hip-hop tracks.

"And so fine!" Bailey fires back. The women share a laugh. "But there's also Laydee, Nash, McKay Alexander."

"Do you mind reaching out to all of them? Not sure which way we wanna go yet, but it'd be good to know who's available, interested, and what their rates might be," Dani says.

Bailey nods her agreement, making a note on her tablet.

This has been the last hour of my life. The planning meeting that was supposed to be for the four of us has really been the three of them firing off ideas and feeding off of each other's energy while I just sit here. My last suggestion of having exotic animals was met with judgmental eyes, so I've since shut up.

Tanya said go big or go home, but the women told me to take my ass home.

Nisha and Bailey recap their takeaways from the meeting before we finally call it quits for the day. As we're all packing up, Mr. Townsend walks through the front door in one of his signature suits.

"Mr. Townsend. Hi, uh, what are you doing here?" Dani asks.

He unbuttons his jacket as he greets everyone, his eyes never once betraying his thoughts. "You mentioned your planning meeting tonight and I wanted to stop by and give you this." He pulls a small envelope from the inside pocket of his blazer and holds it between us. Our names are written in Tanya's distinct handwriting across the front. One of Tanya's hobbies when she was younger was calligraphy. She said she stopped doing it because she grew tired of people asking her to make them invitations and cards, but it always stuck with her. The exaggerated curves around the *H* in my name and the *D* in Dani's are eye-catching. They almost connect as if they belong together.

"What is this?" Dani asks.

"It's your first clue."

Dani's hand freezes midair, allowing the envelope to slip through her grasp. It lands with our names facing up, mocking us for our hesitation.

"Am I missing something here?" Mr. Townsend questions with his eyebrows raised.

I lean over to rescue the lost envelope from the floor, grasping it between my fingers as if it might disintegrate if I don't hold on tight. My mind is swirling with ideas of what this envelope could unleash. I turn it over in my hand and Dani's hand lands on top of mine.

"Stop," she pleads. Her fingers start to tremble, so I shield them with my own. "Thank you for bringing this, Mr. Townsend. I just . . . I'm not ready." She mouths the words "I'm sorry" to me.

For the very first time since meeting him, Mr. Townsend's eyes soften as he takes in our hands and Dani's gentle features. "You can call me Victor. And I understand. You don't have to open it right this moment. But I wouldn't take too long." He leans in closer. "I find the anticipation becomes scarier than the task the longer you wait."

Nisha and Bailey walk out with Victor, plunging Dani and me into quiet.

I start to say something, but she rushes to cut me off. "I have an idea for our auction item I want to run by you."

Interesting change of subject. "Okay. Hit me."

"So, I think the obvious thing to auction off would be one of your paintings. You've done a portrait of her before, so this one would need to be an elevated version of that."

I nod my head in understanding. "Okay, that's great. But how does that involve both of us?" Tanya was very specific in her letter about wanting the two of us to create whatever we auction off together. Is she planning on standing in front of me so both of us can hold the paintbrush?

"I'll be filming you while you paint. I can do it documentary style, so it focuses on you and your creative process, but also allows us to share memories and anecdotes about Tanya. You can come with me to interview other people who loved her too. I'm sure we'll meet a bunch of them on this little odyssey she's sending us on." She waves her hand toward the envelope still nestled in my hand with a look of torment written all over her face.

She seems to have this all figured out. It's a great idea, one I think Tanya would love. Honestly, she'd probably want us to try to pitch the documentary to Netflix or something.

"What do you think?"

I take one more moment to think it over. "It's brilliant. We can play your video at the beginning of the auction to open things up."

"My thoughts exactly." After she asks if I'd be willing to do a test run, she runs out to her car and comes back with a tripod and camera.

"Do you always travel with camera equipment on you?"

She doesn't look up from her setup as she answers. "I actually meant to tell you my idea earlier but I got so caught up with the girls I forgot."

Once her camera is in her desired position, she transforms into a veteran director, explaining how the shoot will go and what she wants me to do. She grabs a stool from the kitchen and forces me to sit down. I feel like I'm on an episode of *Dateline.*

"Why did you love Tanya so much?" Dani asks, once she calls "action."

I glance off in the distance, my lips turning up into a smile. "That's easy, she saved my life."

I can't see Dani's eyes behind the camera, but I can tell my answer catches her off guard.

"Explain."

"When Chi Chi—that's my aunt Monica to you casuals watching—died, I was lost. I didn't wanna paint anymore. I didn't wanna draw anymore. I didn't wanna be a good human being anymore. What was the point, right? You could spend your entire life doing good things and still get hit by a fucking car on a random Wednesday night. Left on the side of the road to bleed out. It all seemed pointless after that."

I let go of the hatred I had for the man who killed Chi Chi a long time ago. He was caught months later and he did his bid. At the time, I thought it was unfair that he got to go back to his life after three years when Chi Chi never did. I still think it's unfair, but I don't hate the man. Whenever I have to talk about how Chi Chi died, however, that anger seeps back into my blood for only a moment.

"You stopped painting?" Dani asks.

"I threw out all my art supplies. Stopped going to Our Place. Stopped giving a fuck. Some of my boys back then used to hit houses and cars, so I linked up with them. And then one day, my dumb ass hit the wrong fucking house."

Realization hits Dani and she gasps. "No! You tried to rob Tanya?"

I grimace at the memory. "I got in and as soon as I turned my back, I felt cold metal on my side." I hold my index and middle fingers up to my side as I'm talking. I can laugh about it now, but I thought I was cooked then. "She asked me if I wanted an open or closed casket and then she pointed the gun at my head. My boys had left me and all I kept thinking was, *Please don't let my parents find out about this on the news.*"

"What did you say?"

"I said I wanted to be cremated and for someone to mix my ashes in with paint and make a dope ass painting with me. That's not even true. I mean, I do wanna be cremated but I don't want my ashes to be mixed into some paint. I just said that shit, but you know what? It got her to put the gun down."

Dani chuckles, alternating between looking at me and down at her camera. "How very afterschool special of you."

"I know, right. She sat me down and we talked about art for hours. I didn't wanna admit it at the time, but I had been longing for the peace art gave me. Tanya said she wouldn't press charges against me if I started coming to the rec center three days a week. She saved my life. She was the one who encouraged me to make the mural for Chi Chi."

She taught me how to let go of the pain I was holding on to, how to channel it into something I could be proud of.

"Micah. That's amazing." Dani moves the camera from in front of her face, making sure I understand her words are for me and not the video.

"Thanks. I don't think I ever told my parents that story." I look into the camera. "My bad, y'all."

Dani laughs before cutting off the video. We move to Tanya's office for Dani's test shot, working silently side by side to get everything set up once again.

I count her down and then press record.

"I'm here in Tanya's office. She used to spend a lot of time here. So far, we've found some really cool things of hers that we think y'all are going to love."

She keeps going, but I struggle to listen.

What the fuck is that?

Everything from the words she's saying to the way she's standing screams impersonal. I've seen her videos on social media—I know how lively she can be, and this isn't that.

"Dani, I'm really sorry. Can I interrupt you?"

"What's up?"

"It's just . . ." I try to find the words to say what I know I have to say. "Are you gonna do these parts of the videos like this the whole time?"

Her hand finds its way to her hip, and I know I've fucked up.

"What do you mean?"

"Well, you just seem sort of . . . stiff."

"Stiff." She repeats the word in that tone that tells me I'm close to death.

So why don't I just shut up? "You sound like you're a reporter doing a segment on someone you didn't know, not a tribute for a dear friend."

"Hmm," she hums.

"I'm sorry. I just think you should relax. Maybe not treat it like it's a project."

As soon as I say it, I know I'm cooked. Her face turns cold, nothing but harshness in her eyes. I can see the muscles in her jaw bulging.

I brace myself for the verbal beating I know is coming when she surprises me. "Thanks for the advice, Micah." Her smile is almost Joker-like in its fraudulence.

This is worse than I thought. "Right. No, you should ignore me. I don't know what I'm talking about."

"No, you're absolutely right. Why don't we switch? I'll record a second story from you and then we can pick up on mine next time."

"Uh, if you're sure."

"I'm sure." She brushes past me to reposition her camera.

Fuck.

It doesn't take long to record my segment. I throw a proverbial dart at the wall of our memories and share whatever it lands on in my mind.

Once we're done recording, Dani packs up her equipment and heads for the door.

"Wait, Dani."

"Yes?" she says, turning to me with another fake smile.

"I'm sorry. I really didn't mean to offend you."

"You didn't."

"Right. But you're clearly bothered."

She looks me up and down, her dismissal rattling my bones. "Trust me, Micah. I'm not bothered."

Chapter Nine

Dani

I'M BOTHERED.

I mean he really had the audacity to give me pointers like I don't do this for a damn living.

I think I would know better.

My third time rewatching the clip puts an end to any hope of believing that lie.

I do look stiff. I don't even sound like myself. If anything, I sound more like Bryant Gumbel.

Frustrated, I let my head flop down on my desk. I don't know what happened. I felt fine at first, maybe a little anxious, but overall fine. And then Micah pushed record and it was like I floated out of my body. I had a heightened awareness of every word I was saying, every movement I was making, and yet I couldn't change it. I couldn't pivot into something coherent and real.

Micah calling it out only managed to drive me deeper into the pit of despair, so I snapped.

Ugh, and now I'm going to have to apologize to his ass.

I don't know how I'm going to get out of this funk, but this was quite literally my idea, so I have to figure it out.

Meanwhile, Micah's segment is perfect. Annoyingly so. He was so dynamic on camera. His story about Tanya was so simple, but he was so charming that I was tuned in to every word.

Why couldn't I do that?

I freeze my screen right on his magnetic smile.

That's enough of that. If I'm being honest with myself, any hope I had of getting some editing done today has flown out the window apparently right alongside my originality.

Without a second thought, I throw on a workout set and head to the Lab.

I need the adrenaline that dance gives me now more than ever.

Walking into Movement Lab, I can feel my mood elevating and my breath coming easier. This place has always been a sanctuary for me. When I was eight years old, I took a jazz class here and loved every minute, even when I fell on my face during progressions because I didn't spot properly. I started taking every class I could, from jazz to hip-hop to ballet and contemporary. It became a lifeline that saved me more than once.

The owner, Trish, is at the front desk talking to two students. She smiles and motions for me to give her a moment before turning her attention back to the two girls.

While she's speaking with them, I take in the studio. It feels like every time I come here, Trish has transformed the place into something that feels more authentically her. When I was a kid, her mom owned the place. She sought to diversify the dance community for marginalized groups by offering them the versatility of different genres. I had my favorites, but I was a better dancer overall by learning the skills of all of them.

Trish seeks to do the same, but she invests a lot of time in helping students figure out what they want to do with those skills. Not only does she offer classes for different age ranges, she also offers different classes per interest. A person who wants to take dance classes as a hobby or a workout might be intimidated by someone who's taking the class in the hopes of going on tour with artists or getting scholarships into places like Juilliard. She's created environments where everyone can feel comfortable while also getting what they need out of the classes. I can tell by looking at the students she's talking to now that they admire her immensely.

Once she's done with the students, I sidle my way over to the front desk.

"Hey, kid!" she says.

I chuckle at the moniker she's refused to stop calling me since I was ten and she was eighteen. "Hey, Trix! How's life? How's this place?"

"Oh, this place is good. It's doing well. You missed it, we had Laydee show up for one of our classes a few weeks ago."

Laydee is a female rapper from Texas. She's a legend and one of my favorite artists to choreograph to. I haven't seen anything about her visit on social media, but I'm sure the class was uploaded to YouTube, so I'll have to check that out.

"I love that for y'all!"

"Yep and, umm, life is good. Life is very good." Her left hand—previously hidden under her desk—now rests on her face, the rock on her ring finger practically blinding me.

"Trixie, shut the fuck up!" I grab her hand to inspect the ring closer. It's stunning and huge. I clearly have missed a few major things in her life. "Congratulations! It's beautiful."

She gushes as she tells me about her fiancé, Jakobi. I've never seen her with a smile as goofy as this and I'm excited to meet the man who put it there. She deserves it.

We catch up on some of the drama at the Lab before she checks the class schedule to see if there are any open studios.

When I left for New York, Trish's mom, Paige, gave me a permanent invitation to come back and use one of the studios whenever classes weren't in session. I used to take her up on that offer every time I visited home, but since moving back permanently, my time here has been few and far between.

"Bailey's class will be over in like fifteen minutes, so you can use that studio after if you want."

The name gives me pause. "Bailey. Is her last name Wright?"

"Yeah. You know her?"

What are the chances that the sister of the man who put me in this foul ass mood teaches at the very studio where I've danced at all my life? For a big city, Baltimore feels small as hell too often. I wonder if this place is how Bailey has a connection with Laydee.

"Yeah. I know her and her brother."

Trish's eyes light up. "That man is fine."

Don't I know it?

"And so sweet."

Alright, enough already.

She gives me permission to watch the end of Bailey's class if I want and I do. Micah always raved about Bailey's talent, and I always wished I had had an opportunity to witness it.

When I walk back to the studio she's using, all the students are gathered around her while she's giving a speech. She's probably hyping them up before they do their final performances. There's a two-way glass so people can look in on the classes and decide if it's the place for them, but I want to be among the action. I want to hear Bailey's speech and feel the music vibrate the floor beneath me as everyone gives it their all.

I slip through the door, standing at the back in the hopes of not being noticed.

"When you're up there dancing, I don't give a shit about perfection. If you got the moves down, that's great. You're hitting every beat, every *ka ka ka,* that's great. But if they don't feel something when they watch you move, nobody gives a fuck. You've gotta make your audience feel it, and that means you gotta feel it. Right?"

I'm still getting to know Bailey, but so far she seems like the quiet type with a very bubbly attitude. Here in her element, however, she's fierce. Her passion for this craft is palpable in every word she says, and every student is enthralled with her. They applaud and cheer in response to her question.

"Put your own stank on it." She claps after each word. "Don't be afraid to let your personality show when you're doing this. Yes, there's complex movements, but there's also pockets when you can just vibe. That whole third verse, he's so calm and collected with it, but he's talking his stuff knowing he's shitting on a lot of rappers out there. So you can play that how you want to. You can be cool with it, you can be cocky with it, you can be extra with it. Do it your way. You feel me?"

"Yes!" the class echoes in unison.

"Right, because nobody can do you . . . what?" She holds her hand up to cup her ear.

"The way you can," the class echoes back.

They adore her. I feel like I just watched a halftime speech from a coach during the Super Bowl. I'm excited to see the raw talent that's in this room.

"Exactly. Let's fucking go!"

Everyone is hyped as they scatter around the room. The videographer for the class gets in position and Bailey moves to the center of the room. It looks like she'll be going solo for the first performance.

As she gets ready for the music to play, she takes a quick scan around the room. Of course, her eyes lock on me. Confusion makes its way across her features before she nods in approval. She turns to face the cameraman, and I can see the moment she switches her persona on.

The music begins and it's Tobe Nwigwe's "Bravo." There's no lead-in; as soon as the music starts, so does the choreo.

She's incredible. There's so much musicality in her movements. She seamlessly switches between sharp, hard-hitting moves one minute to soft, languid moves the next. The moves are complex, requiring the dancer to use their entire body for the full minute and forty-five seconds of the song. Bailey makes it look easy. Her movements and expressions are arrogant, sensual, and fun at the precise moments.

It's a sight to behold.

When the song is over, she walks off center with the shy smile I'm used to seeing on her. The class, who had been hyping her up the entire time, erupts with cheers, praise, and applause. I notice no one touches her when she's done, giving her love from a respectable distance. Someone hands her a bottle of water that she drinks while the videographer gets set up for the next performance.

Every performance is spectacular. Some of the dancers lean on their group members to make the performance more uniform, while others tap into the creativity that feels right to them. There's no space for freestyling in the song, but based on how the dancers approach it, each choreo looks completely different. I love seeing everyone's take on the steps.

Bailey's body language is much more reserved during the other performances, but her support is clear. She cheers loudly for everyone and gets close enough to hype them up, letting her energy feed them.

When the class is over, everyone exits the room, leaving only myself, Bailey, and one of the dance students.

"Dani, I thought that was you," Bailey exclaims.

"It's me."

She waves elatedly so I return the gesture.

"What are you doing here? You taking a class?"

"Nah, Trish told me I could use this studio to get some freestyling in when your class was over."

"Ahh, okay! Would you mind if I hung out for a little while? I've always wanted to see you dance."

Trish didn't mention that she's ever talked about me with Bailey, so the only person who could've told her about me is Micah. I'm embarrassed by how flattered I am that he told her about me. I smack my hand on the back of my neck, trying to cool myself down.

"Yeah, of course."

"Bails, how you feeling?" the dancer next to Bailey pipes in. They're around Bailey's height, which is shorter than me but still tall, with a slender but toned frame, deep brown skin, and dreads pulled into a bun.

Bailey wraps her arm around their side, pulling them closer. "Dani, this is Justin. They're my assistant dance coach." She turns to acknowledge Justin. "Justin, this is Dani. She's my brother's friend," she says, looking at me with a sly grin.

"Nice to meet you, Dani." They give me a single wave, which I return.

"You too," I say.

Justin turns back to Bailey with a scolding eye. "You didn't answer me."

"I'm a little tired, so I'm just gonna do my stretches and relax. I'm a fly on the wall, I promise."

They rub her shoulder and lean their head on top of hers. "Okay, cool. Also, did you see our little Maddy today? She's growing into a bad bitch right before our very eyes." They pretend to dab a tear and Bailey dramatically lifts her hand to wipe their other eye.

"She was so fucking good!"

The two of them explain that Maddy is a teenage girl who was new to dancing, but the growth she's shown in their class this past year makes them so proud.

Justin turns to grab their bag. "I'm gonna go ask Trish about the schedule for next week, but do you wanna go over 'Top Off' tonight?"

"Yes, boss," she says, blowing Justin a kiss.

She salutes when Justin rolls their eyes and pushes their bag farther up their shoulder. They give me one final goodbye before dashing out of the studio.

"You were amazing today," I compliment.

Bailey sits on the floor, and I join her so I can get some stretching in too.

“Thank you!” she exclaims. “I felt good about it.”

“As you should.”

“You can ask about it, you know,” she says while her head is flat against her shin.

“Ask about what?”

She lifts her head up and purses her lips. “My MS. Judging by how lost you were at Tanya’s the other day, I’m guessing you didn’t know before then. Now that we’re alone, you can ask.”

She seems shocked, a little angry, and a little hurt that I didn’t know before the other day. Why would she think Micah had told me about it? We’re not exactly in a place where he should feel comfortable telling me his sister’s medical business.

Unless . . . unless she thought he would’ve told me before.

My mind trails back to our second demise. The time when Micah left me in New York. I thought Micah and I were building something real back then. Everything was happening so fast considering we hadn’t seen each other in five years, but it felt so right at the same time. I thought we were working toward a future together. In hindsight, I don’t know why I thought that. We were so young. I was all of twenty-five and doubting what I wanted out of life. What the hell did I know about long-lasting relationships? What do I know about them now, for that matter? I don’t know why I allowed myself to wish for it, but I did, and then he left. He went home to Baltimore because Bailey was really sick and needed him. He promised he’d be back, and I believed him. But then the calls got shorter and less frequent. The texts became more sporadic. We went from one hundred to zero in what felt like no time at all, and I never figured out why. The final straw was when I got a job opportunity in London that would keep me there for six months. I tried to glue us back together by asking him to go with me, but the pieces no longer fit. He said no.

And I never heard from him again.

I thought it was about me, but now I see it was about protecting Bailey.

I wish it brought me peace to realize that situation wasn't what I thought, but it doesn't. I suppose I am grateful to realize it was never going to work out, not when he clearly wouldn't trust me enough.

A humorless laugh bubbles up in my throat, but I swallow it down. Right now, this isn't about Micah or me. It's about Bailey.

I spent some time researching MS after I found out, wanting to know as much about it as possible. I still have a ton of questions about her specific case, but I feel guilty asking them.

Bailey shouldn't have to sit here and play doctor to explain her disease to me like she's some sort of lab rat.

"I'm mostly curious about your exact experience, really. I read things about people going blind or needing wheelchairs, but I wanna know what you went through."

"Yeah, honestly, I got lucky. At first, my legs would randomly give out. Literally, I'd be walking and all of a sudden, I'd be on the ground because my legs buckled beneath me. I didn't think too much of it at first, thought I was just tired, but you can imagine my concern when it would happen mid-performance. My entire body would feel sore and bone-tired after the smallest activity. And I was having trouble with my vision. It was fucking terrifying. Like, all this work I've put in to be a dancer and it's about to be over? How is that fair?"

"But then the symptoms went away?"

"No. After I finally learned it was MS, I got treatment and it slowed down the progression. Right now, I'm in remission. Haven't had a relapse in a couple years."

Every answer she gives only sparks more questions in me, but I won't bombard her right now. I'll happily learn as we go along in this friendship.

"And, are you and Micah okay?" I ask. They seemed fine when I saw them at Tanya's house the last time, but there was clearly some tension between them the first time they were there together.

She huffs, stretching her arms above her head. "We're good. Until he inevitably pisses me off again."

"This is why I like being an only child," I joke. "Do you guys get into it a lot about your MS?"

"Too often," she sighs. "I get it, he's worried about me, but I know my body. I'm the one who said something was wrong. And he was by my side the whole time fighting to make the doctors listen to me, but it's like sometimes he forgets I'm the one who has to live with this, not him."

The boy's got a bit of a savior complex. I think most men do. There's a difference between intent and impact, and if Micah doesn't loosen the reins a bit, he runs the risk of permanently damaging his relationship with his sister. I don't want that for either of them.

"Keep setting your boundaries with him. Micah's smart—for a man. He'll get it eventually."

"He better," she snorts.

We laugh more about everything before I turn on my music and start dancing. She cheers me on and shouts out a few tips about footwork and ideas when I can't figure out how I want to move to a song.

Her input inspires me to dig deeper until I'm confident in the piece I put together.

Justin comes back after a while and joins in on the fun, allowing me to teach them the steps Bailey and I came up with.

As I leave the Lab to get in my car, I take out my phone to call Micah.

He answers on the second ring. "Hello?"

"Hi, Micah. Are you busy?"

There's a slight pause on the line before he says, "Am I in trouble?"

I suck my teeth. This fool. "No, I am, I guess. I just wanted to say I'm sorry. I shouldn't have snapped at you." There. I said it. He doesn't respond. Instead, he lets the silence stretch for so long I have to check the screen in my car to make sure the call didn't disconnect. "Did you hear me?"

"Oh, I heard you. I was just absorbing the moment, really savoring it."

"Oh, fuck you."

"To be clear, this is you admitting you were bothered, right?"

"And now I gots to go."

His rich laugh floats across the line like butter. "Nah, wait. Forreal, I accept your apology."

"Thank you." The debate in my head about whether I should tell him what I know about New York is short-lived. He tried to tell me himself at his gallery years ago, but I didn't want to hear it. I still don't. The time to tell me was when it could've prevented our foundation from crumbling beneath our feet.

There is a freedom in knowing the truth, though. It rescues me from the resentment I didn't even realize I was holding on to. It paves the way for a new path, a safer one.

"And I'm sorry for keeping you at arm's length. I want us to be . . . friends. Going forward," I add.

He hums contemplatively before speaking. "Friends, huh? No more friend's husband's friend?"

"Keep it up."

"Hey, hey, I was just clarifying. I'm okay with that. I like the sound of friends."

"Good." *It's your only option.*

"Good," he echoes. "So, friend. On a scale of one to ten, how close was I to getting knocked upside the head when I said you looked stiff?"

My response is immediate. "Twenty-five."

"I could tell. You know we gotta go back to recording those videos at some point though, right?"

Or, I could come up with a new project. *No. Don't be silly.* I know the documentary and portrait are the perfect auction item, so why does it feel so wrong when I contribute to it? "I know that. I'm just frustrated with myself."

The halls of my building are eerily quiet when I get home, still on the line with Micah. The only sound is my sneakers against the ornate flooring as I make my way up to my unit.

"Okay, well, let's talk it out. What is it about this project that's different from your social media videos?" Micah's voice seems to bounce off the walls even when I don't have him on speakerphone.

The answer to his question claws at my throat, begging to be freed. "It's personal," I lament.

"What do you mean?" There's no judgment in his tone, just a need to understand.

I sigh. "Okay so, when I do videos for social media, there's a level of separation from it for me."

"Because?"

I hate admitting this. It makes me feel like a fraud. "Because I'm not really being myself. I mean, I am, but an exaggerated version of myself. At the end of the day, the people watching my videos don't know me and I don't know them. I want to connect with them, of course, but I'm not laying myself bare in front of them. That's just not something I do."

I consider myself an actor of sorts. I signed up for the world to know me in one particular fashion. I signed up to be a face people recognize and for their lenses to be pointed at my every public move. I did not sign up for them to point their lenses inside my home.

"And with this video for Tanya, you have to do just that," he agrees.

"There's no other way to do it," I concede. "I keep imagining her looking down at us and seeing the video. She'd roast me within an inch of my life if I didn't dive deep." I throw my keys in the bowl on my entryway table and make my way to my bedroom.

"Okay. Trigger warning, because you might be at a fifty out of ten after I say what I'm about to say."

I suck my teeth. "A fifty out of ten? At that point, I should just kill you, but I gotta get past this shit, so go ahead."

Ignoring the concern for his safety, he lets me have it. "Back in the day, you used to lay yourself bare all the time. You wanted to be vulnerable with those watching you because you wanted to show them the highs and the lows of the industry. You wanted to be a guiding light for kids who aspired to be like you, and that meant you had to be willing to share the darkest parts of yourself. I think I need to understand why you stopped doing that in the first place to help you figure out how to get back there."

Was I naïve to think I could do that? That I could make a difference for the ones after me? "I've changed," I whisper.

"And that's fine," he says without missing a beat. "But some things you've changed because you evolved. Others you changed because something or someone made you."

Many somethings. Many someones. "I . . . I . . ." The words are right on the tip of my tongue, but when I try to push them out, they get stuck.

"It's okay," he rushes to say. "You don't have to tell me. But you do have to acknowledge what it is."

Something about his reassurance pries the words from my lips. "I don't know how to be soft. Every time I've tried, I've just ended up with another jagged edge."

The silence on the other end of the line doesn't bother me this time. I appreciate him taking the time to consider my words and not rushing to comfort me. I don't need comfort, I need reality. I need to know if I'm broken.

"The thing about jagged edges is, they're not a sign of weakness. They're a show of strength, a battle scar to prove you survived. I think true beauty lies in those jagged edges, but if you want to smooth them out, all you need is a little sandpaper."

"A little sandpaper." I flip the words over in my mind. "Where do you get this stuff?"

His voice is a hairsbreadth above a whisper when he responds, but his tone is so sure it leaves no room for argument. "I just say what I feel."

"What's that like?"

"What's what like?"

"Speaking freely all the time." I'm very good about speaking what's on my mind, but speaking what's on my heart is a luxury I've long forgotten.

"I wouldn't say all the time. There's a lot of things on my heart right now that I'm not saying."

Though I can't see him, I feel him looking right through me. I meant what I said about wanting us to be friends, but the kind of friends who keep things lighthearted and easy, not the kind who push past pretty lies to uncover ugly truths. Not the "sandpaper" level of friends.

Sandpaper. I know I have that in my life. My parents, Janelle, Evie, and even Amerie—all of them would take me into their arms and grind my rough edges into dust. The logical part of my brain knows this, but there's this other part that's screaming, *What if it's too much?*

What if smoothing out the rough edges I've gained takes more than what my sandpaper can give?

What if loving me becomes a burden?

Is that how Tanya felt? Like she couldn't unburden herself of her truths until after she died for fear of becoming the weight of the world on someone else's shoulder?

Before I can even process my own thoughts, I release the words into the abyss. "Micah? I think it's time to open the envelope."

Chapter Ten

Micah

"Art imitates life. You'll find my life where you find my art." —Tanya

THE CRISP FALL AIR DANCES ACROSS MY FACE AS I LEAN my head back against the tombstone.

"I hope you two are up there having a time."

Chi Chi was the person I confided in the most, so sometimes when I need to talk something out, I visit her here. She taught me to go against the grain, and so though it might seem corny to some, I don't shy away from what brings me comfort. Sitting here and being able to run my hands along her name and sink my hands into the grass surrounding her does that. I know she's not here anymore. I know all that's left in that grave are a pile of bones, but I think when I come here, that's when she knows I really need her. It's where I can feel our connection.

"I don't know what to do, Chi Chi. I haven't felt this off balance since I lost you. It hurts. And I'm trying not to let that hurt define me like I did last time, but it feels impossible. And then there's Dani. You remember me telling you about her? She's back. It feels like I finally have another chance, but we're both so different now. She clearly doesn't want to take another chance, so I don't know why I can't let it go—why I can't let her go." I shouldn't even be thinking about Dani right now, not in that way.

Our sole purpose of coming together should be honoring Tanya, not trying to rekindle a flame that long ago burned out, but Dani is branded on my skin, my heart, and my soul. I can't forget her any easier than I can forget how to breathe, and I don't know what to do with that.

I run my hands along the blades of grass. "Tell Tanya she's on my shit list for putting us in this situation." I can practically hear Tanya's response in my head: *Tell him I'll pass him the toilet paper*.

The wind serves as my only response from Chi Chi, and the chime on my phone reminds me that I have to get to the gallery.

I sigh as I stand up and brush off my pants. "I just wish y'all were here, that's all."

I make my way out of the cemetery, and as I do I notice two cardinals perched on a tree branch above me.

Cardinals are a message from your lost loved ones. At least, that's what Chi Chi always told me. When I first met Tanya, right after she held a gun to my head, I could see a cardinal right outside her living room window. Maybe that's what made me trust her so quickly.

Seeing two of them together now is a relief I didn't realize I needed.

Smiling, I take one last look at Chi Chi's tombstone and carry on.

My eyes are starting to cross from looking at this calendar.

This is the part I hate about running a business. Paperwork.

I'm looking at the list of commissions I've taken on and planning my schedule accordingly. I never like to keep someone waiting for work they've paid for, so I want to make sure I'm staying on top of everything. Once Dani and I rip the Band-Aid off this scavenger hunt, I don't know when I'll be back here long enough to work on these.

It's worth it to spend more time in Dani's presence, though. I'm determined to bring those walls crashing down, even if all she'll ever allow us to be is acquaintances.

What I'm trying to figure out is where those walls came from in the first place. Who caused her so much pain that she had no choice but to retreat behind a wall of perfection? I hope it wasn't me. I'm not much of a praying man, but I'll pray to whoever I can to ensure that's not the case. And if I *am* responsible for her walls, I'll pray to that same deity to allow me the chance to fix it.

I could ask Rome or Arnold. Who knows the kind of intel they've gotten during pillow talk, but that idea doesn't sit right with me. I don't want to know about Dani's hurts from a third party. I want them from her. I want her to open her wounds to me and trust I'll accept them. Love them. Heal them.

Needing a distraction from the woman who invades my every thought, I turn back to finish my schedule, then move on to double- check the gallery's operating expenses. My hand is itching for a paintbrush right now, something to release this pent-up energy, but this stuff has to get done.

"It feels almost wrong seeing you behind a desk."

The dulcet tones of that voice float across my office like a siren song.

I never thought I'd see the day when Dani would visit me here. The last time she was here was the end of us. Now, she's casually leaning against my doorjamb like she belongs. Like she wants to belong. That's probably wishful thinking on my part.

She looks gorgeous as always in a brown halter top, cream wide-leg pants, and brown boots. Her gold jewelry pops against her skin.

"Sorry, Bailey let me come back," she rushes to say. She must have misunderstood my look of surprised joy for confused annoyance.

Jumping to stand, I say, "No, no. You're always welcome. I was just surprised. I assumed we would meet at BMA." I gesture for her to step farther into the office, careful to keep my eyes on hers and not the gentle sway of her hips as she does.

"I let Nisha borrow my car, so I had her drop me off. Figured it wouldn't hurt to ride together." As if seeking permission, she looks at the chair across from my desk and then back to me. She never needs permission to make herself comfortable in my space, but I nod.

Dani crosses her right leg over her left, sitting with that perfect posture of hers. I shouldn't move. I should sit down on my side of the desk and leave her to hers. I swear I mean to do just that, but I can't resist the urge to be close to her. My feet carry me to her side where I perch on the edge of the desk, close enough to let the sensual scent of her perfume drift up to my nose.

Her body is racked with tension, but it's not the same kind of tension I felt from her after she cried on my shoulder at Tanya's house. This is more like nervous energy. Making her nervous seems to be a new favorite hobby of mine.

"Sounds good. So, how are you? How's Myomari?" I needle her.

She tries to play off the twitch of her neck, but I catch it. "I'm fine and I assume *Omari*'s fine." She makes a point to emphasize Omari's name without the *my* in front of it. I know what his name is, I just don't give a fuck.

"You assume? I'd think you'd know how the person you're dating is doing."

She narrows her eyes at me. "God, you're nosy. Omari and I aren't dating. We have a specific arrangement."

"Oh really?" I lean forward a bit, taking pleasure in the way her breath hitches at the movement. "And what's that arrangement? You know I'm nosy and all."

She blows out a harsh breath, probably regretting even coming here today, but I fully intend to enjoy this. "We see each other when a need arises, okay?"

"A need," I whisper. Does he fulfill her needs the way she deserves? Does he satisfy her every craving?

"If you ask me what kind of needs, I swear I'll punch you right in your titty."

That catches me off guard. "'Titty' is crazy."

"You got nipples, don't you? Then you got titties. Now, are you ready to go, or you need more time?" She leans back in her seat, looking pleased with herself.

It's so adorable I can't find it in me to push her anymore, so I put some distance between us. "Ready."

She gets up from her seat and I rush to hold the door open for her. "Thanks."

"No problem. Follow me," I say as I turn in the opposite direction we're supposed to go.

Her brow arches and she scrunches her nose, making her dimples disappear. "Why?"

"You want us to do this documentary, right? Trust me, this will be worth it."

I turn my back to her, feeling the heat of her gaze on my neck as I walk farther away.

When we reach the reception area, Bailey is sitting at her desk pretending she wasn't watching to see when we'd emerge.

"Bailey, you need me for anything?" I call out to her.

Her response is a look of boredom and a middle finger, so I smirk and lead Dani away.

I take her to the main gallery area and start walking a path through all the art, stopping to ask her about certain pieces.

"What do you think of when you look at this painting? What do you feel?" I gesture toward the piece titled "Kill Me with Your Tears" by an artist named Ayanna Powell.

It's an oil painting emulating a chronophotographic sequence of a man crying and a woman wiping his tears, the distinct painted frames freezing each phase of their rapid movement.

Dani studies the piece religiously. It's a sight to behold the way her eyes focus solely on the woman and then solely on the man before taking them in together.

"I feel panicked," she says.

I tilt my head, observing the piece. I've spoken to the artist herself and many people about this painting. Many have felt sorrow, anguish, and even joy, but no one has ever said they felt panicked when looking at it.

"Can I ask why?"

"It makes me feel like my time is running out. If you were to see this exchange in real life, it would look . . . sweet. It would seem soft, slow, and gentle. But seeing it this way, with every single detail of this simple gesture on full display, you can see how fast they're moving. It's a reminder of how quickly time is snatched away from us, even the little moments."

We both freeze when she says "the little moments." She probably thinks I forgot about the phrase she told me her grandmom used to say. If I didn't think it'd send her running for the hills, I'd show her just how wrong she is. I'm trapped in this vicious cycle of trying to form a bond between the people we are now without reminding her of the people we were.

"That's an interesting way of looking at it."

Her eyes glance over the painting once more before she pushes her shoulders back and strolls on to the next one.

We walk through a few more pieces and installations, her takes on each growing more refreshing and captivating as we go. I brought her in here to try to get a peek at how her brain works. How she views the world and how she thinks the world views her, and I gained plenty of insight.

As we walk out of the gallery area and down to the ballroom, I enjoy the way she openly admires the space.

"This is really nice. So you rent this out for events?"

She knows this because Bailey told her, which is how the idea of hosting Tanya's gala here came to life, but it occurs to me that she's never actually seen it. She hasn't been here since the quiet disaster that was opening night, and even then, she never made it this far into the building.

"Yeah. A few organizations have rented it out, and we've used it for workshops for kids and families, including some of the children from Our Place."

Having the space to explore their interest in art at Our Place gave them the confidence to share those interests with their families and get them involved. Chi Chi's legacy lives on in them and all the other kids finding their way because of Our Place.

Dani looks at me with a tight-lipped smile, her eyes shining with something unsaid.

"What's that look?"

"Nothing," she says, moving her eyes around the ballroom again.

"Something."

"You stay tryna be in my business."

I am. I'm not ashamed of that, though if she really wanted me to stay out, I'd respect her wishes.

"You'll have to get some shots here. Tanya lives in the very bones of this building," I say.

"How so?"

"Tanya was a not-so-silent investor."

Surprise etches its way onto her features, not at the fact that Tanya invested in me, but that she didn't know about it.

"Yeah. My art was doing really well for itself and the Baltimore Collective was already established, so I was ready for this step, but Tanya didn't want me to front all the capital myself."

That earns a wider smile from her. "And what were her not-so-silent conditions?"

I chuckle, thinking of the many contributions she made over the years that I pretended were too grandiose but always appreciated. "You know Tanya. She always had something to say. Some grand idea."

"And they were grand," she adds.

"Very. We hosted a *Bridgerton* ball here one year. That was all her doing."

"Aww, I love *Bridgerton*. I wish—" She cuts herself off before she can say she wishes she had been there. Because she could've been.

I never would've stopped her, but once again I've inadvertently stepped on one of the bombs of our past.

"I know she came in full *Bridgerton* garb," she redirects the conversation, and once again I let her.

Thankfully, after the awkward moment at Spring House, we were able to bounce back and enjoy each other's company on the way to BMA, even if it wasn't a long ride.

When we get there, Tanya's assistant wastes no time escorting us to her office. Her space is as vibrant as she was, teal and gold prominent throughout all the tiny details, incense in eccentric-looking diffusers, and her desk clear of anything except a statue of two linked hands.

Her back wall is covered with photos. In all the time I knew Tanya, she was never without someone under her wing. She loved to pretend she was this mysterious widow, but everyone knew her heart was ten times the size of her body, and her photo wall of every kid she mentored only proves that point. She took care of so many of us; most of us have her to thank for our success. Staring down the rows of people who went on to become famous in their fields, I'm reminded of her impact.

Dani sighs beside me. "I keep wondering when I'm gonna walk into a space that was hers and not lose my breath."

"If grief was easy to measure, people wouldn't be nearly as afraid of it."

Sometimes, there's no rhyme or reason to the things that trigger us. I think Tanya's loss has the power to change the trajectory of our course entirely.

Dani takes a deep breath before trailing her fingers along Tanya's desk and walking to the other side of it.

"What do you think she wanted us to find here?" she asks, eyes roaming.

"The note said we'll find her life where we find her art. Maybe she just wants us to go through her stuff. See if we learn any secrets about her."

We have no idea where this scavenger hunt will take us, only that the possibilities are endless, which in Tanya-speak means we could end up anywhere in the world for all we know. Our first clue was the note Victor gave us from Tanya about art imitating life.

She snorts. "Even on her deathbed, she was the most dramatic woman I know."

"My junior year of college, I applied for this fellowship in New York and I didn't get it, which was fine, except I lost out to a guy in my class that I hated. When I bitched to Tanya about it, she sent a string quartet to my place to play sad 'get over it' music. Drama wasn't on her, it was in her."

Dani stares at me with wide eyes before doubling over with laughter. "I'm sorry, but that's funny as fuck. Did you let them play the whole song?"

"I mean." I pause. "Yeah, they were really good. But still—"

Her sharp laughter stops me short and it just keeps going.

"Aight now."

"I'm sorry," she says between giggles.

"No, you're not."

"I'm not."

I start looking through Tanya's bookcases, picking up a random pen to throw at Dani when I hear her giggle again.

"Ha, look at this." Dani holds up a letter for me.

It seems that Tanya liked to keep her desk clear in favor of shoving everything inside the desk drawers, so Dani and I are sitting on the floor across from each other going through each one.

I scan the letter and then read through it thoroughly three more times to make sure I'm not seeing things.

"Is this a love letter?"

"Yep," she says around a smile.

"From Prince?"

"Prince."

"*Thee* Prince?"

"The artist formerly known as," she responds.

I shake my head. "That's wild."

She rummages through the rest of the papers lying at the bottom of the drawer. "It looks like it was only one and I don't think she responded. Imagine turning down Prince!"

"You think George up there putting hands on Prince for his wife?"

George was long gone before Dani and I came around, but the very fact that he got Tanya to marry him tells me that George did not play around.

Dani sighs dreamily. "Either that or she's charmed her way into the weirdest, but somehow rightest, poly relationship."

"Now you sound jealous," I mock.

Her eyes jump like she's been caught with her hands in the cookie jar. "I just can't believe she knew Prince and didn't introduce me." She shrugs, accepting her lot in life, and continues searching the drawers.

The drama is strong with this one too.

We look through a few more interesting mementos of Tanya's before I have to stand up to stretch my legs.

My foot hits the wall as I stand, sending one of the hall-of-fame photos crashing to the ground.

"Shit," I curse. Dani starts to help me, but I tell her to stay where she is so I can clean up the glass. As I'm sweeping the last piece, I notice something sticking out of the back of the photo.

I pull it out and unfold it. It's a note, written in Tanya's handwriting.

During Halle's senior year, she was the lead in a play with her boyfriend. They broke up during rehearsals because he cheated on her with her understudy. I went to the opening night of the play and watched her act out a scene where she was supposed to pretend to cut his hair off. She didn't pretend. She cut that boy's 4B curls in front of a packed audience. Everyone gasped in shock. I gave her a standing ovation.

I flip what's left of the frame over to find a picture of Halle Hewitt, a famed Broadway actress, and one of Tanya's past mentees.

Did Tanya write a card to go along with every one of these photos?

I hand the picture and card to Dani and grab another off the wall.

Opening the framed picture of music producer Finesse, I find a similar card with a handwritten memory.

Words aren't needed between Dani and me. We both know all these pictures are coming down. One by one, we remove each memory from its cage, as if we can jump inside them like the chalk paintings from *Mary Poppins*.

We go until there's only two photos left: mine and hers.

"You read mine. I'll read yours?" Dani proposes.

Without another word, we swap.

I motion for her to go first and she clears her throat. "Micah had been getting pretty big commissions for a while, but after he booked the Ravens one, he knew he was never going to go broke again. I asked him what he was going to do with his check, and I'll never forget the look of pure elation on his face when he said he was going to buy his mom's daycare center. I think that's the proudest I've ever been of him."

I can't speak. The words are frozen to the back of my throat. I was expecting a funny recollection or even something kind about my work. I'm blown away and honored that her favorite memory of me was how she viewed me as a son and a man.

Placing my hand on my chest, I look up to the ceiling. "Thank you," I croak, hoping that wherever Tanya is, she's listening. My voice comes out hoarse, but I push through, powered by Dani's reassuring smile. "My turn then?"

She nods.

"Okay, Dani smelled like cheese fries and bad manners."

"It doesn't fucking say that—"

She reaches to snatch the card from me, but I hold it high above her head. Standing on her toes brings our lips dangerously close. I can smell the strawberry Tic Tacs she ate in the car on her tongue.

I expect her to back down from the chemistry that has always brewed between us, but to my delight, she holds strong. Her eyes flutter to my lips briefly before she locks her gaze with mine, a silent challenge laid before me.

Not this time, Dani.

Not until you're truly ready.

I lean forward. "I'm fuckin' with you." I laugh, and she slaps my arm. "It says, 'When Dani launched Promesa, we had a celebratory drink at my house. I have never been that drunk in my life. It was the first time I'd ever felt my age.'"

Dani giggles quietly, the sound somehow both innocent and sinister.

"She sang all the parts of 'Ladies' Night' by herself without taking a breath, and I believe I danced on my table. It was the happiest I'd seen her in a long time. I don't think she remembers saying this to me, but she said, 'It's so nice to wake up every morning and actually be happy about it.' That always stays with me."

Quiet falls over the room.

She didn't want to live anymore. I mean, it doesn't explicitly say she wanted to kill herself, but the message is clear. There was a time when she would've gladly accepted death. I hate that.

Dani's hands tremble by her sides. She reaches up and slips the card from my fingers.

I track the barrage of emotions that fall over her with every reread. "Let me just say this and then we can move on like I know you want to."

"Go ahead."

"I'm glad you're here."

Her eyes shoot up to mine, piercing my chest. "Me too."

Good. Until my dying day, I'll always make sure that's the case. That, I can promise.

Something catches Dani's attention, and she gently moves me from her path. She bends over the linked hands statue on Tanya's desk and pulls a piece of paper from one of the palms. Unfolding it, she reads the words and snorts.

"Did you see the new exhibition they have running right now?"

"Uh, no?" I respond.

She holds the paper out to me. It's another flyer for the BMA, but this one is advertising their new installation: *Art Imitates Life*.

"I don't know if I can handle any more emotions today, but lead the way," I say.

It takes us a minute to reach *Art Imitates Life* as we become enthralled in other exhibitions along the way.

When I first met Tanya, she would bring me here often, letting me appreciate the many artists displayed there, but it was discovering how she curated each exhibition that inspired me to open Spring House. Tanya didn't make art, but she was an artist all the same. I can't walk by and not absorb her talent one last time.

Dani stops suddenly, making me crash into her back. I understand why the moment I register what I'm seeing.

Tanya is in the *Art Imitates Life* collection. There are screens across the installation showing photos and videos of her throughout her life.

The videos are clearly home movies, most of them from her time with George. Visually they're wonderful on their own, but there are headphones stationed at each screen so you can also hear the audio.

Dani approaches the first screen, cautiously grabbing the headphones and submerging herself into Tanya's past.

I move onto the next one, diving in with both feet.

"*George is actually one of the most frustrating men I've ever met,*" Tanya says with authority.

From behind the camera, George says, "*Tell them you love me, baby.*"

She hides her smile behind her hand. "*I'll do no such thing.*"

The camera shifts and George appears on screen, wrapping Tanya up in his arms and lifting her off the ground as she screams in false panic.

"*George Basil Holden, you put me down!*" she demands.

His boisterous laugh echoes across their backyard as he spins her one more time before putting her down.

He keeps his hand planted around her waist and she leans into his touch.

"*Tell the people why you're pretending to be mad at me,*" he says, adoration in his eyes.

She scoffs and turns to the camera. "*This man here put a baby in me and that was not part of the plan.*"

He throws his head back with laughter. "*But are you happy?*"

Her hand grazes her stomach, settling protectively over it. Her smile beams up at him. "*Profusely.*"

I snatch the headphones off of my ears. Tanya was pregnant? Did she have a child we didn't know about? Endless questions circle me like sharks. I look over to Dani, who seems to be engulfed in a happy vision of Tanya.

The light hits the plaque under the screen I just watched, catching my attention. It reads, "If I'd known then what I know now, would it have changed anything?"

I don't know what to make of this. Dani removes her headphones and walks over to me. She looks so peaceful that I hesitate to hand her this pair, but Tanya wanted us to see everything.

I grab Dani's hand and squeeze before placing the headphones in her palm and moving on to the next video.

This time I read the plaque first and it says "Lorraine."

A young Tanya sits in front of a camera.

Her eyes are puffy with tears, the only indication that something is wrong despite her perfectly styled hair, makeup, and blouse.

"*George loves his videos, so I thought I'd try this. I've tried to be strong. I really have. But I keep seeing all the blood. The blood that seeped from my body and told us our baby was in danger. I keep remembering the moment everything went black. She was so still in my stomach, and I knew right then that she was gone.*" She buries her face in her hands, eventually running her hands up to grip the roots of her hair tightly.

"*I know she wasn't planned, but I wanted her. Why did you give her to me if you were just gonna snatch her away?*" she asks the empty room, knowing she won't get an answer. "*Why did you give me the experience of childbirth just so I could hold her lifeless body in my arms? I don't understand. I will never understand.*"

She blows out a harsh breath and picks up a makeup brush. She looks past the camera into a mirror, dabbing under her eyes.

The door behind her opens and a downtrodden George walks in. The two of them make eye contact before Tanya jumps from her seat and rushes to George's side. They slide to the floor, holding each other.

Fuck. Tanya experienced such tragedy and was somehow able to keep going. Even after losing George too, she held on. Death was a prominent figure in her life; now I know why she went so willingly when it came for her.

Turning to look at Dani, I find her frozen.

She's staring at her screen with her mouth agape and her hands plastered to her stomach. I rush over and remove the headphones, placing them back on their stand.

I grip the back of Dani's neck and massage her nape. Slowly, her eyes lower into a long blink, then circle back to me.

"There's no way Tanya wouldn't have a relationship with her child and no way she wouldn't have told me she had one in the first place. Where is the baby, Micah?" Her voice shakes with fear. She knows what's coming. She knows it in her bones, and I don't have the power to make it not true.

I take her hands in mine and lead her to the next screen, laying the headphones on for her, but I don't move to the next screen. I stand behind Dani and rewatch Tanya's unraveling, which is even more devastating on mute. When Tanya and George crumble to the ground, Dani's legs wobble beneath her. I catch her and hold on, wishing I could've done the same for Tanya.

We stay together through the rest of the exhibition, serving as each other's anchor. The rest of the videos are peaceful, with Tanya and George moving from Virginia to Maryland and eventually finding their smiles again. The videos end with Tanya and George celebrating their anniversary. I assume home movies died for Tanya when George did.

Tanya's assistant waits for us by the exit of the gallery. Her brows are pulled inward and her muscles tighten at her eyes. She tilts her head to the right as she holds out a flash drive for me to take. We exchange no words once the flash drive is in my hands. She disappears into the crowd as if she were never there.

Remembering Tanya's computer in her office and not wanting to wait any longer than necessary to see what this device holds, we rush back.

"I can't believe Tanya was almost a mother," I murmur as I connect the device to her computer.

"She was a mother," Dani says. "Whether she had the opportunity to raise her daughter or not, she was a mother."

She's one hundred percent right.

Tanya's face appears on the screen. The tendrils of illness showcase themselves in the heaviness of her eyelids and the dullness of her skin.

"Hello, my loves. Did you enjoy the exhibition? God, I haven't recorded a video of myself in decades. Wasn't George handsome? I think he would've enjoyed his movies being on display for everyone. He always wanted to be a movie director, so I transformed our life into his art."

She squeezes her eyes shut and for a moment I forget that this isn't a live feed, and I can't rush to her to make sure she's okay.

Her eyes pop open and she continues. "Yes, I had a daughter. George and I never planned on kids, but the moment we found out about her, we were ecstatic. Her name was Lorraine."

I had wondered if Dani noticed the plaque under Tanya's video. If she realized that Tanya's late child's name was the same as her middle name. I'm not sure if the death grip she has on the armrest of her chair means she did or didn't. I place my hand over hers, offering the only support I know how. She doesn't connect her hand with mine, but she doesn't move it either, and that's something.

"And after we lost her, I told George I didn't want to go through that ever again. When George passed, I regretted that choice. I regretted not trying again to have a piece of George that would outlive me. But then, I met you, Danielle Lorraine Jenkins. And I knew that was George telling me to let go of that pain. I know these tasks may seem silly, but I'm hoping they'll help you let go of your pain before it's too late."

The abrupt end to the video makes Dani jump in her seat, ripping her hand from underneath mine. "Wait, wait. Go back," Dani asks, eyes glued to the screen.

I grab the mouse and rewind until she tells me to stop. "What's wrong?" I ask.

She leans forward from her chair until her face is practically smashed against the screen. "Right there. Don't you see it? One of the pictures from her wall is missing."

I lean past her, trying to see what she sees. In the video, Tanya is sitting at her desk in this very room. The pictures we took off the wall are lined up perfectly behind her.

"Oh, shit," I say when realization hits me.

When we came in here, one of the rows on the wall had one less picture than the others. I think we both assumed she just didn't have another to fill the space, but in this video, all the rows are even.

So, where's the other photo?

We tear through the remnants of Tanya's office, looking for anything we missed the first time around. A framed photo of Tanya on her bookshelf catches my eye. It's from *Time* magazine article about her, but it stands out because it doesn't match the aesthetic of the rest of her shelf. The other frames are gold and elegant. This one is wooden and looks worn. Tanya wouldn't disrupt her design flow for no reason, so without hesitation I flip the frame over and open it.

Another photo falls from the frame. It lands right side up by my feet. Dani shuffles to stand across from me, but neither of us makes a move to grab the picture. I don't recognize the woman we're looking at, but it's clear that Dani does. Her fingers fly up to her mouth as she takes it in.

"You know her?" I ask.

She looks up at me. "Yeah. That's Daria Drayton. She's a fashion designer I've collaborated with. I just didn't know Tanya knew her."

"Well, it looks like she's the key to our next clue. Wanna do the honors?" I gesture to the photo, and she smiles before picking it up.

Instead of an anecdote about Daria on the back, there's only a one-line note, similar to the one Mr. Townsend gave us that led to the BMA, and an address.

In California.

Chapter Eleven

Dani

"Sometimes rediscovering yourself is easier in someone else's mirror." —Tanya

WHAT DOES THAT EVEN MEAN? THE WORDS WRITTEN on the back of Daria's photo were the only thing on my mind during the entire flight to California. Daria sounded a little too excited to hear from me when I called. We haven't spoken in at least a year, but she seemed like she had been expecting me to reach out.

I met Daria at London Fashion Week years ago. Her luxury brand, Magnolia, was quickly gaining notoriety in the fashion industry, and I had surpassed the level of success I dreamt of as a model, but we were both still eager to cement our place in history. She selected me as an ambassador for her brand and together we took the world of high fashion to new heights.

Micah and I have only just begun this journey Tanya has sent us on and already my heart aches for her. She lived a full life before I became a part of it—I knew that—but I wasn't expecting the very first clue to lead us to a discovery of something so significant it altered her very existence.

"It's beautiful here," Micah says, pulling my thoughts away from whatever it is we're headed toward.

When I turn to look at him, he's looking out the window of the car Daria sent for us with such childlike whimsy it makes the stress wreaking havoc on my body feel silly.

"Have you been to California before?"

He turns to me, pinning me under his easygoing stare. "Can't say I've ever been to Calabasas, but I've been to a few different counties. Actually, the last time I was in California was when Rome lived here. Me, Christian, Jalen, Kam, and his mom came out to surprise him for his birthday. Then we made him take us to Disneyland."

"You made him take you to Disneyland for his birthday?"

"Hell yeah. It was his own fault because he said he was just gonna work. His mom wasn't having that. Next thing we know, we're all on a plane headed to the West Coast. Disneyland was Kam's idea, and what Kam wants, he gets."

Kam is an only child with rich uncles and an even richer dad. He has no choice but to be spoiled.

"Naturally," I agree.

"Exactly. Which is how we ended up performing 'I2I' in the middle of the park." His lips tilt into a faint smile as he starts humming Powerline's classic tune.

A ridiculous image of four hulking men singing and dancing their hearts out to a Disney song floods my mind. "Please tell me there's video evidence of this."

He whistles, rubbing his palm over his beard. "Don't tell Christian I told you this, but Ms. Rochelle definitely has that video and sent it to all her girlfriends."

"I'm gonna have to get her number from Nelle," I say, rubbing my hands together. "You just reignited my childhood crush. Powerline could definitely get it."

He whips his body in my direction. "When you say Powerline, you mean Tevin Campbell?"

I shake my head. "No. I mean, I wouldn't say no to Tevin. But, no. I mean Powerline."

"The cartoon?"

"Are you really gonna sit there and act like you've never had a crush on a cartoon?" I stare at him, waiting for him to unleash an inevitable lie.

"Don't think so." And there it is.

"Velma?"

"No."

"Lola Bunny?"

"No."

"Storm?"

"No. Well, yes, but everyone with sexual desires and a brain wants Storm. That hardly counts."

I throw my hands in the air. "Oh my God."

"Oh, wait. I just thought of one."

"Who?" I lean closer to him.

"Trudy Proud."

Silence hangs in the air. From the corner of my eye, I catch our driver, Sam, who's been doing his best to ignore us this whole drive, crack a smile.

"You know what? That's valid. And also proves my point."

"You're right, I concede." He bows his head in my direction and then lifts his index finger. "But at least Trudy is a human cartoon."

I guess I shouldn't tell him about Kovu from *The Lion King 2* then.

For the rest of the drive, we alternate between admiring the view and debating the merits of crushes on animated characters until a private road leads us to a heavy gate that does little to hide the grandiosity of the house behind it. The visible cameras on the pillars beside it must be a good deterrent for unwelcome visitors.

There's a box on the driver side where Sam inputs a code that peels the gate back and allows us entry. As the car creeps up the driveway, Daria throws her door open and stands in the threshold with her arms wide.

"I feel like I just pulled up to the set of a dating show," Micah whispers.

I agree with him as Sam opens my door, waits for me to step out, then hurries to the trunk for our bags before Micah can get his hands on them.

"Hi, gorgeous," Daria calls out to me, wiggling her fingers in a small wave.

"Hi, beautiful," I respond as I walk into her waiting arms. "Long time no see."

She kisses my cheek. "I know, it's so nice to see your face in person again instead of on my screen." She then turns to Micah with an assessing eye. "And you must be Micah. Tanya said you were handsome, but she did not do you justice."

He smiles as he accepts her hug and kiss. "Nice to meet you, Daria."

"You too. Not to sound like a walking stereotype, but have you ever considered modeling?" The wheels in her head visibly turn, building an entire runway show around Micah right this second.

"Nah. I prefer to create the art, not be the art." His eyes shift to me. "I like to leave that to the professionals."

"I can relate to that." Daria looks between us, but what she sees, I don't dare to name. "Shame. You two on a stage or in front of a camera together would be something special." Her unrelenting gaze bounces back and forth for what feels like an eternity before she gestures for us to follow her.

I allow myself to meet Micah's gaze. It was supposed to be for only a moment, but the heat in his eyes sets my very skin ablaze, trapping me beneath the flames. It's not until he takes mercy on me and relinquishes his hold that I'm able to move my feet in Daria's direction.

She guides us inside to a bright foyer with high ceilings and hardwood floors. "I would offer you a tour, but I'm too excited. So, business first. Tour later?"

"Excited for what?" I question.

Daria's brows pull together. "For you to see my creations come to life. And for you to finally tell me what they're for. I'm surprised Tanya didn't come with you. I just knew she'd want to see my face when all was revealed."

My heart falls to the pit of my stomach. She doesn't know. I look to Micah, searching for any way out of this. Any way to avoid being the one to tell her that Tanya's gone, but I know it won't come. This is our cross to bear.

"Daria." Micah coughs into his fist. "Can we go somewhere and sit? I think we need to get on the same page."

Fifteen minutes later, I'm searching for signs of life in Daria's unblinking stare after Micah and I broke the news to her about Tanya's passing.

Her eyes lower into an unnaturally slow blink before she speaks. "She was an incredible woman. I'm sorry she's gone."

"Do you need a minute? Micah and I can always come back later," I ask. I know how grief can chew you up and spit you out. The last thing I want is to force Daria on this road without giving her time to process.

She closes her eyes and shakes her head, reaching out to grab my hand. "No. I'm okay." She lets my hand fall back to my knee as she gets up from the couch and stands by the fireplace. "Come with me."

Micah and I follow Daria through the house until we reach the door to the backyard, where there's a large pool that overlooks a beautiful mountain backdrop. In the pool, three people follow the instructions of a man in navy-blue swim trunks standing on the grass nearby. Their backs are to us, but I assume the man in the pool is older given his short white curly hair. Daria doesn't open the door, she just leans against it and watches them adoringly.

"My parents live here with me." She points between White Hair and one of the women in the pool as they reach their hands to the sky and bring them back down repeatedly. "And so do their full-time nurses. My dad has Parkinson's, and my mom has Alzheimer's, so they need more help than I can give them. Tanya was the only person who didn't make me feel crazy when I said I was moving them all in. She understood the pain of watching someone you love deteriorate before your very eyes, and why as heavy as the weight of that is, I couldn't hand it off to someone else." She wipes the back of her hand against her nose to hide a sniffle. "My dad is losing control of his body while my mom is losing control of her mind, and there's nothing I can do but watch and make them as comfortable as possible while it happens. I appreciate Tanya for not making me watch her circle the drain too."

I've wondered countless times whether I would be handling Tanya's death better if I had seen it coming. Part of me acknowledges my tendency to spiral would've only made it worse. The version of me that she's left behind, however, is still screaming for some kind of rewind button. I admire Daria's surety.

In all the time I've known her, I don't think we've ever had a conversation that didn't revolve around work. Sure, we've shared funny stories about our pasts, but even those had the underlying pretense of our professional future—me sharing my experimentation with cutting my own bangs for picture day in middle school to try to stand out, her telling me about sewing her first dress with her mom and accidentally sewing it to her pants, and so on. Never once have we shared anything deeply personal with each other, and yet, here I am standing in her house for the first time, staring at her greatest source of pain and joy.

All because of Tanya. Or rather, her absence.

I wish it hadn't come to this.

I bite my tongue to keep the obligatory *I'm sorry* from slipping from my lips. Instead, I offer her the only thing that makes sense to me: reassurance. "You deserve that relief."

She looks to me with misty eyes. "Thank you."

She doesn't take us outside to meet her parents, explaining that her mom is having a good day and Daria wants her to enjoy that time with her dad, uninterrupted. As she leads us toward her office, I ask her a question that's been eating at me. "Do you mind if I ask how you knew Tanya?"

To my knowledge, Daria was born in Ohio and lived in New York and London before settling in California, but never in Baltimore. They both traveled a lot, so it's not implausible that they would've met elsewhere, but I guess I'm curious why I didn't know about it, especially given Tanya's proclivity for arranging playdates for the adults in her life.

Daria hums. "We met years ago at this show at the West End. She was there to see one of her mentees and I was there to see a friend. But we left together after the two of them—who were apparently dating—had a nasty breakup backstage. And then, her mentee threw her tea in my face because she thought I was a side chick."

Beside me, Micah barks out a laugh. He holds his hand out in apology. "Sorry, sorry. That caught me off guard."

Daria smirks in return. "No, it's okay. It's funny now, but back then I almost killed her. Tanya stopped me, and my so-called friend barely threw a napkin in my direction as he ran after her."

"Was the tea hot?" I ask before I can stop myself.

"Room temp. Which is probably the only reason I let Tanya hold me back."

"You couldn't break free of her hold, could you?" Micah jests.

She chuckles. "I really couldn't. She had a strong ass grip. Anyway, after that we stayed in touch. You know, she had this way about her that just made her impossible to forget. One day, we're sending each other the occasional 'hope you're well, hope you haven't gotten any more drinks thrown in your face' message. And the next, we're visiting each other's homes and I'm naming my cat after her."

As if on cue, her black tabby, aptly named Holden, sashays through the room, rubbing against each of our legs, escaping just as Daria bends over to pick him up. She sucks her teeth and swipes her hand in the direction he went.

"Asshole." She turns back to us. "He and Tanya were kindred spirits. And then, a few months ago she came to see me and requested I make you a dress and Micah a suit. Funny enough, I didn't even know you knew each other until then."

"She did that?" As I ask, Daria opens the door to her office and shines a light on the dress and suit in question. I'm stunned by the garments on display.

As a brand, Magnolia is a flawless depiction of Daria herself. It's elegant with a bite to it. You could wear the clothes to a high-profile dinner and then turn around and wear the same outfit to an underground concert.

The bodice and train of the dress are a beautiful soft pink, elegant in a classic way, but the rest of the dress is both risqué and artistic. The right side is sleeveless while the left side has a long sheer sleeve covered in fabric flowers so detailed they look as if they've been plucked from a garden. The flowers continue down the side and over the thigh. The bottom of the dress is also sheer, giving the illusion of flowers floating down a river.

Most of Micah's suit is the same soft pink as my dress, but the right side of his blazer matches the floral effect. Together, we'll make a beautiful landscape.

"Daria, these are . . . these are stunning. I don't even know what to say," I praise.

She does a small curtsy, puffing her chest out as she stands straight again. "I do. You could tell me what I made these for. All she said was that you would need them, and you'd reach out directly when you were ready to come get them."

We tell her about the gala Tanya requested in her will as well as how we figured out we needed to come see her.

"Damn, she's brilliant," Daria says in awe. "There's just one problem."

"What's that?" Micah asks.

"Am I supposed to know where your next clue is? Because I don't."

I've been too busy trying to find out everything there is to know about Tanya and Daria's bond that I haven't even thought about what comes next. I step toward the garments, carefully brushing the material between my fingertips. There's nothing on either the dress or the suit that looks like a clue. And how could there be? Tanya never even saw the finished products. Daria said the only direction Tanya gave her when she requested them was that they be fitting for a formal event and to trust her instinct. She gave no opinions on color, theme, or design.

So where do we go from here?

Tanya's note floats to the forefront of my mind. What is it that we're supposed to rediscover about ourselves?

"No, you did your part. Thank you," I acknowledge.

Daria's lips twist into a frown as her brows pinch together. "Well, then, time for the best part. Time to try them on!" She grabs the clothes off their displays and practically throws them in our hands, pushing Micah into the nearby closet and me into the bathroom.

Like every dress I've ever worn from Daria, this one glides up my body like butter. There's something about her clothes that always makes me feel my sexiest, most confident self, like she's infused her own aura into every stitch.

After Daria helps me zip up the dress, I step out at the same time Micah walks out. He's adjusting his sleeves and hasn't looked up yet, so I soak in the view.

They say there's no such thing as perfection.

They've never seen Micah in this suit. The brightness of the pink against his rich complexion is an exquisite combination. He's the apple in the garden, too tempting to resist.

Micah finally sees me, and I watch every thought march right out of his mind.

"Dani, you look incredible."

"Thank you. This dress is the most glorious thing I've ever put on my body."

"It's not the dress. It's you in the dress."

His words are so firm, I find myself standing a bit straighter.

"No offense, Daria."

"Honey, you keep talking like that, you're gonna offend me right out of my drawers."

He laughs shyly, never taking his eyes off of me.

I clear my throat. "Well, you look great too."

He beams at my compliment. Why does he have to do that?

Every time I think I've gotten a handle on this new dynamic between us, he looks at me in a way that drowns me in what we could've been.

Daria uses that moment to cut through the tension suffocating the air. "Dani, I made yours based on your measurements from the last time we worked together and that seems like it worked out well. Micah, I did my best given the rough estimates Tanya gave me. I think we need to make a few alterations, though." She instructs him to stand in front of her floor-length mirror so that she can mark the necessary adjustments. "This is cute, I've never done a couple's fitting at the same time," she remarks, a safety pin hanging from her mouth.

Micah's eyes shutter closed at her words. He can feel the chill they've just unleashed.

"We're not a couple," I correct.

Daria looks up at me in the mirror then back up to Micah.

"Never?" she asks.

"We never got that far."

"We didn't?" Micah interjects.

A low growl rumbles in my chest, but I do my best to suppress it. What I'm not about to do is air out our history in front of Daria.

"Oop, okay. I've stumbled into awkward territory. So sorry. Dani, why don't you go change while I finish this up?"

Without another word, I rush back to my pseudo dressing room.

A soft knock at the door sends relief through my body that I don't have to go back out there and ask Daria to unzip me.

"Thank you, I—"

My words stop short in my throat because it's not Daria. Standing only inches apart, I notice more details of Micah's suit that I missed before. While the design of my dress looks like flowing water, the jewels on Micah's suit look like small rocks. It's as if the flowers are flowing down my river and landing atop his coast.

Focusing on those details is all I can do to avoid the blaze in his eyes.

"Where's Daria?" I ask.

"I asked her to give us a moment."

"You made her leave her own office."

"Yes. Because I wanted to make sure you were okay."

"Why wouldn't I be, Micah?"

"I don't know, Dani. We just talked about being able to speak freely. I thought now might be a good opportunity to try that out."

I fold my arms across my chest. "I don't have anything to say."

"No?"

As I shake my head, he rubs his fingers against his temple and leans against the doorjamb.

"Okay, well I do. Look, I know we never recovered after I left New York. And I know you don't care to hear why. But our time together meant everything to me. I need you to know that."

I don't need to hear why things fell apart when he left New York. I've pieced it together myself. It doesn't change where we are now, so what's the point in rehashing it? I am not the woman I was back then. The woman I am today isn't meant to be with a man like him.

"Thanks for sharing," I say, placing my hand around the door handle impatiently.

He sighs, defeat descending over his body. "Do you need help before I go?"

My nose wrinkles. "Excuse me?"

He gestures behind me. "Your zipper. Do you need help?"

I chew my bottom lip while I consider his offer. "Uh, sure, yeah, thanks."

I turn my back to him and move my hair to one side of my shoulder. His footsteps are quiet, but I feel the heat from his body at my back. His scent slithers around like a snake, crushing me with its intensity.

A sharp chill rips through my spine when his hand touches my back. Why does his touch still affect me after all this time? It would be so easy to give in to the sexual attraction I've always had for Micah, but we both know that wouldn't be enough for him. He would want pieces of me I can't give him. Pieces I no longer have to give.

He takes his time pulling the zipper down, the metallic zip the only sound between us. My flesh begs him to keep going, to keep pulling until the zipper has reached its end and the dress pools at my feet, but he doesn't. He stops just far enough so that I can do the rest myself.

Leaning down so his mouth caresses my ear, he says, "The rest is on you, track star."

When I turn around, he's gone.

At Daria's insistence, we're staying at her house while we try to figure out what Tanya's next clue could be.

We met her parents briefly before they retired to their rooms. Daria and I find ourselves sitting out by the pool while Sam grabs us some dinner and Micah has disappeared for a sunset hike.

"Sometimes I regret it," Daria says, her head leaning against the back of her chair.

"Regret what?"

"Moving my parents in." She winces as she blows air into her cheeks, as if the words taste like bile in her mouth. "The house is about thirty minutes away from the ranch where they got married, and I thought that would be good for them, you know? They loved that ranch so much. I thought I could take them there whenever they needed a reminder of past times, and everything would be fine, but it hasn't been. I haven't designed anything in so long. Your clothes for the gala were the very last thing, and it felt great to get back to what I'm good at. But ever since, my creative well has completely dried up. It's like I'm afraid to progress my business because I don't want it to take me away from them. And sometimes I wish I could turn a blind eye to their illnesses just so I could have that part of my life back. Is that terrible of me to say?"

"No, it's not." I don't have the words to comfort her. I can't relate to what she's going through, but it's easy to see how much she loves her parents. Wanting the best for them and more for herself is only natural.

"Hmm, if you say so. Anyway, when I told you about my parents earlier, you looked at me like I was some kind of saint. I wanted you to know I'm not."

"Oh shit, so that wasn't a halo I saw on your head earlier?"

She chuckles. "No, but I see why you would think so. I am ethereal," she says, fanning her fingers in front of her face.

"Real goddess-like," I add.

"You get it."

I turn at the sound of a small purr to find Holden sneaking toward the pool. He swipes at his reflection in the water and backs away at the sight of the ripples.

"He does that every time," Daria says to me. "Come here, Holden baby." She makes a clicking sound with her tongue as she holds her hand toward him.

He skips happily over to her, wrapping himself around the base of her lounge chair, then doing the same to mine. When she reaches over to pet him, he reaches his paw out and presses down on her hand.

A loud cackle escapes from the depths of my belly. "He said unhand me."

When she tries to pet him again, she receives the stiff arm. "He only likes to be touched on his terms. Which—I mean, go off, king—set your boundaries. But I'm your motherrrrr."

"You gotta play hard to get. You want it too badly," I tease.

"I guess I was due to be told that once in my life."

We watch the sunset from our chairs and encourage Sam to join us when he returns with our food.

I don't see Micah for the rest of the night.

The next morning, the smell of coffee brings me down to the kitchen. Daria's mom's nurse is pouring himself a cup while he waits for her mom's breakfast to finish cooking. He pours a cup for me and makes idle chitchat until his job in the kitchen is done.

It's quiet once he leaves; nothing but the birds singing in the trees outside can be heard. The stillness of the world around me amplifies the thoughts swirling in my head.

From all the work that needs to be done at home to how I left things with Micah, I can't get my mind to quiet down.

You're okay. You're fine. Everything's fine.

Micah's heavy footsteps into the kitchen are a welcome distraction. "Morning," he says as he makes his way to the pot of coffee.

"Morning. How'd you sleep?"

"I woke up with a cat on my chest. So, I guess good?" Of course Holden is drawn to Micah. The man is walking catnip.

"Did he let you pet him?"

He looks at me like I've grown two heads. "He was sleeping on my chest."

"Right," I say, still waiting for an answer to my question.

"He invaded my space."

"Right," I respond.

"So, yes, I petted him." He holds his hands out as if that answer should've been obvious.

"Not what I asked. I asked did he let you pet him? Like did you force him to let you pet him or he just . . . let it happen?"

"I don't think you understand. We're best friends now. He let me pet him." He takes a sip of his coffee, hiding a grin behind his mug.

"Daria is gonna be pissed," I jokingly admonish.

"If it makes her feel better, he did meow very loudly in my face before he left. It sounded like a scream, it was kinda scary."

I'm not sure if that will help or hurt the sting of betrayal, but since Holden didn't even bother to acknowledge me this morning, I'm definitely snitching.

"So, think there's any of Tanya's clues hiding out in Daria's house that she doesn't know about?" Micah asks.

We rack our brains trying to figure out where else Tanya could be trying to lead us. There has to be another clue we haven't found yet.

"I think we need to find Daria," I concede when my brain feels as if it's going to explode.

We never got the full tour of the house, so Micah and I stumble around, carefully peeking into room after room in search of Daria. There isn't any sign of her, which is strange, because she said she's normally an early riser. I'm hoping to at least bump into one of the nurses so I can ask them where she'd be.

As I start to open one door, I trip and slam through the opening.

"Woah," Micah exclaims. Inside, we find a mini showroom. It's the size of a large walk-in closet packed with mannequins decked out in fabulous clothing.

Before we can step into the room, we hear Daria's voice behind us. "Oh, there y'all are."

"We were looking for you," I say. "But, um, what are these?" At first glance at the outfits closest to me, I can tell Daria didn't design them. They're beautiful, but they're not her. They lean too much on the chic side than the edgy.

"Sorry. I was sitting on the upstairs balcony. These"—she pauses as she joins us at the threshold of the showroom—"are Tanya's designs."

"Wait, what?" I ask.

She smiles as she walks into the room and picks a book off of one of the shelves. She flips open to a random page that has a pantsuit roughly sketched on it before plopping it down on the table below the shelves.

"You know Tanya loved to pick up random skills. She got hooked on *Project Runway* and started learning how to draw clothes just so she could sketch designs with me." She looks down at the sketch, then out to the sea of designs before walking around each mannequin dressed in Tanya's pieces. She strides around each garment with purpose, so gracefully her feet almost look like they're floating, stopping at the exact suit from the sketchbook. "You should've seen this when she first sketched it. It looked like a poncho made for a giant."

And now it looks damn good for a novice. I have to give her credit; she never held on to her hobbies for long, but she never let them go until she damn near perfected them.

Micah grabs the sketchbook and flips through it feverishly, looking up to the ceiling when he reaches one page in particular.

"What is it?" I ask him.

He puts the sketchbook back down with his index finger on top of the page. "She designed this?" he asks Daria.

I look at the sketch and freeze. It's the dress Tanya was wearing in her casket at her funeral.

Unaware of the emotions clogging our throats, Daria smiles at the sketch in question. "Yeah. When I told her that I had started sewing her designs, she asked if I would ship that one to her. She said people had to see her in it."

And that they did. When I saw her lifeless body in that pink dress at the funeral, I wanted to laugh. Only she would pick a hot pink dress as her final resting outfit, but knowing that she designed it herself adds all the color I need to understand why.

Micah and I share a look, silently agreeing not to tell Daria where she wore it, but we tell her that we indeed saw Tanya in the dress, and that seems to give her comfort.

"Good. I'm glad someone saw one of her designs. Actually, do you want to take the rest of them? You can add them to her auction. They deserve to see the light of day."

Micah furrows his brows. "You don't want them? Make them part of your next launch?"

She looks over all the mannequins, tears welling up in her eyes. "They're not mine. I don't know if I'll ever design again, but I can't pass off Tanya's creations as my own. I just wanted to bring her vision to life, you know?"

Tanya wouldn't have cared what Daria did with the garments. She would probably be honored to have her designs grace one of Daria's shows, but I understand where she's coming from.

An idea starts brewing in my head. One that I think would both honor Tanya and help Daria find her way back to her destiny.

"We would love to include these in the auction. But, do you mind if we use them for something first?"

She hums. "Use them for what?"

I clap my hands in excitement. "Leave everything to me. I promise I'll take good care of them."

She taps her finger against her chin. "Secrecy. I like it. Go on."

Is this a bad idea or the best idea I've ever had? I guess Daria's reaction when she gets here will let me know.

When I unloaded my thought process to Micah two days ago, I expected him to talk me off the proverbial ledge. Instead, he pushed me off of it, and now here we are, standing at the ranch thirty minutes away from Daria's house, waiting for her to arrive.

Micah exits the lodge looking like a cowboy straight out of my dreams in dark brown pants with a dark denim shirt tucked in. He's even chewing on a toothpick. "You're gonna put a hole in the ground with all that pacing," he chastises.

"What are you, tryna get into character?" I question, yanking the toothpick out of his mouth. Before I realize what I'm doing, I wrap my lips around it, ignoring the chills that rack my body when his eyes bulge.

"You didn't know I was a method actor?"

"Oh, really? And what else does this method acting entail? Will I see you riding a horse later?"

"No, but if you want, I can show you a few rope tricks."

I'd forgotten how easy it is to lose myself in Micah, to get sucked into his charm and hang on to his every word.

"Oh, Micah." I shake my head. "You know, it actually makes sense that you'd be a method actor."

"Why do you say that?"

"You have this quiet intensity about you." It's unnerving and intoxicating at the same time.

"Quiet intensity, huh?"

Like right now. And I don't even think he realizes he's doing it. "It's not a bad thing." I guess.

"Nah, it's not. And besides, I like knowing what you think about me."

Before I can respond to that, Daria's car pulls up to the ranch entrance.

"Showtime," he says as he plucks the toothpick from my mouth and walks off with it back between his teeth.

Sam opens Daria's door, and she steps out looking like a ray of sunshine in a yellow jumpsuit with her hair falling in soft waves around her maple-hued skin.

"Dani, what is happening?"

"Well, I know you're feeling unmotivated to design, so I wanted to remind you of who you are. We're doing a little photoshoot with your work."

"You mean Tanya's designs?"

"Consider it a collaborative effort. Tanya had a vision, but you brought it to life in a way only you can." She still looks a bit skeptical, so I continue. "Come onnnn, Magnolia x T. Holden. You know Tanya would've paid a small fortune to see that."

She breaks at that. "Yeah, she would've." She takes my hand and lets me lead her to the action.

She gets a kick out of seeing Micah in his cowboy gear. Since Tanya's designs only included women's clothes, we had to improvise his outfits. We thought this look would pair well with the black lace tulle dress I'm currently wearing.

"Y'all look amazing," Daria says.

We cycle through most of her designs, following her direction, while Sabrina, the photographer I hired, snaps away. She's a local photographer I've worked with before and who happened to owe me a favor. I saved it for the perfect occasion.

Daria is in her element among all Tanya's fashion, bringing her own flair. During one of the indoor shots, we use the dressing room area. I'm looking at myself in the mirror wearing a cute sparkly dress, but my makeup is sprawled out all around me and my legs are thrown up on top of the vanity in defiance.

In another shot, Micah kneels in front of me as if he's hemming my skin-tight mid-length leather dress, but the shot is taken from the mirror angle so you can't see his face and you can't tell what he's doing on his knees in front of me. I'm looking back at the mirror with a wink to sell the potential scandal as well.

Daria claps excitedly when she looks at the last set of shots Sabrina took. "These are perfection! You are the moment. Oh wow, Tanya would've loved your smolder in this one."

She thanks Sabrina and prepares to start breaking everything down, but I stop her.

"Actually, there's one more shot I'd love to get."

"Okay, let's do it."

"We're gonna need two more models."

"And . . . will I be pulling them from the sky?" she queries.

I motion for Sam and Hannah to come out and in walks Daria's parents. Her mom is wearing a heather gray pantsuit Tanya designed with a peplum-style waist and a large faux fur neck scarf. Her dad is wearing a classic black suit.

Daria yelps in surprise. "Oh my God, Mom? Dad?"

Her mom is a little stunned at first when Daria shouts out to her, but Sam assures me that she's doing okay.

This ranch is the place her parents got married. When Daria mentioned it by her pool, she didn't give the specific name, so I'm sure she didn't think much of it when she pulled up. The moment she said she was going to donate her and Tanya's designs, I knew exactly where I wanted to have this photoshoot. It didn't take me long at all to find the ranch near her house. There were only two options, and the owners were more than happy to help me when I told them what I was trying to do.

I thought having her parents take vow renewal pictures in something she designed would be an ideal ending to this photoshoot. A way to show her that she doesn't have to choose between her parents' care and her career. Their nurses have been integral in making sure that this would be okay for them, which is why I kept it a surprise in case things changed on the day.

Micah gives me a thumbs-up and a bright smile after we look over and see Daria holding back tears while in her parents' arms.

After the photoshoot, Micah and I leave Daria with her family and head back to the house. We still haven't figured out the next clue, but I think it's time to give Daria and her parents their house back, so we'll head to a hotel if need be. I'm prepared to physically fight Daria if she protests.

"Today was really incredible," Micah says once we're settled in the living room with the TV on.

"It really was." Today reminded me of all the good parts of my modeling career. It reminded me how much I loved it.

"That was all you, Dani. You are . . . otherworldly."

I've never seen this look on his face before, this wild excitement. His body is buzzing.

"I think you've got an adrenaline high."

"I do. Because of you. Seeing you take charge and make that happen for Daria? She's going to cherish this moment forever. You should be proud of yourself."

Thank God the deep hue of my skin does a mostly decent job of hiding when I blush. I pull my pajama shirt away from my neck and force my eyes to stay on his. "Well, thank you. And thank you for being my fellow model today. I really couldn't have pulled this off without you."

His hand gently lands on my shoulder. "I'll be whatever you need me to be."

Something tells me he doesn't just mean in this context.

Daria returns a couple of hours later, sighing dreamily, before she marches up and pulls me into a bear hug.

"Damn, are you Tanya? You're squeezing me way too tight," I joke as I struggle to breathe.

After she lets me go, she plants a big kiss on my forehead. "Thank you. Thank you both for today."

"Of course."

"I think this calls for a celebration." She goes to her pantry and comes out holding a bottle of champagne and three glasses.

"Have you been saving that?" I ask.

"This was a gift from Tanya, so I thought it was fitting. She told me to hold on to it until I found my spark. If this feeling isn't spark, I don't know what is."

"Did she say those words exactly?" My heart starts pounding.

"She said something like until I rediscover my spark, but same thing."

I internally roll my eyes at Tanya's lack of subtlety. *Good one, Tanya.*

"Well, then, yes, let's definitely open that up."

Micah joins us in the kitchen and opens the bottle for us.

The corner of the label is peeling, and this champagne is too expensive for that, so I grab it and pull it free the rest of the way.

"Has that always said that?" Daria asks when Tanya's next clue is staring us right in the face.

Chapter Twelve

Micah

"No matter how far you go, you can always go home." —Tanya

I feel most like myself when I'm painting. My brushes are an extension of me. Sometimes, I like to sketch out my work before I start, but on projects like this, where I don't have a particular subject in mind, I like to let my hands lead me. No plan. No pretense. Just feeling.

After we couldn't figure out where the hell Tanya's note was trying to send us, Dani and I came back home. We tried roping in Victor, but he of course feigned cluelessness. We searched her house for the umpteenth time and still turned up nothing. I know Dani was starting to feel frustrated, so we're both glad to have this short break.

My door opens and Rome walks in, carrying a large carry-out bag.

"How you know I wasn't doing something crazy in here?" I yell from the loft area of my apartment, where I do all my painting.

He sets the bag on my kitchen counter and then makes his way upstairs to the loft. "'Cause you're workin' and you don't do shit else when you're working. Hence why I brought food."

"Aww, bitch. You care." I put on the singsong voice we always use when one of us does something nice for each other.

"I don't know why. Bring ya ass."

I follow him back down to the kitchen where he takes the Chinese food out of the bag and we move to the couch to eat.

"So, how's things with Miss Janelle?"

His entire face lights up. "Really good. She's . . . yeah. I really like her."

"I think everybody knows that."

"Nah, but it's never felt this easy before. You know? It's crazy because it's still new, but I just know it's right. She's my person."

He looks at me, his eyes asking if I understand what he means, and I do. I think I met my person eleven years ago, and it hasn't been easy. It's been far from it. But it's worth fighting for, so that's what I'll do.

We catch up on other things like work and our parents until every scrap of food has been demolished.

"How's things with Dani?" he asks, his brows dancing on his forehead. "J has thoughts about y'all."

I bet she does. I'm very curious what Dani has told the girls about us. Rome knows there's more to the story with Dani and me, but I haven't shared the details with him because I never wanted to betray Dani's trust. I've only ever told Bailey and I only told her because she wouldn't accept me moving to New York any other way.

"Wanna share?"

"She told me not to tell you." He smirks as we finish cleaning up our food.

"What you bring it up for, then?!"

"To fuck with you. Aight, I'm out." He chucks the deuces and leaves me behind.

Dickhead.

I'm still in the zone when a knock on my door surprises me. Checking the door camera only surprises me more.

Dani? What's she doing here?

Shit, it's 8:00 a.m. I worked through the night. It's not the first time I've done it, but usually I'm able to sleep for the rest of the day to recover. If Dani is willingly stepping into my space, though, I won't be going to sleep anytime soon.

I open the door and take in the woman I'd always longed to have in my home, a possibility I'd never let myself expect.

"I texted you to let you know I was on my way." She pushes me farther inside and shuts the door.

Before I have a chance to respond, she grabs my face and looks deeply into my eyes. Normally, I would be all about this, but today the sudden jerking of my head is too jarring to enjoy.

"What's wrong with you?"

"Good morning to you too, Dani."

"Don't 'good morning' me. You look like shit."

"Ouch."

"Did you go out last night?"

I grab her hands and remove them from my face. My ears are starting to ring from all the movement. "No. I was up working."

"All night?" she screeches.

I nod my head, and she shakes hers with disdain. "What's wrong with you?"

"That's the second time you've asked me that today."

"And yet the answer is still unclear."

I look up to the freshly finished painting in my loft and back to Dani. Her eyes follow mine but remain unimpressed.

"At least the painting's done." I'll take it to Spring House later so Bailey can ship it to the client for me.

"At least the painting's done," she mocks me in a much higher voice than mine and then points to the hall that leads to my bedroom. "Go shower and get yourself together so we can go."

"And where are we going?"

"Get your shit together and then I'll tell you."

"I'm sorry, are you mad at me?"

"No. I just think you're an idiot who doesn't take care of yourself."

I look in her eyes, and underneath the indignation and ire, I catch a glimpse of concern. She worries about me. That alone gives me the energy I need to get through this day. "You got it, Storm."

She squints her eyes at that. "Storm?"

"Yep, my little thunderstorm." I don't give her the time to think about that before I head to the back to get ready.

Once I'm showered and dressed, I walk back out to the living room, but Dani's nowhere to be found. I look up to the loft and find her studying my paintings. I stand as still as possible, not wanting to startle her. I want to see how she views my work. I want to see how it makes her feel.

She spends a good amount of time looking at each one, analyzing every curve and swoop made by my brushes. She stares at one of the canvases longer than the others, physically reaching out to lightly swipe her hand against it. I wonder what intrigues her about that one. It's of a little boy holding his baby sister for the first time. Maybe it's the pure innocence captured there that draws her in.

She turns around, catching me watching her, and her step falters. "Oops, I'm sorry. I hope it's okay that I'm up here."

"Of course it is."

She bites her lips and looks at another painting. "You really are exceptional at this."

"Thank you."

"What's under there?" She points to a large canvas covered with a tarp in the corner of the loft.

"See for yourself."

She tiptoes over to it, as if what's under there can reach out and grab her.

From where I'm standing, I can't see her face when she pulls the tarp off the canvas, but I hear her full-body gasp.

"When . . . when did you?" Her voice can't be any louder than a whisper, yet I hear it loud and clear.

It's an incomplete portrait of her.

"A long time ago."

Eleven years ago. I started it after waking up to find her missing. I wanted to memorialize the woman who stamped my heart in a single night, but I could never finish it. I've added flourishes to it over the years, added most of the facial details six years ago after leaving New York, even more three years ago after seeing her at the gallery. But still it isn't finished.

She turns to me with glossy eyes.

Every bone in my body wants to go to her, so I do. I take the stairs two at a time until I'm close enough to lend her my strength if she needs it but far enough to give her the space she needs to absorb what she's seeing.

"Why didn't you finish it?"

"It didn't feel right to when our story was incomplete."

She swallows a big gulp of air.

"Maybe one day I'll get to finish it."

She scans the canvas one more time, as if committing it to memory, and then she does the one thing I expect her to do: she changes the subject.

"Are you ready to go? I want to go back to Tanya's."

I gently take the tarp from her hands and then turn and motion for her to walk in front of me. "I'm ready, Storm."

She charges down the steps, but when she turns the corner, I catch her glancing up at the painting again.

I follow, grabbing my keys from the kitchen counter, when she swirls around to face me.

"Keys."

"Huh?"

"You're working off of no sleep, so I'll drive. Keys."

"Okay." I toss them her way, amused when her jaw drops.

"Really? I thought you'd put up more of a fight."

Her assumptions about me are always entertaining. "Why would you think that?"

"I don't know. I just thought you'd be more possessive over your car."

I guess she forgot I literally left my car at a gas station for her. I eliminate the space between us, pushing her hair off her shoulder as I cup the back of her neck. "Believe me, Storm. There's a lot of things I'd be possessive over. A car isn't one of them."

Is it still considered stalking if you have good intentions?

I'm pretty sure it is, but that doesn't stop me from clicking the next post.

Dani is physically so close to me and yet she still feels as far away as she did when this journey began. Ever since seeing Tanya's note on her photo, I've been desperate to get closer to her. To just get a peek behind the curtain and make sure she's okay. Hell, we could go back further than that. I've had this deep-seated desire to know and understand every facet of Dani since the day I met her in Tanya's den. That hasn't stopped, even when hurt, time, and distance stood between us. Watching her during the photoshoot in California, she seemed genuinely happy, but she's so good at masking her feelings that I truly don't know.

So now, while she's only inches away from me, I'm scrolling through every picture she's ever posted trying to see if I can see the signs. The signs of her unhappiness.

It's her eyes that give her away. And her hands.

People post only what they want people to see, and Dani is no different. Her page is expertly crafted. Her videos are always on brand, and she always exudes a level of charm that distracts viewers from the fact that they didn't learn anything too personal about her during the video. I'm grateful my locs hide the earbud nestled in my ear. Her pictures are always effortlessly beautiful, eliciting envy from those who wish they were in her place or by her side without rubbing in their faces that they're not. It's a careful balance and she toes the line impeccably.

If you look closely, however, you can catch the moments where she slips. Her smile never changes, but her eyes fade away. There are photos that may come across to someone else like she's smoldering, but there's nothing there. Her eyes are empty, like she's been drained of all the will to keep going. There are videos where you can see her disassociate even though her voice doesn't skip a beat. In all the pictures and videos where her eyes betray her, her hands put the final nail in the coffin. She grips her purse tighter than usual, her hands ball into tight fists or lie unnaturally straight at her sides, as she mindlessly traces circles while she's talking.

I want to earn her trust back. I want to be the person she can come to when she needs to fall apart. I want to be someone she wants to share her wins and experience joy with. I want to be her sandpaper.

I analyze a few more posts before a FaceTime call from Christian takes over my screen. After I briefly consider ignoring the call, I answer with Dani's permission.

I take my earbud out so Dani can participate if she wants to, although maybe I should've saved her the trouble. "What's up, man?"

"Aye, be real with me. If Bailey wanted to date me, would you let her?"

Now, see. If I'd known he was going to be on some bullshit today, I wouldn't have answered.

Dani's head swings in my direction, her brows pulled up to her hairline.

"The fuck are you talkin' about?" I ask.

When I first answered the call, I was looking at the sky through his sunroof, but now he's picked up his phone so I can see him sitting in his car.

"Just answer the question." He leans closer to the phone with bated breath.

I suck my teeth. "Bailey's a grown-ass woman, so I don't *let* her date anyone. But if she told me y'all were dating, I wouldn't be mad about it."

He lets out a deep sigh and leans back in his seat. "That's what's up."

I laugh. "What's wrong with you?"

"Wait a minute, where you at? Who's driving?" he asks me.

I pan the phone over so he can see Dani. She sends a polite wave his way.

"Oh shit, what's good, DJ?! He got you driving him around and shit? You deserve better."

She glances over to the phone with pursed lips before saying, "Are you supposed to be the better, Christian?"

He grins. "My services are always available. You'd always be my passenger princess."

I turn the phone so he can see my deadpan face. "Well, since I answered your question, I'ma head out."

"Hol'up, damn. I was saying Sophie was making content for the show today and she asked everyone at the station who they wouldn't want to date their sister and everybody said me."

When I don't say anything, he narrows his eyes. "Hello?"

"Hello."

"Ayo. You just said you'd let me date Bailey."

It's like he doesn't hear himself when he talks. "Again with the 'let,' but yeah, I did. But that's off the strength of our friendship. You're my boy, so I trust you wouldn't get involved with one of the most important people to me if you were gonna be on fuck shit like you usually are." I wouldn't call him a man or a friend if I thought he'd do something like that.

He seems to mull over my words. "So you saying my coworkers don't trust me?"

I smack my hand over my mouth. "Ohhh shit, look at that."

"Look at what?"

"The consequences of your actions."

He hangs his head, letting out a short chuckle. "That's crazy. I'm a trustworthy guy!"

Without another word, I add Rome to the call. Christian sinks deeper into his seat when he sees that I'm ringing him.

Rome answers with raised brows and narrowed eyes. "What y'all on?"

I cut Christian off before he has a chance to speak. "If you had a sister and she told you she was dating Christian, would you fuck him up?"

His nose scrunches. "Wait . . . are Christian and Bailey dating?"

"No," Christian and I both answer.

Rome's eyes swing back and forth like a pendulum. "Okay. Then yeah, because why you ain't tell me you were interested in her?"

Christian rolls his eyes. "After you get over that, what's up?"

A softer voice creeps in on Rome's end of the line to say hello. Rome shifts the phone so we can see Janelle standing behind Rome's couch.

"How you doing, Janelle?" I ask.

"Janelle! How you doing, baby?" Christian adds.

"I'm good, how are y'all?"

We catch up with her briefly before Christian turns the conversation back to his hoeish ways.

"Janelle, I would ask you this question, but that might be too soon, right?" His smile is so wide he can't close his mouth.

Janelle holds up her middle finger. "And for that, I hope you step on a Lego."

Christian grabs his heart. "Ahh, Janelle, I was just playing."

She shakes her head and waves him off before kissing Rome on the forehead and walking off, yelling for Dani to text her later before she completely disappears.

"Come baaaack!" Christian sings.

"You ain't shit," Rome laughs.

"The kind of ain't shit that you'd want to be your brother-in-law?" he asks.

"I mean I guess. You know I'd kill you if you hurt my sister, so I wouldn't be worried." He demands to know why we're asking, so I fill him in, and he roasts Christian, insisting he's going to tell Evie next time he sees her.

Dani assures him she's already on it.

"All we're saying is maybe if you treated all women like they were mine and Rome's sisters, you wouldn't have a reputation." I shrug. It's such a simple concept, and I can't wait until the day Christian finally understands it.

He pleads his case some more, but we're not trying to hear it. Janelle's voice chimes in again, telling him that she's going to pick up their food. She tried to argue that he should stay and talk to us when he says that he'll go with her and drive, but he shakes his head. The last thing he says is "fuck them" before he flips us off and hangs up on us.

Christian jokes about him being whipped, but I can't bring myself to do the same.

I had no idea Rome was harboring feelings for Janelle for so long. I thought I'd recognize that level of desperation in someone else, but I missed all the signs. I'm just glad to see my boy happy now, even if I'm a bit jealous.

"He is so interesting," Dani comments under her breath once Christian and I hang up.

I howl with laughter. "That's probably the nicest thing a woman's ever said about him."

"Damn. Let me walk that back then. Evie would kill me if she knew I damn near complimented the man."

"Your secret's safe with me," I promise, zipping my lips shut and pretending to throw away the key.

She looks at me with a hint of something in her eyes. I wish I knew what it was.

Not too much later, we're pulling into Tanya's driveway.

It gets a little easier to walk into Tanya's house every time. It doesn't feel so much like I'm trespassing, more like I'm house-sitting. I only sometimes have to remind myself that she's not coming back to take over the job.

Taking a deep breath, I look to Dani for direction. "Okay, so did you have a thought about what our clue means?"

"Yes." She holds her chin up high. "Well, kinda."

I wince. "You had me in the first half."

"No, no, hear me out. I was thinking that Tanya isn't from here. She was born and raised in South Carolina, so what if the home she's talking about isn't this one?"

I always forget about South Carolina being Tanya's home state. She never talked about her childhood much. Any stories she shared about her parents always seemed as if they existed in a vacuum, removed from any one place.

"That makes sense. So, what are we doing here?"

"Well, we don't know where she lived in South Carolina. I think it was somewhere close to Columbia, but I'm not sure. And we know Victor's ass ain't gonna help. So, there's gotta be something here that's gonna lead us to that home."

I nod in understanding. "Okay, then. I'll take downstairs, you take upstairs?"

I don't want to admit defeat, but at a certain point Victor has to take pity and give us something, right?

The urge to put us out of our misery and call him grows stronger with every minute, but I won't do it. I can hear Tanya in the back of my mind giving me shit for giving up. *"That kind of attitude is why you could never beat me at chess."*

I need some air. I step outside, letting the brisk breeze bite my bare arms. If not somewhere in this house, where is Tanya trying to lead us? The note from Daria's champagne bottle said, *You can always go home.* Is home referring to a person rather than a place? An odd sensation prickles my feet, catching my attention. When I look down, I realize I haven't put my shoes back on before stepping out here. The welcome mat scratches the pads of my feet through my socks.

Welcome mat.

The fucking mat literally says "Welcome home." It never crossed my mind to check. I'm both relieved and irritated when I lift the mat and find a storage locker key.

I race back inside to show Dani what I found, and she finds a receipt for a storage unit at a place close to the house.

"One eighteen, here it is," Dani yells as we pull up to the outside unit with the number that matches our key. "I'm telling you right now, if this isn't the right place, I'm beating Victor's ass."

Her words make me choke on air. "Now, why are you threatening that man?" I ask once I'm able to stop coughing.

"Well, I can't beat Tanya's ass, now can I?" She slaps the back of her hand. "But she'll get it too whenever I arrive to the upper room." She looks up to the sky as if daring Tanya to do something about it.

"You keep playing. Me and Daria tried to tell you that lady was strong."

She balks at me. "And see? Now whenever I get up there, I gotta body-slam her all because you talk too much." She looks up to the sky again. "I'm sorry in advance, Tanya."

"Don't come crying to my corner of heaven when she knocks your soul back down to your body and you gotta float all the way back up again," I say with my hands up.

Her eyes fall into tiny slits. I can't lie, it's adorable. "Get out of the car, Micah."

"As you wish, Storm." I take a sick pleasure from seeing how the nickname riles her up, but the name is so fitting. Dani is an alluring thunderstorm. She's indestructible and fragile at the same time, and the contradiction of that creates this electricity she can't control. I'm willing to let that storm consume me.

I join her at the door to the unit and slide the key in the lock. We each let out a tiny breath when we hear the unmistakable click.

"Victor's ass lives to see another day," Dani murmurs.

"Tanya's is still in danger?" I needle.

"It will be if you keep running your mouth."

I once again zip my lips shut, but before I can throw out the imaginary key, she pretends to snatch it from my hands and trample it with her foot. Message received. I try not to smile as I pull up to the unit's gate.

I wasn't sure what I was expecting when we found this key, but it definitely wasn't a light blue 1965 Lincoln Continental.

Is it an original? If it is, it's in great condition. But why would Tanya have it in a storage unit and what does it have to do with our next clue?

Dani lets out a sharp whistle as she runs her fingers along the hood of the car. "This is nice. She would have this lying around."

Unable to resist, I move to the driver-side door and tug on the handle, ecstatic when it gives way to my pull and opens. I lower myself into the seat carefully, not wanting to damage anything, while Dani pulls out her phone and wordlessly takes a picture of me in the car.

She slips into the passenger seat and starts searching. When she flips open the visor, a postcard falls out. On the front, there's a picture of a house that says "Newberry Cove, South Carolina" beneath it. On the back is a line in Tanya's handwriting. "*If I could give anyone anything, it would be the gift of music.*"

Dani pouts her lips as she types something on her phone. "Not sure what she means by the note about music, but look." She holds her phone out to me. "I just looked up Newberry Cove and they only have a population of seven thousand people. I bet if we go there and throw a rock in any direction, we'll hit a family member or someone who knew Tanya."

"When did you become so violent?" I say in jest.

She lightly jabs me in the ribs right as her phone rings. "Well, hello, Victor. Did you get my picture?"

She winks at me as she puts the phone on speaker.

"I did. That's a very nice car."

Nice is putting it lightly.

"It is a nice car. You wouldn't happen to know anything about it, would you?" she asks.

"Mmm, nothing that comes to mind." There's no inflection in his tone. Nothing to indicate whether we're on the right track or not. I get the feeling he's getting a kick out of us playing detectives. This must be why he and Tanya got along so well. He seems like a stick in the mud, but he's got a petty side to him that I'm sure Tanya appreciated.

"Just when I was starting to like you, Victor."

His laugh lasts only a fraction of a second, but its effect is instantaneous. Dani holds her free arm out toward the phone as if she's reaching through it to strangle Victor.

"The car looks like it's in really good shape. The owner probably took great care of it from the time they bought it," he adds.

Yeah, he's definitely getting a kick out of this.

"And if you had to guess, when would you say the owner probably bought this car?"

"Hello, Micah. Glad you two are sticking to the rules. If I had to guess, I'd say the owner probably had that car since they were nineteen. They probably used every dime they saved up from working since they were fourteen to buy that thing. If I had to guess."

I still have my first car. It's at my parents' house for safekeeping. Honestly, the only reason I bought a new car was because Bailey made me. She little-sistered her way into my pockets to buy a brand-new car that she could also drive, so I understand why Tanya kept this baby.

I'm honored she's leaving it in our care.

"Well, Micah and I were thinking of visiting Newberry Cove, South Carolina. Just feels like the right next step, you know?"

I don't hear his response because while Dani talks, I slip out to run my hands along the wheel wells. When I was younger, my granddad used to always hide his spare keys here. I wonder if Tanya had the same idea. My hand hits metal on the driver's rear side and I'm able to free the spare from its hiding spot. Bingo.

Sticking the key in the ignition, my eyes close when the engine purrs to life. What memories did Tanya have in this car? I can imagine her racing down the beltway with her hair tied up *Thelma & Louise*–style to keep the wind from destroying it. Sitting in the driver's seat makes me feel as though she's right here next to us.

I tune back in to hear Victor's next words. "Safe travels, you two. Oh, and if I had to guess, I'd say a car like that probably rides best with the top down." He hangs up without ceremony.

"That settles it. To Newberry Cove we go," Dani exclaims.

"Right. I do just wanna say that taking a seven-hour road trip in a fifty-eight-year-old car is a choice." And maybe not the best one.

Dani raises her brows and chews on her bottom lip.

"Yeah, but the seats feel so nice." She snorts when I look less than amused. "Come on, what's the worst that could happen?"

"Remember when you asked what's the worst that could happen?" I ask as I put the hazards on and work my way to the shoulder of the road.

We got on the road first thing in the morning, and four hours into our drive, just as we were about to get through Lynchburg, Virginia, the car sort of tapped out. It still moves, but it won't go any faster than twenty-five miles per hour, which might be fine on back country roads, but not the highway we're currently on.

Dani grits her teeth as I'm finally able to get to the shoulder. "In my defense, it could definitely be worse. At least it still runs."

"Yeah, at this speed we could probably get there by tomorrow morning."

She huffs at my response. "Well, now what?"

A sly grin stretches across my face. "Now, princess, we pop the hood." I get out and wait for her at the hood of the car, peeking around it when she doesn't join me.

She sticks her head out the window, her brows knitted in confusion. "I'm sorry, you actually wanted me to join you?"

"Why do you think I said 'we'?"

"You've taken up French in Duolingo? I don't know!"

The first night we met, we played the assumption game. We wanted to know everything about each other, and that seemed like the quickest way. One of her assumptions about me was that I spoke Arabic, which I don't. I don't even remember why she thought that, but I remember how adorable she looked when she was explaining her thought process. So, first Arabic, now French. She thinks I'm a damn polyglot.

My lack of response works though, and she joins me.

With her lips in a full pout, she asks, "Need me to hold a flashlight?"

"Nope. Just wanted your company." I practically wheeze at the way her jaw drops.

It takes me a few minutes to realize one of the hose clamps broke in the engine. It's an easy fix, I just need a new one. The problem is getting one.

I explain the issue to Dani, and she pulls out her phone. "There's a general store five miles out," she says softly.

"Okay, why are you saying it like that?" I ask, looking down at her foot tapping on the ground.

"I just don't love being stuck in a city with the word *lynch* in it." She rubs her hand up and down the front of her neck with her lips turned in a frown.

I throw my head back and laugh. "How about this? I can put the hose back in, but it's just gonna fall back out until we get the part. We can ride with our hazards on until we get to the next acceptably named city."

She claps and jumps in place. "Yes, please."

"Oh, fuck off!" Dani shouts to the car beside us. Since we've been crawling down the road, cars have been speeding around us, some going about their day and some, like the one on Dani's side, have taken to honking and flipping us off.

"Idiot," she whispers to herself as the car finally moves on.

"I didn't take you for a road-rage person."

She balks at me. "Please. If you think that was road rage, you've never been in a car with Evie. I've seen her throw soda cans at cars that pissed her off."

I chuckle as I make a mental note not to get in a car with Evie behind the wheel. "Fair point. Pass me a peach, please."

She holds a peach ring up to my mouth and I make a show of biting it.

She shakes her hand as if I bit her too. "Animal." She turns to look out the window and I catch sight of her weary reflection. "God, it's been so long since I've been on a road trip."

"Why's that?" I ask, eager to learn any part of Dani's story.

She turns to me slowly. "No time. I usually have to get in and get out."

I run my hand along my beard. Curiosity nicks me like a sharp blade. For someone who sells experiences to the masses, it doesn't seem like she's had many experiences that were strictly her own.

"When was your last road trip?"

Her responding smile is laced with memories. "When I was seventeen. Me and my parents drove to Michigan to see the Wolverines play."

My jaw drops in shock. "You like the Wolverines?"

"My dad does. Me and my mom just like my dad."

There was a time when I used to imagine Dani's parents. I used to envision meeting them, growing close to them, knowing them as more than just a passing anecdote.

"And? How was the game?"

She laughs. "They won, but we didn't see the shit. We missed an exit and ended up in Canada."

Her voice is soothing as she tells me about the highway that leads to Canada without the option to turn around. She smiles fondly as she recalls how frustrated her dad was when they were held up too long to make it to the game, since none of them had their passports on them.

"I've never seen my dad crash out like that. He said he was never going to Michigan again."

"The whole state getting banned for one missed exit is crazy."

She slides her eyes over to me. "Please. One thing my dad gon' do is talk shit. He's been to three games since then."

My arm slides up the steering wheel as I laugh. "Your dad is wild."

She answers with a tight-lipped smile, caught up in the haze of her reminiscing. "That was my last family trip before I moved to New York. We still travel all the time, just not road trips. More flying and enjoying events I can include them on."

"If you could take a road trip anywhere, where would you go?"

"Hmm, road-tripping to California might be fun. It's clear across the country so there's so many fun stops you could make."

"That does sound fun. It would probably be a long trip too."

"The longer, the better." She sighs. "What about you? Where would you go?"

"I'd probably go to Canada. But, you know, on purpose."

Her shoulders shake with laughter. "But can you even say you've lived if you haven't gone by accident?"

Once we get the new hose clamp and are able to drive at a normal speed, we get to Newberry Cove right as the sun is starting to set.

I drive us to the hotel we booked for our stay. It's not the five-star luxury hotels I'm sure Dani is used to. It's a family-run business, but something about this place called to me, and with everything we've seen so far, I'm hesitant to ignore anything that feels like a sign.

"Let's see if we can get some answers here." I nod to the hotel entrance.

We walk into Hotel Serenity and are transported to a nature site.

The ceilings are made of shiplap and have green vines hanging from the slots. There are potted plants in varying sizes on the shelves along the walls that give the lobby a comfortable feel. Somehow the air even feels drastically lighter in here than it did outside.

There's a wall made of stones behind the front desk, not one of them looking the same as another.

The receptionist looks up from her computer and smiles at us. Her sisterlocs are pulled up into a bun and her white blazer is pristinely pressed.

"Welcome to Hotel Serenity. How can I help you?"

While I sort everything out with the reservation, Dani examines the lobby, studying every minute detail before she turns her sights on the woman helping us. Taking in her body language and tone, I watch her transform into Dani the professional right before my eyes.

"Can I ask you a question, Traci?" she asks, reading the woman's name tag.

"Of course."

"We're actually here because our friend who recently passed grew up here."

Traci puts her hand over her heart. "I'm so sorry to hear that."

"Thank you. We're trying to visit some places that meant a lot to her. I'm wondering if you could help us. Did you know a Tanya Holden?"

Traci takes a moment to consider, shaking her head after some thought. "Doesn't ring a bell. I'm sorry."

"How about Tanya Gaten?"

Her maiden name feels so odd to hear. She wore the name Holden like a badge of honor that could never be stripped from her.

Recognition spreads across Traci's face. "Oh my God!" she screams, making Dani rear back. "Sorry. I didn't know her personally, but she's a legend around here. Her whole family is."

That doesn't surprise me at all. Of course she comes from a long line of legends. I've always been curious about Tanya's family. As far as I know, none of the Gatens ever visited Baltimore, and we know she wasn't going home to Newberry Cove often, if at all. It's good to see her family legacy is viewed in a positive light, even if she didn't stick around to add to it.

Traci gives Dani the rundown of which Gaten family members we should talk to, her tacit admiration for one cousin in particular crystal clear.

Dani chats with her like they've known each other for years. This is the version of her I'm used to seeing, effortlessly charming, bending anyone to her will. Traci's entire demeanor has changed from ultimate professional to Dani's gossiping best friend.

A phone call to the front desk breaks the pair apart, freeing me to grab our room keys.

As we're walking to the elevator, Traci calls after us. "You should go to Mackey's tonight. Guarantee you'll find at least one of the Gatens there." She pushes a button on the phone and goes back to her call.

When we get in the elevator, Dani sighs. "I really hope Mackey's is a restaurant. I'm hungry as hell."

I laugh as the elevator creeps up the floors. "I'm hungry too. Let's drop our bags and head out?"

She looks at me like I've grown two heads. "Um, no. I'm gonna shower first. I smell like I've been on the road for six hours."

I match her expression. "You have been on the road for six hours."

"Exactly."

"So, what does that smell like exactly?" I lean toward her neck and take a deep inhale, pleased when her body shudders beneath me. "You smell fine to me." Better than fine.

She licks her lips as the bell dings and the doors open to our floor. She moves first, sidestepping around me into the hallway.

"Is there a different odor associated with being on the road for five hours? Or seven?" I continue as I catch up to her.

She huffs. "I don't know, and let's be clear, I smell fantastic all the time. Sometimes a girl just needs a reset," she insists.

She'll get no argument from me.

She stops at the door marked 312, my room. "I can take my bag from here, Micah."

Her room is only a few doors down at 318, so I allow her to slip her weekender bag off my shoulder, but the way she holds my eyes while her hands caress my arm has me suddenly regretting being a gentleman and booking separate rooms.

"See you soon," she says as she reaches her door.

"Soon," I echo.

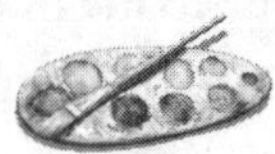

By the time we get to Mackey's, the dinner crowd is in full swing. Dani looks relaxed and confident in her black sleeveless jumpsuit, white button-up, gold jewelry, and black heels. Her chosen fragrance tonight is subtle. It's soft and clean, with a faint essence of roses lingering in the air as she walks.

She catches the attention of many people as we approach the sports bar—unsurprising, but comical nonetheless.

There are a couple of seats here and there at the bar, but we opt to stand at the end, slightly removed from other guests. Of the three bartenders, the middle-aged man with the short curly fro and kind eyes is the one to approach us.

"How you doing, guys? What can I get you?" he asks with a jolly smile spread across his round face.

I start to ask about Tanya and her family, but Dani puts her hand over mine. "Can I have a Tequila Mockingbird? With watermelon juice and no crème de menthe?" She looks over to me, waiting for my order.

"Uh, can I get an old-fashioned, please?" I ask.

He nods his acknowledgment before turning back to Dani. "Top-shelf or well, sweetie?"

She flashes him a sickly sweet smile. "Top-shelf, of course. Oh, and a food menu, please?"

Somehow, his smile becomes even more jolly. "You got it," he says as he passes her a menu and walks off.

She ignores my raised brows in her direction, opting to focus all of her attention on the menu.

"That menu is riveting, huh?"

"Yeah, should I get fried green tomatoes or no?"

"Dani," I say, barely keeping the laugh out of my voice.

"Hmm?" she hums.

"Care to share why you stopped me from asking about Tanya?"

Finally, she takes her eyes off the menu. "Because you have to ease into these things."

"Really? Because you got straight to the point with Traci."

She rolls her eyes as if her logic makes perfect sense. "That was different. It was just the three of us there. You can't just walk into a bar full of people and start asking about a whole family. Especially a family that apparently everyone knows. You've gotta build a rapport. So, just sit back, relax, and let me do my thing."

The person closest to us leaves, so I grab their chair for Dani and remain standing. "Okay, fine. Do your thing. And yes, you should get fried green tomatoes."

She smirks as she passes the menu over to me.

The bartender comes back with our drinks, ecstatic when Dani gushes over the taste of hers. She orders our apps and entrées, even the one I told her I wanted earlier.

Dani learns his name is Aaron, and from then on, she has Aaron eating out of the palm of her hand. He checks on her constantly, making sure her glass is always full and her smile is always prominent.

The fish and chips she ordered are delicious, so I'm happy to let her continue taking the lead.

Aaron sets a small container of sauce in front of Dani. "Brought you this. It's chile-lime sauce. I promise it's gonna really set those wings off."

Dani wastes no time dipping her hot honey wings into the sauce and digging in. "Aaron, you are a God among men," she exclaims.

Once again, he looks awfully proud of himself. "I've been told that a time or two before."

Oh, brother.

After the dinner crowd somewhat dies down, Aaron comes back over to us. "Where you folks from, anyway?"

Dani uses that opportunity to finally tell Aaron why we're here.

"Tanya Gaten," he exhales. "I was sorry to hear she passed."

Dani tells him about the hunt Tanya has sent us on, and he's captivated by her every word. "I gotta ask, is everybody in Tanya's family as dramatic as she was?"

He holds his stomach as he belts out a laugh. "That's like asking if water is wet. Matter fact . . ." He pauses to survey the bar, his eyes landing on his target. "Tony!"

A tall, brown-skin man with glasses looks over from one of the high tops as Aaron waves him over. Tony approaches with caution. Another brown-skin man covered in tattoos and a brown-skin woman with a shaved head follow closely behind.

"I ain't even do nothing yet, Goose," Tony says to Aaron.

"Shut up, fool. This here is Dani and that's Micah. They were friends of Tanya." He turns to Dani. "The three stooges here are Tony, Michael, and Ella Gaten. Tanya's cousins."

Michael assesses us carefully. "You look a little young to have been friends with Tanya. Were you some of them wayward children she loved to take in?"

Ella smacks him in the shoulder. "No decorum-having ass." She turns to us both. "I'm the only one with an ounce of intelligence in this group, so you can talk to me."

"She got about as much smarts as she does hair," Michael mocks.

"Two scoops," Tony echoes.

Ella flips them both off without looking their way. She asks Dani what we're looking for and when Dani tells her, she holds her finger up to her lips and pulls out her phone.

A woman with a raspy voice answers Ella's call on the second ring. "What you want, Ella Reese?"

She gives us a sympathetic smile. "Auntie, you know anything about some kind of deathbed scavenger hunt Tanya set up? I got two people who say Tanya sent them."

The woman is silent on the line. She's silent for so long that Ella checks to see if she hung up. "Auntie?" Ella goads.

"Tomorrow morning. Tell them to come see me," the woman says before hanging up.

Dani and I share a look of horror. What the hell has Tanya gotten us into?

Chapter Thirteen

Dani

MY STOMACH IS IN MY ASS WHEN ELLA PICKS US UP from the hotel the next morning to take us to see "Auntie Joyce," who didn't sound happy when Ella called last night.

Ella pulls up to a quaint ranch-style home with a white vinyl exterior and a dark green roof. I wonder how much time Tanya spent at this house. There isn't a single detail, at least on the outside, that looks like she had a hand in it. She gave Victor a glass-covered rose just to give his office a fraction of light; her touch is nowhere to be found on this house. Is that because of her or because of the family member living here? Ella shuts her engine off and looks to me in the passenger seat and Micah in the back seat as if she's sending us to our deaths.

"We're here. Everything's gonna be fine, just . . . don't look her in the eye when you meet her, okay? She doesn't like that."

"What?!" I shiver.

She holds her stomach as a loud laugh bursts from her mouth. "I'm just playin'. You just seemed so nervous, I had to. Come on."

Damnit, Ella.

She doesn't knock before walking into the house. She leads us past the living room, which is filled with furniture that seems like it's been well-loved for generations, and into the brightly lit kitchen, where the scent of maple syrup permeates the air. Still no sign of Tanya's presence anywhere.

Who I assume to be Auntie Joyce sits in a chair next to the kitchen window, staring out with a lit cigarette hanging from her fingertips.

"Hey, Auntie, here they are, as requested."

She doesn't turn to look at us, but the sound of children's laughter streams through the window, drawing Ella's attention. "I'll go check on them." As she slowly backs out of the kitchen, she mouths the words "Don't look her in the eye" to me, prompting me to flash her my middle finger.

"Come sit," Auntie Joyce's voice booms throughout the kitchen.

There's one chair opposite her at the kitchen window and more at the table right behind her. I silently plead with Micah, so he takes the chair opposite her, but of course the moment I sit down, her head shoots in my direction.

Auntie Joyce has a short black fro with streaks of silver throughout. Her cheeks are soft where her eyes are hard. One of her eyes has more wrinkles beneath it than the other, which somehow makes her look more endearing than intimidating.

She holds her hand out to touch my face, but only briefly, before doing the same to Micah. "So, you're Tanya's kids," she says, matter-of-factly.

My chin wobbles as Micah holds his head up high. "Yes," we say in unison.

She takes a puff from her cigarette, blowing the smoke out the window, then she puts it out in the ashtray sitting on the windowsill. "I wasn't sure when you'd make it here. You were the other shoe I was waiting to drop."

She tells us that Tanya revealed her diagnosis and said we'd be visiting sometime after she passed. Joyce is a great-aunt to some and a cousin to others, but everyone in the family just calls her Auntie, though being one of the sisters to Tanya's father makes her Tanya's actual aunt. To have lost your brother so long ago is already a monumental pain. But to then have to secretly carry around the knowledge that you were also going to outlive the only living legacy of that brother is a burden I never wish to know.

No wonder she sounded so upset on the phone. She's been waiting for us much longer than we knew.

"Come on, let's take a walk." She turns to yell out the window. "Ella, I'll be back. Don't be letting them run in and out the house."

We faintly hear Ella's response as Auntie Joyce shuts the window and rises from her seat.

She's much shorter than I expected, no more than five foot four. Her housecoat almost touches the floor. She shakes it off her shoulders, leaving her in a lightweight sweater and linen pants.

Micah offers the crook of his elbow to her and she takes it, using him as support at the front door when she slips on her comfortable shoes.

We walk through the neighborhood, Auntie Joyce regaling us with stories about the generations of Gatens that have come up in this town. She points out the houses of several of her relatives along her street. I wonder how Tanya felt about having most of her family within walking distance growing up.

She stops outside of another ranch-style home, this one made of brown brick with a table and two chairs on the porch.

"I know this place," I say, more to myself than Micah or Auntie Joyce. "Micah, can I see the postcard?"

He pulls out his wallet and hands me the card, which he had folded to fit.

There it is. The exterior is a bit weathered now compared to the photo, but there's no mistaking that this is the same house from the postcard.

Auntie Joyce leaves Micah's side to join me. A smile creeps onto her lips. "This place has had two new roofs since this photo was taken." She walks up the steps and throws the door open without announcing her presence.

I can't imagine, in this day and age, feeling safe enough to leave your doors unlocked. But I suppose those are the perks of having more Gatens in this town than anyone else.

"John! Dee!" she yells into the ether.

A screaming toddler runs toward us, a clean diaper mushed between her fingers. A man with reddish-brown skin, no shirt, and black shorts runs out after her.

"Come here, you stinker!"

The little girl laughs harder as she pushes her little legs as fast as they can go. He catches her before she makes it to wherever she decided the goalpost was.

"Gotcha!" He blows a raspberry into her belly, her giggles echoing throughout the house. "Hey, Auntie. What's up?"

"She stage a prison break again?" Auntie Joyce says, tickling the toddler's foot.

"I think I'm gonna have to start handcuffing her to the changing table." He looks behind Auntie Joyce with a raised eyebrow at Micah and me. "Everything good?"

Auntie Joyce introduces us to John Gaten, one of her great-nephews. This is the house Tanya grew up in, but now John lives here with his wife, Dee, and their three kids. Apparently, this is the Gaten way. Homes don't go up for sale, they simply pass around ownership through the generations.

"I never thought I'd meet anybody from Tanya's other life," he says in awe.

Tanya's worlds are colliding, and though she kept us apart in life, I think she'd be happy to see us finally coming together.

"Dee's at work and the other kids are at daycare, but you'll meet them later, I hope."

He takes us on a tour of the house, and my imagination runs wild thinking of how the house looked when Tanya lived here.

John opens the door to one of the bedrooms where toys cover every inch of the floor and even the two beds on both sides of the room.

"Was this Tanya's room?" I ask.

"I don't really remember. I think it was Andrew's room, though," John responds.

"Who's Andrew?" Micah asks, stealing the words out of my mouth.

Auntie Joyce and John look between each other. Auntie Joyce is the one to rip off the Band-Aid. "He was Tanya's twin brother."

My heart sinks.

Twin brother.

Since when did Tanya have a twin brother? Stupid question, because the answer is since birth, but it's unfathomable. I assumed she had at least one sibling. She always said kids, plural, when she talked about her mom. But because she never said anything else about them, I always assumed they were estranged. I didn't realize she shared a womb with said sibling and that he died.

I understand Tanya not telling us about everyone in her family. There's so many to mention and she hadn't been home in quite some time, but a twin brother? Seems worth mentioning.

"She—she had a twin brother." My voice is shaky, unrecognizable to my own ears. Why was Tanya tested time and time again?

Auntie Joyce lets out a deep exhale. "She did. He died when they were twenty-three. Fishing accident. I lost them both then."

"What do you mean?" I ask, hanging on to her every word by a thread.

"After Andrew died, Tanya couldn't bear to be here anymore. Too much loss. She and George packed up and moved to Richmond, to his hometown, and from then on her visits were few and far between. Then they stopped completely."

"She always called, though," John interjects. "She called after each one of the kids was born. Sent gifts for holidays and birthdays."

"Not the same as holding her, though." Auntie Joyce's words are laced with so much hurt. The pain of missing out on so much of Tanya's life must have created a void in her soul not easily healed by phone calls and gifts.

John releases a somber laugh. "When she came to visit all those months ago, the town damn near threw a parade for her. I thought maybe she was gonna start coming around again, but then we heard she was gone."

Tanya must have known that visit would be her last. She wanted to see the family she left behind one more time before she shared her fate with Auntie Joyce.

I still can't believe we didn't know she had a twin brother. So much loss. The death of any sibling would be like losing a limb, but losing a twin has to be like walking around with a heart that doesn't fully beat.

I know it hurt Auntie Joyce and the rest of the family, but I can't blame Tanya for putting this place in her rearview. Everyone who lived in this house with her growing up was gone. Every memory tainted by the stench of death.

I probably would've done the same. Maybe that's why Tanya is making us do this. She doesn't want us to make the same decisions she did.

With three kids, all the bedrooms in John's home are occupied, but he kept all the things Tanya left at the house in a shed out back, so he takes us there to look through them with toddler Ava on his hip.

Micah and John bond when John realizes we have Tanya's Continental. He always thought she was the coolest person in the world for having that car. While their conversation slowly turns into gibberish for me the more they talk about cars, Auntie Joyce and I focus on sorting through the lost artifacts. It hits me that I'm going through Tanya's things with someone who knew her longer than me. I have this image in my head of what Tanya was like as a kid. Before my grandmom passed away, she loved to tell me funny stories from my mom's childhood and I loved hearing them. And now, I'm in a town full of people who could do the same with Tanya. My eyes start to feel misty, so I look to the sky to keep it from getting worse.

"It's odd," Auntie Joyce notes, her gaze planted firmly on me.

"What's odd?"

"You sort of look like her." She tilts her head to the side, taking me in from every angle. "Very strange. Maybe it's because I see so much of her in you."

That's the best compliment I could hope to receive.

A book falls out of the box I just grabbed, a cloud of dust escaping its edges.

When the World Gets to Be Too Loud

That's the title stitched onto the cover of the book. When I open it, it's a collection of poems. Some by well-known authors, some by authors I've never heard of, and some appear to be handwritten. The words have faded on the pages over time, but they're still legible. The initials *A.G.* are stamped in the corner of each one.

"Are these . . ."

Auntie Joyce answers my question before I can voice it. "Andrew's book of poems. He was so embarrassed for anyone to read his work, but Tanya was his biggest fan."

There's a small warp on one of the pages, right in the middle of the poem. It looks as if the paper got wet a long time ago. My finger traces the ripple, wondering if it was Tanya's tears that struck this page or someone else's.

"Auntie Joyce, do you mind if I keep this?"

"You don't need to ask me." She winks as she slides her hand over another one of Tanya's boxes, takes a dozing Ava from John's arms, and slips out of the shed.

"She never comes back here. It was probably a lot for her," John clarifies.

"I understand." All too well.

I place the book of poems to the side, my hands itching to read every page, but that will have to wait until later.

"Hey, Storm, look," Micah calls out. When I turn, he's holding up an old music box. "The gift of music?" he questions.

A soft melody fills the space when he flips the box open while a Black ballerina twirls in place.

"I'm pretty sure her mom gave her that. I remember my two sisters begging our mom for one after she showed them because a music box with a Black ballerina was hard to come by back then."

"If I could give anyone anything, it would be the gift of music."

Hearing you loud and clear, Tanya. We'll make sure someone special gets this gift. Micah hands me the music box to sit on top of my book.

Micah and I knew Tanya the woman well, but uncovering the makings of Tanya the girl is a gift I couldn't be more thankful for.

John provides as much context as he can for the things we find but encourages us to talk to some of the other family members for more insight.

I plan to do just that.

When we leave the shed, we find Auntie Joyce sitting on the porch smoking another cigarette. Her thin eyebrows furrow with each puff.

She stamps the cigarette out when she sees us, dabbing her knuckle beneath her eye subtly. "Ava's sleeping in her bed. Ready to head out? I gotta get to the store and buy some celery." She hands John a baby monitor.

"What you making?" Micah asks.

"Potato salad for the cookout later. John, you bring the kids by when they get home, okay?" He nods his agreement and Micah acts as Auntie Joyce's handrail down the steps.

"When did she say we were having a cookout?" Micah whispers in my ear when Auntie Joyce walks a little ahead of us.

Maybe it was in her head, because it definitely wasn't out loud.

Turns out, this is a regular Auntie Joyce occurrence. She calls for a cookout on a random day and the whole family drops everything to come together.

Within hours she has the potato salad chilling in the fridge, and family members start showing up with burgers, hot dogs, wings, baked beans, soda, pies, and other dishes. One cousin literally rolls his grill down the street and parks it in Auntie Joyce's backyard to fire it up.

Before long the cookout is in full swing. Drinks are flowing, kids are running around the yard, and a game of dominoes is growing heated.

One of the little cousins, Jamie, marches up to Micah and looks up at him with determination in her gaze. "Why you so tall?" she blurts.

He doesn't bend down to her level, he just looks down at her like the giant he is. "Why you so short?" he responds.

"I'm still growing!" She stomps her foot.

"You sure about that?"

She turns her nose up in disgust. "Yes. I just grew two inches last month."

"Congratulations."

She considers him for a moment, planning her next move. "You got a dollar?"

His lip twitches, but he's able to stop any expression from showing on his face. "I do."

She pauses, waiting for him to offer it to her on a silver platter. "Can I have it?" she asks when he doesn't.

He crosses his arms across his chest. "Tell you what. I'll give you one dollar for every inch you've grown in the last year."

She grabs his hand and tugs. "Mom!" she yells out. "I need to check the board thingy!" She keeps screaming out to her mom as she drags Micah along behind her. He looks at me and shrugs as he allows Jamie to make him into a rag doll.

As I walk toward the folding tables in the yard to grab a plate, a soft voice calls out to me. "You're Tanya's girl, right?"

I turn and find a table of older and younger Black women, the one who spoke to me a spitting image of John.

"That's me, yeah. I'm Dani," I say as I walk closer to them.

They invite me to sit down, shifting to make space. "I'm June. This is my sister Cora, her daughter, Serena, and my daughter-in-law, Nicky."

Each woman waves as their name is called. Serena compliments my nails, telling me I should come by her shop for a fill-in before I leave town.

"You must be John's mom." I look to June for confirmation, pleased when she nods. "Then that means you two"—I point to June and Cora—"are Auntie Joyce's sisters?" That would make them Tanya's first aunts.

"Yep. There's nine of us total." Cora breaks down the family tree, explaining that Auntie Joyce is the oldest after Tanya's dad, Larry, which is why everyone calls her Auntie. Once Larry passed away, Joyce became the head of the family, and she's worn that title proudly ever since. Cora is the youngest of the siblings, only a few years older than Tanya herself. Serena is Cora's middle child, and Nicky is married to June's oldest daughter, Tiara.

I get lost somewhere along the tree, but the bottom line is they are a close-knit family, able to trace their roots back generations.

"You know, Tanya joining Larry, Ruby, and Andrew is one whole branch gone," Cora says, choking back tears. Serena rubs her mother's back, while Nicky grabs her hand.

"But at least they all get to be together again. I'm just glad Larry and Ruby went first. Parents aren't supposed to bury their kids." Her words make me think about Lorraine. Were Tanya and George even able to find a casket that small? As nice as it is to be surrounded by Tanya's family, I have to wonder about Tanya's mental state. Too much loss can really change a person, and I don't know if she took care of her mental health the way she maybe should have. I don't think anyone in her shoes could withstand this without someone to talk to, professional or otherwise. Did she have that? Those are questions no one here can answer for me and that makes me sad for Tanya.

"Anyway, dear, we're glad you're here. It's nice to meet someone who knew Tanya in her older years," June adds.

"Yeah. What was she like?" Nicky asks. "I never got to meet her, but I heard so many stories."

Where do I even begin? "She was dramatic."

June snorts. "Glad to hear that never changed."

"She was protective."

June and Cora both grin at that.

"She was wise. And she never made you feel less than when she imparted her wisdom on you."

Cora agrees with that wholeheartedly.

"Okay, I gotta ask. Did she pick up random hobbies as a kid too?" I question.

Cora's face lights up. "Oh my God, Junebug, do you remember when she started playing the violin?"

June's smile grows wider. "Lord, that child was not musically inclined. Daddy stole her violin out of our room one night and sold it at a pawn shop. Pretended like the damn thing grew legs and walked out."

"And then she tracked it down and bought it back using money she got from people in the neighborhood who paid her not to sing," Cora imparts.

"All to sell it back to the pawn shop a month later."

The stories go back and forth between the three of us until we're all in stitches.

"Excuse me, ladies, Dani, I brought you this." Micah towers over me with a plate full of food.

"You didn't have to do that. Thank you," I offer, thankful all the same, because as wonderful as this conversation has been, I realize I didn't get to make my plate before we launched down memory lane.

"Oooh, a gentleman. We like that." Serena whistles.

Micah rubs the back of his neck with a shy smile. “Can I get you ladies anything?”

“Oh, no thank you, baby. You already brought us a tall drink of water,” June says.

“You’re shameful.” I laugh. “How much did you have to pay up?” I query, referring to his little bet with Jamie.

“A whole three dollars. I rounded up to five, though.”

The ladies have no idea what we’re talking about, but they’re all too happy to have Micah in their space. Serena pushes Nicky so that Micah can sit between them.

“Did you ask them about the doc?” he says to me.

A light bulb goes off in my head. “Oh my God, I didn’t even think about that.” I tell the ladies about the documentary we’re making for Tanya’s gala and ask if they wouldn’t mind sharing stories about her on video.

June urges me to go grab my camera while Cora runs back to her house to freshen up.

A few hours later, long after the party has died down and only Micah, Ella, Tony, Auntie Joyce, Cora, and I are left standing, Micah has me dancing in the middle of Auntie Joyce’s yard to a Mary J. Blige song.

“Did you have fun today?” he asks with his eyes seared into mine.

“You know what? I did.” There’s a lot of love here. I know that Tanya felt it even if she couldn’t bring herself to experience it in person. “Did you?”

“I did.” He starts to say something else but cuts himself off.

“What?”

“Nothing. I just know the documentary is gonna turn out amazing. You’re great behind the camera.”

"Just not in front of it, right?" I joke, mocking him by bringing up our earlier fight.

"When you're ready to get in front of the camera, it's gonna be incredible. The only person who doubts that is you."

"Why do you always know what to say?"

"Based on your numerous threats to punch me in the titty, I don't think that's true." His expression turns somber, laced with regret. "And if that were true, I would've known what to say when you asked me to go to London with you."

I wince from the sudden plunge of a metaphorical knife in my chest. "The truth would've been a good start."

"You're right. I'll always regret the way I handled that."

"It is what it is."

He holds my eyes and pulls me closer. "Why can't it be what we make it?"

Because we always seem to make a mess.

What if we don't this time?

Our conversation is cut short when Ella cozies up next to me, wrapping her arms around both of us. "This is so precious."

"Oh brother," I sneer.

"I'm serioussss. You look like this wedding photo I saw of Tanya and George."

Micah and I looking like a married couple is a subject I don't want to broach, but I would love to see that picture of Tanya and George.

"See, she's not vibing with that, Ella. I did get three marriage proposals at Mackey's earlier, maybe I should hit one of them up."

I stick my tongue out at him, refusing to take his bait.

"Mackey's would be the perfect place. It's where they had their wedding reception."

Micah's hand falls from my waist as my jaw drops. "It is?"

"Yep. Aaron said his dad still talks about their wedding to this day."

I can't explain it, but something tells me Mackey's is the key to our next clue. Ella and Tony are the only ones who take us up on our invitation to Mackey's, so we all pile into Tony's car and head that way.

"You're back," Aaron exclaims. "And you didn't bring me a plate?" he asks Tony and Ella.

"You work at a bar with food." Ella holds her hands up as if Aaron should be ashamed of himself.

"And you could've come to get your own plate. I know your ass hasn't been here all day," Tony teases.

I lean up on the bar to pretend to whisper. "I heard June saved you a whole half a pie."

He beams at my remark. "Thank you, sweetie. And that's why June's my favorite. And why you two can go to hell."

"A whole half a pie? She told me there wasn't any pie left!" Ella bangs her fist on top of the bar.

"There wasn't. For you," Micah comments.

As Aaron steps aside to grab coasters for us, I notice a card pinned to the wall behind the bar. It blends in with a host of other cards and pictures pinned there, but this one looks familiar. It looks like the postcard that led us here.

"Aaron, could I see that, please?"

He raises his brow but pulls the card down and hands it to me.

I don't recognize the building on the front. I can barely make out that it says "Legacies" above the door, but the bottom of the card says "Richmond, Virginia," which is George's hometown. Tanya's handwriting on the back only further confirms we're on the right track.

Micah looks at it over my shoulder. "I guess we're going to Richmond."

I don't want to leave. I feel closer to Tanya now that I've met her family, and I want to bask in this glow for longer, but we have to keep going. She needs us to finish this.

"We should hit the road tomorrow morning." We'll have to say our goodbyes to everyone first thing because Virginia is not a short drive. I wonder if Serena would be able to squeeze me in for a nail appointment before we go.

"Sure. There's just one thing we have to do first."

The next morning, Micah honks the horn in front of Tanya's old house. We're leaving much later than intended, but Ella kept us out late and we wanted to make sure we were able to say goodbye to the family that welcomed us with open arms.

John's family walks out of the house, John rubbing his eyes, Ava firmly seated on Dee's hip, and the other two kids trailing closely behind.

The sight of Tanya's Continental does the job of waking John all the way up. "Aww man, y'all are leaving already?"

"Yep. We got some things to take care of," I say, leaning against the car.

The kids come running down the stairs to hug Micah and I goodbye while Dee gives us kisses on the cheek and Ava bites our noses.

"Don't be strangers. We family now. And anytime you wanna bring this baby back to see us, I won't be mad." He rubs his hand on the driver's side mirror.

"Actually. We were hoping you'd hold on to this car for us." Micah holds out the keys.

Dee pushes John's mouth shut when his jaw nearly falls off its hinges. "Are you serious?"

"Yeah. No doubt in my mind Tanya would want you to have this."

Tears spring to his eyes and the kids waste no time climbing into the back seat as Micah and I make our way to our new rental car.

It feels good to leave this piece of Tanya where it belongs.

717

Chapter Fourteen

Dani

"Keep the seeds of your garden watered." —Tanya

IMAGE SEARCHES ARE NOW MY BEST FRIEND. THE PICTURE on the postcard turned out to be a community center in Richmond, Virginia, called Legacies that Tanya and George started. According to an online article, George's niece Janine now runs it.

Tanya's secrets are really piling up.

It's relatively empty when we walk into the community center, only a few kids doing quiet activities by themselves. The loudest voice comes from a grown woman coloring and singing as she sits with one of the kids.

A little boy looks up from his Lego Sonic set and yells, "Ms. Janine, somebody's here."

Recognition takes over her face as she jumps up, brushing her floor-length boho skirt before coming over. "Dani and Micah."

I guess she was expecting us too.

Janine's the spitting image of George, just with softer features. She has the exact type of face you'd want on someone who works at a place like this: warm and inviting. She can't be any older than her forties, yet she has the aura of a sweet old soul, capable of melting away all your problems.

"I'm sad that Tanya waited until after she was gone to tell you about this place, but I've heard so many stories about you two over the years."

Why *had* she kept it from us until she wasn't here to share it herself? Considering both of our connections to the rec center back home and Micah's connection to Our Place, she had to know we'd love it here. Then again, I know all about wanting to keep a little slice of heaven all to yourself, and this was the place she built with George.

"Nice to meet you, Janine. Sorry we caught you right before you close, but we can come back tomorrow," Micah promises.

"Oh, you're right on time. Follow me back to the house."

I'm sorry, what?

"Oh, we don't want to put you out. We can stay at a hotel," I offer.

"Nonsense. Family stays at the house," she insists.

A house, it turns out, with one guest bed.

Janine lives with her husband and their two kids, so there's only one spare bedroom, which has exactly one bed.

She wouldn't hear of Micah trying to sleep on the couch, so he's having a good old laugh while I'm stuck staring at this bed that's almost too small for the two of us.

"Dani. I can sleep on the floor if it bothers you that much."

"No, no. I'm fine. I just wasn't expecting this. Janine is very pushy." Very pushy.

"Mhm. Okay then, are you coming to sleep? Because I'm exhausted after all that food." Janine ordered enough takeout to feed an army, and she insisted we eat until I thought the buttons were going to pop off of my pants.

Again, very sweet. Very, very pushy.

Tanya is probably having the time of her life watching all this.

"It's been hours since we ate and I still feel like I'm gonna explode," I complain.

"Same, but her son was about to kick my ass for beating him in *Mario Kart*, so I think I'll stay in here."

Her son definitely has Janine's pushiness. He demanded we play so many rounds with him that I thought my eyes would start bleeding.

I really hope we find this next clue quickly.

I climb into bed next to Micah, lying flat on my back, until I feel pillows hitting my side. "What are you doing?"

"You're acting very shady, so I'm protecting my virtue," he says as he adds another pillow to the wall between us. I reach over it and pluck him in the neck. "Aht aht, stay on your side, ma'am. The goodies are locked up tight."

"Hate you." I turn away from him and then reach back, grab a pillow from the wall, and slam it into his head.

He laughs so hard he snorts.

The lights have been off for some time, yet sleep hasn't managed to find me yet.

"You're a very loud thinker," Micah's voice drifts over the mountain of pillows.

Shit. I thought he was sound asleep. "Have you ever considered that maybe you're just a light sleeper?"

"Considered it. Determined it to be a lie."

I roll my eyes as I lean over to turn on my bedside lamp. "Okay, so why are you up listening to me think, then?"

He turns so his arm is resting atop the pillow wall. "Because I'm thinking too."

"What are you thinking about?"

"Tanya. Does it bother you? That she kept so many things from us?"

I turn my body to face his. "It did."

"But it doesn't now?"

I shake my head no.

"When did that change?"

"When we gave John that car." Seeing him enjoying Tanya's first car with his family made everything click for me. "I kept thinking that maybe Tanya didn't think we were capable of handling the rougher parts of her life. I thought some part of her must not trust us enough. But when I saw the joy on John's face, I realized that she trusted us the most out of anyone. She knew that her death would start a collision course of all her different worlds, and she trusted us to help them navigate through it."

This gala is just as much for all of us as it is for her.

"Hmm, that's a good way to think about it."

"How are you doing with all the secrets?"

He leans back to look up at the ceiling, keeping his arm pressed against mine. "It's not that she had secrets. It's knowing that she carried them all by herself. No one should have to do that."

He and I are on the same page there.

"I'm really glad we're doing this together, Storm. It doesn't hurt as much when you're around."

We lock eyes and for a moment everything falls away. All the pieces of our puzzle that don't fit suddenly do and every jagged edge feels smooth.

"I feel the same way."

He smiles as he grazes my arm before moving it back to his side of the pillows. "Good night, Storm."

This new nickname he's bestowed upon me always makes me think of the day we met. Forced into quality time by Tanya's meddling ways, we spent one unforgettable day together that bled into a night spent chasing down the moon in his car. To this day I have never been kissed the way he kissed me that night.

"Good night, Moonchaser."

I didn't get a wink of sleep. Every time I moved, I thought I was going to fall off the bed. Micah, however, seemed very peaceful. How nice for him.

He stretches his arms in the air dramatically as he opens his eyes.

"Well, good morning, sleepyhead. Proud of you for staying on your side."

Lack of sleep is a dangerous thing; it brings out the worst in you. I guess that's why I find myself in a full-blown pillow fight with Micah.

"Hello? Have you lost your mind? How dare you strike me?"

"Hello? I'm gonna do a lot more than strike you. You and this fucking pillow wall. Take these damn pillows off my side." I slap him repeatedly until he snatches the pillow from me and does it right back. We go back and forth until he blocks one of my hits and the pillow flies across the room, knocking things off the desk in the corner.

"Look what you did," Micah reprimands.

A glint of silver shines in the sunlight peeking through the window. I jump from the bed to pick it up. A trowel. And underneath the pillow are gardening gloves.

"Doesn't it seem strange to you to keep your gardening tools in a bedroom?"

Maybe the seeds of the garden Tanya mentioned are more literal than we thought.

After showering, brushing our teeth, and getting ready for the day, we run outside to Janine's garden.

"We can't just start digging in someone else's garden, can we?" Micah asks. It's barely a garden. It's more a patch of dirt. Not a single flower, fruit, or vegetable is growing here.

I'm ready to leave Richmond, so whether it's him or me, somebody is going to get to digging.

He holds up his hand to hide from my murderous glare and then starts. I wish I had brought some water with us. It's such a nice day out I didn't think I'd need it, but I also wasn't expecting to be subjected to Micah on his knees in nature with every muscle he has bulging out of his clothes. Jesus, why does he have to walk around looking like that?

"Oh, I'm so glad this garden is getting some love. I really wanted to have a green thumb, but I just don't," Janine's cheerful voice rings in my ear. She's watching us from the porch with her head in her hands. "The garden's been so popular lately, I think I'll leave it up. Maybe someone else can get something to grow."

"Who was here last?"

"Oh, Tanya's friend. Victor. He came by a few months ago and asked if he could plant some things for me. I don't know what he planted, but I hope his blooms turn out better than mine usually do."

"Victor was here, you say." Micah's voice is full of amusement. So, we know we're on the right track.

"Dig faster," I mouth to him.

"Well, didn't you know that? He's the one that said you'd be alright sharing that guest bedroom and bought *Mario Kart* for Charlie so that you could play it with him."

Oh, now Victor has a sense of humor.

"Must've slipped my mind," Micah responds.

Janine leaves us to our "gardening" and Micah digs faster, coming up empty. He sits back on his haunches and wipes the sweat from his brow. I would clean that sweat for him with my tongue if he asked.

Get a fucking grip, girl.

"I really do feel bad digging up Janine's garden like this. We could at least plant some stuff for her," Micah says.

"What do you want to plant?"

"Really?"

"What do you think I am? A monster? She thinks she's getting a garden back here, so we should make that happen." I'm not sure if they'll survive, but we can try.

We take a break from treasure hunting to peek in the shed where Janine keeps her gardening tools. She has an abundance of seed packets here ranging from vegetables like cabbage, carrots, and radishes, to early season flowers like daffodils and pansies. We decide to focus on the vegetables and take a nice haul back to the "garden" with us.

While Micah gets back to digging, I search YouTube for tutorials on planting because I don't know a damn thing about it.

Ting. Micah's trowels hits something hard and metal.

There in the dirt is a lockbox that requires a code and a large key with a strange owl symbol on it.

717

Chapter Fifteen

Micah

JANINE HAS TO GO TO A PARENT-TEACHER CONFERENCE at Charlie's school, so she'll be joining us at Legacies later. Now that we know she's not a Peeping Tom insisting Dani and I share a bed just because, her cheeriness doesn't creep me out as much.

Dani and I spend a good chunk of the car ride to the center plotting our revenge on Victor. Though I won't tell Dani this, I'm actually proud of the old man for pulling a prank on us. I wasn't sure he had it in him.

Dani yanks on the lockbox again, but it doesn't budge. We've been fidgeting with it since we found it, inputting any code we could think of.

"I mean how many combinations could there be?" she asks.

"Literally thousands."

She cuts her eyes over to me as another code fails her. "There has to be another clue at Legacies," she insists.

I just hope we're not overlooking something.

Legacies has a lot more kids during normal business hours. According to Janine, most of the kids come right after school, but some are too young for school and their parents can't afford daycare. It reminds me a lot of Our Place.

I knew Tanya and Chi Chi would've been great friends.

The volunteers at Legacies are kind, and they don't hesitate to put us to work when we offer our services.

Dani is swept away helping a few of the kids get a snack, while I'm putting together an arcade-style basketball hoop for some of the older kids. Tavion floats to the forefront of my mind. He'd enjoy doing stuff like this and helping kids—without beating the shit out of bullies—could be a good outlet for him. I wonder if Sammy would be okay with him working at Our Place. I'll have to check in with her when I get back, whenever that'll be.

One of the kids stands out. He was here when we first showed up, sitting in the corner by himself, his nose tucked into a sketch pad, and he's still sitting there drawing. Every so often, his gaze floats over to a little girl who's playing classroom with a few others. Something about this kid feels like a magnet. Once I finish with the basketball hoop, I ask one of the volunteers about him.

"Oh, that's Kenji. That's his normal spot. He really doesn't engage with us too much, but he comes every day to look after his sister, Raena."

I think that's why I'm so drawn to this kid: his protectiveness. "And he just sits there by himself every day?"

She confirms, cementing my decision to talk to him.

"Mind if I sit?"

He gestures for me to join before focusing back on his sketchbook.

"What are you working on?"

He sighs in frustration, turning his work toward me rather than speaking. He's drawing a comic. The figure in the sketch looks more antihero than hero, but he's cool as hell all the same. Instead of a traditional superhero costume, this guy has on street clothes and sunglasses. He's got a knife in his hands, his fingertip pressed against the sharp end, but no blood falls to the ground. Perhaps he's not one hundred percent human.

"Where'd you learn to draw like that?" The details—from his slate-gray-and-muted-gold palette to his use of shadowing to add density—scream of a professional.

I don't expect him to answer me, but his deep voice catches me off guard. "My dad."

"Is he an artist?"

"He was. He's locked up now. Won't let us come see him."

Ah. That's a feeling I can understand. When you lose the person who inspired you to do what you love, it's hard to figure out where to put your anger. Sometimes the only place is in the thing you're most passionate about.

"That's shitty." There's no sugarcoating it. He doesn't want an apology, and he doesn't want an explanation. He wants his dad.

He looks surprised but seems to soften a bit. "Yeah. It is." He waits a beat before speaking again. "Are you an artist?"

"I paint, yeah."

"Cool."

I have to fight to stay composed. *Don't get all cheesy on him now.* "Have you ever thought about sending your comics to your dad?" His dad may not want his son to see him in prison, but I'm sure seeing his son's art would make his time there a whole lot easier. It might make Kenji feel better too, to know his dad has seen his stuff.

"I thought you could only send letters."

I won't pretend to know all the rules of prison mail, but it's worth investigating. "I could help you look into it."

He nods his head slowly at first and then quicker, his eyes wandering back to Raena for a moment with a small smile. "That'd be cool."

"You got it."

"You, um, wanna read what I have so far?"

"Hell yeah."

I don't know how much time passes while I look through Kenji's comics and he tells me about the world he's built before Dani taps me on the shoulder.

"You okay?" she asks me while smiling at Kenji.

"I'm great." I look back to Kenji. "Kenji, do you mind if my friend Dani sits with us?"

He looks her up and down with mild disinterest before going back to his sketching. "I guess."

"Thank you for letting me in your space." Dani looks like she's won the lottery as she slides into the seat across from Kenji. She lets him set the pace, staying quiet while he feverishly adds to his drawings. His sister runs over to Dani for help tying her shoe, and when she leaves, Dani gushes about how sweet she is. Kenji doesn't speak up to say that's his sister. He doesn't even give an indication that he heard us, he just rips out a piece of paper from his sketchbook and passes it over to Dani with a pack of colored pencils.

Dani doesn't understand this sudden inclusion, but she can barely contain her excitement. When she shows him the dog she attempted to draw, he silently takes his pencil to it and makes some adjustments for her. How did I get bumped from the best buddy category already?

That's the power of Dani Jenkins.

Kenji shares the next panel of his comic with me as Dani gets up to find some construction paper. When she comes back, the volunteer who told me about Kenji walks over to us.

"I'm sorry I got caught up. Did you need help with anything else?" I ask.

"Oh no, we're fine. I actually came over because I noticed your key," she says to Dani. The key we dug out of Janine's yard has been hanging from her belt loop since we found it.

"What about it?"

"I've seen that symbol before. Come with me." She leads us to the back office, where there's a small safe that has the same strange owl symbol as the key.

"Oh shit," Dani exclaims.

"Do you know what the symbol is for?" I ask.

"Honestly? I don't think it stands for anything. This safe has been here since I started and only one random guy has ever come and opened it."

Of course.

Dani sticks the key in the safe and turns.

Inside the safe there's a broken watch, forever frozen on the time 12:05. Next to the watch is one of Tanya's notes that says, *"A broken clock is right twice a day."*

"Tanya said she would always remember the exact time her heart stopped beating," Dani says in a hushed tone.

George must've been wearing this watch when he fell. I'll never forget Tanya telling me about the day George died. They were in the grocery store when he collapsed. She rushed him to the hospital, and he never left. Heart attack.

I run out to the car to grab the lockbox. "Do you think that's the code?"

Dani looks at me with a haunted stare. We both know it's the right code. We've learned the hard way during this scavenger hunt that there's no way to prepare ourselves for what Tanya has left behind. All we can do is face it together.

She types the four digits into the lockbox and it pops open.

There are two things in the box. Our next clue, written on the back of a deposit slip from some random bank in Chicago, and a marriage license. Dated after George's death. For Tanya. And another man.

Chapter Sixteen

Dani

"Sometimes you have to fall to find your way." —Tanya

MARRIED. MARRIED? TANYA WAS MARRIED TO someone we didn't know about? How could that be? If she did, I'm happy for her, but Tanya only ever talked about George. He hung the moon in her eyes. I don't see anyone coming close to that for her.

"Is it just me, or did Victor sound even drier than normal when we told him we were headed to Chicago?" I ask Micah. After we finished with Janine's garden last night, we called him to let him know we found the next clue and were headed straight for the Windy City.

"Yeah, he sounded sort of sad."

The flight to Chicago is short and sweet. This constant travel reminds me of the height of my modeling days, but I'm enjoying the time.

Traveling with Micah is nice. When he's not trying to get under my skin and shoving pillows into my back, we mesh well together.

"You gotta be kidding me," Micah mumbles when Victor's face is the first one we see as we make our way to baggage claim.

"Why didn't you tell us you were meeting us? How'd you get here so fast?" He must've hopped on the first plane out as soon as we called.

He greets us with the poise we've come to expect. He's like a royal palace guard. I'm determined to see him break character. I know Tanya must've accomplished it.

"I go where I'm needed." Dry as ever. "I hope you had a good flight. Your baggage claim carousel is this way." He leads us to our assigned belt, which spits out our bags soon after.

As we're walking to Victor's car, Micah speaks. "Since you're here, maybe we can squeeze in that game of chess you owe me."

Victor smirks. "This will be a short trip for me, but my office is open to you anytime."

Tanya tried to teach me how to play chess a couple of times. It didn't interest me, but I loved how much she enjoyed it. I can't say I'm surprised that Victor is also a fan.

Victor is subdued as we drive to the bank that was on the deposit slip clue. He shows the woman at the front desk the proper documentation to gain entry, and then we're escorted to the back room.

"You'll need this," he says, handing us a laptop.

"You're not gonna stay?" I ask.

"Like I said, I go where I'm needed. You don't need me for this," he confirms. He and the bank employee close the door behind them to give us some privacy.

"What do you think is in here?" I ask once the door shuts. It feels like whatever it is has the power to send us both flying into orbit.

"Only one way to find out." Micah puts his hand on top of mine and we open the box together.

There's a flash drive that makes the reason for Victor's laptop clear. And then there's a deed to a house and a copy of the marriage license we saw in Richmond.

"I'm almost scared to watch this one." The flash drive feels like it weighs a ton in my hand.

We connect it to the computer and Tanya's face appears.

I can see her only from the waist up, but I can tell she had lost a ton of weight. Her fingers are bony and her skin is slightly paler. We are watching her wither away right before our eyes.

My stomach flips.

"Hi, my loves. You must be very confused because the name on that marriage license is not George Holden. I met Roger Lucas exactly one year after George died. I was still a wreck. I had taken about all I could take. I was offered a job here in Chicago and I considered taking it."

Her words are interrupted by the harshness of her cough. Her chest rattles with every move. Still, she's determined to push past her obvious pain.

"Excuse me. Where was I? Oh yes, I considered taking the job in Chicago, but I also didn't want to give up the home I shared with George. It was the last place he had touched, you know? So I decided I'd go to Chicago for a visit. See if it felt right before I committed. I stayed at the Lennox Bed and Breakfast, and that's where I met Roger. His sister owned the place." She smiles mournfully before continuing. *"He was so like George in a lot of ways. It was like talking to his ghost. I let that coincidence tell me it was something more and I became swept up in all that was Roger. Within two months, the man had proposed and bought us a house. I said yes when I should've said no. I knew it didn't feel right. I knew when I saw our names side by side on the marriage license that I had made a mistake. I cried in my bathtub for hours at the thought of getting rid of the last name Holden."*

Coughs overcome her body once again. It takes her a solid minute to recover. A familiar hand presents her with a cup of tea from behind the camera.

"These coughing fits really do disrupt the power of my story, huh? I'm sure you were on the edge of your seats until I hacked up a lung."

Micah and I laugh at that.

"I'm getting to the point now, I promise. As you probably guessed, Roger and I didn't get married. I hated breaking his heart, and like the kindest man he was, he didn't get angry with me. He even insisted I keep the house. I left the reminders of Roger in Chicago because that place belonged to him. Everywhere else belonged to George. So now, when I said I was leaving you everything, I meant everything. The house is yours. I always wanted to do something special with it, but I never figured out what that was. Maybe you'll have better luck."

Her mention of luck sends my hand up to the necklace lying around my neck.

I've never even been to Chicago for anything longer than a layover, and now I co-own a house here.

What is life?

Not having the energy to face the house yet, we decide to visit the bed and breakfast Tanya mentioned. Maybe Roger's sister still owns the place, and we can ask her some questions.

Victor is quiet when we meet him back outside the bank. This part of Tanya's story seems to be greatly affecting him. I'm not going to voice my thoughts on the situation. As Micah loves to point out, I run from my feelings, so I'll be damned if I call someone out for doing the same.

When we ask him if he can take us to Lennox Bed and Breakfast, his GPS shows that he was already headed that way. A lucky guess, he claims.

After we pull up to the building, he lets us know he'll have a car sent our way for the remainder of our trip. The man flew all the way here just to turn back around the same day. That's a level of dedication I don't think all clients get from their lawyers. It's a level of dedication I doubt all of Victor's clients get from him. I've been hard on him, and I haven't been considerate of how Tanya's death must have affected him on a deeper level.

"Hey, Victor, are you okay?"

He gives a single nod and says, "I'll be just fine."

I can't help but notice he didn't say he *is* fine.

Walking into Lennox feels like walking into your grandmom's house. The smell of cookies wafts through the air. The furniture looks inviting. The couch looks like it makes for a great nap while the TV stand appears handcrafted.

A woman walks into the foyer with long twists pulled up into a bun. "Oh, hello. Welcome to Lennox. Have you booked a stay with us?"

"We haven't. But do you have any rooms available?" Micah inquires.

"Absolutely. Come with me."

We follow her to a desk that looks a bit more modern than the rest of the decor. "And would that be one or two rooms?"

"One," I say.

"Two," Micah says at the same time.

Heat rises up my neck. How fucking embarrassing. "Right. Two."

"I just thought you'd be more comfortable that way," he explains.

I don't meet his eyes. He's right. I just figured that after we survived sharing a room in Richmond, we'd be fine. This is why you shouldn't assume. "Please let me wallow in my humiliation in peace," I jab.

He runs his hands down his face, a hint of a smile peeking through the slits of his fingers.

To her credit, the woman doesn't acknowledge the blunder and instead types furiously on her computer. "We happen to have two rooms left, so I'll go ahead and book you if that's okay."

We give her our information so we can complete our check-in. A man a few inches taller than her, with a low-cut Caesar and a tattoo of a bird on his neck, walks down the steps. He's got a bit of a baby face, but he stands with all the confidence of a man who knows exactly who he is.

"I'm Kelly, by the way. And this is my son, Slater." She holds her arms out for the man, and they half hug. "We run this place together, so we're happy to help with anything you need."

"Ahh, nice to meet you. Your last name wouldn't happen to be Lucas, would it?"

"It was once upon a time. Why do you ask?"

"Well, I believe your brother, Roger, and I had a friend in common."

"Oh really? Who?"

"Tanya Holden."

Her smile falls into a deep frown while Slater's eyes widen. "Tanya. Yes, I knew her. She won't be joining you, will she? She's not welcome."

"Mom," Slater chastises, and she brushes him off.

This is the first person we've met on our journey that didn't have the utmost respect for Tanya. My claws want to come out in her defense, but I know Tanya would want me to swallow my pride to carry out her wishes.

"She's dead. So, no. She won't be joining us." The snark in my voice can't be helped.

"Tanya's dead?" Slater whispers. Whatever his mom thinks of Tanya, he clearly doesn't share her sentiments.

Micah steps in to tell them who Tanya was to us and how she mentioned Roger, so we just wanted to see the place they met. He seems to think that would soften Kelly up a bit, but if you ask me, that only makes her more frustrated that Tanya even mentioned Roger's name.

"Yes, well, she broke my brother's heart. I hope she doesn't think sending you two here will somehow grant her Roger's favor in heaven."

Fuck Roger's favor, bitch. My tongue itches to bite back with that, but Roger doesn't deserve my harsh words. He seemed to be a good man. Kelly's probably a good woman too. But I don't take kindly to people disrespecting my family.

"How about I take you up to your rooms and get you settled?" Slater urges us to the stairs and I look back at Kelly, who's watching us closely. He continues, "So, you missed breakfast obviously, but it's served at 9:00 a.m. every morning. Dinner is served at 6:00 p.m. each night and tonight we're having lasagna. It's family-style, so we all sit at the table together, but no pressure to join. I know you didn't get the warmest welcome."

"That's not your fault," Micah excuses.

"No, but still. Um, okay, Dani, this is your room. And Micah, your room is just down the hall. I'll walk you there next."

"Thank you." I'm ready to get inside and decompress for a bit.

"Just so you know," Slater says before I can step into my room. "I always liked Tanya. She was really nice to me. Uncle Roger would be glad you're here."

Once I've showered off my attitude, I'm debating if I want to look for a snack and risk running into Kelly, when there's a knock on my door.

Without a doubt, I know I'll find Micah on the other side.

"How did I know you'd come find me?"

"I expected you'd have some sort of plane odor you wanted to wash off, so I gave you some time, but do you wanna go out with me?"

"Go where?" I was in the middle of applying lotion to my legs so I go back to doing just that, but now the simple task feels far too intimate with him here. His eyes follow every swipe of my hand hungrily. It's not an obvious hunger. If I didn't already know what Micah looks like when he's trying to control himself, I might've missed it. But I do know, and the desire to tease him into action keeps growing stronger.

"I know we should be visiting that house or looking for our next clue, but you said you've never really been to Chicago before, right?" he asks once I've broken the trance by putting my lotion back on the nightstand.

"I did."

"How'd you like to be a proper tourist?"

Absolutely, yes. I don't even care where we're going. If I'm going to keep resisting the temptation that is Micah, then we need to get far away from places with doors and beds.

"Thank you for today. I do feel like a proper tourist," I say, carrying the bear Micah made me at the Build-A-Bear at Navy Pier. He's decked out in all Chicago gear, which means absolutely nothing to me, but he's adorable and I've named him Chauncey.

Micah chuckles beside me as we climb the stairs to our rooms to change. "You should. You've done every touristy thing imaginable."

I tip my imaginary hat to him. "I hope ol' Kelly's lasagna is good because we could've had dinner at the John Hancock." Having dinner with that view would've been unreal, but I didn't want to let Slater down.

Micah licks his lips, leaning against my door and giving me his rapt attention. "Did you smell all those spices when we walked in? That lasagna gonna be bussin'. So you think you'd wanna come back here?"

"To Chicago? Yes. To the Lennox? Mmm, jury's still out." It depends on the treatment we get from Kelly tonight.

"Noted," he affirms.

I probably will always associate Chicago with Micah now, but I find that I don't mind that so much. We are friends, after all.

Dinner with Slater, Kelly, and the rest of the guests is enjoyable. Kelly gives us a wide berth, while Slater naturally commands the attention of everyone with his charm.

After dinner, some of the guests decide to watch TV while others go back to their rooms. I pull Slater aside before I lose track of him. "Hey, would you be free tonight?"

"Oh? What'd you have in mind?" His eyes trail my body for far too long.

Don't get me wrong, he's definitely attractive, but I've got too much on my plate right now. "Sorry, I meant to meet up with me and Micah." That didn't come out right either.

"I could be into that," he says.

"God help me." I tell him about the documentary for Tanya before any more images of having Slater and Micah at the same time can cloud my mind and my judgment.

He accepts my offer to be part of the documentary but agrees it's for the best that Kelly not know about it.

The three of us meet by the fire pit once most of the guests have gone to bed. The light from the fire adds an old-school camp aesthetic to the video that I think Tanya would love.

"Did you and Tanya keep in touch?" I ask once the camera is rolling.

"Oh, yeah. She even came to my college graduation. She sat in the way, way back because she knew my mom would be upset about her being there, but she didn't wanna miss it. She was good people."

"And what about the house? You didn't want it for yourself?" Tanya never used it. At the very least, I'm surprised Kelly didn't demand she release it to the family.

"No." He waves me off. "Uncle Roger got that house for her. It could only ever be hers. I did offer to maintain it for her, though, in case she came back."

"Meaning?"

"All the least fun parts about homeownership. I made sure it stayed clean, got repairs when things started to wear down from age, kept the grass cut. Stuff like that."

"Just because she was nice to you back when you were in college?" At this point, I've forgotten about the documentary; I'm genuinely intrigued by the depth of his generosity.

He chuckles. "When you say it like that, it sounds crazy, but yeah. My uncle was the best man I knew, and he loved Tanya with everything in him. Even after she left, he still said her name on his deathbed. And even though she couldn't give him her heart, she continued to handle his with care, and that's enough for me. She'll always be good in my book."

Once we're finished recording, Slater bids us a goodnight, the twinkle in his eyes letting me know he'd still be up for what he thought I proposed earlier. I won't be taking him up on that, but my thoughts keep drifting back to Micah as I lie in my bed.

I'm confident that he'd be better off finding someone else to satisfy his emotional needs, but I can't help but remember how good we are together sexually. Why shouldn't we be able to re-explore each other's bodies and leave it at that? What's the harm in proposing that to him tonight? What's the worst that could happen? I mean, I was already humiliated in front of Kelly, so if he rejects my offer, maybe I'll be able to finally let go of the idea.

I throw on my socks and tiptoe out of my room—avoiding the creaky floorboard I noticed earlier—toward Micah's door.

I knock as softly as possible, hoping it's loud enough for him to hear me.

He opens the door in just his briefs.

Yeah. I'm going to fuck the shit out of this man.

"You need something, Dani?" His voice is sinfully scratchy. A voice I have vivid memories of waking up to.

"I do, actually."

"Wanna come in and tell me what it is?" He rests his hand on the door above his head. He knows what he's doing.

"Yes."

As I move to step around him, he lowers his arm to block my entrance. "Be really sure you want to come in here before you do, Storm."

I'm so fucking sure. I reach for his waist when a loud siren pierces my ears. We both duck and cover our ears.

A fire alarm? At this time of night? That can't be a random test.

Other guests come trailing out of their rooms in various stages of sleepiness, not paying us a lick of attention as they file down the stairs.

"We should go," Micah instructs.

How bad do we think the fire really is? No. No. Pull it together.

As we file outside quickly, I catch a glimpse of flames coming from the kitchen. We hear the sound of fire extinguishers well before the fire truck arrives.

One of the guests tells another that someone tried to heat up the leftover lasagna in the microwave without taking it out of its metal tin.

While the firefighters head inside, I see Micah shiver slightly. "Aww, you cold? That's what you get for coming to your door like a whore," I mock.

He squeezes my arm. "Mhm, I'll remember that."

And I'll forever remember being clitblocked by a lasagna.

It doesn't take long for everyone to be allowed back into the house, but Kelly and Slater are waiting for us when we do with solemn faces.

"Sorry for the inconvenience, everyone," Kelly announces. "The fire is out, but it damaged the kitchen and dining room pretty badly. We won't have use of the kitchen until repairs are done."

"Because of that, we'll be issuing refunds to everyone who wants one. We're also happy to help you find other accommodations if you'd like. We understand not wanting to sleep with the smell of smoke," Slater offers in apology.

The crowd takes the news rather well and a couple of the guests even opt to stay. Before Kelly gets to work with the guests looking for new accommodations, she excuses herself into the kitchen, while Slater starts helping those who need a refund. I am not a Kelly fan by any means, but the look in her eyes has me following her. I motion for Micah to stay.

What were once beautiful white cabinets are now completely charred. The microwave is lying face down on top of the melted stove. The damage stretches across the entire back wall of the kitchen and the dining room as if they had put the fire out and then it caught them off guard and came back with a vengeance. Kelly is bent forward with her hands on her knees, her cries sounding like dry heaves.

I lift my shirt over my nose and mouth and move closer to her, tapping her on the shoulder. "What can I do?"

She looks stunned to see me. Her lips remind me of a fish the way she opens and closes them multiple times. "I don't know." Before I realize what's happening, she wraps me up in a tight hug, resting her head on my shoulder as the sobs take over her body.

I'm sure watching her beloved business almost go up in flames was a traumatic experience, and no one deserves that, not even Kelly. So I hug her back.

Once Kelly is good, I reunite with Micah to head upstairs for our things, but Slater calls my name. "Hey, sorry about all this." He looks around for listening ears before continuing. "I would say you guys could stay at your new house, but I'm having work done to the HVAC system, so it's not really comfortable there right now. Want me to help you find somewhere else?"

Micah looks up from his phone, smiling at Slater. "I got it handled, but thanks, man."

News to me, but okay.

We say our goodbyes as we finish climbing the stairs. "You got it handled?"

He has a gleam in his eye. "Trust me."

The view from the Viceroy is gorgeous.

When Micah said he had it handled, I did not think he meant booking us a penthouse suite.

"Micah, this is incredible," I tell him.

"I'm glad you like it," he says.

"What made you bring us here, though? You're not usually a flashy kind of guy."

He pins me with a stare that sets my body aflame. "I thought you'd like it. I don't know if we'll get a chance to have dinner at the Hancock building this trip, so I wanted you to have your nice view in some other way."

"And to think, yesterday you didn't even want to share a room with me."

He scoffs. "Get your facts straight, Dani. I was just following your lead."

He steps toward me, and I don't know what makes me do it, but I step back.

The move makes him freeze in place. I was so sure mere hours ago. My body is still sure, but that fire alarm allowed my head to fill with doubts. I can see it's too late for me to say anything. Micah has retreated back behind the boundaries I set.

Fuck.

My phone rings and I yank it out of my pocket.

Micah peeks and chuckles, unamused. "Myomari's calling."

Oh my God, give me a break. When is the last time I even talked to Omari? He's texted a few times since he last stayed at my place, but they've all gone unanswered. I silence the call. "Thanks," I murmur.

"Don't feel like talking tonight?"

"Not really."

"How come?"

I sigh. "We don't have anything to talk about, really."

There's only one person my body is humming for and I'm royally fucking up my chances there.

"Why can't you tell him you're not interested, then? I can't see you being in a relationship with a finance bro, no offense."

"I can't see me being in a relationship with anyone," I exhale.

That stops him in his tracks. "What?"

Our eyes meet and I hold strong. "I just don't see the point. I'm never gonna fall in love, so why waste someone's time, and my own, just to say I'm in a relationship?"

His frown grows deeper. "So, you're saying you don't believe in love?"

"No, I believe in love. I see it every day when I look at my parents. Even when I look at Rome and Nelle. I know it's out there. I just don't think it's out there for me."

"Why is that?"

"Because I don't think I'm capable of letting my guard down enough to find it."

The city of Chicago looks up at me from my hotel room window and I smile before lifting my head to let the sun's rays kiss my cheek. The view is beautiful and the bed is luxuriously comfortable. I roll my neck and put on the complimentary hotel robe before stepping out of my room in search of coffee.

We retreated to our rooms pretty quickly after the Omari conversation last night, so I wasn't expecting for him to be sitting on the couch sketching this early.

"Good morning." I try to keep my eyes off his shirtless frame.

His grin tells me I've failed. "Morning. Was the bed everything you dreamed of?"

"And then some."

"Great."

"You think we should go look at the house today?" I'm both excited and nervous to see it. To see a life Tanya almost had here. If she had taken that job and married Roger, we wouldn't be sitting here today. We never would've met Tanya to begin with.

"Actually, if you don't mind staying another day, I thought we could go look at the house tomorrow," he says.

"Oh, sure. Is there something else we need to do today?"

"Not 'we.'" The phrase adds another foot of distance to the flimsy bridge between us. "I was gonna go out and take some pictures. Just to clear my head."

And now I feel like shit. I've probably given him so much whiplash because my body and my head can't get on the same fucking page. I don't argue. He needs his space and all I can do is give him that.

Hours later, he's still not back. I've been confined to these walls all day. I could've spent the day out, and maybe I should have, but I moved my body from the couch only when room service arrived.

My mind is crowded with thoughts of Micah. Where is he? Is he out with someone? Is he even coming back tonight?

Stop holding yourself back from all the things you want. Just let go. Let go of all your inhibitions.

Slowly, I trail my fingers down my body, imagining they're Micah's calloused hands.

A moan escapes my lips the moment my fingers make contact with my nipple. I tweak it until it starts to pebble.

How would Micah do this? He'd make me suck his finger first so that the cool air on his wet finger would drive me crazy as it swirled around my nipple.

I run my finger back up to my mouth, swirling my tongue around it in soft, lazy circles, releasing it with a pop. I suck in a breath at the cool sensation against my nipple. Reaching my other hand up to take care of the other one, I flick it a few times because Micah would never let me get too comfortable. Torturing me with the delicious balance of pleasure and pain.

Biting my lip to keep the volume of my moans down, I let my fingers find their way down my stomach and into my shorts. Pushing my panties to the side, I'm already wet for him.

If this were him, he'd take his time swirling his finger around my clit, making me dizzy with need before finally slipping at least two fingers inside of me. The sounds of my wetness fill the room, and I sink farther into the couch, pressing my feet into the cushions to keep myself grounded.

This isn't enough. It's good, damn good, but I need him. I need the flat of his tongue against my clit and the weight of his fingers inside me.

The pressure of my thumb forces a guttural groan from me at the same exact time the door swings open.

I freeze in place, my hands still in my shorts and my nipples exposed.

Fuck. I don't have to lift my head to know Micah is staring at my mostly naked body, fully aware of what I was doing. Why didn't I bring a damn blanket out here so I could at least cover up?

I hear the sounds of his heavy footsteps heading my way, but instead of approaching me, they pass me. A bag hits the kitchen counter and the fridge opens. I stay as still as possible, not wanting to bring the slightest bit of attention to myself while Micah opens what sounds like a bottle of soda.

"Don't stop on my account. Good night," he says, his footsteps retreating to his room.

What. The. Fuck?

I slip my fingers out and put my panties and shirt back in place. I'm frozen.

I want to go back to my room. But if I do that, he'll know what I'm doing and that doesn't sit right with me, even though it shouldn't matter because he's already been given a show.

This was supposed to take some of the pressure off, but now I've made it worse. And to top it all off, I'm left here frustrated and unsatisfied.

My breath hitches when Micah's door opens again. I silently beg him to put me out of my misery and stay in his room for the rest of the night, but his footsteps continue growing louder, more focused.

"What do you want, Dani?" he asks in a husky voice.

I look up at him and the ravenous look on his face has me clenching my core. "What do you mean?" My voice quivers.

"Do you want to come?"

I bite my lip. I desperately do.

"Answer me, Storm," he barks.

"Yes."

He sinks to his knees behind me, his lips resting on the shell of my ear. "Then put your fingers back inside your pretty little pussy and start again."

Just the sound of his voice when he's like this has me close. I lift my hips off the couch so I can pull my shorts and panties down. I want him to see what he's doing to me.

"Shirt too," he demands.

I lift the tank top over my head and throw it across the room.

"Good. Now, what are you waiting for? Make yourself come, Dani."

My fingers slip inside my pussy again, and this time I add a third, trying to stretch myself the way he would. I pump my fingers in and out, alternating between fast and slow strokes.

He makes a *tsk* sound in my ear, and I bite my lip until it almost bleeds. "Is that how I would do it, Dani?"

Oh fuck.

"Is that how I would fuck you?"

No. He'd make me fuck him back. Slamming my pussy down on his fingers or his face, taking as much as I was being given. "No," I whimper.

"Then do it right or don't do it at all."

I swirl my hips around in circles, lifting them off the couch again to meet my fingers, thrust for thrust.

"How does it feel?" he asks.

"Good. So good," I say in between pants.

He stands up and my breath catches in my throat at the thought of him leaving me, but then he walks around the couch so that he has a front-row view of my dripping pussy. "We can do better than that, can't we?"

God, yes, we can. I nod. I want him to touch me. I want my fingers replaced with his. I want the softness of his lips and the roughness of his beard. I want the curve of his dick.

Shit. My head flies back to the arm of the couch.

The couch dips and I look up to see Micah kneeling between my legs staring with laser-like focus. I made fun of this ridiculously long couch when we first checked in, but now I'm thankful for it. I throw my feet behind his hips, hoping I can tempt him to fall into me.

As if punishing me, he holds firm, watching but never touching.

"What's taking so long, Dani? If this were me, you'd have come twice by now. Maybe you need a reminder of how I fuck you."

"Yes!" I scream. Yes, please.

His laugh is sinister. "You're not ready for that. You'll have to do this by yourself."

I groan my frustration, but I'm so close it turns into a whimper.

"I'm tired of waiting. Come, Dani. Now."

I fall apart at his assertiveness, letting out a low-pitched scream as I come crashing back down to the ground. When I can finally bring myself to open my eyes, he's still kneeling between my legs, his fists clenched tightly against his thighs.

"You know what to do now," he says.

Licking my lips, I pull out my fingers and make a trail up my body with the remnants of my release. Micah watches with hungry eyes, tightening his fists to the point of pain when I swirl my release around my nipple.

He stands from the couch and gives me a long kiss on my forehead. "Good night, my little thunderstorm."

"Wait," I call out, my voice weak.

"What?"

"You're just gonna leave me like this?" My voice is pleading with him.

"You're a greedy girl, aren't you?"

My chest heaves with need. This alone will fuel my dreams for nights to come, but I want him to touch me. I need him to fall apart in front of me. "I wouldn't say greedy. You're not even gonna clean me up?"

His fingers twitch by his side and when he walks toward me, I feel victory coming my way.

He once again sinks to his knees, this time beside me. My stomach clenches when I feel the hot air from his breath against my waist.

"You're greedy, Dani." His tongue touches my belly and follows the trail I created up my body, teasing my nipple just barely enough to wipe away the evidence. He makes a show of swallowing the proof, planting his hands on both sides of me. "And greedy girls don't get their way."

I was wrong. So very wrong.

I thought giving in to my sexual desires for Micah would ease some of the pressure and make it possible for me to focus again. It's only made me more feral.

He's had a smug grin on his face since we left the hotel to go see our new house, and I've never wanted to slap him more.

And then maybe slap my pussy in his mouth.

Before I can let that happen again, we have to have a conversation. I need to make sure he understands exactly what's on the table.

But that's a problem for later. Right now, we have a house to investigate.

As promised, there's a crew here working on the HVAC system, so it's noisy and hot inside, but it doesn't take away from the vision.

Roger picked a perfect place for Tanya. Original wood doors, four floors of spacious, grand living space, the exact type of dramatic light fixtures Tanya loves. She just wasn't the right woman to live here.

"What are we gonna do with a house all the way in Chicago?" I whisper to myself.

Micah lays his hand atop my shoulder, heat radiating from his skin. "We don't have to have all the answers right now."

Yes, but it would be nice to have any sort of answer to any question swirling around my mind right now.

We take our time, going through the house and taking pictures so that we don't have to rely on our memory once we're back in Baltimore. I keep trying to think of what we could do with it, and nothing comes to mind. It doesn't seem like Tanya wants us to sell it, but what the hell else would we do?

Micah slaps my shoulder every time he says he can feel me asking that question. Ass.

The primary bathroom has its own linen closet and inside there are two suitcases.

If no one has lived here since Roger bought it, what are they doing here? Micah helps me pull them out and open them. Each suitcase has one item in it, a snowsuit. One with my name on it, the other with Micah's.

"I know Chicago gets cold, but I don't think we're gonna need these here."

When Micah unfolds his snowsuit, our next clue comes tumbling out.

Chapter Seventeen

Micah

"In spite of all the ugliness, there's so much joy to have and so little time to experience it. Don't waste time." —Tanya

THE CLUE TANYA LEFT FOR US ISN'T MUCH OF A CLUE at all. Snowsuits and a note about not wasting time. It doesn't narrow down the options nearly enough.

Dani paces, occasionally staring back at the two open suitcases.

After last night, I want nothing more than to sink deep inside of her. It's all I could think about when I went back to my room, and all I've been thinking about since we left the hotel. But I don't want to push her too far. When I tried to get close, she backed away. There's some part of her that's still hesitant to take the plunge, even though her body responds positively to me.

I only want to give her what she's ready for.

There's so much joy to have and so little time to experience it. My mind keeps going back to that particular sentence. But why?

Joy.

Joy.

Joy.

A memory of a map in Tanya's house comes to mind. That's it!

"I have an idea," I say, causing her to stop pacing and turn to me with her hands on her hips.

"I'm all ears."

"We need Bailey."

When I call Bailey and tell her what my thoughts are, she hangs up and calls me back once she reaches Tanya's house.

"Okay, so what do you need me to find?" she asks.

Tanya has a map of the United States hanging in her office upstairs. It has pins all over it and instead of reading "United States of America" above it, it reads "United States of Joy." I always assumed that the pins represented places she's visited.

Once Bailey has found it, I ask her to turn on her camera.

"Is there anything that stands out to you about the pins?"

She squints her eyes as she looks it over. "Ooh, yes! So all the pins are gold, but there's one that's blue."

"Where's that pin go to?" Dani chimes in.

"Mmm, looks like Colorado." She takes the pin out of the wall. "Hold on, I think I found something." She puts the phone down, but we hear wrestling noises and tearing before we see her face again. "What would you do without me?" She beams.

"That depends. What'd you find, Franky?"

"When I pulled the pin out, I could tell it was stuck in something underneath, so I took the map off the wall. Ripped it a little, sorry. And look what I found?" She holds up a coaster with a logo for a cabin in Ouray, Colorado.

"We'd be so lost without you, Bailey." Dani bows down to her.

"You would," she agrees.

Next stop: Ouray.

Tanya really knows how to pick her vacation spots.

"This is a beautiful area," Dani says, admiring the gorgeous mountain views from the car window.

"It is." It has nothing on Dani, but it's beautiful all the same. Every location has been more breathtaking than the last.

"But do you think we'll run into bears? I've heard bears are an issue out here."

We get out of the car, and she looks around hurriedly as if a bear is going to run out of the woods straight for her. She is so cute.

"I think we'll be okay."

We go to the main cabin to check in and are greeted by a woman with honey-brown skin and blue curly hair. A goldendoodle perks its ears up from its bed and a white and brown cat looks unbothered from atop the desk.

"Welcome, welcome. How can I help you?"

We tell her our names, and she claps excitedly. "Oh, thank God. I was starting to think you guys were mythical creatures."

"I do think I was a mermaid in a past life, but what do you mean?" Dani questions.

"Oh, I like you. The gentleman who called to book your cabin didn't have firm dates, so they booked it for a few weeks."

Did Victor book the cabin right before Tanya died? Jesus.

"Shit," Dani curses under her breath. A moment later she plasters on a happy face. "Sorry to disappoint; we are real people."

The woman waves her off. "Eh, it's fine, I'll meet my dragon one day. So, welcome to Black Creek Pines, soon to be your favorite cabin in Ouray. I'm Yara Andrews. I'm the manager." The cat lifts its head to hiss then goes back to sleep. "Along with my co-managers, Gingersnap

Josephine." She gestures to the cat. "And Jellybean Theodora." She waves down to the goldendoodle, who has now decided it's time to greet us. She stretches off her bed and cozies up to Dani first, then me before coming back with a toy and pushing it into Dani's hand. "Throw that thing at your own risk. She could play fetch for hours."

Dani shrugs. "I'm easy." She walks back outside with Jellybean and starts throwing the toy repeatedly.

"Just so you know, we also call Jellybean Mrs. Steal Your Girl, but it's never happened that fast."

"Oh, I'm not worried." I've waited this long for Dani, I can definitely outlast a dog.

"Says a doomed man." Yara goes through the process of checking us in and informing me of everything there is to know about the cabin, including the possibility of snow today, but they're not expecting much. She suggests we either head back to town to get groceries just in case or provide her a list so she can do it.

Dani opens the door, and Jellybean runs inside chasing her tail until she eventually flops back down on her bed.

"You actually wore her out?"

"I promised her I'd throw more later."

"Ah, well, she does hold a grudge, so you have to keep your promise."

"Scout's honor," Dani swears with the complete wrong fingers up.

Yara laughs. "Okay, well, before you go, I forgot I'm supposed to give this to you when you check in." She slides a letter across the desk, our names on the front of the envelope.

"Thanks, Yara."

She salutes us on the way out.

Our rental isn't far from the main cabin, but it's too long of a walk with all our bags, so I drive the car up, handing Dani the letter. The moment we get inside the cabin, she tears open the envelope.

Hello, my loves,

Welcome to Ouray!

I'm simply too tired to make another video. I hope you understand.

I admit, there's no secret house, baby, or family here. There isn't anything to find or learn about me. This place was mine and George's dream vacation. We were both used to southern heat, and we wanted to feel snow on our tongues and drink hot chocolate by a fire.

We didn't get a chance to come here together, but I did come alone. I wanted you to experience the peace this place brought me. Enjoy it, together, for me.

If there's a place you dream of going, don't wait. If there's a place that brings you peace, go there.

Don't wait for life to pass you by.

Love you deeply,
Tanya

"Wow. I guess this is the end of the road." Dani sighs.

"I guess so." I don't want it to be. I want it to be the start of something real, but that's up to her.

"I gotta admit, I was skeptical at first. And there were times she ripped the rug out from under us. Most times, really. But I had fun."

"Me too." I think the things we learned about Tanya are going to make her gala even more special. I drop Dani's suitcase on her bed and turn to leave for the second bedroom in the cabin.

Dani grabs my arm. "Micah, wait."

I stop. Not wanting to face her, afraid that looking her in the eye right now might push her away from where I hope she's going.

"Are we gonna talk about it?" she continues, dropping my arm.

"Talk about what?" She's going to have to spell it out for me.

"What happened in Chicago?"

I step toward her, noting the shiver that slides down her spine. "What happened in Chicago that you wanna talk about, Dani?"

She puts her hand on my hips. "You're so fucking annoying."

"And you're so used to not saying what you really want to say."

I take another step toward her, and she steps back like she did in Chicago. But this time, she reaches for me as she does it. When I take another step forward, her eyes start to soften. We continue this little dance until I have her backed against the window.

"Say what you want."

"You. I want you."

My nose flares, a deep rumble vibrating from my chest. "You want me to what?"

"I want you to fuck me."

It's a start. Before I can think too deeply about what she didn't say, I crash my lips down onto hers. Her mouth immediately opens to welcome my tongue.

She moans into my mouth when I grab two fistfuls of her ass, pulling her up enough so she can wrap her legs around me.

The evidence of my need for her pokes her stomach and she slides a hand between our bodies to wrap around it.

"Ah, shit," I hiss when she tugs from base to tip.

"Put me down so I—" She stops midsentence and her whole face changes. Her eyes become unfocused and her head lolls to the side.

"Dani?"

"Put-put me down." The way she says it this time does not sound full of sexy promises. I set her on the bed and she puts her head between her legs.

"Talk to me, what's wrong?" All the fire and need drain from my body, concern for her the only thing on my heart.

"Nothing, it was just a head rush." She stands up and immediately wobbles before pushing past me and running to the bathroom just in time to empty the contents of her stomach.

Altitude sickness.

The mountains have sent my girl into a tailspin.

She's spent the last six hours puking her guts out, while I've been helpless to do anything but rub her back and force-feed her toast.

The worst part is, we can't even go to a lower altitude because we were hit by a much more severe snowstorm than Yara expected. Thank God, she brought us some essentials before it got too bad.

"You gotta drink this water, Dani." I urge her to sit up.

"Nooo," she whines. She mumbles something incoherent under her breath.

"What'd you say?" If she's slurring her words, I'm even more concerned.

She groans. "I didn't mean to say that out loud."

"What did you say?"

"I said, 'You're okay, you're fine, everything's fine.' It's my motto."

I nod. "When you're feeling better, maybe you'll tell me more about it?"

Her eyes are bloodshot from all the puking, but they still sparkle with a smile. "Maybe I will."

"Good. In the meantime, Google says staying hydrated helps with altitude sickness," I insist.

She tells me and Google to fuck off, which is too funny to me. "Micah, please. Save yourself. Leave me here to rot."

"You're so dramatic. I'm not leaving you."

"I wouldn't blame you if you did. I'm probably in desperate need of What That Mouthwash Do? right now."

When I met Dani, the extent of her modeling catalogue was a toothpaste commercial for a brand not well-known called Plaque Where?

What That Mouthwash Do? was a brand Dani came up with that night that we definitely should've sold to the Plaque Where? conglomerate.

We both laugh at the old joke from that night, but the sudden movement seems to make her stomach lurch. At this point, I don't think she has anything left in her system to throw up.

"Come here." I motion for her to lay her head in my lap and she does. "You're okay. You're fine. Everything's fine. I got you," I say in a low voice.

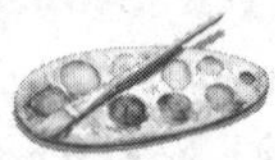

It takes three days for the snow to melt enough for us to venture out of our cabin. Yara's essentials were a lifesaver, but it'll be nice to go out today and get other things.

Dani's doing better, no sign of vomiting or dizziness.

I go outside to investigate the snow while she's in the shower. When she's done, she joins me outside.

"You sure you're feeling okay? Want more toast?"

"If I never see another piece of toast again, it'll be too soon," she says. "No, I drank an entire bottle of mouthwash and brushed my teeth a million times, so I feel better. And thank you for taking care of me."

It's my pleasure. "You're welcome."

Our investigation shows us that while we can leave our cabin, there's still too much snow and ice to drive down the mountain. We're stuck.

As we're walking back, Yara pulls up beside us on a snowmobile. The light brown skin you can see under her snow gear is slightly reddened from the cold. Her blue curls poke out from under her helmet.

"Hey, Yara."

"Hey, y'all. Do you guys have enough food? The roads are gonna be trouble for at least one more day, so I'm checking on all the guests. I can get to the store for any emergencies."

We take Yara up on her offer and give her a small list.

"And tell Jellybean I haven't forgotten about her," Dani says.

"I did tell her you were sick, but toy throwing waits for no one, so you can expect some attitude when you see her again."

"I deserve that." She giggles.

As we're walking back to the cabin, a rustle in the nearby trees catches our attention.

"Is that a bear?" Dani whisper-shouts.

"It's not a bear, Dani," I say. At least, I don't think so.

The trees rustle again and none other than a black bear steps out into the clearing.

"It's a fucking bear!" She grabs my wrist to haul ass back to the cabin, but I stand firm.

"Don't run! It'll think it should chase us."

We're having a stare-off with a fucking bear.

"I'm pretty sure that's just for dogs."

I look at her and she looks at me, neither of us sure who's right.

"Fuck it," we say in unison, running for our lives back to the cabin.

When we slam the door shut behind us, we're both out of breath from running and laughing. She slides down the door to the floor as I double-check each and every lock.

"A bear almost had you for lunch," she says around a gulp of air.

"Me? It looked like it had room for both of us."

"Yeah, but I beat you back. Therefore, he would've gotten you, not me."

I balk. "Because I stayed behind you for protection."

"Your first mistake," she clarifies.

Unable to resist anymore, I grab her face between my hands, planting a deep kiss on her lips. I don't want to let her go, but when I do, she raises her fingers to her lips, as if committing the feel of my lips on hers to memory.

Glad I'm not the only one affected.

We wait for Yara to get back with the groceries and then we drink hot chocolate by the fireplace in our room.

I open the window so we can watch the night sky, too.

"Life's little moments," I whisper.

She looks up at me, grin as wide as can be. "Life's little moments."

Her phone pings and when she leans over to check it, her whole body goes stiff.

"Storm? You okay?"

Her hand was warm moments ago, but now it's slick with sweat.

"Yeah, I'm fine," she lies.

I know by now when she's truly fine and when she's holding everything inside. "Dani. You don't have to be fine with me."

Her eyes search for something in mine. I face her stare head-on to convey to her that I'll do anything to give her whatever she's looking for.

She scoots her back and grabs my hand. "That ping was someone sending me an article about a man I used to know."

"Okay," I say, void of any emotion for fear of fucking up.

"His name is Nigel Pierce. He owns a modeling agency. He's not a good guy."

"I figured that." My fist clenches involuntarily.

"When I was younger, he demanded things of me. Things I didn't want to give him, but he told me it was the only way to secure my future. I was scared after my first agent had screwed me over and taken all my money. I couldn't start over. I thought it would kill me. And he held all the realms of possibility in the palm of his hand." She looks as though she might be sick all over again, but she pushes it down.

"You did what you thought you had to." It's not a question. It's an escape. I'm trying to release her from the prison she's undeservedly put herself in.

She shakes her head. "I didn't do it. He got a phone call, and I took that as a sign to run like hell. I think I'm more embarrassed at the fact that I would've done it. I was so desperate I would've given up such a large part of myself to hold on to an industry that didn't give a fuck about me. I spent the rest of my time in New York constantly looking over my shoulder, worried that he'd corner me again or that I'd run into someone else like him. Even when I became a big name, that fear still kept a grip on me."

"Men like him should be embarrassed, not you. He took advantage of someone he was supposed to look out for. That makes him weak."

"But I didn't say anything," she croaks. "Nothing happened, so I didn't think there was anything I could say that would stop him. How many other girls suffered because of my silence? That article? It was about him and a newer model he's taken under his wing. What does that even mean? He doesn't have wings, he has talons and they are deadly. My silence left him free to continue abusing his power."

"That's not on you. That's on him being a predator." Although I would like to find a way to get whoever this new model is far away from him.

Once I get Dani settled to sleep, I hit up Rome asking him to help me locate a certain Nigel Pierce.

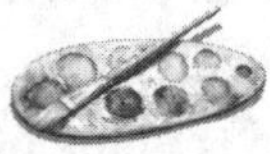

"I'm thinking we should put those snowsuits to use," Dani says as we look out the window at the row of cabins that are much clearer to see than they were yesterday. She seems clearer as well. Her confession about Nigel last night left her bone-tired, but she seems to be in better spirits.

"What do you wanna do?" I ask.

"Let's go skiing."

"Do you know how?" I ask, genuinely curious.

She glares at me. "Now why would you ask me a question like that?"

I shake my head with my mouth pursed.

The answer is no. Dani cannot ski. Eventually, we switch to snow-tubing since she's spending most of her time on her butt anyway, but her smile never dims. This is a look I could get used to.

When we climb back up the hill for another round, Dani sits between my legs on the snowtube. We've been riding together without issue, but this time is different. This time, we pick up more speed and when we hit the peak of the slope we catch air, separating us from the tube.

"Oh, shit!" Dani screams as I reach out to grab ahold of her. Our bodies roll until Dani lands right on top of me in an embankment of snow at the bottom of the hill.

"Jesus. I saw my life flash before my eyes," Dani pants. We fall into a fit of laughter. Only we would have a near-death experience on a damn snowtube.

The longer our bodies stay entangled, the more our laughs quiet down. Our breaths mingle and our eyes lock. One minute, my gaze rises to her lips, the next our lips are colliding into each other. She sucks my tongue into her mouth, moaning when I bite down on her bottom lip.

"Micah?"

"Yes, Storm?"

"Take me home and fuck me."

My fucking pleasure. I roll her onto her back so I can stand and pick her up.

The drive back to the cabin is a blur and when we get inside, all bets are off. Somewhere between the front door and the bedroom, the boots, snowsuits, and gloves get left behind.

Dani presses me against the wall and rubs her palm against my dick. I groan in her ear, firmly rubbing my hands along her sides, determined to let her set the pace.

"If you want something, Storm, come and get it."

She slides her hand up to the waistband of my briefs and pulls.

I'm happy to oblige her needs. I push her onto the bed and rip the rest of our clothes off. She grips me tightly in her hand, rubbing circles around the tip with her thumb.

My low, rumbling groans turn into a full-blown growl when she slides my dick between the warmth of her lips.

"Fuck, Dani." I tilt my head to the sky, slipping my dick free of her mouth. "Not yet."

I bend down to take her ear between my teeth and tug. Slipping my hand under her side, I flip her onto her stomach.

"You gonna be okay like this?" I ask, squeezing her ass with all the final threads of restraint I have.

"I'm good."

That's all I need to hear. I press down on the small of her back, forcing her head farther into the sheets, and her ass lifts even higher.

I swipe my finger at her clit, then slowly trail it down to her entrance. One finger slips inside of her, quickly followed by two more.

She cries out into the ether, as her body starts rocking back and forth. My greedy girl.

I crook my fingers inside her, trying to drive her as crazy as she drives me. "I want one on my hand and one on my tongue before I give you this dick. You understand me, Dani?"

"I want it all," she mewls.

"You'll get it." *I'll give you anything you want.*

She rocks back to meet the force of my palm, so I ease the pressure, letting her take the lead. But when she lurches forward, mewling about how she feels me everywhere, I slap her pussy to make her come back to me.

"I'm gonna come," she cries out.

"Let me hear it," I command.

"Micah!" she screams my name as her orgasm overpowers us. I love that sound. I've missed that sound. I don't ever want to be without it again. I don't ever want to be without her again.

"Keep saying my name like a prayer, baby. I just wanna be your blessing."

She screams my name again and again until her throat is dry.

I don't give her any time to recover. I loop my arms around her thighs and pull her pussy back to meet my tongue. The flat of my tongue laps her up while my arms keep her body locked in place when her legs start to shake.

"Not you shakin' already. I'm not done with you yet."

"I can take it," she says, knowing damn well I'll make her pay for that.

"You sure about that, Storm?"

Reaching back without responding, she grabs both of her cheeks and pulls up, giving me more access. Challenge accepted. I latch onto her clit and suck her into my mouth.

I'm relentless in my carnal pursuits and she's right there with me.

She bites down on her pillow to keep the scream to a minimum when another orgasm comes for her. I'm drowning in her release, but I don't shy away. I want more of it. I soak up everything she has to give me and when I'm sure there's nothing left, I run my tongue up her spine with her wetness dripping from my beard.

That is one hell of a thunderstorm.

I slowly sink into the bed, careful not to let exhaustion take over. I haven't had the main course yet.

She hops from the bed and starts rummaging through her bag, fishing out a condom before doubling back and getting a whole strip.

She's wanted this as much as I have. Good to know.

She climbs onto my lap, pushing on my chest until I give in and lie flat on the bed.

The ravenous look in her eyes dissipates a bit when she sees something else in mine.

"Micah, you do understand this is all I can give you, right?"

My eyes darken. "Yes, Storm. I understand."

"Do you really? Because I know you want me—"

I cut her off. "I don't want you."

She jumps back, but I grab her hips to keep her in place.

"I don't want you, Dani. I crave you. I crave everything you'll allow me to have. Please don't deny me."

A storm brews in her eyes as she slips the condom down my length and then crawls up my body until I meet her entrance. I grab her by the back of the neck and pull her into a hungry kiss as she sinks down on my dick.

We moan into each other's mouths once she's fully seated, taking a moment to relish how good we feel together.

This part is always good for us. This part is all she's saying she can do? Then let's make it our best.

She claws at my chest as she rotates her hips. I'm mesmerized by the sight of our bodies connecting. Needing control, I lean up to thrust into her. She bites the side of my neck, so I grab a fistful of her hair to pull her back, sucking one of her nipples into my mouth.

Her eyes roll in the back of her head, her hand moving between us to rub circles around her clit.

"Oh fuck!" she screams, letting the waves of pleasure wash over her.

I stay with her while she rides out the wave, but I feel my release coming so I slap and squeeze her ass again.

"I'm gonna come, baby. Where do you want it?"

She throws her leg off me, so she can stand and rip the condom off. Sinking to her knees before me, she presents her body like an offering at my altar.

"Paint me with it."

Fuck, she is sin incarnate.

Sliding my hand up and down, eyes never leaving hers, I demand more from her. "Open."

The moment she does, the threads of my release hit her tongue, neck, and breasts, painting a picture of our passion.

Chapter Eighteen

Micah

I find myself at Victor's office, hoping to get some clarity.

Being home doesn't feel right.

There should be more. While I couldn't be happier with how things went in Colorado, Tanya's scavenger hunt feels . . . unfinished.

Everything we've learned, everything we've seen, all that to end with a mini vacation? It just doesn't seem like how she would end things.

Maybe she ran out of time. Maybe the illness made it so she couldn't finish it the way she wanted to.

"Micah, come on in," Victor says, walking around his desk and greeting me with a handshake.

"How's it going, Victor?"

"Just fine. Have a seat," he instructs, lightly running his fingers over the glass-covered rose on his bookshelf as he takes a seat. "Something on your mind?"

A lot of things. "I'm just—I'm trying to understand, I guess."

"Understand what?"

"Why the ending of Tanya's quest feels so sudden. Are you sure there weren't any other clues for us to follow? Any more videos to watch?"

He leans back in his chair, tapping his fingers along the top of his desk. "Care for a game of chess?" he asks.

Confused, I agree, watching as he pulls out a wooden chessboard that looks awfully similar to the one in Tanya's home.

He glances at me as he sets the pieces up on the board. "I've given you every clue I had to give you."

He doesn't say there aren't any more clues, just that he's given us all the ones he had to give us. Did we miss something in Colorado?

"Do you think that maybe you just didn't want it to end? No matter the circumstance, it must've been nice hearing her voice again."

Well, of course part of me wants to continue in the hopes that we'll get one last video message from Tanya. One final chance to see her face and hear her voice. But that's not the reason I feel unsettled. My gut is telling me this isn't over. Victor knows more than he's letting on, but I suppose it's not time for me to know.

"Did she leave any videos for you?" I'm not sure why I ask or even if I should, but I find myself more curious about Victor and Tanya's relationship.

He takes his move, the ghost of a smile on his face. "She left me one."

"And how many times have you watched it?" I consider my options carefully before deciding to move one of my pawns.

He opts to castle kingside, which leaves me reconsidering my approach. "More times than I can count," he says.

Right. "Does it help? Hearing her voice?"

He nods solemnly. "It does. But it helps more knowing she's at peace. At the end. It had been a tough road, but on the day she passed, it was like all the suffering ceased to exist. She was happy. Do you want to know what her last words were?"

My heart is beating out of my chest, waiting. Dani will want to hear them too. She'll be so happy to know Tanya wasn't alone in the end.

I tip my head forward. "Yes."

"She said, 'They're gonna be alright.'"

I won't make a liar out of you, Tanya.

After I beat Victor in two of our three games of chess, I leave.

I start to head to the gallery, but Bailey texts me that she won't be in today because she's having an MS day. On its face that's not concerning. Multiple sclerosis can rob you of the strength in your muscles. It does in Bailey's case, at least. It's been hard to see my baby sister go through this, but I've come to terms with the fact that sometimes the fatigue wins and she has to allow her body the time to rest.

Bailey's apartment is shrouded in darkness when I walk in. That's not surprising because she lives like a vampire most of the time, but the silence is off-putting.

Bailey can never sit in silence. The sounds of music or TV are always booming through the halls of her place. She usually has her AirPods in at the office so she can constantly listen to whatever playlist or podcast she wants. She can't even sleep without some kind of sound playing, so the overarching quiet doesn't sit right with me.

She's not on her couch, so I rush back to her bedroom, not even bothering with knocking before barging in.

"Now why the hell would you be sitting here like that?" Her weird ass is under the covers, sitting straight up with her arms folded across her chest.

"Because I knew your Papa Smurf head ass was gonna come over here, and I wanted to hear you coming. I was about to fall back asleep, so I'm glad you came when you did. I needed my bit to pay off." She pushes a button on her phone and a cover from Vitamin String Quartet starts playing through her speaker. I laugh when she turns over and pretends to snore.

"But forreal, you tired, sore, or both?"

She sighs. "I'm exhausted like no amount of sleep will fix it and my legs feel really heavy. But do not start doing the most. I just need to rest. I don't need you to do a damn thing."

"So you don't want the salad I got you from DiPasquale's?"

She blinks one eye open and sits up again. "Well, go on and get it. I can't, I'm simply too weak." She holds the back of her hand up to her forehead and sighs dramatically.

I grab a sweater off the chair in her room and launch it at her.

"You do know you don't have to come over every time I'm MSing, right?" she asks, not looking at me as she bites into a piece of eggplant from her salad. Not long after she was diagnosed, she started referring to having flare-ups as "MSing." She found that it was easier to explain her symptoms to us when she related them to PMS symptoms.

Of course I know I don't have to come over for every rough day, but she's my baby. I know she can take care of herself, but it's my job to protect her. She has a habit of not asking for help, so I like to see her face-to-face to know if she's being honest with me and herself about how she's feeling.

"I know, Franky. Pass me the remote." This is our normal routine when she has an MS day. I come over with food, she reminds me I don't have to do that while eating; I turn on *One Piece* for us to watch until she falls asleep; and then I clean around her house and take stock of things she needs so I can make a store run.

She tosses the remote at me, still chomping away at her salad. "Let's watch the Marineford Arc. I could use a good cry," she says around a mouthful.

I've seen all the episodes of *One Piece* only because I've been watching it since it came out in the nineties. Bailey hasn't because we tend to skip around, ignore some filler episodes entirely, and revisit her favorite arcs rather than progressing.

I settle into her swivel chair, which is probably the most comfortable chair I've ever sat on, and she moves the remnants of her salad over to her nightstand, sinking deeper into bed.

I expect her to audibly sigh when Ace meets Shanks the way she does every time we watch these episodes, but she doesn't. Instead, she's watching me warily.

"You good?" I pause the TV.

"Why didn't you tell Dani about my MS?"

The question knocks me so off guard, I have to blink slowly to process. "Wait, what?"

She pushes herself up farther, flopping her hands in her lap. "Why didn't you ever tell Dani about my MS? Weren't you two dating or whatever when the signs first started showing?"

All those years ago, when Bailey's symptoms were—rightfully so—scaring the shit out of her, I made the decision to come home from New York and help her find out what was going on.

I didn't tell Dani because I didn't know what to say. I was scared too. We didn't know what was going on with Bailey, why her legs were failing her at random times and why her vision kept getting drastically worse, and the doctors we went to either couldn't figure it out or didn't care to listen to her complaints.

Our mom and dad wanted to drop everything to take care of her. Our mom was ready to walk away from the daycare center she dedicated her life to in order to spend every minute of every day running Bailey back and forth to different hospitals. When she wasn't doing that, she was helping our dad, who had injured his knee badly at work and needed surgery and then months of physical therapy.

I couldn't let my mom give up the center and watch her and Bailey stretch themselves thin, so I took over. I moved Bailey in with me to keep an eye on her. I took her to doctor after doctor, fighting with everyone who tried to turn us away. I stayed up all hours of the night, letting Bailey cry on my shoulders because she thought her dreams of becoming a dancer were being stripped away.

And through all of that, it never seemed right to tell Dani what was going on. With her, I felt pure bliss. Long distance was challenging, confined to mere phone calls and texts, and I didn't want to spend what little time we had drowning her in my fears.

By the time Bailey was diagnosed, Dani had long removed herself from my life. It's been weeks since Dani learned about Bailey's MS and I had no idea Bailey was harboring these emotions, but I feel awful.

I tell Bailey all this and her posture relaxes with every word.

"That makes sense," she says.

"Did you think I was embarrassed of you or some shit?" I ask incredulously.

"A little." She shrugs when I balk at the ridiculous suggestion. "I mean I remember you telling me about Dani. You never said as much, but you had it bad. I've never seen you like that. You were prepared to move to New York just to give the two of you a real shot and I remember being jealous that I wasn't gonna see my brother every day. And when you came home, you talked about her less and less, then not at all. You never told me why things ended between you, but I was sad because you had been doing so much for me, and then you lost the thing that was just for you."

I never told her because I didn't want her to blame herself. It wasn't her fault, or Dani's. It was mine.

"Part of me was mad at her because I thought she left you when you really needed someone on your side, but when she looked so lost after I brought up my MS, I was mad at you. I thought you were trying to hide it from her."

"Bailey, I'm not embarrassed of you or your MS. It's simply a part of what makes you, you. I was just scared back then." To be honest, I'm still scared. She's been in remission for a while and her treatment seems to be slowing the progression of the disease, but still, it's unpredictable. It looks different for everyone, so there's no way to tell what this disease will look like for her years from now. The uncertainty terrifies me more than the disease itself.

"Okay," she says. "Good. That makes me feel better."

"You have nothing to worry about. At least not about that, because I *am* embarrassed of that big ass head you carry around. How's that thing even stay on your shoulders?" I smack her forehead the way I used to when she was younger.

She smacks my hand with a chuckle. "Fuck you. At least my eyebrows don't make me look like Krillin."

"Nah, you're just giving Temu Rihanna in the forehead."

"Temu?!" she screeches.

We roast each other some more until she starts getting sleepy, so I fix her some tea and resume our episode of *One Piece.*

When she falls asleep, I pull myself out of my chair to start cleaning.

"Hey, Chopper?" Bailey calls. Her eyes are closed and her voice is dreamlike.

"Yeah, Franky?"

"I like Dani a lot." She murmurs something else I can't understand and then fades back to sleep.

Me too, sis. Me too.

Me: Can I come over?

Dani: Absolutely

I'm pleasantly surprised by Dani's response. It's one thing to spend time together, just the two of us, when we're in a different state where nobody knows us, but it's something different when we're home. It's a step in the direction of everything I've been wanting.

She's made it very clear where she stands: she's only willing to give me her body, so I'm prepared to meet her where she's at. Tonight, however, I'm only after one thing: her friendship.

After spending the afternoon with Bailey, I want to get a few things off my chest and clear the air. I hope Dani's willing to give me that.

She opens her door in a silk pajama dress that accentuates her every curve. She was definitely looking for more benefits, less friendship tonight.

"Come inside," she says, her voice heavy with implications.

I accept the sultry kiss she plants on my lips, but I stop her from lifting my shirt.

"What's wrong?" she asks.

My eyes flit to the sight of her hip beneath the slit of her nightgown before I catch myself. "Nothing. I was hoping we could talk."

"Talk?" She clenches her nails into her palms, a telltale sign that she's nervous, and takes a slight step back. "About what?"

I take her hands in mine to keep her from retreating any further, hoping like hell rubbing my thumbs against her palms calms her. "I could use a friend."

I tell her how Bailey was upset with me for never telling her about the MS and Dani's eyes widen before softening to glassy pools. "We're gonna need some tequila."

She guides me to her couch before disappearing into the kitchen and returning with a bottle of Promesa and two glasses. She runs back to the kitchen for two cans of ginger ale and passes me one.

"You think I need a chaser?" I joke.

She coughs around a laugh and holds up her hands. "It's called being a good hostess. I was just giving options."

"Mhm," I say in disbelief. "When it comes to you, I don't need a chaser."

She crosses one leg over the other. "You mean when it comes to my tequila?"

"I mean what I said."

Leaning forward, she holds her glass toward me. "Cheers to that."

"Cheers to that." I clink my glass against hers, getting lost in her eyes as I down the shot. That is damn good tequila. I've been a fan of her brand since she launched it, but it's nice to actually share a glass with her now. "Who would've thought the woman who once gagged and cried over this stuff would go on to make the best tequila I've ever had."

Her fingers trace the rim of her glass. It's a risk, bringing up our past. The last thing I want is for her to shut down on me. I know we're different people now, but our history shouldn't be this unapproachable subject. I want to be with the woman she is now, but she was born from the woman she was then. She deserves acknowledgment.

Her resounding smile is all the payoff I need. "First of all, fuck you. I didn't gag or cry."

I tilt my head with pursed lips.

"Okay, fine. I did gag. Second of all, thank you. I'm glad you like it. So, tell me about Bailey."

With that, I launch into the full story, explaining why I disappeared on her all those years ago and apologizing. I tell her why Bailey was so upset that Dani didn't know, cringing as I remember the pained look on Bailey's face. I let it all out, and to Dani's credit she listens with rapt attention.

When I'm done, she finishes her drink, licking her lips as she sets her glass on the coffee table. "I, um, I don't really know what to say to that."

"It's a lot to digest, I know. But I don't wanna keep letting people down."

She sighs, looking away from me before granting me another glance. "I get that. For what it's worth, you didn't let me down. I've long since forgiven your disappearing act and I hope you can forgive me for mine."

It's worth a lot. Since Dani and I have come together this last time, I feel like I've been fighting an uphill battle with her. Being able to stop and catch my breath is a nice feeling. I hold my hand out for hers. "Forgiven."

She accepts, shaking it gently. "I think we've come a long way."

"Oh, we've definitely made progress. I've gone from your friend's husband's friend to your friend. I'm ecstatic."

She kicks her leg toward me, but I'm serious. When this all started weeks ago, I never thought we'd get to a place where we could even have a conversation without sinking into the quicksand of our insecurities.

"I'm happy too, I suppose. Are you and Bailey good now?"

"I think so." Everything seemed fine when I left her place, at least.

She holds the bottle toward me, waiting for confirmation before pouring another glass. "Have you ever considered group therapy?"

My head reels back. I can't say I was expecting that. "Group therapy? I haven't, why?"

"I looked into it. They have support groups for people with loved ones who have autoimmune diseases. It might be good for you to go and talk about Bailey."

I scoff. I'm not the one who lives with the disease, so why should I need to be consoled for it? "I don't know about that."

"Stopppp. I know what you're thinking. Seeking support isn't you trying to have a pity party. And it's not just about you. It's for Bailey too."

My brows furrow. "How so?"

"I think it might be good for you to learn how to support Bailey in a way that works for her, not yourself."

Ah, I see. She's saying I'm too overbearing. I know that I can be sometimes and I'm trying to work on that; it's just always been instinctively a part of me.

"Just think about it," she says in a rush. "I can send you a link for the ones I found."

"Okay. I will. Thanks."

She pulls her phone out immediately and mine pings a moment later. She's really given this some thought, and that makes my chest feel warm.

"Just out of curiosity, how long have you been researching these support groups?"

Her fingers hover above her phone before she slowly meets my eyes. "Since the day I met Bailey at Tanya's house and you two got into it."

I do my best to keep my emotions off my face, and when that fails, I take a long sip from my drink. Even before she was willing to open up to me, she still wanted to help. Things like that are what draw me to her flame.

She clears her throat and lowers her head before speaking. "I've, uh, I've been thinking about going back to therapy myself."

"I didn't know you had done therapy."

"Yeah, a while ago. The therapist I went to just wasn't a good fit for me, and I . . . well, I used that as an excuse to not find another one. But I think it's time to go back."

"Well, that's great. I'm proud of you for making that decision."

Her lips tilt up into a smile. "Thanks. When we were doing the scavenger hunt for Tanya, I just kept thinking, all the shit she went through, did she have anyone to talk to about it? Did she ever seek professional help or did she just deal with it on her own all those years? I feel like in a way she was telling me that it's okay to find someone to unburden myself to."

"I think you might be right," I agree.

We're gonna be alright, Tanya. We're gonna be just fine.

Chapter Nineteen

Dani

"Don't you fucking stop, Micah," I cry out, on the verge of ecstasy and hoping this time he'll let me grab it. My hips jerk with need when his fingers brush against my clit for the millionth time.

"You telling me what to do now, Storm?" He changes his pace, slowing his strokes so that I can get a taste of glory without giving me enough to reach it.

"Oh, fuck. Please, Micah, please."

"Which is it, Storm? Are you begging me or demanding me?"

This is the game we've been playing this morning. Him bringing me to the brink but never letting me fall off the edge. It's been tortuous and intoxicating at the same time.

"I'm begging you." I think. I can't even think straight anymore. My vision is hazy, but I can see him clearly. He looks like my judge, jury, and executioner, here to dole out punishment after mind-blowing punishment.

His hands roam my body, confusing my senses even more. I try to lift my ankles off his shoulders, but he grabs them to keep me in place.

"You sure about that? The right answer might make me let you come. Don't you wanna come, Dani?"

More than fucking anything. "Yes. God, yes," I pant.

"Final answer, then," he says as he pumps into me once more. "Begging or telling?"

Shit. I don't know what the right answer is, so I let my instincts take over. "I'm telling you. Make me fucking come. Now."

He wraps his arms around my thighs and fucks me into oblivion. When I fall over the edge, I can hear all the colors in the room. I clench the sheets beneath me into my fists as I scream his name.

He kisses my ankles as I come down from the high, shifting so that my legs lie in his lap after they start to shake.

"You okay?" he asks, leaning forward for a quick kiss while massaging my thighs and calves.

"I'm amazing." I let out a deep exhale. "So, 'telling' was the right answer, then?"

"Oh, the right answer was whatever you said. I just wanted to see which one you'd choose."

"Ass," I hiss halfheartedly.

He hums contentedly as his hands make their way to my sides to knead the skin there. "Roll your neck for me," he instructs, demonstrating the stretch he wants me to do.

I follow his directions, coming back into my body little by little.

Once I fully come down, he disposes of the condom in my bathroom, then grabs me some water and my bag of TruFru.

This has been the last couple of weeks for us. Nights of passion that bleed into the morning.

Silently, he holds his hand out for me, knowing I'll take it because we've done this so many times before. He knows where my shower cap is, the exact setting I like my shower, the temperature I like my towel warmer, and the playlist I like to project through the bathroom speakers. He knows because this is our routine. He fucks me like I'm his greatest enemy and then cares for me like a priceless piece of art.

He turns me so my back is to him and then grabs my African exfoliating net and starts scrubbing my body.

"How are you feeling about today?"

I'd been so engrossed in my pleasure, I forgot the reason the torture started this morning was to ease my nerves about my first therapy session today.

I'm definitely calmer than I was when I woke up, but I'm still scared. I'm scared of who I'll be without these walls to keep me safe, but I'm even more afraid that if I don't get help, these memories and emotions of everything I've suppressed over the years will crush me beneath their weight. Something has to change.

"I feel fine."

His hands stop, hovering just above my shoulders. "Actually fine? Or the 'fine' you tell people when you don't wanna talk about it?"

I hate when he clocks my tea. "The fine I tell people," I sigh.

He turns me around, running the net across my chest, staring straight into my soul. "Okay. At least you can admit that. It's going to work out, and if it doesn't, that's okay too."

I breathe in his words, letting them wash over me like cool rain as I watch him wash his own body.

He does his best to ignore the water streaming down my naked form, resolved to do nothing more than take care of me, but his hardened dick pressed against my stomach reminds us how well our bodies communicate. One more distraction wouldn't hurt, right?

"Storm . . ." he starts when I run the tip of my nail down his length.

"Yesss?" I sing.

Instead of answering, he reaches behind his back to switch the water off. He steps out first, grabbing my body oil spray from under the sink to coat my body in it. He kisses my wrists as he rubs the oil up my arms, my chest as he massages it over my breasts, and my stomach when he sinks to his knees to give my legs the same treatment.

When he stands to drape my towel over me, he gives me one final kiss on my forehead. "Let's get you ready."

I've never felt more turned on by a rejection in my life.

I get to Dr. Aria Goode's office fifteen minutes early, but I don't go inside until two minutes before my appointment.

The first thing that comes to mind when I step into her office is that it's bright. The walls are colored a bright and soft blue, the lights are blinding, and the furniture is a mixture of pastels and wooden accents.

I hate it.

The whole aesthetic feels like it was ripped straight out of a how-to guide for getting your clients to spill their guts.

Dr. Goode is dressed in a green sleeveless jumpsuit over a white dress shirt. Her megawatt smile sets off alarm bells in my head. Too friendly.

She motions for me to take a seat, and I dig my nails into my palm as I do.

"So, Danielle."

"Dani. It's just Dani," I correct.

She smiles. "Dani. How are you today?"

"I'm fine." One day, I hope to abolish that word from my vocabulary.

"That's great," she says.

"What's Goode with you, doc?" I outwardly cringe at the play on her name I'm sure she's heard a thousand times before.

To her credit, it doesn't faze her. "I'm good today. Thanks for asking."

I acknowledge her words with a nod and then the silence sets in. The silence goes on so long, I start to fidget in my seat, my sweater clinging to my neck with sweat.

"So, how does this work?" I ask. Do I start or does she?

"How do you want it to work?" she asks.

I inwardly sigh. Great, she's going to be one of those "How does that make you feel?" doctors. I'll be back to searching for a new therapist tonight.

"Aren't you supposed to tell me that?"

She crosses one leg over the other. "I'm not into cookie-cutter bullshit."

The nonchalance of her statement throws me for a loop. "I'm sorry, what?"

"I'm not here to tell you how your therapy should go. It's your session, so we take it at your pace. If you wanna sit here and stare at each other for an hour, we can do that. If you wanna talk, you can do that. If you want me to ask you some questions, I can do that. But I won't tell you which one you're supposed to choose. There's no right answer."

I might like her after all. "And what if I wanna sit here and stare at the wall for every session. That's okay?" I call her bluff.

"Again, it's your decision."

She seems so unbothered, the stubbornness in me can't help but test the theory. I plunge us into silence for fifteen minutes. And for fifteen minutes, she sits perfectly comfortable in her chair, not giving a fuck.

"I don't know where to start," I admit.

She sits up higher. "Well, why don't you tell me what you hope to get out of coming here?"

"So, start at the end and work my way backward?"

She smiles. "Something like that."

It all sounds so simple. I really hope it is.

In the end, we don't talk about the past at all. We talk mostly about where I want to go. What I'm hoping therapy can do for me. She doesn't make any false promises, which I appreciate. She doesn't even pressure me to book a second session, but I do the moment I leave.

I feel a bit lighter now that the first session is out of the way. I'm optimistic about Dr. Goode.

I force myself to call my mom and tell her about it, when really the person I want to call is Micah. That terrifies me. This is only supposed to be sex and friendship, but it feels dangerously close to the last time we were together. Maybe I should stop ignoring Omari's texts and meet up with him. I've only been seeing Micah and perhaps the unspoken exclusivity of that is fucking with my head. Yes, I should link up with Omari and let him fuck those thoughts right out of me.

When I pull up to my place, I pick up the phone to do just that, but reality stops me. No matter how much dick Omari throws me, my mind will be on Micah. He's wormed his way in there so deeply, it would take the jaws of life to get him out. I am fucked, and not in the way I prefer to be.

I have only a couple of hours to myself before everyone is due to come over and discuss their auction items for Tanya's gala, and I spend most of that time trying and failing to figure out how I'm going to take a step back from Micah.

He, of course, is the first to arrive. I've greeted him at my door plenty of times, but this time when he leans down to kiss my cheek, I turn away.

"Did you just curve me?" he asks around a laugh.

It was meant to be a step for self-preservation, but I hated myself the second I did it. It's so ridiculous, but I don't know what the fuck I'm doing when it comes to this man. I shrug. "Well, I don't know, that greeting was giving relationship, no?" More bullshit.

He hides it well, but there's a layer of hurt beneath the surface of his nonchalant facade.

I don't want to hurt him, but I don't know how else to keep myself safe. If I could speed up this therapy healing process, that would be fantastic.

"I'm well aware we're not in a relationship, Dani," he says, voice low and firm.

"I know you know, but—" I reach for his arms, falling short when he steps back. "No. Not 'but.' I overreacted. I'm sorry."

He studies me for a moment, eyes zeroing in on my hands plastered to my sides.

"Forgiven." He steps past me to get inside, lightly gripping my hip to keep me steady as he does. "How did it go today?"

I have to stop letting our sexual relationship interfere with our friendship. It's not fair to either of us.

Words from Tanya's letter spring to my mind: *You deserve all the good things. Grab them and hold on tight.*

After everything I've been through, I deserve a friendship like the one I have with Micah. And he deserves for me to give him the same effort.

"You know what, it was a good start. I'm actually excited to see her again," I admit.

He flashes a smile and then marches over to scoop me up into a hug. "That's amazing. I'm excited for you."

I squeeze his middle again. "Thank you. And remind me again why I scheduled therapy on the same day we gotta deal with our misfit crew?" I mean, not only will we have to deal with Christian and Evie's nonsense, but this will also be the first time I've seen Ri around Nelle since the wedding.

"Lack of foresight?" he teases.

I pinch the bridge of my nose. "They're gonna drive me to drink."

By the time Evie and Christian are done bickering and everyone stops holding their breath waiting for Arnold and Amerie to show, I'm on my second glass of wine.

We've managed to nail down most everyone's items:

Evie is going to make all the invites and the signage for the event, which is a huge help. Jalen is auctioning off private basketball coaching with him. Rome is auctioning off the chance to be a character in his studio's next game. Janelle is partnering with The Dahlia Resort to offer an all-expenses-paid trip for two.

"Okay, Christian, what are you auctioning off?" I say, ready to add his contribution to my Notes app.

A cheesy grin crosses his face and he clears his throat like he has a big reveal. "I'm gonna auction off a date."

"A date?" Janelle asks.

"Yeah. A date with me." He holds his head up high and I'm proud of myself for holding back my laughter.

Micah makes eye contact with me across the table and smirks.

Evie scoffs. "Christian, it's supposed to be something people would like, not a punishment."

He sucks his teeth. "Play your cards right, and I'll take you on a date after."

She gags, and the two of them start going at it again until Janelle cuts in and Jalen puts a calming hand on Evie's waist.

Micah's phone pings, and he reads the message out loud. "Ay, Arnold just texted and said him and Ri ain't coming."

"Obviously," Evie interrupts with what I guess she would call a whisper.

"He said he's gonna auction off a meet-and-greet with the Ravens and Ri is gonna auction off a custom-made dress, though."

Janelle chews on the inside of her cheek while Rome rolls his eyes.

I'm not surprised Arnold and Amerie didn't show their faces tonight. Things between Amerie and the girls are, at their worst, nonexistent, and at best, rocky. Plus, Micah told me that things got heated between the guys and Arnold in the last Baltimore Collective meeting earlier this week. Apparently, Arnold brought up the idea of selling one of his buildings to someone whose business practices directly go against what the Baltimore Collective stands for.

Rome let him have it for that one and they hadn't heard from him since.

I'm not willing to spend any time worrying about the two of them right now, though, so I end the meeting. Christian leaves, but everyone else stays for another drink before heading out.

Micah catches my eyes and winks at me as he goes.

Hours later, my phone ringing shocks me out of my sleep.

"Do you even know what time it is?" I ask once the audio call connects.

"Yeah, it's eleven o'clock. What are you, ninety-two?" Micah mocks.

Feels like it some days. "Sir, I am a child of the Lord and I'm in the bed rubbin' my feet together. Is that a problem?"

"What if I was calling to get some ass?"

I sit up in bed. "Get some ass? Who even says that?"

He laughs. "I thought it might resonate with your ninety-two-year-old spirit."

I force out an exaggerated yawn. "Boohoo. What are you calling Granny for?" If this really were a booty call, he wouldn't have called.

"Come take a ride with me." Seconds later, there's a knock on my door.

Well, shit. I consider pulling the covers over my head and ignoring him but dismiss the thought as quickly as it comes.

I drag my feet over to the door and yank it open. He's leaning against my doorway, looking like he's up to no good. He adjusts the skully on his head as he takes me in.

"Take a ride with you? Are you a teenager?"

"Don't get excited, cougar. My virtue is still intact."

I snort. "Ha, now that's a lie." That virtue was left behind in a cabin in Colorado. I look down at my sleep shorts and thin shirt. "Let me go change."

We've been driving around for thirty minutes. No destination in mind, windows down so the cool air kisses our skin, and Victoria Monét serving as our soundtrack.

I let my eyes fall shut and stick my arm out the window to let it fly with the wind.

"I like seeing you like this." His voice is quiet at first; it almost blends in with the sounds of the night.

My eyes pop open. "Like what?"

"Relaxed."

"You tryna say I'm high-strung?" I joke.

He glances over, making me roar with laughter.

"Damn. You never miss an opportunity to get on my fucking neck, huh?"

"It's not a bad thing."

I have literally never heard it used in a good way. "Being high-strung isn't a bad thing? Or you being on my neck isn't a bad thing? Because you will be sent my medical bills."

"I'll get you a special-grade neck brace. And I'm just sayin', it's understandable when someone has so much on their shoulders and doesn't try to pass off any of the weight."

I playfully roll my eyes, then whisper under my breath. "Can't a girl just be delusional sometimes?" I turn to him. "I'm gonna go back to relaxing now, so you can shut up." I poke him in the side of the head before closing my eyes again.

He doesn't respond, but I hear the music get louder.

It does feel nice to let go sometimes, to exist without the worry of what comes next needling you. I want more of this feeling.

Five minutes later, I let my eyes flutter open. "Hey, Micah?"

"Yeah?"

"Do you still chase the moon?"

He looks up to the sky to find a full moon sitting right above us. His right hand moves over to my thigh, and he squeezes it with a smirk as he slams on the gas.

He doesn't tell me where we're going. He doesn't need to. We know where the moon is taking us. We park by one of the trails at Loch Raven

Reservoir and get out to walk around, neither of us feeling any pressure to talk. Words aren't always needed.

We end up sitting on a large rock by the water and I wonder if this is the same spot from all those years ago. If the surrounding trees and rocks could tell their story, would they remember us? Would they have expected us to end up back here?

Time passes as we pick up smaller rocks nearby, tossing them in the water and listening to the ripples cascading from the impact.

"I haven't been honest with you," he says as the water settles.

"Okay," I say shakily. "Be honest with me now."

He shifts so that our knees are touching. "You told me what you were willing to give, and I told you I was fine with that. I lied."

A herd of elephants stampedes through my stomach. If we're really being honest, I knew from the beginning it wouldn't be enough for him, but I was willing to take his words at face value to get what I wanted. What kind of person does that make me?

"Or at least I thought I did."

"You thought?"

"Yeah. I have always wanted more with you. I've always wanted the whole picture and this time was no different, so I said what you needed to hear, thinking maybe down the line I could convince you to take a chance on us. But then when you backed away from me earlier, I thought, damn, she may never get to that point."

I hang my head, the familiar tinges of shame creeping up on me.

Micah lifts my chin with his finger, a tender smile on his face. "And that's when I realized I'm okay with that."

I shake my head, trying to comprehend his words. "I don't understand."

"I realized that having you in my life, in any form, is more important to me than having you in my life in the way I want you. I get that I have bigger feelings about us than I let on, so I would understand if you wanted to cut off the benefits factor of our friendship. It's you that I can't lose."

I freaked out about a kiss on the cheek earlier and here he is telling me that he would stay in the friend-zone forever if it meant he got to keep me in his life. He is unbelievable. "You're serious?"

"Dead serious," he confirms.

The Goode doctor is going to have a field day with me next time I see her.

What if I stop calculating my every move and let life happen? At some point life has to be about living and not survival, right?

"I don't wanna cut off the benefits," I rush to say.

He chuckles. "Well, okay. Is there more to that?"

"I can't say that I'm ready to commit to 'more.' But I'm done fighting against the possibility. So, what if we just let whatever's supposed to happen, happen?" I'm tired of turning us into a self-fulfilled prophecy.

"I like that," he says, holding his pinky up between us. "To whatever comes?"

I lock my pinky with his. "To whatever comes."

We weave our fingers together and watch the moon illuminate the water before us.

Chapter Twenty

Micah

THE SMELL OF FOOD AND THE SOUND OF MUSIC SEND me hunting for Dani.

When I get to the kitchen, she's cooking eggs with my T-shirt draped over her body, dancing to "Get Me" by Justin Bieber and Kehlani.

Watching her move is majestic. Every step is the picture of grace. From the way she twirls on her toes when she needs something from the fridge to the way she balances on one leg when she stirs her pan.

Simply put, I'm in awe of her. I walk up and kiss the back of her neck, surprised when she leans in rather than pushing me away.

After our conversation last night, I brought her home so she could pack a bag, and then we made our way back here into my bed. I want the whole Dani package, every piece of her, but I'm not willing to lose her again by pushing my own agenda.

"Since when do you cook breakfast?"

She transfers the eggs onto a plate, turning in my arms and wrapping hers around my neck. "Since I woke up starving after someone burned off all my calories last night."

I step away from the stove, pulling her with me until we're swaying with the music. "Hmm, I don't recall. Maybe you should refresh my memory."

She leans up to kiss me, moaning as I bite her lower lip. "Mmm, no, no, no. Back it up," she says as she drops her hands to my stomach to push against it. "The eggs are gonna get cold fucking with you."

That's the goal. I go in for one more kiss before holding my hands up in surrender. "Breakfast is the most important meal of the day."

"Exactly."

We sit at my kitchen table, eating together and planning our day. It's impossible not to imagine a future where this is our routine, but I release those thoughts in favor of enjoying the now.

"I don't know what to do about my video for Tanya," she says. "All the footage I got from you and everyone else has been amazing, but mine still isn't coming out right."

"Yeah, but you're working on that. Give yourself some grace." Leave it to Dani to have exactly one therapy session and think she should immediately move past all her mental blocks.

"We don't have time." She waves me off. "I mean, we don't have forever. The gala will be here before we know it."

We've been moving full speed ahead with planning since coming back from Colorado, but we still have plenty of time before the date.

"You will get there. The words are in there." I place my index finger against her heart. "And when they're ready to be spoken, you'll know." Matters of the heart don't take kindly to being rushed.

She lets out a deep exhale, her shoulders loosening with every second. "I guess you're right. I wish I were an artist like you, then I wouldn't even need words."

An idea takes root in my mind. "Will you try something with me?"

She nods without hesitation, unleashing a fire inside of me.

I guide her up to my loft and have her sit on a stool. I search through my supplies until I find one of my white paint markers. "Do you trust me?"

She considers me carefully.

I'm waiting with bated breath for her answer until she sets me free.

"I do."

Thank fuck. "Good. Then—I mean this in the most nonsexual way possible—I need you to strip."

She folds over herself with a howl of laughter.

Once she strips off my shirt and I grab her bra from my room for her to put on, she's left in her bra and underwear.

"Now what?" she asks.

Now, I get to work. "Leave it to me."

I sink to my knees before her and push her legs apart. Her soft gasp starts a rumble in my chest. There's no plan in motion when I bring the marker to her skin. I don't have a design in my head or even an inkling of an idea. All I know is I have the quintessential canvas in front of me, so nothing can go wrong.

Her skin bubbles under the first stroke of the marker. I soothe the goosebumps with my other hand, relishing her softness. With each swipe, her body relaxes more and more, becoming putty in my hands. Eventually, I don't even have to tell her when I need her to stand and when I need her to sit. We set an unspoken rhythm.

Almost on instinct, I start to make the design on her other leg symmetrical, but an invisible force stops my hand midair. I want to show Dani how I see her. There is beauty in her fearful symmetry. She has a formidable strength that intimidates the world around her, yet a softness that even she doesn't see. She is a host of imperfections that add up to create the perfect picture.

The designs I drew on her other leg were more delicate. Flowers that transform into running water; soft lines that blend into soft curves.

This side is all sharp lines and edges. Lightning that sinks into harsh waves.

The branches on the tree I draw on her stomach extend over her arms, no leaf exactly the same.

When I'm done, I escort her to stand in front of my floor-length mirror.

"Woah," she heaves.

Leaning down so that my head can rest on her shoulder without messing up the paint, I say, "You don't need to be an artist when you are living, breathing art."

She holds her arms out to her sides, inspecting them closely, her mouth agape. "This is incredible. I look incredible. I never wanna take this off." She even does a full three-sixty in the mirror so she can get a glimpse of the designs all over her back.

"I hear not bathing is in these days," I joke.

Deservedly so, she slaps my chest. "Shut the fuck up." Her eyes move back and forth in the mirror, widening every time she notices a different design on her body.

I think I could watch her all day.

She turns to me with a shy smile. "This might be silly, but could you take a picture of me?"

Capture her covered in my art for the rest of my life? I'd love nothing more.

I take out my phone and start snapping pictures. This is when she's in her element. She comes alive under the camera's gaze, knowing exactly how she wants to be displayed. She is the muse they write about in history books.

Both of us had plans for the day, but those plans morphed into doing absolutely nothing together and I have not a single complaint about it.

Bailey comes over to hang out, wanting to introduce Dani to some anime, and we get into a debate of what anime should be first. Both of us agree that *One Piece* has too many episodes to keep Dani's attention.

Bailey insists on *My Hero Academia* while I push for *Demon Slayer*. We put on the trailer for both and let her decide. Bailey is over the moon when Dani sides with her.

"Before we start, can I ask one question?" Bailey begins, her eyes ping-ponging between us.

"What's up?" Dani responds.

"What the hell is all over you?" Bailey flicks her hand up and down the markings she can see under Dani's T-shirt and sweat shorts.

Dani stands with her feet wide apart and holds her arms out. "I'm a work of art, baby," she gloats.

Bailey tries to ask more questions, but Dani simply grabs her hand and leads her to the couch.

While Dani gets to know Deku and his classmates, I check in with Rome via text. I had asked him to help me locate a certain Nigel Pierce and he seems to have found information that will come in handy.

"Is Bakugo ever not yelling?" Dani asks with her lips twisted in a snarl. We're starting the first episode of season two and so far, all of Dani's complaints have centered around the character Bakugo and his propensity for anger.

Bailey grimaces with an innocent smile. "Well . . . no. He has his moments, though! I'm telling you, he's gonna grow on you," she claims.

"Are we sure?"

She looks over Bailey's head at me and I hold my hands in the air. "Hey, I voted for *Demon Slayer*."

Bailey grabs the throw pillow beside Dani and whacks me in the side. "Fuck you, this is a good show."

It is. It's one of my favorites, but I do love to fuck with Bailey any chance I get.

“And why is this girl’s titties all the way out? She’s like twelve,” Dani says, referring to the character Momo.

Bailey and I look at each other, then back to Dani. “Anime,” we say in unison.

Once our takeout arrives, we decide to eat in the kitchen and give our binge-a-thon a break.

Dani asks how classes at Movement Lab are going and about a girl named Maddy, which ramps Bailey up to gush over the girl’s progress.

“I need to come for a class,” Dani adds.

Bailey claps her hands excitedly. “Yes! You probably should soon because I might be taking a break from the Lab.”

This news makes me rear my head. “Why? What’s going on?”

“I might be going on tour.” She beams.

“No, you’re not.” *Shit.* I want to take the words back the moment I say them, but Pandora’s box has already been opened.

Bailey gawks at me as Dani whips her head in my direction. It’s as if all the sound in the house was sealed into a vacuum.

“What did you say?” Bailey’s voice is eerily calm.

“I didn’t . . .”

She holds up her hand. “No. No. Repeat what you said.” Dani starts to chime in, but Bailey cuts her off. “I wanna hear him say it.”

Gripping the back of my neck, I sigh. “I said, ‘No, you’re not.’ ”

“No, I’m not . . . what?” she goads.

“Going on tour.”

“Please explain to me how you’ve decided I’m not going on tour. I’d really love to know how, without asking me a single fucking question, you made that decision.”

I wince at the ire in her words. I shouldn’t have said it. I know I shouldn’t have. It was as if the words invaded my body, spewing out their poison before I could regain control.

“I didn’t decide. I shouldn’t have said that. I just meant that touring would be a lot on your body.”

Her eyes lower into slits as her leg bounces up and down. "You don't think I know that?"

Dani clears her throat. "Okay, let's take a step back."

"I don't wanna take a step back," Bailey hisses. She points her fingers at me. "I wanna understand why my brother thinks I'm so fucking useless."

I jump up. "I've never said that."

"It's how you act!" she shrieks. "You act like I can't possibly take care of myself. You infantilize me. I tell you news that should be exciting, and instead of being happy for me, congratulating me, or even asking who the fucking tour is with, you immediately tried to shut down the idea."

My skin feels like thousands of needles. She's right. I stomped all over her joy before she even had a chance to express it. "I'm sorry," I offer. It's not enough, but it's all I have in this moment.

She scoffs, jerking back from the table to stand. "Fuck you, Micah." Pushing past me, she grabs her coat and storms out.

When I start to follow her, Dani grabs my arm. "Let her go."

"I fucked up." I hang my head.

"You did. I know you want to protect her, but all you're doing is keeping her trapped. You would be the very first person to say her disease doesn't define her, right?"

"Of course."

"So, then why is it that every time you see her, all you do is look for the MS in her?"

Ouch. I don't think I do that every single time, but I can understand that it comes across that way. I've lost so many people in my life, I just don't know what I'd do if one of them was her.

"I'll make it right," I say, more to myself than Dani.

"I know you will."

When sleep finally comes for me that night, it transports me to the hospital where Bailey received her MS diagnosis.

I'm sitting in the waiting room with my head in my hands.

"You're better than this."

I jump at the sound of Tanya's voice. When I look up, she's sitting in the chair beside me. "I know I am. I can't get her disappointed face out of my head."

"Come with me."

She leads me through the halls of the hospital, stopping in front of Bailey's room. At least, I think it's her room. I rub my hands over my eyes, but I still can't see her clearly. Everything inside the room is blurry while everything out here is crystal clear.

Tanya brushes past me, and when I turn to follow her, I'm stunned by the sight of everyone I've ever lost standing in a row with solemn faces. Tanya doesn't acknowledge any of them as she walks to stand at the end of the line.

"She's not us. Stop treating her like she is, or she will move on with her life without you."

I start to respond when I hear shifting behind me. I turn around to find the hospital has changed into a stadium and Bailey is on stage dancing her heart out. I can't make out anyone else on the stage or in the audience, but I see our parents run over to her after the performance to hug her. Dani's there as well. Everyone in Bailey's life is there except for me. There's music playing somewhere, but when I reach out to her, the music cuts and Bailey gives me the look of contempt she gave me when she left my house tonight.

Tanya places her hand on my shoulder. "Do you hear me, Micah?" Her voice sounds so far away even though she's right beside me.

I shake my head. "I'm sorry, what?"

"Do you hear me? I said WAKE UP!"

I jolt awake covered in a layer of sweat. Knowing sleep won't come back anytime soon, I sit up in my empty bed and pull up the link Dani sent me.

Chapter Twenty-One

Micah

GO IN OR DON'T, BUT STOP STANDING HERE LIKE A *creep*, I scold myself as I stand frozen outside the support group Dani sent me. I need to go in. Losing Bailey to MS would be devastating, but I would never recover if I lost her because of my stubbornness.

Taking a deep breath, I step into the meeting room.

There are padded stack chairs set up in a circle in the middle of a neutral-colored room. Some people are already sitting while others are gathered around the snack table.

"Welcome in," a Black woman with micro twists, a burnt orange oversized sweater, and black jeans greets me. "I'm Kaylan. I'm the facilitator here."

I shake her hand, still taking in my surroundings. "I'm Micah."

"Is this your first meeting ever or just here?"

"Ever. I'm not really sure how this works."

"Well, there's no formula. Some people have been coming here for a while, some not as long. You can choose to share your story, but you don't have to. Just be willing to listen to everyone who does."

That sounds easy enough.

I follow her to the middle of the room, grabbing a chair. As everyone files in, there's a calm quiet that settles over the room.

"Alright, let's get started. Welcome to everyone returning and new. How 'bout we dive right in and open the floor? Does anyone have anything they'd like to share?" Kaylan poses the question to the group.

A man named Carlos is the first to speak. His wife has lupus, which has led to severe damage to her kidney, and they're on the transplant waitlist. "It's been four years, and we're still waiting. It feels like we haven't gotten anywhere. Georgie is always so optimistic, and I love that about her, but I'm scared. I'm scared and I can't tell her that because I don't want her to be like me. I want her to keep being fearless. I don't know, I feel like I come here and say the same thing every week and it helps for a little bit, but the feeling always comes back."

"And that's okay," Kaylan assures him. "Your concern for Georgie is valid, and for as long as you're dealing with this, that fear isn't gonna go away, right? But the point of this group is for you to have somewhere to voice those fears and know that you're not alone."

The group nods along with her.

I feel a kinship to Carlos. I understand that fear of the unknown, fear of the inability to prepare. It affects every interaction you have with that person.

A woman named Rachel is the next to share. Her partner has Cogan syndrome, which has led to him losing his hearing. "So, John and I just found out that we're expecting."

The group erupts into cheers and congratulations. One woman snatches Rachel up into a hug, rocking her side to side while tears stream down her cheeks.

Kaylan hands her a tissue when she sits down. "Thank you, guys. We're really excited. Well, we're trying to be. The insurance is still giving us a hard time about approving him for the cochlear implant, and so the other night, John broke down crying. He just kept signing, 'What if I'll never be able to hear our baby's voice?' I didn't know what the fuck to say to that!" She holds the tissue up to her eye as she sucks back a deep breath. "He has really taken this disease in stride. He accepted the hearing loss as part of his life, and then there are times like this where it hits him what this disease has really taken from him and it breaks my heart all over again."

A few nod in understanding. Kaylan offers her some words of encouragement.

A woman named Helena coughs softly. Her focus seems to be on one particular spot on the floor, but then she looks up at everyone and offers a kind smile. "Most of you know my daughter has MS."

My ears perk up at that.

"Last night, I held her while she cried for what felt like hours because she got into a fight with her friend. Her friend Sidney, who I want to point out I've never liked, got mad at her because Iris was too tired to play with her. She had just missed Sidney's birthday party over the weekend because she was having a bad day, so Sidney wanted her to come over and play yesterday to make up for it. Iris was still too tired and that really pissed Sidney off. This girl accused my baby of being selfish and not caring about her. Iris was just sobbing in my arms wondering how she could fix things and all I wanted to do was rip Sidney's throat out. They're only ten, so I get it. Sidney doesn't understand Iris's disease. None of her friends really do. It's hard for them to comprehend that Iris even has a disease when physically she looks to them like a typical kid. But why should Iris have to shoulder the brunt of their lack of understanding?"

Helena is out of breath by the time she's done speaking. My heart goes out to both her and Iris. Bailey didn't get her diagnosis until she was twenty, so it was a little easier for her to articulate what was happening to her body to those around her. Iris probably barely understands it herself.

Her story makes me feel compelled to share mine.

"Hey, I'm Micah," I start. "My sister isn't speaking to me right now. She also has MS." I look over to Helena and she gives me an earnest nod before I continue. "She has relapsing-remitting MS. I'm told it's one of the more common types of MS, as if that gives us any sort of comfort. She's been in remission for the last year and a half, which is great, but I find myself always waiting for the other shoe to drop. I think my problem is that I can't fix this. I've always looked out for my sister, but with this there's no blueprint on how to handle the disease. I know no case is exactly the same, but I wish I could know what to expect. I can't predict when or if she'll relapse. I can't predict when the disease will progress. If I don't know what's coming, how am I supposed to know I'm doing everything I can?"

For a moment, I forget other people are in the room; I'm just spilling all my fears out loud to myself. "She's a dancer. All she's ever wanted is to choreograph for artists and go on tour. But when she got her diagnosis, she scaled back on that. At the time, she was in the thick of her symptoms and her body couldn't manage it. Now that she's in remission, she can. And she has an opportunity to do just that, and I shit all over her dream."

When I held her as a baby, I vowed to always protect her and fight for her dreams. I never thought I'd be the one her dreams would need protection from.

I'll never forget the look on her face when she accused me of thinking she's useless. It will haunt me for the rest of my life.

Kaylan's voice brings me back to reality. "So, we're seeing there's a balance that comes with caring for someone with an autoimmune disease, right?" She holds her hands up like a scale. "You don't wanna dip too far into this side where you're piling everything onto yourself with no help and you don't want to be too far on this side where your attempt to care for them strips them of their independence."

That's exactly what I've done to Bailey. Without meaning to, I've stripped away a core part of who she is. If someone tried to tell me I couldn't make art anymore, I'd make them pay.

Helena chimes in. "Maybe it's a good thing we don't know what to expect from this disease? At least that way we can't expect the worst. I don't know. That's what I tell myself, but I don't know if I really believe it."

Maybe that's how I should be looking at it. But that's easier said than done.

Kaylan checks in with me after the meeting to see how I liked it and offers a few other resources to look into. I check my phone to see if Bailey has returned my calls and texts, but no such luck. What I'm not about to do is ambush her and try to force her into forgiving me, especially when I haven't earned it, so I'll respect her boundaries and give her space.

I approach Helena as she's about to leave, wanting to pick her brain. We sit and talk about Bailey and Iris, finding common ground in the way we've approached their care at times. She offers a lot of helpful advice for how she's coped, and I offer her insight into how Bailey is able to lead her life now, which makes her feel optimistic for Iris's future.

I check my phone for any sign from Bailey to no avail, but I do have a message from Dani waiting for me when I leave group.

Dani: You are confirmed for your appointment at The Salon. Please arrive for your appointment at the designated time. Looking forward to seeing you.

Below the text, she's dropped a pin with her location and another text that says the appointment time is right now.

What is she up to? When I realize the pinned location is just her place, I waste no time racing over there.

She opens the door dressed in a black jumpsuit with a white button-up shirt and a black apron over it. The apron has clips all over it and combs in the pockets.

"What is going on?" I question.

"Welcome to the Salon of Dani. You are extremely fortunate to have gotten an appointment here. Usually, I'm all booked up," she brags.

"Oh, is that so? And what services did I book for today?"

"That head needs a wash and retwist. I just came from picking up some products so let's go, chop chop." She claps her hands and steps aside so I can enter.

"By any chance is this a distraction from the fact that my sister doesn't fuck with me right now?"

"It might be. Will that stop you from having your appointment?" she asks with her hand on her hip.

Hell no. I want everything she has to offer. I settle for a simple "Not at all."

"Then move." She smacks my ass and pushes my back, pouting when I don't budge.

When we enter her kitchen where she's set up a shampoo bowl, she gives me the five-star treatment. She puts on some lo-fi hip-hop and then proceeds to sit my ass down like it's a professional shop.

It feels good having her hand in my scalp. Admittedly, the detoxing, two rounds of shampooing and rinsing, and ringing out my hair lulls me to sleep.

She pours something else in the front of my hair and sits in my lap, which makes me sit right up.

"What's that?" I ask, not really caring because I like this seating arrangement.

"A hydrating shampoo. Just wanna get some moisture back in your hair after cleansing it." She's very focused, massaging the shampoo deep into my scalp.

I run my hands up the back of her legs.

"Stoppp, I'm busy."

"But I'm your favorite client," I pout.

"No, that would be Evie."

I tickle her some more until she fights me to stay still.

After my hair is thoroughly washed, she sets me down between her legs so she can start the retwist.

I'm used to being the one caring for everyone. I'm not used to being catered to like this. Even if she never gives me forever, I'm so grateful to have even a fraction of this woman's affection.

She slathers some gel on the back of her hand and takes out one of her small-tooth combs.

"Where did you learn how to do this?" I ask, impressed.

She smirks. "Just because I personally always choose a forty-inch buss down doesn't mean I'm not capable of other things."

I smack my own forehead. "Of course, how dumb of me."

She chuckles as she turns my head the way she needs it, clipping my locs into sections. "When I first started modeling, I got fucked over a lot when it came to my hair and makeup. I learned how to do it all myself, so I'd be prepared in case they sent me to someone who didn't know what the hell to do with my complexion and hair texture. And then I found that I really enjoyed it, so I kept learning from stylists I met over the years. Now, I really only do Evie's hair when she asks. So consider yourself blessed."

"Oh, believe me, I know I am."

She licks her lips and ignores me in favor of focusing on my hair. She works in silence for a bit before speaking again. "You went to the support group today, right? How did it go?"

"It was really good. It was nice to get some new perspectives." I tell her about my conversation with Helena while she works on my head.

"I'm happy it worked out."

"Thank you for finding it for me. It really means a lot." I pull away from her grasp on my hair so I can face her. I want her to see my sincerity. Going to this group is going to do wonders for my relationship with Bailey, and Dani deserves all the credit for it.

She drops her head bashfully. "That is something you never have to thank me for."

"Okay, then, let me thank you for my appointment at the Salon of Dani." I press against her knees so I can raise myself up to reach her lips.

She presses her lips together and scoots back. "Um, sir, I don't know what kind of establishment you think I run here, but I accept tips in cash, not dick."

I lay my head against her breasts, enjoying the jerky rise and fall I know is coming from her amusement. "Aww, damn. I forgot my wallet."

She raises her finger to point to the door. "Get out."

Laughing, I take out my wallet and pull out a stack of cash to wave in front of her. Before I realize it, she snatches the stack out of my hand and shoves it down her shirt. She pops me on the shoulder with her comb, then makes a twisting motion with her fingers. "Well, come on and turn around. I got other appointments today."

"Ma'am, yes, ma'am," I salute as I pocket my now lighter wallet and sit back down.

"How is therapy going?" I ask once she gets in the groove of twisting and palm-rolling each loc.

"Things with the Goode doctor are going well. I . . . uh, I told her about Nigel during our last session."

"You did?"

She smacks me with the comb again. "You always wanna look somebody in their eyes, stay still!"

I burst out laughing. "Sorry."

"Mhm. Anyway, yes, I did. She wanted to know where my mantra came from."

Not wanting to get hit again, I keep facing forward despite my need to see her face. My fists clench involuntarily. I hate hearing about Nigel. I want to destroy him for all the pain he's caused Dani. Rip him limb from limb until he's unrecognizable to anyone who has had the misfortune of knowing him. "And how did that conversation go?" I don't want to pry into her therapy sessions, but I do want her to know I'm here to listen to anything she wants to share.

"Better than I was expecting. She basically said I use the words 'I'm fine' as a crutch to force myself to be okay when I'm not. And I know she's right. So, we talked about maybe trying out other mantras when I feel . . . a moment coming on."

"And you're open to that?"

"That's why I said the conversation was better than I was expecting. I actually am. I think my mantra started off being helpful and then it ended up doing more harm than good. So, we'll see."

I'm extremely proud of both of us for putting in the work to become better versions of ourselves. My ultimate wish for us is that our growth waters the roots of the trees we planted long ago, so that our branches may bloom in a way that leaves us inextricably linked.

When she's done with my retwist, she sets me under the dryer and disappears to call Nisha about something. The heat and the lack of sleep from last night start to take their toll on me and my eyes begin to close against my will. The clear vision of a future with this woman upon every long blink is what makes me give in to the temptation.

Chapter Twenty-Two

Dani

Heavy thuds against my door catch Bailey's, Nisha's, and my attention.

"You got a warrant out or something?" Bailey asks.

"Not in this state." I stick my tongue out at her as I make my way to the door.

An excited Evie waits on the other side, carrying a large white box with a gold ribbon wrapped around it.

"Interesting time for you not to use your key."

"You don't see this big-ass box in my hand?" Hearing voices behind me, she bends to try to see past my arms, almost stumbling. "Who all over here?"

I lead her to where the girls are.

When Nisha sees her, she jumps up for a hug. Evie plops the box down on my kitchen counter to reciprocate.

Evie looks at Bailey, stunned for a moment before smoothing out her features.

"Evie, this is Bailey. Micah's sister," I introduce the two. There's no reason to hide their relation. Their parents literally hit copy and paste when they had them.

She tips her head back. "Ahh, that makes so much sense. I kept thinking I knew you from somewhere. And then I was like, is this my gay awakening? What's happening?"

Nisha and I cackle while Bailey flashes a bright smile and dips into a curtsy. "Oh my gosh, I love you already," she says to Evie.

They gush over each other for another minute before Evie finally makes her way over to this mysterious box. "Okay, okay. So, I have a sample of the invites for Tanya's gala and I had to show you."

A sample invite? In that huge box? "That whole box is the invite?"

She beams. "Yep! You said make it extravagant, sooo . . ."

Instead of finishing her sentence, she unties the ribbon and presses one of the sides. The box opens outward until it lies flat and as it does a group of beautiful paper butterflies flutter into the air. When the last butterfly is out, our attention is drawn to what's in the center: a smaller, flatter box with a tent card on top.

I flip it open. It reads: *"Please make art with me one last time."*

When I lift up the lid of the second box, there is a blank card, a paintbrush, and a strip of watercolor paints inside.

My curiosity too great to wait, I grab the items and spread them out on my counter. The girls gather around closely as I run the brush under my kitchen sink and dip it into blue paint, spreading it across the card with reckless abandon.

The words come to life on the page under each stroke of the brush. Details for the gala typed in an elegant font. Bailey gasps.

I turn to Evie with watery eyes. "Evie, this is beautiful. It's . . . it's genius."

She takes a little bow with a proud smile. "Thank you. You said Tanya had a flair for the dramatics, so I figured she'd like this."

She'd absolutely love it. She'd probably have Evie make a dozen extra just so she could open them all and pretend to be shocked every time.

We look over the invitation to make sure all the details are correct before working out the logistics of sending them out. Evie volunteers to handle delivery as part of her contribution, and Nisha emails her the guest list.

"Okay, I gotta go. I will call you later," Evie says, blowing me a kiss and saying her goodbyes to Nisha and Bailey.

"Okay, love you. Tell Jalen I said hi."

"Love you too, I will," she responds before realizing what she's said. She stops in her tracks and turns back to me. "Oh, fuck you."

The sound of my howling laughter follows her out the door.

Once she's gone, Nisha goes back to typing on her laptop. "We got a few more auction item submissions today, so I'm organizing those into categories. Is Micah coming? I got a question about one of the paintings he's auctioning."

Bailey's tone is forceful and shadowed by betrayal. "Who cares?"

"Oop. Okay, I'm guessing you two haven't made up yet." Nisha whistles.

My heart pangs. I know it's killing Micah that Bailey won't speak to him. I'm not sure if they've ever gone this long without talking. He doesn't even know I'm meeting with her today, because I couldn't bear to see the hurt in his eyes.

"Nope." She pops her lips around the *p*.

"What will it take for you to forgive him?" I ask.

She looks me up and down. "Are you gonna run and tell him if I tell you?"

"If you're asking me not to, then I won't." As much as I want them to make up, I won't betray Bailey's trust. Besides, Micah knows he was wrong and he's working hard to make it right. He doesn't need my interference.

"Okay, good. I'm asking you not to. Honestly, I'm not even mad anymore, but my feelings are hurt. He's pissed me off with his hovering ways before, but that was the first time he's made me feel small. And I don't know how we come back from that."

Injured pride can be hard to overlook. Especially when the one who deals the killing blow is someone who's supposed to be in your corner. It's a wound that never heals quite the same as it was before, but with the proper care, the scar can be minimal.

"Look, I can't tell you what to do. But I can say that I know you love each other very much and your bond is worth fighting for."

She swallows hard, her arms hugging her stomach. "I'm gonna go. I gotta meet up with Justin to prep for class." She thanks me for my thoughts with a hug then turns to Nisha. "Call me later?"

Nisha nods and Bailey grazes her hand with her pinky before leaving.

I squint at Nisha, folding my arms over my chest.

She lets out a small huff. "No comment."

I press my lips together to hide a smile. "Mhm. Okay, fine."

"Actually, I'll tell you if you tell me what's up with you and Micah."

"Okay," I say, shrugging my shoulders back.

She hunches over. "Damn, I thought you'd tell me to fuck off. Okay, I changed my mind." She closes her laptop and attempts to run from her chair.

"Nah uh, get over here! Come hear about all the fantastic sex I'm having!" I yell as I chase her down.

Signing up to lay myself bare and confront my ugliest truths is probably the wildest thing I've ever done.

And what do I get at the end of it? Personal growth? Yippee.

Dr. Goode and I have hit our stride in our relationship. We work well together in the sense that even when I feel a bit raw after our sessions, I never leave feeling broken.

Sometimes, though, on days like today, the realizations make me wish I had never opened this can of worms.

"So, you think the argument you had with Amerie the other day was silly?"

I blow out a harsh breath. "Not at all. I just think it's silly that I should have to explain to someone who's supposed to be my best friend that this event is important to me and her planning a trip at the same time is rude and inconsiderate." I wouldn't think I'd need to tell her that this event I've been planning for months in honor of my dead mentor should probably take precedence over a trip she just started planning when she could have picked any other time. The more I think about the conversation we had yesterday, the more mad I get. She had the audacity to say, "It's just a party."

My feet are tired from pacing around the office, but I need to dispel this energy somehow.

"I see you're taking deep breaths to re-center yourself. Why?"

That gives me pause. "What do you mean 'why'? Shouldn't I be trying to calm down? Not be so angry?"

"Sure, but you haven't given yourself a chance to simply be angry first."

"I don't wanna hold on to that, though."

"Let me ask you a question."

Questions from the Goode doctor are never fun. Questions from her always make me question myself. "Yeah?"

"I've noticed that when it comes to your friendships with Janelle and Evelyn, you all seem to have a system where you hold each other accountable. When you fight, you process it and move on. But when it comes to Amerie, you go out of your way not to hold her bad behavior against her. I'm curious why that is."

That's less of a question, more of an observation, but go off. "Well, I wouldn't say I go out of my way not to. I hold her accountable." I was the one who talked to her after her wedding and told her she was wrong and needed to make things right with Nelle.

"I didn't say you don't hold her accountable. I said you don't hold her bad behavior against her. It's like you feel bad about yourself when you're mad at her, even when your anger is justified."

I freeze. My feet meld themselves to the floor, wanting to run away from what's coming but knowing I can't. I do feel bad about myself when I'm mad at Amerie. She frustrates me because there's a familiarity I see in her, and I hate when she holds that mirror up to my face.

Slowly, I deflate into my chair. "I don't wanna be like her."

"You don't wanna be like Amerie."

Again, not a question. A cold, hard fact lingering in the air, slapping me in the face.

"Well, why is that?"

Amerie has a habit of lashing out at the people who care about her, isolating herself from us. Sometimes I think the walls I've put up to protect myself from outsiders keep the people I want in out as well. I don't want to isolate myself from them. I don't want to become unlikable. "I don't want the seeds of my unhappiness to plant themselves in my relationships."

Maybe that's why I can't bring myself to give up on Ri. I don't want to believe she's too far gone, because what does that mean for me?

Dr. Goode considers my words. "I have a challenge for you."

"Should I choose to accept."

"Exactly. I want you to take yourself on a date."

"Take myself on a date? Like dinner and a movie?"

"If that's the type of date you like, sure. I want you to go out into the world and spend some time alone. Check in with yourself."

"I feel like I spend plenty of time with myself," I object.

She shakes her head. "You spend a lot of time with yourself when you're overanalyzing everything you do. It's great that you care about your loved ones and that you want to protect them from the walls you've built. But I don't think you'll be able to take those walls down until you feel safer with yourself."

Well, damn. "So just go out alone? When do I have to do this by?"

She takes a sip of her tea to hide her smile. "Let's call it an ongoing challenge. Things don't have to be done perfectly the first time around. You can work your way up to it, however that looks for you. You love dancing, maybe try that in a new place where you don't know anyone? Try something you've always wanted to try? Go somewhere you've always wanted to go?"

"You know I'm going straight home to Google ideas, don't you?"

"I did think you might do that, yeah."

Later that night, I'm lying in bed on my laptop, with Micah in my ear. I haven't seen him in a couple of days because he's been swamped trying to finish a commission. How I've gone from dreading being in a room with him to not being able to go twenty-four hours without hearing his voice, I'm not sure.

"What about a picnic?" Micah suggests.

"Mmm, nah."

"A concert?"

"Nah."

Poor Micah has been trying to help me plan my first solo date, and I've been rejecting all his ideas. None of these are speaking to me.

"What about a hike?"

I scrunch my nose. "You can't see me, but I'm side-eyeing you." I love to be outside in the sun, but I like to keep my encounters with nature very much sedentary.

"Ha, well, I'm fresh out of ideas, Storm."

I can make out the faint sound of the bristles of his brush hitting a canvas. There's a musicality to the way he paints. Each brushstroke sounds like precise chords in the song he's composing.

"It's okay, I'll figure it out. How's your painting coming?" As I speak, I find a link for a candle-making class in Fells Point.

I do love a good candle.

"It's coming along. I should be done by tomorrow morning." He tells me more about the client who commissioned the painting while I find the class schedule and discover the next one is tomorrow. After wrestling with myself, I book a spot in the class.

"Well, good. I guess we'll both be doing good things tomorrow. Guess who's got a date?"

Micah: Have a great date. Be yourself and I guarantee she'll love you

Micah: And remember, you're grown. So if you wanna give it up on your first date who gon check you?

Pocketing my phone after reading Micah's texts, I have to fight to wipe the goofy expression off my face when I walk into the Wick at the Knees store. This fool.

The front of the store has an airy feel, with wooden showcases covering every wall. Each shelf is lined with different-sized candles grouped by color. A dessert bar is set up in the center of the room, but instead of sweets, it holds mini candles. A rack next to the station holds tiny shopping bags so people can create their own sample packs.

I have to bring Nisha here; she would love this.

A sign points me toward a back room where the class is being held. Clear chairs surround two long tables. Each station is set up with a burner, a pitcher, and these adorable instruction cards. I must be the last to arrive because all but one station is occupied.

"Welcome, everyone." The velvety voice of a woman with chestnut skin, braids in a Burmese bob, and lips painted a deep purple cascades over the room. "This is the Candle Bar Experience. My name's Samira, I'm the owner here at Wick at the Knees. Today we'll be making coconut soy wax candles. Our class is ninety minutes, but the last thirty of that will be leaving your candles to cure. So, any questions before we get started?"

Samira instructs us to go over to the far wall and select as many scents as we'd like for our candles so that they're ready when we get to that step. One of the couples and one of the single women seem to think they're in a competition show and they race over to the wall, sifting through the options as quickly as they can. I pick my first scent immediately—lavender—but then I take my time sorting through the others until I find two that make the perfect complement: geranium and rosemary. Something about these together feels like a warm hug.

Samira walks us through the steps of getting our water boiling, measuring our wax into our pitchers, and setting our wicks in our jars.

The meticulousness of the steps is soothing for me. I like that I can rely on exact measurements and temperatures. Doing this at home would probably be the perfect activity when I'm stressed out.

Samira glides around the room, helping those who need it and making suggestions. When it's time to add our fragrance oil, she instructs us when to pour it into the wax and how long to mix it. She compliments everyone on their scents and I wonder if she really likes all of our combinations or if she's gone nose blind from doing this.

Around the one-hour mark, she announces, "Okay, everyone. Your candles now need to cure for at least thirty minutes before they're travel safe. Please feel free to grab a snack while you wait, or you can do a little shopping. And don't forget to take your cards with you when you leave today in case you want to continue your candle-making journey at home."

I grab the card and shove it in my purse. I end up buying candles for Nisha and my mom and then picking Samira's brain on materials to buy to make more at home. I'm starting to realize why Tanya was always picking up random hobbies; she was consistently dating herself.

We're given labels to put on our candle jars so that we can create custom names. I struggle to find a name for mine, so much so that I'm the only one still lingering in the classroom by the time I come up with it. I grab the Sharpie and write *Little Moments* across the label.

When I get home, I hop in the shower to get ready to christen my new candle. Once I'm clean and I've slipped into my silk robe, I light the wick with my lighter and slide between my sheets.

The aroma shifts through the air, coiling itself around all my senses.

Damn, I made a good choice.

It's crisp and earthy with a subtle softness to it. It's familiar.

Images of Micah take my mind hostage until I find the courage to voice my thoughts: *I miss him.*

That's the terrifying yet freeing truth. I miss Micah. And I shouldn't, because he's here and he wants to give me everything.

I'm not ready for everything.

But I am ready for . . . something.

I grab my phone and dial his number.

"Your date over already?"

I turn over so I'm lying flat on my back and put the phone on my chest. "Yep, it's over. I decided not to put out this time, but she did take me to a nice meal before the class."

"Ahh, okay, well, did she bring you flowers?"

I hum. "Nope, she didn't."

"That bitch," he gasps. "You deserve better than that."

"Oh, yeah? Maybe you can show her how it's done."

"I sure can. Give me her number, I can put her on with the local florists around here."

I snicker as I sink deeper into my sheets. "I'll get right on that. In the meantime, I was hoping you and I could go on a date sometime."

The silence on the other end is deafening. It stretches so long, I check my phone to make sure I wasn't speaking on mute.

"You asking me on a date, Dani Jenkins?"

Finally. "Yes, Micah Wright, I am. What do you say?"

"I say I'd love nothing more. Oh, and Dani?"

"Yeah?"

"I think I'm a red carnation kind of guy."

And then he hangs up. Such an ass.

Chapter Twenty-Three

Dani

THIS MAN HAS LICKED, SUCKED, AND FUCKED EVERY crevice of my body, yet I'm nervous for a date.

I change my sweater for the third time before throwing on a pair of chunky heels and calling it a day.

"Okay, deep breaths, bitch. It's just a little date," I mumble to myself. I'm trying not to say *It's okay, it's fine, everything's fine* quite as often. I don't know if I've found a suitable replacement yet, but the breathing exercises seem to offer a modicum of relief.

I grab the stupid ass red carnations off my table on the way out the door.

Micah fans himself and gushes as he opens the door. "Ooh, you came all the way to my door to pick me up. This date is starting off great."

"You're incredibly annoying," I say with a roll of my eyes as I reveal the bouquet of red carnations hidden behind my back.

If you've ever seen a grown six-foot-seven man hold a bouquet of flowers up to his nose to inhale, then you know it's sickeningly adorable.

"I could be a lot worse, trust me. Come in real quick. I wanna put these in some water."

In his kitchen, he has a vase waiting, like he knew I'd bring his ass flowers. I can't stand him.

He walks behind the counter and pulls out a bouquet of gorgeous pink and orange tulips, along with a second vase. "And these are for you."

Okay, I can stand him a little bit.

"Thank you." I watch him closely as he trims the stems. He looks good, really good. The hunter green button-up against his deeply melanated skin looks downright regal. I'd love to see the gold chain against his bare chest as it dangles above my face.

"Did I mention how beautiful you look tonight?" he asks as he strolls over to me.

"I don't recall you mentioning that, no."

He cups his hand around the back of my neck. "Allow me to rectify that, then. You look incredible." He places a tender kiss at the base of my throat, making it hard to catch my breath. "You smell incredible, too." Another kiss on the other side of my throat.

"Change of plans, we're staying in."

He shakes his head, licking a small path up the front of my neck. "I wanna be wined and dined tonight, Storm. Maybe then I'll show you what you do to me."

A frustrated groan rumbles deep within my chest. "Well, let's go then, tease."

He smiles as he reaches back to swipe his keys off their hook.

"What you grabbing your keys for? If I'm wining and dining, then you're passenger princess."

"You know, I might be into you bossing me around a lil bit."

I move his hand off my throat to wrap my hand around his and lean up to whisper in his ear. "Get in the fucking car."

He leans away with a glimmer in his eye. "Oh yeah, I like that shit."

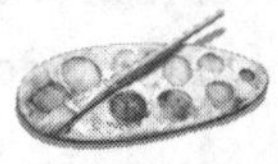

Why is this man good at everything?

I bring him to Topgolf, thinking it'd be something cute, but he's about to be whisked away on the PGA Tour.

He drops his head onto my shoulder. "Ohh, don't look like that. You're doing great!"

I look over to the scoreboard, then back to him. "I'm doing well, but I'm nowhere near beating you, and I don't like that."

"I'm so sorry to let you down."

Mushing his face with my palm, I walk over to grab my club and take my turn. I know I must look dumb as hell up here, but I find myself not caring. My swings are wild and ridiculous, usually missing the ball entirely at least once before finally connecting. It's fun. I'm having fun. With Micah. And for no other reason than I want to. I'd forgotten how nice it is to just be with him. Time and hurt can take a heavy toll on your good memories.

As I'm taking my next swing, I catch sight of another round of drinks being dropped off at our table. I sashay over to Micah and fall into his lap.

"Are you having fun?" he asks as he wraps his arms around my waist.

I bite my bottom lip. "I really am. You're not a bad date."

"You really have a way with words," he chuckles.

"I know, I won a poetry contest at school when I was in fourth grade."

"Forreal?"

"Yeah. If I remember correctly, it was a poem about friendship."

He tilts his head, impressed. "Okay, *Color of Friendship* head ass. You're full of surprises, Dani Jenkins."

"Gotta keep you on your toes." I kick my legs in the air and then take another sip of my drink. "It's your turn, by the way."

"I know. But I really like the position I'm in right now."

I grind my ass down onto his lap and he grips my hip.

"Storm, if you think I won't spread you open on this table so everyone can watch me take care of that perfect little pussy of yours, you're sorely mistaken."

I clear my throat and jump up from his lap. I'm not about to fuck around and find out. "My God, today, please, go take your turn." I point in the direction of the bay.

He slides his hands down the front of his pants as he stands. "Maybe on the second date, then."

After our first game finishes, we still have time left on our reservation, so we decide to make things a little more interesting.

"Truth or dare, Storm," Micah asks as he sends the ball flying.

"You don't even know if it's gonna land in the right spot."

"I do know because I haven't missed yet." He holds his hand over his eyebrows dramatically as we watch the ball land in the right target.

Son of a bitch.

We've been playing truth or dare, but we can ask only if we hit our ball in the target the other person picks. Micah has been wiping the floor with my ass. You'd think he'd take pity on me and miss at least one, but no.

"Ugh, fine. Dare."

He taps his finger against his chin. "I dare you to let me post any picture I want on your story with no context. And you can't delete it—you have to let it run for the full twenty-four hours."

Oof. My hand twitches in my back pocket and I stomp my foot when I realize I probably won't get very far if I run. I hand him my phone. So far during this little game, I've had to call Victor and pay him a random compliment and I've had to start talking to our server in a British accent. Now who knows what he's going to post on my social media for the world to see.

He disappears with my phone and when he comes back, he hands it back to me silently. What the hell did he do?

"Should I even bother looking?"

"Look or don't look. You can't take it down either way."

Oh lord, let me mentally prepare now for all the texts and calls I'm bound to get because of whatever foolishness he's posted. I navigate to my socials and bust out laughing when I see what he posted.

He apparently went into the bathroom and took a selfie, but the top half of his face is cropped out and it says, "Before I get attached, does this belong to anybody?"

"Have you lost your mind?" I ask.

"That is quite possible."

"And who says I'm gonna get attached to you?" As if I'm not already.

"That is the hope," he says as he winks.

"I'm so over you. Move over." I bump him with my hip so I can take my turn.

Thankfully, it lands where it needs to, so I get to ask him to make a choice now.

"Hmm. I will take truth."

"Boring." I yawn.

"Oh, peer pressure won't work on me, sweets."

"Fine. Why do you think we keep finding our way back into each other's lives?" Something keeps pulling us together despite my best efforts. It's no coincidence that he and I would have the same mentor all those years ago. That we would bump into each other at a random New York club years later. That years after that, our friends would start dating and force us back into each other's orbit.

"Easy. I told you before I believe we're inevitable."

That he did. When he chased me down as I tried to sneak out of his gallery opening, he tried to tell me that. I didn't want to hear it then. I'm inclined to believe it now.

"You really believe that?" And if that's true, why the hell has it been so hard?

"I believe in that more than I believe in the stars in the sky."

I don't know what to say. Could I believe in us that strongly one day?

We stare into each other's eyes and the only thing I can think to do when the server walks by is ask for the check. Date night is officially over; I'm ready to have Micah between my legs.

When the server drops off our check, I see that it's not a check at all. It's a receipt. Because the bill has already been paid.

I squint to make sure I'm seeing this right and then over to Micah. "You paid already?"

"Absolutely. You didn't actually think I'd let you pay, did you?"

"Yes. That's part of the whole wining-and-dining thing."

He stands and holds out his hand for me to grab. "And I hear you. But I have my limits."

I take his hand, but when he moves, I don't move with him. I hold firm in place until he turns back to me. He lets me pull him in close so I can whisper to him. "You know I have to punish you for that, right?"

His wicked grin sends chills straight to my pussy. "I'm looking forward to it."

When we get back to Micah's, I use his body to slam the door shut. He leans back against the door and lifts my thigh into his hand, his other hand grasping the back of my neck.

"I had a nice time tonight, Storm," he says between kisses.

"I'm glad. But I'm mad at you." I'm absolutely not mad, but I enjoy the growl that rumbles from deep in his chest when I say it.

"Mad at me, huh? How can I make it up to you?"

I press my hand into his chest and free myself from his grasp. I turn away from him, but when I hear him follow me, I whip back around. "I didn't tell you to move."

He licks his lips, motioning for me to carry on. Swishing my hips, I make my way to his couch. I make a show of stripping off every article of clothing except my panties. When I sink down onto the cushions, I lift one leg over the armrest and pull my panties to the side. "You wanna know how you can make it up to me? You can be a good boy and make me come."

He starts to stalk over to me, but I once again lift up my hand to stop him. "Uh-uh. Crawl to me."

His responding laugh is quiet, almost foreboding. When he's in control again, he will make me pay for this, and I'm looking forward to that.

Slowly, he sinks to his knees and locks his eyes with mine. He lifts his shirt over his head, tossing it across the room. He looks like an animal stalking its prey as he makes his way over. My pussy clenches with anticipation.

Once he's eye level with my pussy, he looks up to me for permission.

"What are you waiting for? Show me what a good boy you can be."

He grabs me by the hips and pulls me down so my ass hangs off the couch. He tosses my legs in the air and lays his tongue flat against my center.

"Oh my God," I cry out.

He moves his hands under my ass so he can lift my hips up in the air. The sound of fabric ripping brings my soul back down to its body in time to see the scraps of my panties float to the floor.

When I meet his eyes, there's not an ounce of remorse. His only concern is the sounds I make as he wrings every drop of pleasure from my body.

He latches onto my clit and uses one of his hands to trace the rim of my ass. When his thumb dips into my puckered hole, my entire body screams.

It's so good. It's too fucking good.

I don't even have a chance to tell him I'm going to come before I'm coating his face with my release. He swallows me down like I'm the best drink he's had in a long time and he can't get enough.

"Jesus, you are definitely a good boy," I sigh.

"Nah, fuck that. I wanna be the best." He scoops me into his arms and carries me to his bedroom.

He throws me onto the bed, but I scramble to my knees before he follows me down. "I didn't give you permission to take control, did I?"

He growls his displeasure. "No, you didn't."

"No, what?" I climb from the bed, eyes glued to him as I strut around until we're face-to-face with his back toward the bed.

He licks his lips as he takes in my naked form, my inner thighs glistening with my own release. "No, ma'am."

I tap his nose, laughing when he blinks in surprise. "Good boy. Take off your pants."

He pulls down his pants, stepping out of them with no issue. When I lift my eyebrow, he rushes to ditch the briefs as well.

"You really are good at following directions."

"For you? Always."

"Hmm, we'll see about that." I grab his wrist and yank him toward me, turning our bodies in the opposite direction. "Now get on the floor," I say as I give him a slight push.

He lets me move him as he falls to his butt. "How can I serve you now, Storm?"

I like the sound of that. I disappear into his bathroom for condoms and come back to find him perfectly still, waiting for my next instruction.

I walk behind him and lean over his shoulder until I can grab his dick. Slowly, I slide the condom down his form as I suck his earlobe. He grunts and I smile with his ear between my teeth when I see his fists clenching by his sides.

"You still wanna serve me, Moonchaser?"

He nods profusely as his gaze tracks my movements until I'm standing over him. "Till I take my last breath."

There's a pang in my heart at those words, which I fight to ignore. No more teasing. As I sink onto his lap, he holds his dick up to my entrance so I can slide down effortlessly. Careful not to sit on his ankles with his legs crossed, I wrap my legs around his back and my arms around his neck, loving how stretched I feel.

"Fuck, don't move yet. Please," he begs.

"What's the matter, Micah. Is it too much?" I whisper in his ear.

He rolls his neck and hugs me tight to his chest. "Never."

"Then stay still." I grind my body into his as he matches my rhythm.

We share soft kisses and promises as our bodies become one.

Chapter Twenty-Four

Micah

I STACK THE LAST CHAIR IN PLACE RIGHT AS KAYLAN finishes cleaning up the snacks and coffee from today's group meeting.

A jolt of excitement runs through me at the sight of Bailey's name on my screen.

"Hello?"

"Hi, Micah. Could you please come over? I need your help with something."

"Sure, is everything okay?"

Her tone is sharp and clear. "Everything is fine. Just come over."

"All good?" Kaylan asks when I hang up the phone.

"Yeah, that was Bailey. She asked me to come over."

Her eyes sparkle. "That's great! This is the first time she's talked to you in what, two weeks?"

Eleven days. The longest silent treatment I've ever gotten from her. She hasn't even been working reception at Spring Hill, leaving that to our office manager, while she works remotely. If

I'm being honest, the only reason I haven't given in to my temptation to barge into her place is because Dani and my parents have been telling me how she's doing.

"Almost, yeah. Is it weird that I'm kinda nervous to see her?"

"No, I get it. You're worried about what will happen if this conversation doesn't go well. But worry about the bridge you're on right now. If you try to look ahead to the bridge coming, you're just gonna end up in the water."

Right. Be in the now.

When I first walk into Bailey's apartment, my eyes shift around every part I can see. She peeks out from the kitchen area and motions for me to join.

Her kitchen has an explosion of groceries scattered over her table. There's a cluster of plastic bags condensed together from the groceries that have already been put away, and a pile of food storage containers lining the counter.

"The crap gap?" I ask.

Her eyes soften as she nods. Usually, around a month prior to Bailey's next Ocrevus infusion, she starts experiencing MS symptoms again, so she likes to meal-prep in advance and freeze her leftovers so it's one less thing on her plate when she's already fighting for energy.

"I got all the stuff I need to make my recipes, but I'm too tired to make it all. That's where you come in. I was hoping my big brother would help me out." She always loves to lay on the big brother thing when she wants to get her way, as if I wasn't going to say yes already.

"I got you, sis." Bailey is vegetarian and she keeps her meals simple, so I should be able to knock this out in no time. I start prepping the food while she sits at the kitchen table. "I'm glad you called me."

"Me too. You see how I do ask for help when I need it? So, you don't have to assume I always need it."

"You're right."

"I know I am. Glad you agree because I don't like when you get on my bad side," she responds.

"I'm gonna try not to be on that so often. And I really am sorry. I was wrong to shut you down like that and I promise to do better." Helena says that protectiveness is a sign of love and that overprotectiveness is a sign of mistrust. I trust Bailey to take care of herself and I need to prove that to her. "And for the record, I think you're the furthest thing from useless."

"So you think I can't handle myself?"

"I know you can."

Where her diagnosis sent me into a panic, it gave her relief because she finally knew what was going on with her body. She immediately put her all into learning about MS, its causes and treatments. She searched everything she could on maintaining a career in dance with MS and things to do outside of work. When she wasn't happy with her injection treatments because they left her with scars and was taxing on her schedule, she researched her options so she could make an informed decision. Ocrevus is an infusion therapy that she receives every six months. She talked through the pros and cons with her neurologist at length before deciding it was the right match for her lifestyle. Bailey is more than capable.

"But even if you didn't have MS, I would still be extremely protective of you because, well, you're my little baby. You're a brilliant woman, but you will always be my baby girl. I will do my best to ease up on it, though."

She wraps me up in a tight hug and smacks an obnoxious kiss on the side of my face. "I love you, Chopper. And thank you. I really appreciate it, forreal."

"I love you too, Franky. Alright, alright, get off me." I shake my entire body until she lifts herself off me, flipping me the bird. "So, did I make my way off the shit list because you wanted me to cook your food, or that's just a happy coincidence?"

"Do you want us to be cool or nah?" She picks up a piece of raw broccoli and throws it at me, hitting my eye.

"Not if you tryna blind me and shit."

"Whatever. Just cook my food, fool."

Once I'm finished cooking her meals and fixing us both something for dinner, I sit with her at the table. "So, about the tour. First of all, congratulations. That really is a big fucking deal." This is all she ever dreamed about when she was ten years old dancing along to Michael Jackson videos in our living room. "Second of all, tell me more about it. Who's it with? Where y'all going?"

"It's not set in stone yet, I still haven't made up my mind. It's for four solo rappers and they're calling it the Legends and Icons Tour. They want me to be the choreographer." She gives me more details about the tour and her role in it, and all the while her body is buzzing with anticipation.

"If you're this excited, how come you haven't told them yes?"

"I don't know. I guess I'm playing hard to get."

Or did I manage to ruin the excitement for her? "Don't pass on a great opportunity that could bring you so much joy because of your dumbass brother. Okay?"

She turns her head away to wipe her eye. "It's not because of you. Well, not entirely. It's a lot to think about! I wanted this once upon a time, but do I really want it now or do I think I should because the opportunity is in my lap? Because I really love teaching at the Lab."

"The Lab would still be there." Bailey has really found herself a family among the people there and I know she would always be welcomed back.

"I know it would. But still. I'm weighing my options, okay?"

"Okay." I won't push her in either direction. Whatever she decides will be the right decision for her.

With one final brushstroke, I've finally finished the portrait of Tanya.

I can't believe it's over. I've purposefully drawn out this process, not wanting to let her go too fast. And yet, it still wasn't long enough.

"Wow. You're done," Dani says in awe from behind her camera.

We've been recording some footage for the documentary, but when the end was nearing, words failed us. All we could do was watch this final visual of Tanya come together.

"I'm done. Huh. That's kinda crazy," I say blankly.

Staring back at me are the different versions of Tanya. It's a four-panel portrait meant to show how multifaceted she was. The top left panel shows Tanya sitting behind her desk, her legs propped on top with a queen chess piece in her hand. She's donning a no-nonsense face, wearing an all-white power suit. Tanya was sweet and she was kind, but she was no fool when it came to business. She had her hands in many different pots, and she was always able to keep a firm grip on every single one of them. She used to say that loving her job is what made her so good at it, but it also made her a shark willing to bite the heads off of anyone who threatened her ability to do that job.

The top right panel shows Tanya on a stage accepting a philanthropic award for her volunteer and mentor work in the city with her head thrown back in a fit of laughter. Her shadow doesn't match that image, though. Her shadow is her in a fetal position on the ground with her hands clutched to her face and her shoulders up to her chin. Tanya had a larger-than-life personality, but she was also a complex woman who suffered many losses. She carried the weight of those losses on her own shoulders and never dared to let anyone else see them.

The bottom left panel shows Tanya slow-dancing with George. The image is a replica of a wedding photograph Auntie Joyce gave me when we were in South Carolina. Tanya had the fortune of finding her once-in-a-lifetime love so early in life and the cruel misfortune of losing him too soon, but she never stopped loving him. She had fourteen years with him, which seems like a drop in the bucket when you consider that she spent forty-one years without him by her side, but he was a part of her until the day she reunited with him.

The bottom right panel shows Tanya sitting in a chair with a bright smile on her face. Standing behind and all around her are me, Dani,

Daria, and all of Tanya's other mentees. In her arms lies a sleeping baby wrapped in a soft blanket. Tanya was a mother. She was a mother to Lorraine, a mother figure to all of us. We are her legacy.

"Micah," Dani breathes. "I know I always say your work is incredible, but you've outdone yourself. She would lose her mind over this."

While Dani zooms in with her camera, I look back at the portrait, trying to see it through Tanya's eyes. I hope that she would feel seen looking at this.

Dani interviewed me throughout the course of making this painting. Now that it's done, there's not much else for her to ask me. Instead, she asks me if I have any final words about the painting or any more stories I want to share about Tanya.

"Not really. I think the painting speaks for itself. Tanya Holden, you will be very missed. But you will never be forgotten."

She cuts the camera off. "And that is a wrap for Micah Wright. That was perfect."

"Yeah?"

"Yeah. We got everything we need." She looks back at the painting. "Fun fact, sometimes I find myself wanting to cry because I miss her so much, and then I imagine her calling me a nerd for crying over her. Believe it or not, it helps."

"Bet it dries those tears right up."

"With a quickness."

Once we move Tanya's portrait out of the way so it can rest and dry, Dani is in no rush to leave and I'm in no rush to let her go. She sits in my lap with her head on my chest while I rub her back. Neither of us is sleeping or even tired, we're just existing. Existing is a thousand times better when I'm doing it with her.

I've fallen for this girl. Again.

The first time I fell in love with Dani, it was after we got caught in the rain on the day we met. She was soaking wet, in total shock that the rain had come down so hard, and when she looked at me, something in me said, *I could do this for the rest of my life.*

The second time I fell in love with her was instantaneous. I hadn't seen her in years since our first and last encounter. But the moment I saw her again, standing in the middle of a New York club looking like heaven on Earth, it was as if my heart had been beating irregularly until she came back into the picture to set it right.

This time, I don't think there was a specific moment. It just was. It's always been.

"I had an idea," she mumbles.

I tug on her hair so she's forced to look at me. "What is it?"

"I want you to make me into art again."

"Okay, I can do that."

"But." She pauses. "I wanna turn you into art too." She runs her hands up and down my arms, the heat from them searing my skin.

"You wanna make art together?"

"I liked how I felt when you painted me. I wanna feel that again with you."

I'll give her anything she asks for. "How did you feel, Storm?"

"Like me," she says quickly. "I felt like myself."

I ease her off my lap and take her hand in mine. I grab a tarp and a large canvas and show her my collection of body paints. She carries them over to the middle of the loft floor.

While I lay everything down, she sets up her tripod in the corner, in perfect view of the canvas.

"Let's make art," she says as she turns on the camera.

I pull her to the center of the loft and show her the bottles of body paint sitting there.

She crouches down to open them, revealing different shades and colors. She looks up at me from the floor. "Show me how."

I help her up and lift her shirt off her body, throwing it over the railing down to the floor below. She returns the favor, sending my shirt flying after hers.

With determined eyes, she bends to pull her pants down, staying in her squat position to free my dick too. I grab one of the bottles of blue paint and dip some onto my finger. Gently, I swipe the paint across the base of her throat.

She picks a yellow bottle and lets it drip onto my shoulder.

We keep going back and forth, covering each other in innocent places until I smear some green paint across her breasts. She hisses from the cold, her eyes hazy when she looks back at me. Licking her lips, she picks a different color and pours it down her chest until she's almost completely covered, then she smashes our bodies together. Her lips seek out mine, tangling our tongues together as her paint-covered hands explore the planes of my chest.

I pick her up and wrap her body around my waist before sinking to my knees and laying her on top of the canvas.

I lean up to grab a condom and stop to admire her, a living embodiment of art. She watches with hooded eyes as I sheath myself and then welcomes the cold touch as I pour more paint between our bodies and slide inside.

"Ahhh my God," she shivers.

Her hands curl against my stomach, making my muscles contract. I pick up her hand and stretch it behind her head, enjoying the imprint she leaves behind on the canvas. Stretching her arm high like this arches her body upward, her gorgeous figure like a statue.

"Keep your arm there," I command as I let go in order to smear paint all over my hand to cup her breast, branding her with my touch.

Her pussy clenches around me, plunging me forward so my nose is buried in her neck. I feel the paint plastering itself to my nose, chin, and beard. I just don't care. The scent of her perfume clings to my nose. It's rich in its complexities, unapologetically spicy yet sweet. It's intoxicating, much like the woman wearing it.

"Micah," she moans, biting her lip to keep from screaming.

"Be free with yourself, Storm. If you wanna scream, then scream. These walls can take it."

She reaches for the yellow paint and dips her fingers in it. Watching me, she rubs her paint-covered fingertips over her nipples.

"I should discipline you for moving your arm when I said not to."

She tweaks her nipples more. "Are you going to?"

Fuck, is she tempting.

I sink my arms into the blue and red paints until they're almost elbow deep. Paint drips from my fingers as I pull them out. "No, princess, but I am going to make a mess of you."

She sucks in an intake of air when my hands connect with her throat and glide down her body. I caress the underside of her breasts before dragging my hands down the front of her stomach. She arches into me as I pump into her.

I grip her hips and knead them, fueled by her mewls and whispers of pleasure. My hands make their way to her ass, holding it for what I hope is long enough to leave perfect handprints.

"Mmm, Micah, I need more," she cries.

My lips tilt up to a maniacal grin. I'm always willing to give her more. I'd give her anything. I lean down to kiss her, sucking her tongue into my mouth before pulling away. "I got you."

I glide my hands up to the back of her knees, pushing until her legs stretch out past my head. I kiss her ankle and then push her legs until they're spread wide on both sides.

"Shit, that feels good," she gasps.

Gripping her hips again so I can lift myself to get a better angle, I slam back into her as her head rolls backward.

There are no more words to be used. No commands or challenges. We let the art speak for itself. The only sounds are the smacking of my body into hers and our groans of ecstasy.

After we've washed the paint from our bodies and our hair, we watch the video we made and recreate it again and again without the paint. We're still on the floor from our latest go-round when my phone pings with an email.

What the fuck?

The email isn't from Victor. It's from Tanya herself.

From: tanyaholden@gmail.com
To: micahwright@springhouse.com
Subject: One Last Request

Micah—
This place shaped who you are. Embrace it.

Love you deeply,
Tanya

That's all the email says.

One last request? Really, Tanya? I really hope they're handing you some kind of heavenly Oscar up there.

Dani's phone pings too and when she practically jumps out of her skin, I know what she's seeing.

"You got one too?" I ask.

"What the hell is this?"

"I'm guessing this is the true ending of our scavenger hunt." This must be what Victor was hiding. He knew these emails were scheduled to go out, but I wonder how she decided when we'd get them.

"What does yours say?" she questions, her voice shaky. I tell her and she taps her fingers across her lips. "Our Place?"

"That's the one."

"What does she want you to embrace about it?"

My place there. Or what she deems my place should be. She knew about Paris and Penelope's offer, and she also knew I had turned it down. Is she really expecting me to just change my mind because she sent an email from beyond the grave?

Dani lifts my chin with her hands once I've finished telling her my interpretation of Tanya's email. "Micah."

"Yes, Storm?"

"What did Tanya say in her letter about you thinking you don't deserve good things? You're proving her point right now."

"I'm okay with that. Because I'm right in this case."

"Debatable."

I gasp. "Rude."

She chuckles. "Don't deflect; that's my game. Moonchaser."

That nickname does something funny in my chest.

"You are deserving of good things. Tanya saw that. Your aunt Monica saw that. Paris and Penelope see that. I see that. And deep down I think you see it too. Your vision is just clouded by the guilt of surviving."

She's right about that. I have a hard time celebrating life's wins because ultimately I end up thinking about the ones who should be standing there with me.

"How about this? I agree to have a conversation with them. I can't promise anything more than that right now." I'm not ready to sign any contracts or anything, but I am ready to say I'd like to get there.

"I'll take it."

"Good. Can we talk about your email now?"

JULY
IV

Chapter Twenty-Five

Dani

From: tanyaholden@gmail.com
To: djenkins@promesa.com
Subject: One Last Request

Dani—
This place took something from you—take it back.

Love you deeply,
Tanya

Fuck.

Take it back? Take it back?! What if I don't want to get it back, Tanya? Did you ever think about that? Whatever I lost there was meant to be lost and stay that way.

My softness? My belief in humankind? My naivety? New York can keep all that.

What about the piece of you that never recovered from that hotel room? You don't want that back?

Shit, could she really be asking me to face Nigel? To take back what he took from me?

That's very on brand for her, but I'm not sure I'm ready to do it.

I look over to Micah's furrowed brows and smooth out the wrinkle between them with my thumb. "Why so serious?" I ask.

"I don't like this. I don't want you to do something you're not comfortable with. Not when it comes to this and . . . him. I love Tanya, but you come first."

Why does he always have to make me feel things? I was trying to approach this dilemma with logic, and now my heart has entered the conversation and it's very loud.

"You'll be with me, won't you?"

He looks at me with dreary, half-lidded eyes before his eyebrows jump up to his hairline. "Oh, that was a serious question."

"Now, why else would I ask?"

"Storm, I told you from the jump we're partners in this. I'ma be wherever you are."

I take a deep breath and say what's on my heart. "Then I'll be okay."

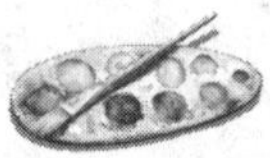

Micah and I will head to New York in a couple of days, but today I'm going with him to Our Place to talk to his cousins.

I haven't been back here since the day we met. I always wanted to, but I had drawn a line in the sand. All places associated with Micah were off my radar.

I'm excited to see the inside of this place. All I had ever seen was Micah's mural on the back wall, which I'm glad to see is untouched, but I always wanted to immerse myself in the place that meant so much to him.

When I step inside, I immediately understand the magnitude of this place.

The layout is pretty standard for a community center and there aren't any decorations that particularly stand out. It's the energy.

When you walk in, there's this overwhelming sense of . . . joy. This isn't just a place where kids go to be a warm body in a seat until they can go home. This is a place where they can explore who they want to be in this world. I saw a little girl tell a teenager that she wants to run for her class treasurer but was afraid she'd be made fun of, and the teenager has been helping her ever since with making signs for her campaign and a cute slogan. The kids here understand the importance of a place like this, and they do everything they can to protect it.

Two women walk up to Micah and me. The one with box braids in a messy bun is wearing a brown blazer over a white T-shirt and jeans. The other, with coily hair framing her face, wears a cardigan over a tank top and jeans. The woman in the blazer, whom Micah introduces as Paris, has a kind smile, while Penelope, the woman in the cardigan, has a kind face until she smiles. Her smile and laugh are a bit diabolical sounding and looking.

"This is Dani—"

Paris interrupts Micah before he can say anything else. "Oh my God, *you're* Dani."

Penelope elbows her and she winces.

"Shit, I mean. Hello, kind stranger I've never heard of."

Micah rolls his eyes. "Bailey told y'all my business, didn't she?"

Penelope holds her thumb and index fingers up. "Lil bit."

Normally, I would be furious at my business being on front street, but this feels good. This feels like I'm on the path of something great.

"I'ma have to beat her ass," Micah says casually.

"Umm, no, you won't. Because who told Bailey all our business, hmm?" I chastise.

"Oh yeah, I like her," Penelope says.

We follow the women back to their office and they direct us to sit while Penelope grabs the chair across from us and Paris stands at her back.

"So, you ready to hear us out?" Paris asks.

"I guess so," Micah says in a somber tone.

I grab his hand to offer solidarity. He's been there for me a lot over these past few months, and I'm honored to now be doing the same thing for him.

I squeeze his hand all throughout Paris and Penelope's proposal, reminding him he's not alone in this. His face is generally blank during their presentation, so I can't get a sense of what he's thinking except for when he squeezes my hand back. He'll seemingly zone out and then squeeze my hand three times to let me know he's back and focused.

This keeps going while Paris explains Micah's function as a partner and Penelope breaks down the numbers. When they're done, they look so proud. Micah looks unamused.

"I remember all this from the last time you made this pitch. I guess I just still don't understand why? Being on the board I get, but why do you want me to be a partial owner?"

Paris groans in frustration. "Ugh, isn't it obvious? It's what Mom wanted!"

The waves from the bomb she dropped rip through the room at an alarming speed. It hits Penelope first, causing her to squeeze her eyes shut. It hits Micah next, his jaw practically hitting the floor. It hits me last, leaving my stomach in knots.

"What do you mean? Chi Chi left the place to my mom because you two were too young. What does that have to do with me?"

Penelope picks up where Paris left off. "Sometimes, it's hard for us to remember what Mom's voice sounded like. Last year, we found ourselves wanting to hear from her again, so we looked through our keepsake box and there was a note stuck on one of the last pages of this book she used to read to us as kids."

"I don't know how we missed it before," Paris adds.

"But it was a login for an email account. She had this whole separate account that she used strictly to email herself all her dreams and aspirations. Sometimes, they were just detailed accounts of literal dreams she had the night before."

Paris pulls out a printed copy of one of the emails and hands it to Micah. He reads it out loud, bringing the girls to tears as he recounts his aunt's wishes that one day the three of them run the center together. How she always envisioned it that way because they were the reason she decided to stop dreaming about opening Our Place and actually do it. How she wanted them to be proud of her and wanted to leave behind something they could be proud of.

Monica must have intended to change her will to say just that once the three of them were of age, but she never got a chance. She was taken from them when Micah was just fifteen, Penelope eleven, and Paris ten.

Micah lowers the paper, tears welling up in his eyes. "I was always proud of her," he manages to say.

"Us too," Paris agrees. "So we asked you to be a partner because we wanted to honor her wishes."

"Why didn't you tell me this before?"

"You weren't ready to hear it. You pretty much shut down the conversation before it really got started. We didn't want to tell you about Mom's note and guilt you into it. We hoped you'd want to be a part of it," Penelope responds.

"But you're telling me now."

Paris sucks her teeth. "Because if you didn't want this, you wouldn't be sitting in that chair. Look, you can still say no. We're not trying to force your hand."

"Right," Penelope cuts in. "But for what it's worth, we always saw the three of us doing this together too."

It's easy to see how much they admire Micah. I hope that one day he can fully grasp the impact he makes on this world.

He stands from his seat and walks around the desk to pull Penelope and Paris into a group hug. When they part, all their cheeks are stained with tears.

"I still need to think about it. But I promise I'm considering it, okay?"

Paris bobs her head up and down while Penelope offers a curt nod as she dabs a tissue under her eye.

"The Pee Pee Girls plus Micah. It does have a nice ring to it," Micah sings.

Paris and Penelope freeze. They look at each other before Paris pretends to strangle him and Penelope pretends to kick him in the groin.

As we're leaving their office, I lean over and whisper to Micah, "'Pee Pee Girls' is insane, by the way."

"It writes itself!" That's his only response.

A tall, muscular teenager with sepia-hued skin walks through the front door, a fitted cap covering his head. He spots Micah and rushes over to him with all the urgency of a young child.

"What's good?" he says as he holds his hand up to Micah.

Micah daps him up and pulls him in for a hug. "What's up, Tee? I didn't know you were working today."

Ahh, this must be Tavion. Micah told me about his godson and how he lost his dad. I knew Micah had hooked him up with a job here, so I'm glad I'm getting a chance to meet the kid Micah adores so much. But if I keep letting myself become so ingrained in his life, I won't be able to pull myself out. Is that really what I want?

"I'm not. There's a kid here who walks home every day but has issues with some of the kids in his neighborhood, so I try to come by and walk with him whenever I can."

Oh, this kid is a mini Micah in the making.

"Which kid is it? Want us to drive him?" Micah asks.

"Nah, I got it. Those kids don't mess with me."

Micah seems to accept this response. He wraps his arm around my shoulder. "Tee, I want you to meet Dani. Dani, this is my godson, Tavion."

Tavion looks at me like he's got a secret, or rather knows a secret. I think it's more than just Bailey that Micah spilled his guts to. "Nice to meet you, Dani. You can call me Tee."

I step into his open arms and return his hug and sentiment.

Since the boy Tee's here to escort isn't ready to leave, he and Micah decide to shoot around at the basketball hoop out back. I have no interest in doing that, but I do offer to catch their rebounds.

"Hey, can I ask, what did you and my parents used to do around here?"

"Anything, really. If I wasn't shootin' hoops with your dad, I was usually painting something. Your mom used to play the flute, did you know that?"

He does a double take. "No, I didn't."

"Yeah, she was in the marching band at her school, but she could never practice at home because her dad worked nights and would be sleeping when she got home from school. So, she'd come here to practice. Me and Taron used to go to her school's games, and he'd be the loudest motherfucker there cheering only for her."

He laughs. "I bet she loved that," he says with a pinch of sarcasm.

I'm guessing Sammy is not a woman who likes the spotlight.

"She did only when it was him."

"What kind of stuff did he like to do? You had art, Mom had music. Was he focused on basketball?" He takes a shot, the ball bouncing off the rim and tipping into the net.

"Actually, he really loved kids. He would tutor here, help them with their homework. He'd even stay late to cook dinner for the ones who couldn't go home. I think he probably would've ended up being a teacher."

Tee stumbles over his dribble, but he recovers quickly. He's clearly processing Micah's words and maybe realizing that he's more like his dad than he ever imagined. From how highly Micah speaks about Taron, I hope Tee is proud of that fact.

"What do you think he would've taught?"

"He could've taught any age, but younger kids really loved him, so I could see him teaching elementary school. He also loved science. He was always volunteering to help kids build baking soda volcanoes or balloon-powered cars."

"That sounds dope."

"It was. He was."

They play for a little while longer while I watch contentedly, despite Tee's urging for me to play H-O-R-S-E with them. Once I show him how terrible I am by attempting a shot and ending up with an air ball, the requests conveniently stop.

"I've been meaning to ask you something," Tee says as he sinks another shot.

"What's up?"

"Do you think maybe you could take me driving? Mom wants to, she just doesn't have enough time with all her shifts and classes."

I can see it written all over Micah's face that he's going to happily say yes, but he paces over the free-throw line to draw out the moment. He may not admit it, but he's got a touch of Tanya's dramatics too.

"Yeah, I guess I could do that."

Tee starts to celebrate, but Micah holds up his index finger.

"On one condition."

"I'm listening."

"No more suspensions."

Tee stands up straighter. "I can do that."

"At least learn to deal with the bullies off school premises."

We all bust out laughing and Micah makes him swear not to tell his mom what he said.

I'm heading over to Nelle's place because I need to borrow a pair of sneakers from her. I realize that the very few sneakers I have are not made for the kind of walking required in New York City, and I love Tanya, but I'm not getting blisters for her.

And maybe I'm looking for a little self-assurance before I let myself walk into the lion's den that is that city. I've been back to New York since moving home. My career doesn't exactly allow me to avoid the place, but I've never gone back alone, and I always get out of there as soon as possible.

I won't be alone, of course, but I know I won't be getting out of there unscathed this time.

When I let myself into Nelle's place, Evie turns around in her chair like a Bond villain.

"Jesus! You scared the shit out of me!" I yell.

She rubs her hands together maniacally as Nelle walks out from the back. "She's been waiting for your ass."

"Why?" I ask, hugging Nelle and making my fingers into a cross toward Evie.

"Oh, you know. You're just about to go to New York with fine ass Micah. I wanted to see how you were feeling about that."

Oh, brother. Here we go. Evie used to flirt with Micah relentlessly, which I always found entertaining, but now she's more into figuring out what's going on between Micah and me. I say let's go back to the flirting.

"I feel fine about that," I say, keeping my tone as flat as possible. Him going is the only reason I feel fine about this entire trip.

"Mhm. So, are you gonna admit that you and Micah are feelin' each other?" she asks, looking over to Nelle, who nods.

Now's my chance. My chance to come clean with two of my favorite people in the world. I want to let them in. I want to share this part of myself the way Micah has with Bailey. I've never gushed over a man with them before; the only one I ever felt inclined to do so about was Micah, and when it ended so suddenly, it felt like confirmation that I should never bring that part of me to light.

I can either rip off the Band-Aid or keep letting this wound fester.

"Actually, yeah, we are. We're kind of dating." Is that what we're doing? It feels inadequate to call it that, but anything else feels too heavy for my mind to comprehend.

"Skrrrrrrt, hold the fuck up. You're dating now?" Evie asks, her tone giddy.

"Rue, when was this?" Nelle adds.

"I mean, I did ask him on a date, and we went, so—I guess we're dating." I shrug.

Evie turns to Nelle. "Did she just say she asked him?"

"She did." Nelle turns back to me. "Say more about that."

The knock on her door is just the distraction I need. When she answers, I hear Rome's deep voice float through the halls. Moments later, they walk back to the kitchen arm in arm, an iced coffee in her free hand.

"Oh, hey, ladies. I'm sorry, I didn't know y'all was here. I would've gotten y'all coffees."

"That's okay, Rome," Evie chimes in. "You can make it up to us by answering some questions."

"Okay, like what?"

"Did you know Micah and Dani are dating?"

Here she goes.

"Damn, look at the time, I gotta get going." His eyes widen and he disentangles himself from Janelle, giving her a sweet kiss as he tries to escape.

Poor, unfortunate soul. He's never going to make it out that door.

"Uh-uh. Hold up!" Evie literally chases him and drags him back.

I make a mental note to buy my own damn sneakers next time.

Nelle makes Rome hide out in her room while I tell them the truth for the first time. The whole truth. Every part of mine and Micah's history and every part of our present. Their mouths are practically on the floor by the time I'm done.

"I wasn't expecting to tell y'all all that when I came over, but there it is."

"Holy shit, you two are in love," Evie gasps.

"You always have to take things too far."

Evie scrunches her nose and tilts her head. "Riiiight. Because that's such a stretch. Either way, I'm so fucking happy for you. You deserve this level of happiness."

"And it looks good on you," Nelle adds.

"Yes, consistently fucked and blissfully happy might be my favorite look on you," Evie says, waving her hand up and down my frame.

I hide my head in my hands. "Okay, okay. Thank you. We're just seeing how things go. That's all. No pressure."

Evie and Nelle share another look. "Mhm," Evie says.

"Yep," Janelle responds.

"No pressure," Evie adds.

"No pressure at all," Janelle echoes.

"Are you two done?"

"For now," Evie confirms.

"You know, you never even told us what you're going to New York to do, just that you got one final task from Tanya," Nelle notes.

"Right. I do wanna tell you guys about that. I'm just not ready." Not to go into details at least. I don't want to dredge up all those feelings right before I'm going to face the man responsible, but I want to get better at being honest with my friends.

Nelle grabs my arm. "Wait, are you okay?"

"Yeah, I'm good. Or I will be. But I promise to tell you everything when I get back."

"You don't have to if it's too much," Evie assures me. "Just know that you can."

"I know."

"Does Micah know whatever it is you're not saying?" she asks.

I nod slowly.

"Good. Do not let him out of your sight. I don't know if it's a person or a thing that put that faraway look in your eyes, but I do know if it's not us that's gonna have your back, Micah damn sure will."

For once, my heart and my head have no objections to that.

"Do you wanna free Rome from his prison cell?" I ask.

"No, this is his punishment for not telling me about you and Micah sooner. I mean, what am I giving up the cookie for if he's not doing pillow talk correctly?"

Fucking Tanya. The longer I sit on this bench, the longer I'm cursing her name.

I'm already itching to leave this city, but I didn't come this far to let it tear me down.

"And your friend was sure this is the time he comes?" Micah peers around the bench we're sitting on, which is situated across from the spa that Nigel frequents. When I told Micah that I wanted to confront Nigel, I knew I wasn't going to reach out to him to do it. I'll be damned if I give him the satisfaction of letting him know he still has an effect on me after all these years, but what I will do is stage a little run-in. I called Anya, as she's still modeling in New York and part of Nigel's circle, much to her chagrin. She and Pedro were more than willing to help me set this in motion.

"She said he's still a creature of habit and this is his appointment time every week."

At 3:00 p.m. on the dot, I pretend not to see him approaching the door to the spa. My teeth chatter as if they know the moment he spots me.

"Dani? Danielle? Is that you?"

My skin crawls at his use of my full name, as if he knows me well enough to do that.

Micah's eyes never leave mine and I'm grateful for that because they keep the proverbial walls from closing in just slightly.

The voice calls out to me again, this time closer, and when I jump up on instinct, Micah moves me behind him.

I can't run from this. I won't let him chase me away from this.

"Hi, Nigel."

"Wow, it's been too long. You look amazing." His voice is dripped in a tone that makes my blood run cold.

He holds out his arms for a hug, but Micah doesn't move from in front of me. I can't see Micah's face, but I've seen his eyes when they turn dangerous and I'm sure—based on the way Nigel stepped back—that's exactly how they look now.

Nigel, never wanting to concede his supposed alpha male spot, clears his throat and pivots his approach. "Well, how have you been? I saw you stopped doing runway and started doing little, um, videos, right?"

Please. His comments on several of my posts were practically begging me to notice him. Now he wants to pretend they were barely a blip on his radar. "Yep. Best decision I ever made." My voice conveys a strength I don't feel.

He smiles, just barely covering the sneer I know he wants to send my way. He's deemed my career change inadequate because it's taken me out of his web of control. I know this, and yet it still eats me up to see him do it.

"Good, good. Well, how long are you here for? We should get dinner to catch up," he offers.

"Nah," Micah responds. He doesn't offer any excuse or try to soften the blow, he just shuts the possibility down with one word. It's incredibly attractive.

Nigel, noticeably avoiding Micah's gaze, waits for a response. As if Micah's was invalid.

Normally, I would say something along the lines of "sorry, we're actually heading out now" or "maybe next time," anything to make myself seem unbothered, but Micah's strength feeds mine, pushing me to say what I really want.

"I would rather chew on a jean jacket than share a meal with you."

Nigel balks at that. "Excuse me?"

"You're disgusting. You're a predator who has to rely on his status to force your way into women's lives. Men like you don't deserve to draw breath, so no, I don't want to 'grab dinner and catch up,'" I say in quotes. "I'm embarrassed to even be talking to you."

His stunned expression shifts into a maniacal grin. "Wow. You're serious. Danielle, if I hadn't discovered you, you'd still be—"

I don't give him the chance to finish. "I'd still be what? Does it make you proud to say you find women when they're young and vulnerable and take advantage of them? Does that make you a man in your eyes?"

"I never took advantage of you. I gave you what you wanted." When Nigel's gaze wanders down my body, Micah clenches his jaw.

"You didn't give me anything that I didn't earn."

He lets out a small chuckle.

"Men who get a ton of work done to still be a five should never laugh," I add.

All the color drains from his face.

My fingers start to twitch and spots cloud the corners of my eyes. We have to wrap this up. Nigel will not win. I'm not sure he's ever been in this position before. He's used to being the one to make people—women in particular—cower before him. When he saw me, he thought he'd get a quick boost to his ego and disparage me. I hope he chokes on regret for approaching me today.

When he opens his mouth again, Micah speaks first. "Do you have anything else to say?" he asks me.

"No. I'm finished."

Micah looks back at Nigel. "Then I suggest you walk away while that's still an option."

Nigel makes up some excuse to get as far away as possible.

I don't turn to blatantly watch him, but I do keep him in my sights until I can't anymore. Then, I fall apart.

The thumping of my heart is so loud in my ears, I'm sure my eardrums are about to burst. My trembling hands have given way to full-blown tremors. I try to grab my right hand to stop its shaking, but it only causes the shaking to spread through the rest of my body.

"Dani. Hey, hey, look at me."

I hear Micah's voice, but it sounds so far away, lost in the spinning void that is my head.

Deep breaths, Dani. Deep breaths.

That does nothing to ease the tremors.

You're okay. You're fine. Everything's fine.

I keep repeating the mantra to myself, but my head keeps spinning. It's getting so bad I have to close my eyes to keep from tipping over. My breath becomes shorter and shorter until I hear myself choking from somewhere outside of my body.

Micah keeps calling my name. At least, I think that's what he's saying, but his voice is faint and foggy.

"You're okay. You're fine. Everything's fine. Everything's fine. Everything's fine." Saying the words out loud doesn't make this feeling subside. Maybe giving in would be the better option. Just let the sensation overtake me until it decides to spit me back out. I resolve to do just that when I feel my feet leave the ground. I register a hard surface pressed against my body.

"Dani. Listen to me, okay? Follow the sound of my voice. I need you to tell me five things you see around you. Okay? Just five things."

I squeeze my eyes shut, and when I open them, I see we're in a bathroom. Not a public bathroom—we're in someone's home.

I blink repeatedly until the features of the room start to get less blurry. "Sink. Shower. Mirror. Cabinet. Tile."

"Good job. Okay, can you tell me four things you can touch?"

Trying my best to focus, I start swinging my hands around. "Floor." My hands settle on the cold, hard floor beneath us, my body finally recognizing another temperature other than boiling. "Nose." I touch the tip of my finger to the tip of my nose. "Lips." I let my finger slide down my face until it reaches those lips, just to make sure they're still there. "You." I hold his wrist in my hand, counting the beats of his pulse.

"You're doing so good, Dani. Now give me three things you can hear."

"Pulse. Clock. Laughter." Laughter drifts through the open window in the bathroom. It sounds specifically like children's laughter.

"Two things you can smell."

I don't hesitate. "Lavender. Musk."

His features are more prominent now, so I see the edges of his lips twist into a grin.

"You're almost done, Dani. One thing you can taste."

I lick my lips, the flavor of my ChapStick coating my tongue. "Cherry."

He takes a few deep breaths, motioning for me to do the same, and I do.

The trembling in my hands subsides and I can finally hear myself think over the sounds of my heartbeat.

"How do you feel?" he asks, scanning every inch of my face twice over.

"Better." And it's not a lie. I'm so grateful for my breaths coming easier that I don't have the emotional capacity to feel embarrassed that Micah is seeing me like this. "Where are we?"

The bathroom, though nice, feels very clinical. It's a stark white and there are no personal touches anywhere.

"We were right by a hotel my boy owns. I got him to get us into a room real quick."

I must've been pretty bad if I didn't notice any of that.

"Got it. Well, tell him I said thank you." The shame is starting to creep into my consciousness now.

"Don't do that, Storm."

My head flies up at his authoritative voice. "Don't do what?"

"Don't be ashamed of this. You're safe with me."

And I know he means that. I feel it every time we're together and even when we're not. I nod my acknowledgment, and he relaxes.

Let go, Dani. Let him be there for you.

Hot tears scorch my face, and as fast as I swipe them away, more keep coming.

"Is it okay if I touch you?"

I nod vehemently and he pulls me into him, burying my head against his chest and planting soft kisses on the top of my scalp.

"None of it is your fault."

That's all he says. It might take some time for me to believe that, but I want to get there. I let myself be held by him for a while longer, not even caring if my makeup is transferring onto his shirt.

When the tears finally stop falling, I sit up and watch in awe as Micah gracefully moves around the bathroom, running a washcloth under water and using it to dab the tears from my face. He steps out to give me privacy to touch up my makeup.

I pop a pain pill when the signs of a tension headache start showing and take a minute to observe the woman in the mirror. She looks like hell, but she feels lighter. That's a start.

When I open the bathroom door, Micah is sitting on the edge of the bed concentrating on something on his phone. He looks up and he doesn't look at me like a disaster. He looks at me like a gift.

We walk out of the hotel, and it feels like an entire day has gone by. I want to go home and crawl in my bed, but I'm doing what Tanya asked of me. It will take more than this one confrontation, but I'm stealing my life back from this city.

"Can we go home now?" I ask. I don't care if it's his home or mine, I just want to stay with him.

"Of course we can."

A short plane ride later, we make it back to my house and Micah takes such good care of me. He pulls me into the shower, scrubbing every inch of my body. He dresses me in my favorite silk pajamas and he holds me while we watch a movie.

Long after he falls asleep, my body is calm, but my mind is still reeling. I'm full of disappointment that I wasn't able to keep my emotions at bay, gratitude that Micah was there with me, and rage at Nigel's boldness.

I tap into that rage as I grab my camera to set it up. Rage I can do well, and it's time I direct its laser at the people who put it there.

I don't bother setting up any aesthetics for the video. I just sit in front of the camera and press record.

"We need to talk about why Nigel Pierce and men like him are dangerous to this industry."

Chapter Twenty-Six

Dani

One point two million views.

Three hundred thousand likes. Two thousand comments. Four thousand saves. Thirty-five hundred shares.

Those are the stats on the video I posted about Nigel and other assholes I've come across in the industry two days ago.

There's some trolls in the comments calling me a liar or saying I should've just kept my mouth shut if nothing actually happened, which I expected. Usually, I eat internet trolls for breakfast, lunch, and dinner, but the high of finally getting all that off my chest has me not caring to engage.

Most of the responses have been overwhelmingly positive. Other women have already started to come out to tell their stories about Nigel. Some of them weren't as fortunate as me to get away and I feel guilty for that. I know I wasn't the first woman he tried to take advantage of, but would it have made a difference for the ones after me if I had said something sooner?

"Can I ask what you're thinking about?" Dr. Goode prompts.

For a moment, I forgot I was in her office, that I was thinking about the video because she asked me how I felt about its success.

"To be honest? I don't know."

She gives me time to elaborate.

"I feel amazing about the video. I'm proud of that, but I still feel disappointed."

"Disappointed, why?"

"For not speaking up sooner."

"You spoke up when you were ready to."

"That's not good enough," I spit. My harsh tone ricochets through her office.

She doesn't try to cut through the tension of my outburst. She lets us sit in its heaviness. Her eyes aren't angry, judgmental, or pitying. They're just accepting. She uncrosses and recrosses her legs before speaking. "Were there any other reasons you felt disappointed?"

The words feel like bile coming out, but I let them out anyway. "I let him affect me. I . . . the first panic attack I ever had was because of him, so it's like, yes, it's great that I finally shared the truth out loud but . . ." The rest of the words glue themselves to the roof of my mouth.

"You feel like because he triggered a panic attack for you before and he did again this past weekend that you haven't really made any progress," Dr. Goode offers.

I turn to the wall, hating that she was able to so clearly put my emotions to words. That's exactly it. What good is allowing myself to be vulnerable if the sight of Nigel is still going to reduce me to a blubbering mess? "Yes," I acknowledge.

"Okay, I see what you're saying. So, let me ask you this. We've talked about your friends Amerie and Janelle and their relationship. Will you think less of Janelle if she does make amends with Amerie?"

"Of course not."

"Why?"

My blood starts to boil at that. I haven't been opening up to her for her to try to get me to look down on my friends. "They're sisters. Of course it's not gonna be easy for her to suddenly go no-contact. She may not even want to do that and that's her choice."

"And other victims of sexual abuse and sexual harassment, do you look down on them for not speaking up right away or at all?"

"Never."

"So, why is it that you can extend grace to everyone but yourself?"

The question sits atop my chest like an anvil. "Well, my situation is not the same as Janelle's."

She tilts her head. "You're willing to acknowledge that Janelle's relationship with her sister is complicated and that her healing process may not be linear, but you think yours should be?"

I open and close my mouth three times before giving up completely.

Dr. Goode presses on. "You acknowledge that women who have been in your situation deserve grace and respect and the freedom to take whatever course of healing suits them best, but you're not included in that?"

Tears burn my eyes and Dr. Goode passes me a tissue before the first one falls. "He doesn't deserve my tears," I cry.

She passes me another tissue. "He doesn't. But you do." A beat passes before she adds, "Dani. You can't expect the panic attacks to just magically go away. That's not realistic. Who knows, maybe the third time you see him, you won't have a panic attack. And maybe the eighth time, you'll have another one."

I hope I never get to eight times of being in his vicinity again. Hell, I pray I never get to three.

"Regardless of whether they happen or not doesn't mean you're not progressing."

I let her words sink in, truly sink in. Deep down, I know she's right. I just have to get to a place where I'm okay with believing that.

"Okay, Goode doctor, I hear you."

She laughs at the moniker I've given her. "Good. Remember, a few weeks ago you weren't even willing to call them panic attacks. That's progress in itself."

She's got me there.

We spend the rest of our session talking about ways to manage panic attacks. She's very impressed with Micah for knowing the five-four-three-two-one method. I'm very impressed with him for a lot of reasons.

When our session is over, Micah is waiting for me in the parking lot. He greets me with a kiss that makes my toes curl.

"How'd it go?"

"She read me for filth, yet again. So, good," I admit.

He squeezes my thigh with a smile. We're headed to Victor's office to pick up his item for the auction. With the gala getting closer, we're sorting out the very last details.

When we get there, Victor doesn't spend too much time on small talk, which he knows I appreciate. He turns to his bookshelf and grabs the glass-covered rose, placing it in front of us.

"Wait, you're auctioning this away?" I say in disbelief.

"Yes. Tanya gave me this one month after we started working together. She said she couldn't bear to sit in my office for another day without some color to remind her she wasn't in a mental institution. And for years, this thing brought all the color and light to my office. I'm hoping it can do the same for someone else now."

I've never seen Victor more clearly than I do in this moment.

"Did you ever tell her?" I ask.

He scrunches his nose. "Tell her what?"

"That you were in love with her."

He doesn't try to deny it. He closes his eyes with a serene smile. "No. No, I didn't."

"But why?" I know I said I don't understand why people fall in love, but if you're already on the ship, why sink alone?

He lets out a light huff. "You saw the same videos and read the same letters I did, Dani. Tanya had a huge heart, and she shared it with so many. She loved me dearly, as a friend. But when it came to romance, she had room in her heart for only one man, and she's with him now."

Sorrow seeps into my skin for this man that I once detested. He sat by Tanya's side without a care in the world for his own feelings, simply because she needed him. Even I have to admit how painfully beautiful that is.

My mind slips, as it so often does, to the man beside me. One who shows up for me in that way even when I don't want to accept it. I turn to find Micah's eyes already gazing back. Yes, Micah terrifies me. But do I want to have the same ending as Victor?

"Do you wish you could've just loved her as a friend? Would that have been easier?"

He ponders. "Easier, maybe. But, no. I don't wish I could've changed my feelings." He looks to the ceiling. "It was an honor to love Tanya. Even if she couldn't love me back the way I wanted."

Somehow I knew that's what he was going to say.

Micah and I walk out, the rose nestled against his side. As we reach the car, he stops and grabs my hand with his free one. "I think it's my turn to ask you on a date, no?"

There go those butterflies, taking flight in my stomach again. "I do think it's your turn, yeah."

"Okay." He lets go of my hand and walks over to the passenger door to open it for me. "Hey, Dani?"

"Yeah?"

"Will you go on a date with me?"

I can't bring myself to say it yet, but I could see myself going on a lifetime of dates with this man.

"Gladly," I say as I take my seat.

"What are you up to today?" I ask as I rub circles on Micah's naked chest.

These days we don't spend many nights apart, so I'm curled up in his bed, my body wrapped around his.

"I gotta meet up with the guys. We're scoping out this building we may wanna buy."

"What are you gonna do with it if you buy it?"

"It's an apartment building. We heard that the owner is considering selling the place to a development company. If that's true, we'll offer to buy it and keep it as is."

The work the Baltimore Collective does has always impressed me. "Got it."

"What about you? What are you doing today?"

"I think I'm gonna go to the rec center."

He sits up in bed, his hand falling from my back to my ass. "Our rec center?"

"Since when is it *our* rec center?"

"That place brought us to Tanya and she brought us to each other, so it's ours."

"Mhm, right. Well, then yes, I'm gonna go to our rec center."

"How come?"

I always visited Tanya at the rec center even after I left home, and I know Micah did too, but when she stopped working there, it wasn't the same. Management didn't put their all into the place like she did, so I stopped coming by. "I had a dream about her last night," I confess.

"About Tanya?"

"Yeah. It was nice. We were at the rec center running lines for some movie. Don't ask me what the hell the movie was about, but Tanya was giving it her all."

"Of course," he snickers.

The dream felt like a sign. A sign that something is waiting for me there. I intend to find out what that something is. Maybe it's just a chance to experience her again; that would be enough for me.

I tell him this and he offers to come with me, but I decline. I feel it in my bones that I need to go alone.

When I get to the rec center, it's quiet. I wasn't expecting a bunch of kids at this hour since it's a school day, but I was expecting someone. Some sort of adult class, people playing basketball, anything. Instead, there's just one woman sitting on one of the couches with her headphones on, writing furiously in a notebook, and another woman pacing back and forth while reading a stack of papers to herself quietly.

I walk over to the woman with the papers, not wanting to make the woman on the couch remove her headphones. "Hi, is there someone working today?"

She turns to me and that's when I see she's not a woman at all. She can't be any older than fifteen, maybe, but she's only about an inch shorter than me. "Oh my God, oh my God," she yells.

The woman on the couch squints over at us, lifting her headphones off one ear, but returns to whatever she's doing when I give her a thumbs-up.

"Sorry, I shouldn't be so loud, but you're Dani Jenkins, aren't you?"

"That would be me."

Her voice jumps a half octave. "You're my idol!"

I slap my hand against my chest. "That is so sweet, thank you."

Her legs start shaking and she hides her stack of papers behind her back. "I have so many questions for you, oh my God." She shakes her head. "No, you're busy. I'm sorry, I shouldn't bother you."

I look at this girl, beautiful yet awkward in her stance. I approached her, and yet she apologized for bothering me. Her white blouse looks fantastic against the russet color of her skin, but she tugs on the bottom of her shirt like she's dressed inappropriately. Somewhere along the lines of her life, she's been told that she's too much and that she needed to take up less space. I wish I could wrap my hands around the throat of every person that's ever told her that and squeeze until they couldn't fill her head with lies anymore.

"I'm not busy and you're not bothering me. Do you want to sit down?"

Her eyes bulge out of her skull. "Really?"

"Really."

She starts to skip over to the bleachers, but then looks back at me, embarrassed, and slows down to a stroll. I catch up to her and skip past her, all the way to the bleachers, happy when I see her doing the same.

"So, what's your name?"

"Veronica."

"It's nice to meet you." I hold my hand out to hers and she nearly rips my arm out of its socket with how fast and hard she shakes it.

"Sorry, sorry. Nice to meet you too."

"You said you had questions for me?"

She rubs her hands down her face, letting out a small shriek. "I don't even know where to start. Umm, how did you get into modeling?"

I happily give her a brief rundown of what led me here and I can see her mouth moving as I talk, trying to memorize every word.

"Are you interested in modeling, Veronica?"

Her hand flies behind her to the stack of papers she stashed there when we sat down. "Sort of. I want to model, act, and sing."

"A triple threat, I like it."

I expect her to smile at that, but she doesn't. She looks away, suddenly very interested in her nails.

"Did I say something wrong?"

Her eyes jump to mine as she frantically waves her hands. "No, no, no. I'm sorry, I didn't mean to offend you."

"Is it okay if I grab your hands?" I ask.

"S-s-sure."

I take her hands in mine and take a deep breath. "You didn't offend me. We're having a great conversation, okay?"

She mimics my deep breath. "We are."

"Okay. So, tell me about the modeling, acting, and singing."

Another deep breath. "People tell me I could be good at modeling, because I'm tall. But most people say I don't have the right vibe to be famous."

That gives me pause. "What's the right vibe?"

She hums. "More calm, I guess. They say I have too much energy to be able to do interviews and stuff. They say acting takes a finesse I don't have."

Again, who is "they"? And where can I find them? "You know what that sounds like to me?"

"What?"

"Jealousy."

"Oh, I don't know about that," she says, a hint of red creeping up her neck.

"I do. Anyone who tries to dim someone else's light has no light of their own. Let them rot in the dark."

Her hands fly to her mouth and her eyes peek behind her once again. After seemingly wrestling with herself, she finally grabs the stack of papers. "Um, I was thinking of auditioning for my school's musical."

"Yes! That sounds amazing. What is it?"

"*Little Shop of Horrors.* I really want to play Audrey."

"Those your lines for your audition?" I motion toward the papers. It can't be a coincidence that this girl is here running lines by herself the night after the dream I had.

"Yeah. The audition is in a couple weeks, so I'm practicing. But I don't even know if I should do it."

"Do you want to do it?"

"I do."

"Then you will. Hand it over, we can run lines together."

She perks up. "Are you serious? But weren't you here looking for someone?"

"Looks like I found 'em."

After ninety minutes of running lines in between Veronica prodding me with questions, she leaves to head home, while I'm the one left buzzing.

Veronica was a gift I didn't know I needed. Once upon a time, interactions like that were everything I wanted out of this industry. In all the pain I experienced, I allowed myself to forget that.

I won't let myself forget again.

Chapter Twenty-Seven

Micah

"You know, it is possible for you to just tell me where we're going sometimes. It ain't always gotta be a surprise," Dani complains with her eyes closed in the passenger seat as I make another turn.

"I could. But admit it, you like the surprises." Last night when Dani came over, she couldn't stop gushing about her trip to the rec center and meeting Veronica. She had this renewed passion for her work that I haven't seen in a long time. It was wonderful.

"I admit nothing," she teases.

"Whatever you say, Storm."

She reaches out to hit my arm but misses since her eyes are closed. She looks so cute swinging aimlessly, so I move my arm within her range.

"Did you move your arm?" she asks, her nostrils flaring.

"I couldn't keep watching you flail around."

"Flail? That's insane, actually. I've never flailed a day in my life."

"Considering you just did, I don't think that's true."

She swings at me again, huffing when she misses. "Put your arm back."

Laughing, I put my arm back in the line of fire. "All yours."

She thanks me as her hand connects. "Anyhoo, did you guys end up buying that building?"

"We're putting in an offer today. Hopefully he accepts it, but he was basically fangirling over Jalen the entire time we met with him, so I think he will."

She keeps her eyes closed but turns her head toward the sound of my voice. "That's awesome, Micah. We should all go out and celebrate."

Funny she should say that, since the purpose of today is to celebrate her. "I'd be down for that."

Dani blindly reaches out in search of something and when she finds my hand, she grabs it and squeezes. "It's an honor to know you."

Damn. That has my heart jumping out of my chest. Her words mean more to me than she'll ever know and I squeeze her hand back in thanks, but as she flashes a bright smile my way, all I can do is laugh. "I'm sorry. You just look so ridiculous." With her eyes squeezed shut and her cheesy grin revealing her bright white teeth, she looks like a kid with a secret.

She gasps and yanks her hand away, making this all the more amusing. "Oh, boy, fuck you! I should open my damn eyes."

I pull up to our destination. "Go ahead. We're here."

She sucks her teeth, but then her jaw drops when she opens her eyes and sees where we are. "We're at my parents' house?"

I step out of the car and walk to her side to open the door. "We are. And before you say anything, just wait and see."

She blinks a few times, taking in the sight of me in front of her parents' house, and then she makes my day and smiles. "Okay. I trust you."

Music to my ears.

We walk up and I knock twice before her dad opens the door.

"Peanut!" He wraps her up in a big bear hug before turning and dapping me up. "Micah. Nice to meet you in person."

"In person. I'm just wondering how you met any other way," Dani muses as she steps past her dad into the house.

"Girl, you don't know everybody I know."

She turns back to him, eyes crinkling in the corners. "Yes, I do."

I get the sense that she's about to start naming everyone he knows until her nose turns toward the kitchen and she starts sniffing. She walks away without a word, her nose turned up.

Her dad nudges me with a smirk and follows. When we walk into the kitchen, Dani is completely still, facing the spread of food laid out before her.

"A pancake breakfast was in order," Julian says.

I hear her sniffle before she turns to us. "Oh, really? For what?"

Julian rolls his eyes at her. Her parents know about her video on Nigel. Her mom called her maybe ten minutes after she posted it. "You know for what. And Micah says you're mentoring someone too. You always wanted to do that, Peanut. I'm so proud of you."

Dani and her dad talk animatedly, and when her mom comes downstairs, she's just as animated. Dani is a perfect blend of her parents, with her dad's smile and her mom's mannerisms. The love in this house is easy to find.

We sit down to eat and I devour the pancakes. They're just as delicious as Dani always hyped them up to be.

Her mom asks me about my career, and her dad and I talk about Tanya's Lincoln. Dani has a giddy look on her face while she shoves bite after bite in her mouth. A drop of syrup lands on her chin and I wipe it off without hesitation.

She raises her brows at me, and I know what she's thinking. *This gives relationship, no?* The thing is, it's been that. For a while now.

After breakfast, her mom refuses to let me help clean dishes, much to Dani's chagrin, but her dad pulls me aside before she can plead her case on why I should help and not her.

"I wanna touch base with you because she didn't introduce you as her boyfriend, but you're the first man linked to her that's ever walked through those doors. So, what's up?" He's asking a question without a simple answer.

"Sir, all I can say is I care about your daughter. A lot. And it's my goal to make sure she always knows and feels that."

He nods slowly. "Well, she might not say it, but that smile on her face tells me what I need to know."

I sure hope so.

When we leave her parents' house, she squeezes her parents tight. Her mom whispers something in her ear that makes her face light up, and then she does something I wouldn't expect her to do in front of them. She links her hand with mine.

We drive in a comfortable silence to her place. The lingering happiness on her face fuels me to bring up a topic I've been sitting on for a while. I overstepped with Bailey. I took away her choice and I can't do the same thing with Dani. We have too much on the line for me to mess up now.

"I have a confession," I say as I park in front of her house.

Her eyes drift over to mine. "And you buttered me up for it by taking me to see my parents first?"

"I could see how you would think that, but no. I just can't keep it in anymore."

"Well, please, unburden yourself," she says with a wave of her hand.

Here goes nothing. "When you first told me about Nigel, I got Rome involved. I didn't tell him why I needed the information, but I had him look up anything he could find on him."

"Why?"

"Because he caused you pain and he needed to suffer."

Her eyes widen. "What did you do?"

"I didn't do anything. Yet. But we did find out that Nigel doesn't own his agency. He's a figurehead. The real owner is more than willing to negotiate terms of sale because Nigel isn't making him the money he wants." He's even more motivated now that Dani's video has demolished his reputation.

Her head starts shaking rapidly. Her words coming out in a stutter. "W-wait. Woah. Hold on, so you're planning on buying Nigel's agency?"

"I was." I wanted to pry it from his hands and serve it to Dani on a silver platter. I didn't care what she'd do with it. If she wanted to burn it to the ground, I would hand her the match. "But then I realized I'd be taking that moment from you. If you want it at all."

"This is a lot right now. I need you to spell it out for me. What exactly are you saying?"

I brush a flyaway hair behind her ear. "I'm saying that if you want his company, say the word. I will make it happen for you. Or I can introduce you to the owner and you can make it happen yourself. Or if you're satisfied that he's suffered enough, I can walk away and leave this be. Whatever you want to do, we'll do. But I want it to be your decision." Selfishly, I don't want her to pick the last option, but if that's what she chooses, I'll accept it.

She stretches her neck, rubbing the back of it with her hand. "I would've been pissed if you had just outright bought it and gave it to me, so thank you for realizing that. And I think, prior to meeting Veronica, I might've said it wasn't worth it. But after meeting her, and seeing the videos from his other victims, I don't want him to have access to us anymore. He deserves ten times the hurt he's dealt. He needs to be stripped of all his power and every fucking thing he has."

Warmth settles in my chest. "Now it's your turn to spell it out for me, Storm. What do you want me to do?"

Resolve settles over her features. "Bring me his head."

"Consider it done."

Chapter Twenty-Eight

Micah

Today's the day of Bailey's treatment.

When I get to her place, she's shoving her iPad into her bag.

"You nervous?" she asks me.

Of course I'm nervous. I always get nervous when she has treatment, but I'm just happy she invited me to come with her this time.

"Me? Nah. I've got nerves of steel."

She coughs into her hand. "Liar," she mumbles between the coughs.

"Wowww, that's crazy."

When we get to the hospital, she introduces me to a nurse who will be monitoring her throughout her treatment today. She runs through Bailey's medical history with her and asks if she has any questions. Usually, Bailey doesn't have any because she has a later appointment with her MS team of specialists, including her neurologist, but this time she looks to me.

"Go ahead, Chopper. Ask your questions." She motions for me to start talking.

The nurse stands around waiting patiently for me to ask, but I don't.

"Actually, I think I'm okay." I trust Bailey to take the lead on her own care, and if she needs me to help, she knows I'll always do so.

"I'm very impressed," Bailey offers.

"I told you I was gonna be better."

"That you did."

"I have a lot of help."

"Oh yeah? Who? Daniiiii?" she sings.

"She's definitely a big part of it. But, I'm, uh, I'm going to this support group. It's for people with family members suffering from autoimmune diseases. The people there are really cool."

Bailey is teary-eyed when I look at her. "You started going to group therapy for me?"

It's for both of us, really. I want to be better for her. For Dani. For everyone in my life. "Actually, I started going for the cookies, but you were a bonus."

"Just tell me you love me, you big dumb idiot."

I smile. "I love you, sis."

"I love you too. Always."

Dani texts to check in on us, and that pulls at my heartstrings.

"Okay, now that you can't go anywhere, lemme see what questions I wanna ask you."

"You waiting until I'm hooked up to this thing is diabolical."

I rub my hands together evilly. "Let me see, have you made any decisions about the tour yet?"

"Still not one hundred percent onboard, but I am meeting with all the artists over FaceTime later this week."

"Well, that's good."

"Yeah, Justin said I'd be a quote 'dumbass bitch' if I didn't at least talk to them."

I knew I liked Justin. "Well, I'm with them when they're right."

She gasps. "What happened to me being your baby girl? Now you letting people call me a dumbass bitch?"

"The two aren't mutually exclusive." I pretend to bite her finger when she flips me off. "No respect for your elders. Anyway, glad I brought two gifts for your indecisive ass, then."

"Gifts, you say?"

I pull two small boxes out of my pockets. "One is for if you decide to go. The other is for if you decide not to go. When you make your decision, I'll give you the right gift."

"Or"—she holds her hands up—"hear me out. You could just give me both gifts now and who knows? That might influence which route I take."

She tries to snatch the boxes, but I'm quicker. "Even more reason for me to keep them from you."

She sucks her teeth. "Fine, keep your shitty ass boxes." She pretends to knock them off the table, yelping in horror when one actually almost falls. "Let me stop playing before my diamonds get fucked up."

"Now, why the fuck would you think there's diamonds in either of these boxes?"

"Mmm, because I'm your favorite sister and I deserve them?"

"Now's probably a good time to tell you about our secret sister. She's my favorite."

She flicks my forehead. "Good. Then she can take you off my hands full-time."

"Whatever. Next question."

"There's more?"

Ignoring her, I press on. "How was your date with Nisha?"

Her entire face lights up. "It was nice. It's been a long time since I've been on a date, so I was antsy, but I liked it. I like her."

"When's the last time you went on a date?"

Her mouth twists into an uncomfortable grin. "When I went on a date with Roc."

I do a double take. “So I’m not crazy, there was something there.”

“Yeah, but it was just one date. We make way better friends. And, I don’t know. I don’t really like to date.”

“You like dating Nisha,” I point out.

“Well, we haven’t had our second date yet, so this could all go up in flames.”

I ask for more details, and she tells me all about the cooking class they went to, excitement flying off her every word. I know how my sister gets, and she really likes this woman. Who would’ve thought my little sister might end up with the assistant of the love of my life?

Once her infusion is done, she’s very excited. It’s like they pumped all the energy back into her muscles and she’s ready to party.

I remember this throwing me off the first time I saw her after an infusion. I was concerned they had given her too much or something, but now when she asks me to go mini golfing with her and some of her friends from the Lab, I go.

As I’m driving home, I’m about to call Dani to see what she’s up to, but I don’t need to.

I see her out at dinner—with Omari.

Chapter Twenty-Nine

Dani

"I haven't decided if it's really the right move for me, you know?"

Omari asked me to meet him tonight to pick my brain about the tequila business. His brothers want him to go into the whiskey business with them, but that's not something he's ever considered.

He really is a nice guy, and I feel bad about basically ghosting him, so here I am listening to him drone on over steaks.

"Well, you can't rush into a decision like this. Switching careers is life-changing."

He ponders my words. "You're right. I've been thinking I need some sort of change in my life. Something big. I just don't know if this is it."

I take another bite of my steak, apparently oblivious to Omari staring me down. When I finally notice, I pause with my fork halfway to my mouth. "What? Do I have something on my face?"

"No. Nothing like that. I'm just looking for the right words."

Uh-oh. Nothing about his tone sounds good. Maybe coming here to end things with Omari in person was a mistake. "Omari, before you say anything, I feel like I need to go first."

His face drops into a mask of nonchalance. "Sure, go ahead."

"I came here tonight as friends because you wanted to pick my brain. But I'm seeing someone now, so that is all I came for."

He wipes the side of his mouth with his napkin. "Is it serious?"

More serious than I ever intended when this started. "It is."

"I figured as much when I couldn't get a hold of you."

Omari stopped texting me a while ago. I think we were still in Colorado the last time he messaged me, and it's been weeks since I even thought about responding. I should've ended things definitively then. I don't know why I didn't. Maybe I was trying to sabotage what Micah and I have been trying to build. Who am I kidding? That's definitely what I was doing, but I'm here trying to rectify that now. "I'm sorry."

He sighs. "It's okay."

"No, it's really not. You're a great guy, Omari. And you deserve someone who sees that and appreciates it. I'm sorry I wasn't her."

He holds up his drink. "Cheers to finding the right person at the right time."

I clink my glass with his. "Cheers to that. Now, let's get back to whiskey."

After dinner, I hug Omari goodbye and stick around to order some dessert to-go. My mind is stuck on one person and one person only, so that's where I'm going to go.

Micah opens his door in a T-shirt and sweats. "Hi," he says.

"Hi." I hold up the takeout bag. "I brought dessert."

He steps aside to let me in. "What'd you bring?"

"Tiramisu."

He quietly leads me to kitchen where he grabs two forks and pulls out my stool for me. There's something in his eyes that doesn't sit right with me. It's sadness with a hint of something else I can't quite decipher.

"Did everything go well with Bailey's treatment?"

"Yeah, it was cool," he says around a bite of dessert. I wait for him to give me more, but he doesn't. He's been psyching himself out for this appointment for weeks and all he has to say is "It was cool"?

"Are you okay?"

"Hmm. I don't really know. But I'll figure it out."

That doesn't inspire a lot of confidence in me. I'm beyond happy with Micah. Our connection now is even stronger than it was when we were together before, but this time it feels different. Like it could last.

But damn if his response doesn't trigger an onslaught of hurt within me. "Okay. Well, can I help you figure it out?"

A war brews behind his eyes. It's a battle I've fought many times between letting those you care about shine a light on you or remaining in the dark. The darkness won far too many times for me, but all I want is for us to step into each other's light.

"I have this fear. It's a fear I don't have a right to have, but it rules me."

I take his hand in mine. "Okay, what is it? What's your fear?"

"Losing you."

I blink in surprise. Why does it seem like the possibility of losing me has been on his mind heavy tonight? Last time we spoke everything was good. "I don't understand. Why would you lose me?"

"I guess first let me start with my confession. I saw you and Omari out at dinner tonight."

"You did?"

"Yeah and I hated it. I wanted nothing more than to go in there and pull you away from him. But then I realized I have no right to do that. You and I aren't exclusive, and you can do whatever you want."

What I want is the man standing in front of me. No more, no less. "Is that what you want? For us to be exclusive?"

"Yes," he says with zero hesitation. "I have wanted you and only you since I was twenty-three years old, that hasn't changed. But I'm not willing to cross your boundaries to have that. I want to do things right this time around."

I move the plate of tiramisu to the side and stand from my chair, forcing him to do the same.

"In that case, it might help to know that I went to dinner with Omari strictly as friends because he had legit business questions. It might also help to know that I did make it clear I was seeing someone and that it was serious."

His eyebrows rise. "You did?"

"I did. Believe it or not, I'm pretty satisfied only dating you."

He laughs. "Pretty satisfied? That's all I get?"

I wrap my arms around his neck. "That's all you get."

"I'll take it for now. I hope you know I'm gonna be insufferable from now on, calling myself your man officially."

"I would expect no less, Moonchaser."

"Oh, I'm retired from that business."

"Is that so?"

He smiles. "Yeah, I don't chase the moon anymore. I only chase storms."

My heart leaps out of my chest. Sometimes, you meet the right person at the wrong time, but if it's truly meant to be, it finds its way back around.

He grabs my legs and pulls me up his body, giving me a kiss that touches my soul.

Chapter Thirty

Dani

"YOU GOTTA STOP PACING, BABY. EVERYTHING IS GONNA be fine." Micah loops his arms around my waist to stop me from wearing down the floors.

The night of the gala is finally here. Everything we've been working toward for months all comes down to this one night, and the nerves are still getting the best of me.

"I know, I just want everything to be perfect."

"We put our all into this, so it's going to be perfect. Tanya would be thrilled."

"You're right, you're right." I take a few steadying breaths to bring myself back to center. Dr. Goode and I have worked through a few new coping mechanisms to get me through panic attacks. I'm learning that there is no one-trick pony that works every single time, so sometimes I have to adjust, but I'm getting better at doing just that.

When the room stops spinning, I can see Micah clearly. He looks too sexy in the suit Daria made for him. "Damn, you look good. Did I say that already?"

"Once or twice. Maybe you could show me better than you could tell me?"

I bite my bottom lip, looking over to the locked door of our dressing room. "I definitely could." I push the jacket of his suit off his shoulders. "This jacket looks fantastic on you." But right now, I think it looks better on the floor.

"Thank you."

I get down on my knees and free his dick from his pants. "These pants are the perfect fit for you."

He hisses when I take him in my hands, tugging from base to tip. "Shit. I'm glad you like them."

"I really do. You know what else I like?"

"What's that?"

"The taste of you."

He looks down at me with hooded eyes. "Get a taste, then."

I take him in my mouth, using my hands for what doesn't fit. When he hits the back of my throat, I gag around him and then take some more.

"Fuck, Dani."

I hum with content at his loss of control. It does it for me every time.

He yanks me to a standing position and turns me around to face the vanity mirror in the room. He makes eye contact with my reflection as he pulls my hair to gain more access to my neck. "How was your taste?"

I lick my lips and stick out my tongue. "Delicious."

His head falls to my shoulder, planting a small kiss there. "Spread your legs for me, Storm."

I do as he asks, enjoying the view of him flipping the train of my dress up to expose my ass. He grabs a fistful, rubbing his dick between the globes before sliding his fingers around to my clit.

His thumb rubs circles onto my clit while three of his fingers pump inside of me. I arch my back, wanting to feel more of him.

"More," I demand.

I reach back for his dick, but he swats my hand away. "You know the rules, Storm. You come, then we come."

He pumps his fingers harder, and I bite down on my lip. "Shit, right there. I'm almost there."

When his fingers send me over the edge, I hear the telltale signs of a condom wrapper before I feel him stretch me wider. "Does my greedy girl wanna come again before she has to go on stage?"

"Yesss," I sing. So desperately.

He slams into me, the legs of the mirror rattling loudly.

I want to scream, but I don't want anyone coming back here to interrupt us. I slam my eyes shut to keep the sounds down.

"Want some help with that?" Micah's voice lures my eyelids to open.

I look at his reflection, cautiously nodding.

He holds up his finger, the one coated in my release. "Bite down."

Without a second thought, I grab his finger and suck it into my mouth. I swirl my tongue around his finger, making him melt into me. Releasing his finger with a pop, I say, "Come with me."

"Fuck," he groans.

"Now, Micah," I command.

My release hits me like a freight train and he follows right behind me.

We've just finished making ourselves presentable again when a knock at the door makes us jump.

"Come in," I call out.

Daria enters, stunning in a red gown that has her signature style. "Hello, my loves." She greets us both with a hug and a kiss.

"Daria! So glad you made it, you look amazing," I say.

"Thank you, thank you. My parents send their love."

"How are they doing?" both Micah and I ask.

"Good. My mom's non-lucid days are becoming more frequent, but we're managing. Anyway, I didn't come back here to stir that up. I wanted to make sure you got your letters."

Micah and I look at each other. "Our letters?"

She beams with pride. "I knew I sewed them in there too well. Come, come." She pulls a small pair of scissors from the top of her dress and ushers me over.

She silently gets to work cutting a tiny incision into my dress, and when she does, she pulls out a small folded-up note. Tanya's handwriting is on the front.

"What is going on?" I ask.

She ushers Micah over and starts cutting into his suit as well. She pulls out a note with the same writing on it and hands it to him.

"Tanya asked me to sew these into your garments and not say anything until the day you wore them."

That woman really thought of everything.

"I will leave you to it. Whatever these notes say is bound to make me cry and I don't wanna have to fix my makeup." She blows us a kiss and a wave as she backs out of the room.

So, this is it. After this, we won't have any more letters coming from Tanya. I've come to rely on these letters as confirmation that she's still looking out for me. Every time I read one, I swear I can hear her voice so clearly. I never want to forget what it sounded like.

The thought of forgetting any detail of her brings tears to my eyes. I guess it's just fuck my makeup then. I hold my letter out to Micah. "You read mine, I'll read yours?"

"Deal."

We switch letters and he starts reading immediately.

My dearest Dani Girl,

I can't leave this earth without telling you how special you are. You have been through a lot and you're still standing. You are incredibly resilient, but please hear me when I say this.

You don't have to be.

You don't always have to be so strong.

This country was built off of our strength. Sometimes, we need to tell them to hold their own damn heads up.

We deserve rest.

Rest, Dani Girl.

Let it go.

Love you deeply,
Tanya

P.S. Remind Victor to take a damn vacation. He needs it.

I snicker at the line about Victor. The man definitely seems like the type to have to be forced to take time off. And look at me—caring about that. I don't know when Victor changed from a man I barely tolerated to one I admire and respect, but I know Tanya is probably moved to tears up there knowing she brought more than just Micah and me together.

Unfolding Micah's letter, I take a deep breath before starting.

My dearest Micah-Angelo,

I see so much of myself in you.

Your life has been plagued with so much loss that you cling to everyone you have left with all your might.

I understand it.

But that loss has also made you question why you were spared.

It's because you were destined to be exactly where you are now.

Do not let life pass you by, or else we have all died in vain.

Live, Micah. And enjoy doing it.

Love you deeply,
Tanya

P.S. Remind Victor to take a damn vacation. He needs it.

At this point, I'm too much of a blubbering mess to even form words. Micah tries to wrap me in his arms, but I back away. "No, I don't wanna get makeup on you."

He scowls. "You can always leave your mark on me, Dani. Now, come here."

This time I give in, and we fall into each other.

"Also, clearly we have to book a vacation for Victor," I say once we break apart.

"Clearly."

When we walk into the banquet hall, we're greeted by Bailey, Nisha, Nelle, Evie, Rome, Christian, and Jalen. No sign of Arnold or Amerie. I'm hurt but not surprised by that, and I refuse to spend even a modicum of tonight focused on their absence.

The women look incredible in their gowns: Nelle in emerald green, Evie in periwinkle, Bailey in light pink, and Nisha in orange.

Everyone compliments us on the turnout of the event before taking their seats.

"You ready?" Micah asks, handing me a mic.

I step onto the stage and those nerves I was feeling moments ago dissipate the moment I look into the crowd of smiling faces.

This is a beautiful event, and Tanya would be proud of what we put together. She would be over the moon to see all the people she valued in life gathered in one room. But then I look back to Micah and I think this is what she would be most proud of, us finding each other again.

"Hi, everyone," I greet the audience once the applause has quieted down. "Thank you for being here. Everyone here knew Tanya, and so I'm sure it's no surprise to you that this event is reminiscent of a lavish wedding, rather than a homegoing."

Another round of applause and laughter.

"Tanya was . . . she was special. She was the type of person who changed your life from the moment she entered it. She was always there when you needed her, and even when you didn't."

The audience's laughter helps me keep back the tears.

"I had planned to come up here and make this entire speech about how magnanimous she was, but she once told me not to start listing off all her accomplishments or I'd be there all day. I think what she would really like for me to do is stand up here and share with you all a few words from someone she loved who didn't get to share these words himself."

I flip over my speech card and take a deep breath. "This is a poem by Tanya's late brother, Andrew. It's called 'Gone Are the Days.' I hope you enjoy.

Gone are the days of innocence.
Gone are the days of blissful ignorance.
Gone are the days of wonder and adventure.
Time strips them away without warning or pretense.
It wraps itself around you and molds you into who the world needs you to be.
Time takes, yet it also gives.
It gives experience.
It gives wisdom and freedom.
It gives forgiveness.
Time gave me you.
And so how can something that gives me someone so treasured be bad?
Gone are the days of storm clouds, for you've shone your ray of light onto me.

Gone are the days of despair, for you've given me joy.
Gone are the days of being alone, for now I walk beside you."

When I finish reading the poem, I look out into the audience, searching for one person in particular. When I find Auntie Joyce with tear-stricken cheeks and an approving smile on her face, I'm happy.

The servers come out of the kitchen, brandishing trays of covered plates. "Dinner is being served now, and in a little while we will open the gallery for your viewing—and buying—pleasure. In the meantime, please enjoy this documentary made in Tanya's honor. I believe that the only way a person can truly die is if we stop talking about them. Everyone featured in this documentary had wonderful stories to share about Tanya. I encourage each and every one of you to continue telling those stories. Thirty years from now, I hope your kids, your kids' kids, and their kids all know who Tanya was. She'll live on forever in all of us. Thank you."

Micah waits off stage for me, so I take his hand and let him guide us to our seats.

The lights dim as the documentary plays.

It starts with Micah's very first interview, the one we did in Tanya's house. The audience is immediately enthralled by his story.

It cuts to him working on her portrait, with me peppering him with questions about his artistic choices.

Throughout the video, the footage keeps cutting back to Micah painting the portrait of Tanya. I start chiming in more and more as it goes on.

One of the last interviews Micah and I recorded was one of my own. My heart starts to race when I see my face on the screen, hoping I didn't gaslight myself into thinking the footage was good when it wasn't.

"Can I ask you a question?" Micah asks off screen.

"That is kinda what we're doing here." I laugh.

"You right. Did Tanya give you that necklace?"

In the video my hand flies up to rub the very necklace lying against my chest as I grab the same necklace in real time.

"She did. How'd you know?"

"A lot of times when we talk about her, you touch it. I don't even think you realize you're doing it. It seems like it just comes naturally for you."

On screen I rub the necklace three more times before answering him. "She gave it to me three years ago. Actually, it was the night of your gallery opening."

The camera can't see him now, but the look of confusion on his face when I said this is still fresh in my mind. "Really?"

"Yep. She gave it to me and told me it was her mom's good luck necklace. She made me promise to give it to the next person when I felt like I didn't need it anymore. And I used to think how could she possibly think I'm deserving of this? Why would she pass this down to me of all people? But I haven't taken it off since. And it's taken me a long time, but I finally understand that I'm the exact right person to carry on this legacy for her."

Evie reaches over the table and puts her hand over mine. "I'm so proud of you," she mouths.

"I love you," I mouth back.

The video progresses through more confessionals. The interviews with Tanya's family keep the audience laughing and lighthearted.

"How would you describe Tanya in one word?"

"Dramatic," Cora responds.

"Iconic," says John.

"Oooh, um, I'd say carefree," Aaron says during his interview.

June and Tiara interview together. "One word for Tanya?" June says. "I don't even think there's a singular word that exists that fits her."

Tiara smiles at her mom. "Indescribable?" she offers.

"That feels like cheating, but I'm gonna take it," June says.

"Impossible!" Auntie Joyce yells. "She was impossible. Impossibly kind. Impossibly funny. Impossibly driven. Impossibly everything."

"Do you have a favorite moment with Tanya?" I ask.

June, Cora, and Auntie Joyce have the most stories to share. Auntie Joyce shares one about Tanya getting caught smuggling a stray dog into the movie theater as a kid.

June shares a story about Tanya driving June's husband's truck into a mud pit by accident once and coming home covered head to toe in what they thought was shit.

Cora gives details about Tanya's wedding. The audience bursts into tears when she describes how happy Tanya and George were and how she thought they'd last forever.

Janine, Daria, my parents, and Micah's parents all have videos throughout too, each one pulling at every heartstring in the building.

When the documentary is over, I make my way back to the stage.

"Thank you, everyone. As you might have noticed, Micah was working on something throughout that video. We'd like to share that painting with you all now."

Micah pulls the cover off his painting and there's a wave of shock and awe that runs through the crowd.

Ella stands up and starts slow clapping. It doesn't take long for others to follow. I force Micah to take a bow as the claps grow louder.

"This painting is titled *The Many Faces of Tanya* and it is available for bidding. Once again, thank you, everyone, for being here tonight. Tanya loved her life, and she loved you all, so I know she's smiling down on us now. Oh, and she's also reminding me to remind you all to keep bidding on those auction items."

Victor is the first person to approach me after my final speech. He's of course wearing a suit, but this one is forest green, a nice change from his usual.

"Victor, I didn't know you had color in your closet," I tease.

"Well, I thought I'd dig this one up in Tanya's honor." I look at his lapel to see he has a pink flower pin that closely resembles the one he donated.

"And you succeeded." I hold my hand out to him. "Thank you, Victor. We could not have done this without you."

He looks at my hand briefly and then pushes it away and pulls me in for a hug.

Now he's messing up my makeup by making me cry! I'm back to not liking him.

"You did right by her, Dani. Know that." He kisses my forehead before heading back to his table.

Moments later, Ella, Tony, and Michael sneak up and squeeze the life out of me in a group hug.

"Y'all are the worst," I huff as I try to regain my breath.

"And you love us anyway," Ella sings.

I really do. These people have become like family to Micah and me and I'm never letting them go.

"She doesn't really have a choice. We're locked in," Tony adds.

"But also, you did not tell me how many fine women would be in attendance tonight," Michael says as he surveys the room.

"And why would she do that when none of them would want your ass?" Ella teases.

"Who asked you, Two Scoops? I'm leaving here with at least one number tonight, watch."

"It's Tanya's homegoing and you worried about getting numbers. Degenerate," she tsks.

I interrupt. "Right. Michael, have you met Christian? And Ella, have you met Evie? I *really* think y'all would get along." It would most likely be disastrous, but I'm willing to risk it for the sheer entertainment potential.

I point out their doppelgängers and tell them to introduce themselves at some point before I head over to the auction area to check the lists.

Bailey is going to walk away with Tanya's mom's music box. That is so perfect for her.

One of Tanya's cousins is taking Victor's glass-covered rose.

Auntie Joyce is going to win Micah's portrait of Tanya. I couldn't be happier with that turnout.

Christian is standing off to the side with a sour look on his face.

I walk over to Evie and tap her on the shoulder. "What's up with him?"

She snickers, so I know she's up to no good. "He's just mad because no one has bid on his little date."

"No one at all?" I say, shocked. Christian may be a bit much for my tastes, but he's attractive. I can't believe no one would bid.

"I mayyyy have paid whoever came up to his clipboard to walk away."

I slap her arm. "You ain't shit. That money is for charity."

"Please, I'm good for it. But that look on his face is worth its weight in gold."

We cackle when Christian perks up at the sight of another woman walking over to his bidding table, all to deflate as she walks away quickly.

"Oh, and by the way," Evie adds, "I was told to give you this tonight." She reaches into the breastplate of her dress and pulls out something small and folded.

When I unfold it, I realize it's a small swatch of sandpaper. My head flies up, searching for Micah, but I don't see him anywhere.

"Who told you to do this?" I ask, though there's only one person it could be.

"Mmm, I was told if you asked that to simply say, 'I'll be your sandpaper.' So, that's all I got for you."

My vision becomes blurry, but I don't wipe the tears away. I wear them like a medal.

While I'm searching for Micah, I bump into Slater, and I'm shocked to see who he's with. "Hi, Slater. Thanks for coming. And, Kelly. I am . . . surprised to see you here." She looks stunning in a gold floor-length dress.

"I misjudged Tanya, so I wanted to show my support."

"It took you this long to realize you misjudged her?" My curiosity is too great not to ask what convinced her to come.

She pushes her shoulders back. "It took a young woman hugging me while I cried in the remnants of my kitchen after I had been nothing but rude to her for me to realize I had misjudged Tanya. She couldn't have been so bad if she had a hand in raising you."

Wow. I wasn't expecting her words or her genuine expression. "Well, in that case, I'm really glad you're here."

"Me too." She smiles.

Throughout the night, I'm handed swatches of sandpaper from the people I hold dear. I've collected so many that my clutch is about to pop. Another swatch appears in front of me and when I turn to find the presenter, it's none other than Micah.

"May I have this dance?" he asks.

"Of course." We glide onto the dance floor, staring into each other's eyes while Janessa Howard strums a beautiful melody on her violin. "If you had told me at the beginning of the night that my purse would be filled with sandpaper, I wouldn't have believed you." The swatch he gave me is still in my hand, pressed against his shoulder.

He smirks. "I just wanted you to have a reminder of who your sandpaper is. But I still like a good, jagged edge."

I'm learning to like them too. They've gotten me here, after all.

Once the auction portion is over, the gallery is open for people to walk through and observe or buy pieces.

Micah managed the gallery portion of the night, so he handled the final walkthrough. Now, I can just sit back and enjoy the art with Micah's hand in mine. As I'm walking through the rows of paintings, I'm stunned speechless by a new one.

It's the portrait Micah started of me years ago, finally finished. It's titled *The Art of Loving You.*

He wraps his arm around my waist and I melt into him. "Just so you know, the video we made isn't for sale," Micah whispers in my ear.

I spin around so I can look him in the face. "Micah, I—" I cut myself off.

"It's called *The Art of Loving You* because loving you is an art form in its own right. And I do love you. I need you to know that. You don't have to say it back. In fact, I don't want you to. I want to keep earning it."

I get choked up on my words, but I manage to push them out. "You don't mind that I'm not ready?" It's not because I don't feel it, but because I'm not ready to voice it.

"Nope. You take your time because whenever you get to the finish line, I'll be there waiting for you."

I kiss him so deeply that people around us start to cheer.

Epilogue

Dani

THE UNMISTAKABLE SMELL OF PANCAKES DRIFTS TO MY bedroom.

Is my dad here?

I rush out to the kitchen to find the man who has been teaching me a thing or two about letting go. Micah flips another pancake, silently celebrating as it lands perfectly in the pan.

I can't hide my laughter, causing him to spin around.

The smile when he sees me is one I never get tired of. I love the way he looks at me.

"Hey, Storm," he says, holding the pan away from us as he leans in for a kiss.

"Good morning. What you doing here so early?"

"I know Veronica got the part in her play, so I figured pancakes were in order."

My heart squeezes at his thoughtfulness.

He pulls a chair out for me to sit down and then places a stack of pancakes in front of me. They smell amazing. I cut into them, smiling to myself, and then shove a bite in my mouth. My jaw drops. These aren't just pancakes, they're my dad's pancakes. "How did you do this?"

"What, you think I'd give you bootleg pancakes?"

I scrunch my nose. "Micah!" I'm floored and about to fall out sobbing, so I need him to answer.

"I may have asked your dad and he was willing to give me the recipe."

If my dad was willing to give him the recipe that he won't even give me, that means he approves of Micah staying around for a very long time. We're on the same page, Dad.

Micah cuts into his own stack of pancakes and holds his fork up to me. "Good days, Storm?"

A feeling of pure bliss settles into my bones. I cut into another bite of pancakes, holding my fork up to his. "Good days, Stormchaser."

My hands are trembling with nerves.

I invited Micah over here because I have something I want to show him.

I've been working on it for a while, but I haven't been ready to share it until now.

Even though he has his own key, he knocks on the door and waits for me to let him in. My ominous text probably freaked him out. I rub my hands down my pants one more time and open the door.

"Hey. You okay?" he asks.

"I'm a little nervous. Come on in." It feels good to say how I'm actually feeling instead of brushing everything under the "I'm fine" rug.

"What are you nervous about?"

I clap my hands together. "I've been working on something. A work of art, I guess. For you. And I wanna show it to you. I'm just scared."

His eyes light up with pure elation. "You made me something? I can't wait to see it."

I take a deep breath and guide him over to my living room where I have the piece covered with a tarp.

"Oooh. An official reveal." He laughs.

"Shut up. Ready?"

"Very."

I pull the tarp free and watch Micah take in what he sees. His brows pull inward and the rise and fall of his chest grows faster with every moment he looks at it.

"Are you serious?" He turns to me.

It's not really a painting—I will leave that skill to Micah—but it is a collage of sorts. I had photos of us printed and I cut them into letters to spell out *I love you*. It's corny, sure, but I wanted him to feel how deeply I mean the words.

The moment he said he loved me, I wanted to say it back more than I wanted my next breath. Even when our mistakes skewed those feelings and made us bare our teeth in anger, the love was there. But telling him in that moment would've been a disservice to us both. Because I needed to be sure I loved myself enough to stand tall under the weight of my love for him.

"I am. I love you. So fucking much."

He scoops me up into his arms and swings me around, ignoring my squeals. "I love you, too."

"I know."

Bonus Epilogue

One Year Later

Micah

"VICTOR, I HAVE TO SAY, YOUR OFFICE LOOKS AMAZING," I say, looking around at all the updates.

The space has been modernized with new furniture and fixtures, and the drab colors have been upgraded to brighter, but still neutral, shades.

"Thank you. Dani definitely got her skills of persuasion from Tanya," he jokes.

"I learned from the best," Dani says, stepping around me, letting my hand go as she does.

Victor greets us both with a hug before we sit down.

We've stayed close with Victor over the last year, now that he's our lawyer and all.

He's taken care of the contracts for Dani's modeling agency, now named the Holden Agency, which just had its launch party last month. She's taken great care to make sure everyone who walks through her doors feels safe. They also offer contract reviews, so models don't get screwed over by agents, and she personally covers therapy services for all her clients.

Today, we're here to discuss the launch of Our Place's second location—the house in Chicago. We've been back and forth to visit the house and Slater over the last year, and with his help we realized that something like Our Place would do wonders there.

When I pitched the idea to my fellow partners, they were ecstatic about it. Paris volunteered to move out there temporarily to get the ball rolling, so she'll be doing that in just a couple of months.

"Is Bailey ready to go on tour?" Victor asks while I'm signing the contracts he handed me.

My smile is wide and full of pride. "Yep, she's all ready." The Legends and Icons Tour is taking off this fall and she will be traveling with them as the lead choreographer. She and I have come a long way in our relationship. It's become easier for me to ease up on her and not breathe down her neck. She's even met the people in my group and their families, as they've become important people in my life as well.

"I can't wait to be front row with all the girls at the Baltimore stop." Dani sighs dreamily.

"Damn, just the girls? I'm not invited?"

"Oh, you can come. You just can't sit with us. I need space to throw ass."

Victor chokes on his water.

"Sorry, Victor."

Once I've signed the last page, Dani perks up. "Okay, last order of business. Vacation. You're due for another one, sir." She points her fingers at Victor. We've taken Tanya's memo in her letter to heart, forcing Victor to take breaks from work and enjoy his life.

He scoffs. "Tanya was always fussing. I don't need a vacation."

Dani and I exchange looks, a silent conversation passing between us.

"Tell you what," I say. "Dani and I are leaving for Japan in two weeks. If two plane tickets were to end up on your desk, surely you wouldn't let them go to waste, would you?"

"Two?! Why two?" he balks.

"Aht aht. Don't even try it. You've got a niece in Jersey who would love to go," Dani interjects.

Victor lowers his eyelids, but Dani is unfazed.

"I'll think about it," he concedes.

"Great! Then that settles it." Dani stands from her chair.

"I said I'd think about it, Ms. Jenkins, not that I decided."

She gives him a pitying glance before skipping out of his office.

We laugh the whole way to my car, knowing we'll be seeing Victor and his niece in two weeks.

Dani

Don't smile. Last time he caught you on the doorbell camera cheesing he teased you for hours.

Too late. It's been two months, and I still haven't gotten over calling Micah's place my own. It's surreal, I just break out into a huge smile whenever I walk inside. This won't be our home for too much longer, though, because we're planning to buy something new. Something with a yard so we can finally get the dog I've been harassing him about lately. Deux needs a playmate.

I unpack my haul from my farmer's market run with my mom and rush to change my clothes before I set out to meet with Veronica. I'm scrolling through my socials as I lotion up my legs when I see a post that makes me pause.

It's a video of Nigel trying to avoid looking at the cameras as he enters a courthouse. He looks awful. Like he's lived a total of forty years in the span of ten days. The caption details how the civil cases against Nigel keep piling up. It calls for abusers to stop being able to inflict pain on others without consequence. It alleges that the seven women who have come forward so far, which does include myself, is only the tip of the iceberg. I have no doubt that's true.

The Goode doctor has been right about so many things, but she really hit the nail on the head when she said my reactions to Nigel would never be one thing. When I was called to be a witness at one of his trials, because my circumstances were similar to the plaintiff's, I was filled with nothing but rage at hearing what he had done to the young woman suing him. There's been other times where the panic became so strong I needed to take the Hydroxyzine I'd been prescribed to calm down.

I never know what emotions Nigel—or anything for that matter—will draw out of me, but for now, looking at him with his haunted eyes and haggard facial hair, I feel only one thing: glee.

"I hope everywhere you go, you find hell, Nigel," I whisper to myself as I pocket my phone and head out.

When I get to Days of the Week, Veronica is already sitting in a booth sipping a glass of what looks like lemonade.

I slide in across from her. "Hey! I ordered you that matcha blueberry tea you like."

"Thank you. How you been?"

"Good! I'm so nervous for the audition, though." Since getting the role of Audrey in *Little Shop of Horrors,* Veronica has gone on to play Rizzo in her school's production of *Grease* and Effie in her school's production of *Dreamgirls.* She gets more comfortable with every role, but now she's venturing outside of her school.

I allowed her to join the Holden Agency under the condition that she finish high school and not let it affect her schoolwork, and she's done a fantastic job so far. Now, she has an audition for a commercial with a popular brand.

"You belted out 'And I Am Telling You I'm Not Going' in front of a packed gymnasium. You can recite a few lines in front of some boring casting directors."

"Yeah, yeah, I know," she says as she moves her empty glass to the edge of the table. "But this could be the start of . . . more. It's nerve-racking."

"Well, I brought you something that I hope helps with that."

I slide a small box across the table to her, and she eyes it with a sly grin. "What are you up to?"

As she opens the box she starts to tell me about a dream she had, but her words die on her tongue when she sees what's inside. Her eyes fly up to my neck where a certain necklace always used to reside but now lives in that box.

"Dani. Tanya's necklace?" She never met Tanya, but she knows her all the same.

I nod my head.

"But . . . what about your luck?"

I think about my incredible friends and family who always stand by my side, the career I've found a renewed passion for, and the wonderful man who feeds my soul, and I understand how Tanya was able to part with this necklace. "I have no more use for luck."

After Veronica and I leave our lunch date, I give Micah a call.

"What are you up to?" he asks as the video connects.

"I was gonna ask you that."

"Me and Tee just got done visiting his dad and Chi Chi." He pans the phone over to Tavion sitting in his passenger seat.

"Hey, Tee! Did you send them my love?"

"What's good, Dani? Of course we did. And guess what?"

"What's up?"

He grabs the phone from Micah's hands. "My passport made it!"

"Ayeee!" Sammy and Tee are both going with us to Japan, but it's taken forever to get his passport in. He was stressed about it, as if we would actually go without him.

We go back and forth dancing while Micah shakes his head at us. When he gets the phone back, he flashes a smile at me. "Need me to grab anything on my way home?"

"Nope, I'm still out anyway, so I'll meet you there."

"Oh bet, I'll drive slow so you beat me there."

I tilt my head. "Why would you do that?"

"So I can watch you cheesin' on the camera."

"Fuck you, Micah. Bye." I fight to keep the giggle out of my voice as I hang up.

When we get home, at the same time might I add, I smile as I walk by my favorite spot: the wall where our art hangs side by side.

Where they'll stay forever.

The end.

Acknowledgments

To Taj—Thank you for always being fiercely protective of me and my work. Every Black woman in publishing needs a Taj by their side. Love you!

To the Zando team—Thank you for believing in Dani and Micah's story. Transitioning to the traditional lifestyle was definitely an adjustment, so thank you for sticking with me.

To Brad—Thank you for pushing me on those deadlines. Sorry for all the times I told you to get off my ass. Thank you for knowing I'm going to cuss you out again and loving me anyway.

To the Devereoux-Black Family—I can't put into words how much I love y'all. Thank you for always loving me, pushing me, and being strict af with me when I need it. This house ain't got no roaches or nothing.

To SSS and DGM—Nothing beats being on my Zoom with y'all! I love you deep.

My sensitivity readers: Keona, Rita, Becki, Lisa, and Paige—Thank you so much for willing to be so open and vulnerable. You shared your journeys with me, and I do not take that lightly. I hope I was able to create a story that made you feel proud and seen.

To my readers—For my loves who have been rocking with this series since 2023 and waited patiently for this book to come, thank you from the bottom of my heart! I hope it was worth the wait. For my loves who are new here, thank you, thank you, thank you!

To Kim—Thank you for getting me through those sleepless nights.

To Chrissy and Jimmy—Will. She. Wriiiiiite?! . . . she did. I love you guys!

To all the Black girls who need to hear this—We deserve rest. Please rest.

Kd Seegars (@k.seegars)

About the Author

NATASHA BISHOP is a contemporary romance author living in Baltimore, Maryland, with her family and fur baby.

She likes to write about complicated women and the men who love them down.

When she's not writing, she loves to read, travel, play with her adorable dog, and spend time with loved ones.

Stay connected!

Goodreads (https://geni.us/GoodreadsNatashaBishop)

Instagram (@natashabishopwrites)

Threads (@natashabishopwrites)

TikTok (@natashabishopwrites)

Amazon (https://geni.us/NBAmazonAuthorPage)

Linktr.ee (https://linktr.ee/NatashaBishop)

Website (www.natashabishopwrites.com)